IDENTITTI

IDENTITTI

IDENTITTI

A NOVEL

MITHU SANYAL

TRANSLATED BY ALTA L. PRICE

ASTRA HOUSE ∧ NEW YORK

Copyright © 2021 by Mithu Sanyal

Translation © 2022 by Alta L. Price

Originally published in the German language as *Identitti* © 2021 Carl Hanser Verlag
GmbH & Co. KG, München.

The translation of this work was supported by a grant from the Goethe-Institut.

Identitti is a work of fiction. As is true in many works of fiction, this book was inspired
by events that have appeared in the news. Nevertheless, all of the actions in this
book, as well as most of the characters and dialogue, are products of the author's
imagination. The names of some real people do appear, along with some real social
media posts and public quotes, but they are applied, out of context, to the events
of this novel in a fictitious manner. All real quotes and tweets are sourced
in the bibliography.

Astra House

A Division of Astra Publishing House

astrahouse.com

Printed in the United States of America

Library of Congress Cataloging-in-Publication Data
Names: Sanyal, Mithu M., 1971– author. | Price, Alta L., translator.
Title: Identitti : a novel / by Mithu Sanyal ; translated by Alta L. Price.
Other titles: Identitti. English
Description: First edition. | New York : Astra House, [2022] |
Summary: "A satirical debut about a German Indian student whose world is
upended when she discovers that her beloved professor who passed
for Indian is, in fact, white"—Provided by publisher.
Identifiers: LCCN 2022008115 (print) | LCCN 2022008116 (ebook) |
ISBN 9781662601293 (hardcover) | ISBN 9781662601309 (epub)
Subjects: LCGFT: Satirical literature. | Black humor. | Novels.
Classification: LCC PT2719.A59 I3413 2022 (print) | LCC PT2719.A59
(ebook) | DDC 833/.92—dc23/eng/20220225
LC record available at https://lccn.loc.gov/2022008115
LC ebook record available at https://lccn.loc.gov/2022008116

First edition
10 9 8 7 6 5 4 3 2 1

Design by Richard Oriolo
The text is set in UtopiaStd-Regular.
The titles are set in Kanit-ExtraBold.

CONTENTS

FOR DURGA—AND MATTI

THE DEVIL AND ME

IDENTITTI

A BLOG BY MIXED-RACE WONDER WOMAN

About me:

The last time I spoke to the devil he was naked, visibly aroused, and female. So much for social certainties, right? If you can't even count on the devil being male, you might as well shed all forms of identity like you would a worn-out T-shirt—which is precisely what I'd like to do, if only I had one to slip into, let alone out of. That's exactly what this was all about, just like every other encounter with my devil, who's actually a devi—an Indian goddess with too many arms, wearing a necklace made of her enemies' severed heads. Yes, I'm talking about Kali. "Demons, the lot of 'em," she said, in the same dismissive tone my cousin Priti would use to say, "Men, the lot of 'em," and then she shook her necklace until her slain foes' teeth chattered. Sure enough, Kali's demon heads all looked suspiciously like men's heads.

But she'd already moved on to other things. "Let's have a squirting match, whoever shoots farthest wins."

I nodded at her hairy vulva, taken aback. "How do you plan to . . . ?"

"Hah! Jizzing isn't just for cis men," Kali shouted, beaming so triumphantly that for a moment I didn't even notice she'd just said cis. "And why would it be? We had three genders eons before your god was even born."

"But you're my goddess," I reminded her.

"I thought I was your devil . . ."

"What's the difference?"

Race & sex. Whenever Kali and I talked, it was always about race & sex. Meaning—for lack of a more accurate term, or any term whatsoever that won't send us down a rabbit hole—it was about my relationship to Germany and India, my two neither-mother-nor-fatherlands (remember, I'm Mixed-Race Wonder Whatever), and . . . sex. This blog is mostly transcripts of our conversations. If you read on, I'll eventually tell you why I'm always talking to a goddess. My name is Nivedita Anand. You can call me IDENTITTI.

STRANGE FRUIT

1

The day hell's jaws opened and spewed out a slew of howling furies started out like any other day, if any other day normally starts with a rocket launch.

It's not a rocket, it's a satellite, Nivedita read—at least that's how she interpreted her cousin's WhatsApp message. Priti had actually written *tis-NArugula, issaSATELLITE!!!* plus an emoji that looked like a bunch of asparagus. Nivedita gaped up at German Public Radio's twenty-story concrete tower. It was perched precariously atop a spindly plinth that looked like a fiery plume, which seemed to be propelling the building skyward. She texted back: *obvs a rocket!*

At the building's peak, where the Saturn V rocket housed the Apollo spacecraft, flying buttresses formed an iron arrow in the glaring gray sky. Nivedita felt simultaneously sublime and insignificant in the face of this concrete spaceship whose entrance was crowned by a blue inscription: *The News*.

Imagine yr a terrorist who's killed several people, Priti's next WhatsApp message advised, in an even more arbitrary array of letters, *or that yr a terrorist who already faked killing piles o' peeps—this'll be a cinch*. Seconds later, *1 small step for you, 1 ginormous leap for humankind ROFL LMAO*.

The glass doors silently slid open before Nivedita, and she entered the hallowed halls of national radio headquarters. It smelled of candle wax and pleather, a blend of IRS and CIA, if news broadcasters could smell like James Bond films looked. She'd only caught a glimpse of the receptionist's suit through the glass doors, so when she strode over and he looked up, she was shocked to see he was no older than she. But that black uniform signaled that he belonged to a different generation and danced to a different drum—a rather more conformist one than she—unless he were to slip off his staid jacket or she were to shed her radical-chic-meets-I-mean-business outfit. Clueless as she was of the codes, Nivedita had done her long black hair up into a milkmaid braid that morning and, strand by strand, it had been struggling free in silent yet staunch protest all day.

"I'm here to be interviewed about my blog," she said, enunciating the phrase she'd practiced the entire train ride there.

"Where?" the receptionist cryptically replied.

"Uhh . . . here?"

"No, I mean, which department?" he asked, giving her a fatherly glance. For a second Nivedita couldn't even remember her own name. She felt like a snagged zipper, suddenly stuck, but then the midnight-blue phone on the receptionist's desk rang, coming to her rescue.

"Nivedita Anand," she said, just as he hung up and announced, "They're on their way."

Then she did what she always did when she wasn't feeling up to the task— she went to the bathroom. Not because she needed privacy, but so she could look in the mirror and make sure she was still there. The bathroom's frosted glass door bore an inscription, "*Frau* (from Old High German *Frouwa*, 'lady' or 'mistress'): adult female. Definition varies according to geo. loc., hist. era, as well as societal and cultural norms." Her cell buzzed.

"You in?" asked Priti.

"Yeah," whispered Nivedita.

"Why you answering then?"

Conversations with Priti were always on Priti's terms. At some point she'd invariably remember she had more important things to do than chat with

Nivedita, even if she was the one who'd called. Actually, especially if she was the one who'd called. That's why Nivedita didn't bother explaining herself or anything else, and instead said, "You should see this bathroom, the door alone is a veritable intro course in German."

"That's the spirit!" Priti cheered, "Feel superior to the bathroom! Then you'll . . . Wait! Something's come up, Niv." When Priti was in the right mood she'd call Nivedita *Niv*, like the Irish name Niamh, pronounced "Neave." Priti was from Birmingham and had come up with this nickname not because anybody there had a clue how to pronounce Irish names, but because it highlighted that she was different. *As if anyone would doubt Priti was capital-D Different, capital-O Other!* As long as she sprinkled her cousin with the stardust of her approval, Niv felt capital-N Noteworthy rather than Not Worthy. But Priti's moods were mercurial, and when she was feeling less generous she'd call Nivedita *Nivea*, like the *white* skin lotion whose racist advertising regularly sparked scandal.

"Shit!"

"Priti?"

"Gotta go—I'll call you back."

Nivedita tapped the red receiver icon and looked deep into her own eyes. They didn't betray a thing. She desperately wished she could see herself how others saw her, but she just couldn't—hell, she couldn't even see how she saw herself. But she *could* smudge her eyeliner to cast a more intellectual shadow around her eyes, so she did just that.

On the other side of the frosted glass door, a petite woman and large dog were waiting for her.

"Welcome to RadioNew, I'm Verena. May I call you Identitti?" Verena had perfect dimples when she smiled, and Nivedita imagined what it would be like to have sex with her. Then she imagined what it would be like to have sex with her dog, but quickly lost interest, and went back to the first option. Much like the bathroom, the stairwell reminded her of college—brutalism meets parking garage—and for a second she felt like Freida Pinto in *Slumdog Millionaire*, until she glimpsed her reflection in a windowpane and noticed her eyeliner was less smoky-eye and more I-bawled-in-the-bathroom.

When they got to the recording studio, Verena handed her a laughably large headset. The dog plopped down in a corner, all the while keeping his mournful brown eyes aimed at her, as if trying to convey his compassion for the whole human race.

"That's Mona," Verena said by way of introduction, and Nivedita mentally corrected her grammar: *she/her compassion.*

"Hiya, Mona," she said, whereupon the dog shot right up, came over, and stoically let Nivedita pet her.

A lit display in the middle of the recording console gave counterintuitive signals: green light = wait, red light = on air. Verena pulled the microphone closer and dove right in.

"'Where are you from?' is a loaded question nowadays. Is it a form of racism, or just curiosity? What are we still allowed to say? What should we never, *ever* say? What does it all mean, and what does all this say about us? Today's guest is blogger Nivedita Anand, one of *Missy* magazine's 'Must-know POCs.' Nivedita, before answering all our questions, could you explain the term POC, without using the words *people* or *of* or *color*?"

Nivedita stared at Verena as if she'd said, "Can you breathe without inhaling?" or "Can you and your mother hang out without you flipping out about something totally trivial?" or "Can you think of India without feeling a vertiginous void opening up inside you?" Then she heard her own voice saying, "POCs are the folx who always get asked, 'Where you from?'"

"And where are you from, Nivedita?"

Nivedita was beginning to suspect Verena and her dimples were jerking her around. She knew the question was a joke—goading makes for good radio. But she couldn't exactly prod back, so her answer came out sounding defensive, "I'm from the Internet. I live online."

Which seemed to be the precise answer Verena was waiting for. "Indeed, under the name Identitti. Nivedita blogs about identity politics and . . ."

"Tits," Nivedita added. *Two can play at this game.*

"Let's go with *boobs*. Would you say it's more boobs, or more identity politics?" Verena beamed. Her sheer gusto dissolved Nivedita's defenses.

"Not just boobs. I also blog about—can I say *vulvas* on the radio?"

"Let's stick to boobs."

"Okay." For just a second, Nivedita wondered what Verena's boobs looked like, but then quickly directed her brain back to—her own. "It all started when I posted a selfie of my boobs. I'd written on them in eyeliner, 'In ancient Ireland, the Celts proved their loyalty by sucking the king's nipples.'"

"Really?!" Verena's dimples flashed as if to signal this was a two-thumbs-up tidbit.

"NO IDEA. MY cousin Priti heard it on a quiz show, and I just adored the notion of nipple-sucking as a form of social exchange. But then some smart-ass posted a comment about how 'that story could only be found in the saga of . . .'"—Nivedita stealthily peeked at the inside of her forearm, where she'd jotted down key names and dates—"'Fergus mac Léti, in the eighth century, and even there it was meant as a joke, but obviously' I 'have no sense of humor because' I 'majored in gender studies.' So I replied, 'I'm not into gender studies, I'm into postcolonial studies,' to which smarty-pants replied, 'The only other mention comes from Saint Patrick, who supposedly refused to suck the pagan Irish king's nipples, but relying on the word of Saint Patrick when it comes to heathens is about as wise as relying on Donald Trump when it comes to Muslims, but surely you know all that, what with all your postcolonial gender studies!' Before I could even answer, Facebook had blocked my account because it showed nipples, but by then the image had been shared so far and wide that I just knew I had to keep going. By the way, I call my posts a *blog* because it sounds so retro, like CDs, or GTOs, or opposite-sex marriage, but my website is actually just an archive of my threads, rants, posts, stories, and comments because people seem to want to read them chronologically, like a *her*story. Because we humans are more than just a bunch of rando comments on identity politics, you know?"

Nivedita felt her nipples perking up under her T-shirt, as if to boast: You've got us to thank for that—you're welcome.

"That's just outstanding," Verena concurred. "Is that how you came up with the name Identitti?"

"Nah. First my blog was called *Fifty Shades of Beige*, because of my skin tone—y'know, beige."

"Why not brown?"

"Saying *brown* is racist."

"Really?" Verena's dimples vanished, dismayed.

"I dunno. But that's really what all this is about: the fact that we don't have the language to talk about people like me. After all, until quite recently we were strictly *verboten*—forbidden. Like fruit."

"Forbidden?"

"Forbidden," Nivedita reiterated. In all honesty, the college paper she had written on the various "anti-miscegenation laws"—actually, on all the laws forbidding "miscegenation"—was the real genesis of her Internet persona. Intriguing as nipples are, they'd never have sparked such a lasting, steady stream of verbal indignation. Anyway, it had all begun with sex, actually: legal sex, illegal sex, and sex that was so utterly unthinkable that it caused the heads of the lawmakers to explode. "Nazis weren't the only ones who tried to prevent so-called interbreeding. In the United States, *whites* and *non-whites* couldn't marry until . . ." Nivedita peeked at her forearm again, "nineteen sixty-seven, and in South Africa they couldn't until nineteen eighty-five. And here in Germany, when my mother was pregnant with me, her doctor warned her that *Mischlinge* are more prone to depression. But when I told that to Simon, my . . ." she hardly hesitated, "boyfriend, he just said, 'It's always all about you and your Identitti,' and somehow Identitti just kind of stuck."

"You write under two alternating pen-names, Identitti and Mixed-Race Wonder Woman. One of your superpowers is that you can speak with the gods—or at least one of them, Kali, the Hindu Goddess of Destruction. Most of your blog entries are conversations with her. Why?"

Verena might as well have asked Nivedita to take a deep-dive into her own soul, find the golden egg containing life's ultimate truths, and resurface with it intact. But even if such a thing were possible, it wouldn't have changed Nivedita's speechlessness at this very moment—after all, no such egg exists. At best, there might be a shell, and some kind of liquid, which might later turn into some kind of being with feathers, but there's no guarantee. And feathers are indeed one of Kali's attributes, but then again Kali has so many attributes that Nivedita had long since given up trying to keep track. Verena looked at her expectantly—how long had it been already? So Nivedita quickly jumped in, "I have to process all this with somebody. Most people have no clue how to talk about this stuff. Me neither. So I need someone to explain it all to me."

But Verena wasn't all that interested in Kali, she was just using her as a stepping-stone to get to her real question: "Now, allow me to pivot from one goddess to another: from Kali to Saraswati. Not Saraswati the Indian Goddess of Knowledge, but Saraswati the Professor at Düsseldorf's Heinrich Heine University, with whom you took intercultural studies and postcolonial theory."

Nivedita's heart pounded in her chest.

"Saraswati, exactly." *Charismati Saraswati*, as Priti always called the professor they both studied with, although Priti's irony was just an act, since not even she could deny Saraswati's disarming charm and sheer intelligence.

"Why just Saraswati? Doesn't she have a last name?"

Nivedita shrugged, causing the headset to begin slowly but surely sliding off, leaving just one earphone in place. "Beyoncé doesn't need a last name, either," she replied, trying to straighten the headset without too much interference, "nor does the Queen of England."

"But both of them *have* last names."

"Right, Knowles and . . . Hapsburg?"

"Windsor," Verena corrected her.

"Sure, whatevs. Saraswati definitely *has* a last name, too, but she doesn't need one, because *she's Saraswati*, and everyone knows which one you're talking about."

"That's right!"

Nivedita watched, riveted, as Verena silently slid out a sheet of paper, held it up, and read aloud, "In 1999 Saraswati published her first book, *Decolonize Your Soul*, which became an instant best seller and later led to her endowed professorship in Düsseldorf. But she wasn't just read at schools. Saraswati went POP—so very pop that her second book was titled *PopPostColonialism*.

And as with any star, major debate sprang up around her, especially on social media."

Nivedita shrugged again, this time holding her headset tight. "Nowadays, nobody's a serious intellectual until they've sat in the eye of a shitstorm." And anyone who's met Saraswati couldn't help but take her seriously. As Nivedita's *partner* (for lack of a better term) Simon always said: Priti has an innate compass with POWER as its true north, so of course the needle of that inner compass single-mindedly pointed straight at Saraswati. And Nivedita—whose soul was in desperate need of saving—was pulled in just as single-mindedly by the promising title of Saraswati's book *Decolonize Your Soul*. That's exactly what Nivedita had been trying to do when she began studying with Saraswati three years ago.

"But a large part of the phenomenon known as Saraswati isn't just your everyday Internet cantankerousness—at her own university, she's regularly accused of being racist. There's even a lawsuit regarding her treatment of *white* students," countered Verena.

"The people who accuse Saraswati of being racist . . ." Nivedita toyed with the idea of saying *can go suck their own tits*, but then decided to go with "just don't get her. Above all, they don't get what *being white* means to her." In less than twenty-four hours, Nivedita would wish she'd sucked her own tits instead of saying those words on live radio.

"And that's precisely what her hotly debated essay 'White Guilt: Why nobody wants to be *white* anymore,' is about," Verena said, reading from yet another sheet she'd silently slid from the desk. "Last month it was published simultaneously by the *Times Literary Supplement* as well as the French and German editions of *Lettre International*. The TLS called it 'an essential text for an era in which the phrase "old white men" has become an insult.' Is it true that *nobody* wants to be *white* anymore?"

"Well, I sure don't," Nivedita emphatically replied, her sheer enthusiasm covering up her bald-faced lie. She herself had spent half her life wanting nothing more than to be white, and the other half wishing she were darker than she actually was. Anything but the hybrid half-and-half she naturally was, which eluded all existing categories. The color was so fluid and hard to pin down that even Pantone had named the shade after a liquid: Cognac.

"Why not?"

Where to start? "That's 'cause of the term's history. Up until the seventeenth century, there was no concept of *white* aside from descriptions of clouds, or, like . . ."—and in the heat of the moment nothing came to Nivedita's mind but—"sheep. Then came the Transatlantic slave trade, and of course the Europeans had to justify that whole thing somehow, since nobody can just go someplace and abduct people and hawk them off someplace else. So the way they explained it, their justification, was that the *white* race was superior. But in order to do that, they first had to invent this *white* race." Nivedita hadn't just read "White Guilt"—like all of Saraswati's screeds, she'd devoured it as if it were dogma. "Before, Europeans hadn't thought of themselves as *white*, they identified themselves by the part of Europe they came from, or the language they spoke. Where was I again . . . ?"

"*White* supremacy."

"Right," except of course Verena used the German term, *Weiße Überlegenheit*, even though Nivedita and her fellow students in Düsseldorf all used the English loanword in Saraswati's seminar. Postcolonial studies basically viewed white supremacy as the original sin, ground zero of the earthquake whose aftershocks were still reverberating worldwide. "Because of that history, the notion of *whiteness* is inextricably linked to *white* dominance. *White* never had any other meaning. Consequently, *white* people couldn't really view their own *whiteness* through any lens but that of *white* power. For them, there's no such thing as a special *white* culture or *white* music, because everything is *white* to them. It's like living in an endless *whiteout*. Black people are discriminated against as they always have been—there's no question—but at the same time we've come to associate Blackness with notions like revolution, subversion, and Black power. In contrast, we have no progressive associations with the notion of *whiteness*. And that's how Saraswati arrives at the conclusion that *whiteness* is a concept that limits the rights of everyone, *whites* included." For just a moment, Nivedita felt her professor's presence so keenly that she could almost feel Saraswati's dupatta draped over her own shoulders, and her clavicles rose as she subconsciously assumed Saraswati's permanent prima-ballerina pose, shoulders wide, head held high. She remembered Saraswati once said, "Your neck aches in back, mine aches in front." So Nivedita raised her chin, lowered her eyelids, and sized Verena up: "What about you? Do you perceive your *whiteness* as a limitation?"

Verena cast a naked, vulnerable glance her way, and Nivedita thought, *Ah-ha, so that's how Saraswati does it.*

2

On her way back to Cologne's main train station, Nivedita wondered whether she'd just imagined that moment. Afterward, Verena had steered the conversation back to the eternal *Where-are-you-from?* question, and Nivedita slipped comfortably into her little comedy routine: "I once transcribed all the conversations over the course of a month where people had asked me that. 'Where you from?' Essen. 'No, I mean where're you *from* from?' Essen-Frillendorf. 'No, really, where are you *from* from from?' Uhhh, my momma's belly? 'No, I mean, why are you brown?' . . ." but the undeniable climax of the interview had clearly occurred when Nivedita broke the rules, turned the tables, and volleyed Verena's question right back at her.

As soon as she got off the bus, the humid air enveloped her as if the forecasted storm would never come, and she tried calling Simon. She'd once read somewhere that busses were like Faraday cages, so she always pictured the cell-phone signal bouncing back and forth inside the steel chassis until its trajectory resembled a kind of scribbled pencil drawing and all the passengers vanished behind a gray curtain of static. Like both of her last tries, this one too went straight to Simon's voice mail: "Your call is important to me. Please leave a message after the tone, and I'll call you back as soon as possible." Just that he never really did call back ASAP.

Nivedita went to the Museum Ludwig for its public Wi-Fi—she loved public Wi-Fi, such a democratic notion—and posted a soft and cuddly kitty pic she'd found online during the drive to the studio on her Instagram account and blog.

Every time you think a racist thought,
God kills a kitten.
But don't worry,
it's not a German kitten!

She'd initially wanted to paste a cutout of Maradona's hand above the kitty's fluffy head, as the hand of God, but then she realized copyright issues made Simon's hand a safer choice. But, as would soon become clear, Simon also held the IPR to God.

"Why didn't you pick up?" Nivedita complained as her train pulled into Düsseldorf.

"I just did," Simon shot back, with a tone that always got under her skin. Everything he said after that was drowned out by the conductor, who proceeded to announce all the connecting trains to every conceivable destination. The doors loudly whooshed open, the noise out on the platform was even louder, and by the time she could finally hear Simon again all he said was "My ringer was on low," as if his cell phone were somehow superior to her current surroundings.

"But we'd agreed to meet in Cologne three hours ago!"

"I was preparing for my meeting with Campact and lost track of time."

A wave of emotion spread over Nivedita—she was jealous of Simon's smug self-sufficiency. She translated his retort as *I studied law and am destined to save human rights, which is more important than your little goal of saving your own soul,* or, more concisely, *I'm more important to you than you are to me.*

"But I was on national radio!" she howled back.

"Oh," he said.

Nivedita sensed her hurt feelings suddenly turning into full-on irritation. "What?"

Silence.

"WHAT?!"

A young man whose luggage was piled onto a shopping cart glanced inquisitively in her direction, but apparently it's fine to rant and rave as long as you're holding a hand to your ear.

"I'm sensing that you're in need of attention," Simon says flatly.

"Great, then WHY DON'T YOU GIVE IT TO ME!?"

"Where'd you get the idea that people will be extra nice to you if you yell at them?"

"Little Si just can't handle your success," was Priti's take later on. Then again, that was her take on pretty much any relationship problem. But it really irked Nivedita that people were always telling her who she was supposed to be, what she was supposed to think, and why she just loooooves eating rice, to the point that she was almost never able to catch onto others' underlying motivation for saying such things.

Please, please just ask me how it went, she thought, through the phone, as loud as she could without saying a word. But Simon was too busy being Simon to catch on. Another call popped up. Nivedita ignored both it and the body-temperature drizzling rain clinging to every inch of her face that wasn't already clinging to the phone. She strolled out onto Bertha von Suttner Platz, and unlocked her bike. Simon was silent on the other end of the line. A timid clap of thunder piped up from behind the clouds, then also fell silent.

"Did you see my latest post?" she finally asked, trying to keep the non-existent conversation going. And that, believe it or not, was what made everything oh-so-much worse.

IT WAS THE time of day when you turn on the light and it just makes everything darker. Nivedita strode through the front door of her shared apartment, called out "I'm baaack," and the empty space swallowed up her voice just like the insulated walls of the radio studio, except that this time there was no cheerful Verena or melancholic Mona waiting for her. A quick peek into the kitchen confirmed that her first housemate wasn't home. Another peek behind the door with the mandala confirmed that her second housemate was also out. Opening the fridge, Nivedita pushed aside soggy cardboard take-out containers and labeled yet utterly unidentifiable jars of who-knows-what until she found a leftover bit of cheese and spread it on the lone remaining cracker, only to notice she wasn't hungry. Her phone vibrated on the kitchen table. She tried to ignore it, to show Simon she wasn't just sitting there waiting for his call. But because she also counted on him to hang up before leaving a message and then never try calling ever again, after an embarrassingly brief moment of restraint, she dashed over to get it. The voice on the other end sounded contrite enough all right, but it wasn't Simon.

"Nivi?" Priti said through a snivel.

"What's going on?" Nivedita asked, suddenly fearful.

Priti interjected, "Nivi?"

"I'm here. What happened?"

"Nivi?" Priti said for the third time, whereupon Nivedita decided to just yell if she asked a fourth time. Sandwiching the phone between ear and shoulder, she grabbed her bag and a glass of water, and elbowed her way into her own room. "Yup, uh-huh, yeah, this is Nivedita. Now that we've cleared that up . . ."

Priti interrupted her again, but this time uttered the four words that had long since become the formulaic intro to every crisis convo they'd ever had. "There was this boy . . ."

Although *boy* wasn't exactly accurate, since Saraswati's brother was closer to retirement than he was to puberty. "Old but gold."

"Saraswati's *what*?" Nivedita shouted, nearly dousing the T-shirt she'd tossed onto the bed that morning after trying it on.

"Her *brother*, aren't you listening?"

"Saraswati's *brother*?"

"Indeed."

"*Saraswati*'s brother?"

"In-deed," Priti repeated, almost forgetting to snivel this time.

"*Gold* . . . ?"

"You know—*in the sack*!"

"No, I *don't* know, 'cause I didn't even know Saraswati had a brother! And I certainly don't know how he is in bed!"

"Right, the only pants *you* want to get into are Saraswati's," sniffled Priti.

"You're hilarious. But—*Saraswati's brother*?!"

In time, Nivedita would assemble bits and pieces from Priti's disjointed anecdotes to reconstruct the entire epic, but even then she had to admit it might only partially correspond to reality. Priti was into young women, older men, trans people of any and every age—the more controversial, the sexier—and of course *Saraswati's brother* was über-controversial. To sleep with someone like that, with *him*, with *her brother*, was tantamount to sleeping with Saraswati while simultaneously shaking your bare ass, full-moon-twerk-style, right in her face, because—again, according to Priti—Saraswati and her brother hadn't spoken to one another in the last *thirty years*. In fact, they were so thoroughly estranged that Saraswati hadn't even told him that she'd *changed her name* . . .

And . . .

". . . *her color.*"

Just when Nivedita thought she'd hit rock bottom, and that the day couldn't possibly get any worse . . . boy was she wrong.

"She changed her *WHAT*?"

"Uh, yeah, her skin color."

3

It seemed like an eternity before Nivedita found her laptop under the pile of T-shirts. As the pale-blue light leaked from the screen onto her comforter, typos kept finding their way into her password (*milk* as in—yeah, you get it), but she finally nailed it. Ignoring the endless pings blowing up multiple apps on her computer, she opened a new browser tab and searched *Saraswati* and *white*, narrowing the search to the last twenty-four hours. Okay. Oh Kali. Okay. EIGHTY-FOUR THOUSAND results, each one like a punch hitting a different sore spot, striking every inch of her body.

Her stomach: *Scandal Surrounds Star Prof. of Postcolonial Studies* (*HuffPost*, three hours ago).

Her temples: *Prof. Curried Favor under False Pretenses* (*SPIEGEL Online*, an hour ago).

Her solar plexus: *D.U.'s Faux Guru: Düsseldorf, We Have a Problem* (*Die Tageszeitung*, 44 minutes ago).

One thousand and one questions arose in Nivedita's perplexed mind, but she had too little breath left to pose even one of them, even to herself. Instead, she heard her own voice, hanging lightly in the air, as if she'd huffed helium: "I don't believe it."

"There are pictures, too," Priti informed her in a voice dampened by tears, as if sinking into a mud pit.

"What?"

"Well, pics of Saraswati from . . . from before her metamorphosis."

But Nivedita had already found them. She randomly clicked on the first one and immediately regretted it. Saraswati looked like Madonna in her *Blond Ambition* period: the tips of her conical bustier thrust so aggressively through her jacket—a jacket you can be sure was still being marketed as a "men's jacket" back then—that passersby ran the risk of poking their eyes out, or impaling their quickly beating hearts; the only difference was that her gel-spiked coif was ash blond, not platinum. In the next image, a ginormous backpack was propped up against her *white* legs, which were in turn propped up against the Air India counter of a German airport ("They photoshopped that, I'd never have been able to afford Air India back then," she later explained, "I flew Emirates."). The next one showed her as a seventeen-year-old in a typical southern German living room, complete with piano and sectional sofa, alongside her equally many-years-younger-looking brother ("You slept with HIM?"), who even in that snapshot seemed to be trying to command her respect. But Saraswati—or rather the young woman who would one day become Saraswati—was staring straight at the camera lens, her lips pursed like she was about to blow a kiss, as if she'd just said *Foucault*.

COCONUT WOMAN

1

Nivedita was twenty-three when she first met Saraswati, who was almost twice as old at the time.

She had highlighted Saraswati's seminar in the expanded course catalog, ringing it in ink, multiple times. But, whereas most professors understood "expanded" as a cue to add further comment on the course content, Saraswati had instead just riffed "Kali studies—come and find out if you can study a goddess," with an image of Kali underneath. Nivedita's Kali. Nude, Black, sticking out her tongue, wearing a skirt of dismembered arms. The very Kali with whom Nivedita was already and always having endless conversations, albeit in her head, both when the world made no sense and when it made too much sense. The very Kali she'd followed each night of her entire life, who had led her off to sleep or had led her to stay awake, focused on the mere memory of sleep, and had danced through her earliest dreams.

Nivedita was still too young to read on her own, so it must've been her mother who read her *Little Red Riding Hood*. In any case, there she was, smack in the middle of a sentence, standing in a fairy-tale forest that looked suspiciously like a rain forest (maybe it was actually *The Jungle Book* her mother had read to her?), and from the dense foliage she spotted a dark figure waving to her with two arms while using all her other arms to part the branches. Nivedita immediately recognized Kali as the goddess whose image hung all over her parents' home—she even popped up in the family car, as a little figurine stuck to the dashboard, head bobbing, arms waving. So she posed the burning question she'd been asking herself ever since the very first time her little-girl finger had poked at that Kali figurine to bring it to life: "Why do you have so many arms, Kali?" Except in the dream, she formulated it as an exclamation, just like in the fairy tale: "Kali, how many arms you have!"

Kali's long red tongue unfurled from her wide smile. "All the better to hug you with, my child!"

Seeing the course title Kali Studies was like getting a message from that childhood, a world where identities were the stuff of fairy tales in which anything was possible and, just to make sure it wasn't overly harmonious, there was always a bunch of mischievous djinns standing by, ready to turn everything upside down, muddle every norm, and remix every notion of morality. Nivedita had just moved from Essen to Düsseldorf, was settling into a new apartment, and beginning her first year as a master's student in the Intercultural Studies and Postcolonial Theory program. She welcomed this familiar fragment from the past with all the ardor of her own astonishment.

"Kali Studies?" Priti had echoed over Skype those three long years ago, back when they spoke nearly every night, since both had just relocated. Priti had just landed in London, in the Department of War Studies at King's College (in reality, she hadn't gotten into the War Studies program, and had instead enrolled in German Studies, but by the time Nivedita found out it was already too late). "Everyone here is destined for the civil service," Priti continued, undaunted, "or government. While you all . . . I mean, Kali Studies? Where will that take you?"

A knock at the door saved her from having to answer.

"Yeah?"

"Well, what do you say—should we check it out?" asked Charlotte, her second roommate (who of course went by Lotte) as she strolled right in, cheeks aglow. Lotte was one of those giraffe-type women, super tall and lanky, long arms, long torso, and hardly any discernible waistline, so her overall look was less erotic than elegant. And of course Priti, who ranked everyone according to sexiness, didn't refrain from visibly expressing her verdict. Nivedita turned her laptop aside as Priti gestured—slicing her neck one, two, three times with her index finger—trying to keep her cousin outside her roommate's line of vision. All the while, Lotte rambled on with an endless stream of info, room numbers, times, days of the week, so it took Nivedita a while to catch on to what seminar Lotte was even talking about. But as soon as she said the magic name, it unexpectedly clicked.

Nivedita had thought she was the only one interested in Kali. And her intimate knowledge of the Indian goddess now spilled over onto Saraswati, whom she hadn't even met yet, so that in her mind the two of them fused into a single figure that promptly promised to take Nivedita into her many arms. It felt as if Lotte had caught her in the middle of some particularly kinky foreplay.

"Not Kinky Studies—Kali Studies," clarified Lotte, who of course already knew everything there was to know, at least about the professor. "She's a total cult figure," she said, trying to punctuate the pronouncement with a dramatic pause but then failing, as the words just kept gushing from her mouth. "Everybody's talking about her, Nivedita! *Ev-er-y-bo-dy!* Didn't you see her on that talk show? None other than Sandra Maischberger interviewed her—or was it Markus Lanz? Maybe both. I'm just afraid we might not get a spot."

SO IT WAS that two days later Nivedita and Lotte biked to campus together and squeezed into a standing-room-only lecture hall to await the arrival of the legendary Saraswati, who was clearly on her own schedule.

Fifteen minutes past the academically accepted fifteen-minute cushion, she finally stormed in, dupatta streaming, flung her leather briefcase onto the lectern, and paused in front of the blackboard, her back to everyone, as if she had to gather herself for a second before diving into the seminar, unveiling the provocation. Her hair cascaded long and black and heavy down her nape, causing the hair on Nivedita's own nape to shiver with a sensory memory of bristles tickling her skin when Priti used to brush it—an all-enveloping, synesthetic, whole-body ASMR experience of the sort that, otherwise, Nivedita only felt when listening to rain fall on gently flowing water, or looking at paintings by Amrita Sher-Gil, or smoking marijuana.

With a perfectly choreographed twirl, Saraswati turned toward the class, lifted her glasses from her eyes, held them before her furrowed brow while the chain dangled from them, and scrutinized the student ranks now before her. "Okay, let's start: all *whites* out."

Silence reigned as everyone wondered whether they'd heard right.

"C'mon, let's go, we haven't got all day. Grab your stuff. You can come back next semester. This seminar is for students of color only."

It was as if tectonic plates were shifting. Mountains rose up where before there had been empty planes. The earth burst open and something broke off the continent known as Nivedita, drifting out into an ocean of possibilities.

"Umm, I say, that wasn't in the course description," Lotte protested, as Nivedita marveled at her tenacity, if not at her inability to assess dangerous situations.

Saraswati gave Lotte a good long look and, clearly amused, replied, "Is the word *out* really so hard to understand that you need me to spell it o-u-t for you?"

Without another word, Lotte gathered the pencil case she'd bought on Etsy and her Moleskine from the desk. The first bunch of grumbling students had already begun pushing their way out the door when a lithe girl with ivory skin—the shade a chain-smoking elephant's tusk would have, that is—raised her hand.

"Yes?"

"Who counts as a student of color? I mean, where do you draw the line?" the young woman asked with audible uncertainty.

Saraswati clapped, "Excellent question! Who here feels that term applies to them?"

A few students hesitatingly stood up.

"You can stay!"

Lotte also stood up, albeit with her pack all ready to go. "You coming?" she whispered. The hurt visible on Lotte's face pained Nivedita, but leaving would've pained even more.

"I'm staying," she whispered back, and then quickly added, "for a bit," just to console Lotte.

"But you're *white*," Lotte said.

"No, I'm not *white*," Nivedita said, for the very first time in her entire life to a *white* person. She'd already tried convincing Priti, countless times, that she had just as much of a right to claim her mixed heritage as Priti herself did, since they're relatives, after all (Seriously, *Herrgottnochmal*, or should she say *Good Lord!* Or maybe *Hey Raam!* . . .). Up until now, she'd never denied a *white* German their ostensible common ground. But there wasn't a colonial army on the whole planet that could've kicked her out of this seminar.

She sure as hell couldn't say any of that to Lotte, though, without hurting her even more. She might as well have just said "Girlfriend, I belong to a club you can't join." Even though Nivedita also had to admit that Lotte belonged to a ton of clubs that wouldn't admit her. Like the club of girls who could charm everyone with their doe-eyed expressions—whatever it was Lotte was always expressing, since she was constantly deploying her doe eyes to get whatever she wanted. Like the club of girls who always went "home" for Christmas, meaning "home to Hannover, Germany's heartland." Like the club of girls who were always observing that the TV shows they watched every night had too few women in starring roles while at the same time failing to observe that the shows had too few melanated people in any roles.

Yet Nivedita always agreed with Lotte, of course, saying she too would love to see more female role models. Which is exactly why it was now so exciting to see one such role model swaggering at the front of class, before her very eyes, so close she could even touch her if she just clambered up onto her graffitied desk and reached her arm out. Maybe Saraswati wasn't exactly strutting back and forth, but in Nivedita's eyes she was too dynamic to just stand there and lecture.

"Well now!" Saraswati said, brimming with satisfaction as she closed the door behind the last *white* students to leave. "Let us begin. Why did you all stay?" Nivedita's throat swelled with silence, until she was sure all the words she'd never said would now cause her to burst. While her mind was still pondering precisely where to start, her mouth let loose, and out tumbled the story of Kali and the jungle, but this time it didn't end "all the better to hug you with, my child!" Instead, she heard her own voice saying, "all the better to rip your heart from your chest with, and then replace it with a stronger, better heart, my child!"

Saraswati gave her a good long look, about as long as the one she'd given Lotte earlier, and Nivedita considered grabbing her things and running after her roommate, but then Saraswati asked, "What's your name?"

"Nivedita."

"Come by my office sometime this week, Nivedita."

IDENTITTI

Why is Kali so cool? Let me count the ways:

1. She's a goddess. I mean, where do you find goddesses anymore? Okay, that's BS, there are actually tons of goddesses. (Can there be such a thing as enough goddesses? That's a whole other post—stay tuned!) But do any of today's dominant world religions venerate a goddess anymore, not to mention the better question of whether any of these religions boasts so many goddam goddesses that you can't even count them?

2. She's nude without being erotic. Okay, that's BS too, I actually think she's super sexy. In her original form, Kali had not just one vulva, but hundreds. Scooch your cooch over, Venus! Kali's eroticism isn't the modest-maiden-standing-in-a-seashell-shielding-her-bosom-with-one-arm-while-crossing-her-legs-like-she's-gotta-pee type. Nuh-uh. Kali's nudity says: I can strangle a Bengal tiger with my bare hands, so watch out, or I'll eat you for breakfast.

3. She's dark. Yeah, Black. Sometimes she's even dark blue or dark brown, and I've even seen a dark green Kali. But if there's one thing she isn't, it's *white*.

4. She's fierce and furious and drinks the blood of her slain adversaries. That's how I want my goddesses. Okay, that's how I want *myself* to be: fabulous and frightening, inimitable and incalculable, and yeah, I'll say it, I'd love to don a skirt of my enemies' lopped-off arms. Okay, okay, I'd much rather have no enemies whatsoever, because I'd be so frightening that nobody would dare mess with me.

5. During sex, Kali's always on top.

"During sex, Kali's always on top," said Saraswati. "Why does that matter? After all, any old goddess can have sex absolutely any way she wants."

I'm right on this, thought Nivedita, *I'm right!* The thought terrified her as much as it turned her on.

"Because it's not a personal preference, it's a political choice," Saraswati said, answering her own question. "You all know the story of Snow White and the prince." With dramatic flair, she pointed her remote at the projector and the PowerPoint appeared. The first slide, taken straight from a classic edition of *Snow White*, showed a glass casket with a fairy-tale prince looming over it. The next slide had nearly the same composition, but this time the white, lifeless figure lying on the ground was the Hindu god Shiva, and Kali wasn't looming *over* him, she was *on top of* him. Saraswati beamed her Kali-style smile at the class and continued: "Here we see dead Shiva. Shiva is a *shava*, meaning a corpse, because he chose to withdraw from the world as an ascetic. And it's Kali who brings him back to life by . . . nope, not with a kiss . . . but . . . ? That's right, you guessed it: she "kisses" him with her *other* lips. Which brings up a few other intriguing questions regarding consent, but we'll get to that later in the semester. For today, let's focus on the fact that Kali refuses to be invisible. She forces Shiva to see her, to notice her, thereby forcing him to empathize with the world around him. So this myth is about recognizing that everyone and everything has a soul, and that soul must be respected. It's about love as a revolutionary act."

Click, Mahatma Gandhi appears.

Click, Martin Luther King Jr.

Click, bell hooks.

Nivedita took notes like her life depended on it. Normally she doodled her way through lectures, sketching naked ladies all over her notebooks, and every now and then jotting down keywords like *social constructivism*, *brute facts*, or, most recently, *critical race theory*. Saraswati was the first professor with whom Nivedita heard those terms appear in entirely new formulations, and that was because these sentences spoke directly to Nivedita, *and that was because Saraswati's sentences spoke directly about Nivedita.*

"And why is love a revolutionary act? Because it's the first thing you teach people you plan to colonize–slash–oppress–slash–discriminate against: that they don't belong, that they aren't worthy of love," Saraswati continued, as Nivedita took it all down in her notebook. "And that's meaningful because we only feel empathy for subjects worthy of love—hence, consequently, they *are the only ones who can enforce their right to such empathy.* It's no coincidence that all groups and individuals who experience discrimination share a common sense that they're less worthy, and worth less, than others. More specifically, that they don't deserve as much love. 'Nobody could ever love someone like me' isn't a personal declaration stemming from a personal problem, rather it's a social declaration pointing to a social problem. Of course a social problem can turn into a personal problem—but that's a whole other issue. For today, let's stick to structural problems."

A girl in mustard-yellow glasses and a wax-print turban sitting next to Nivedita whispered anxiously, "I thought this was about racism . . ."

Nivedita whispered back, "Hey, this *is* about racism," and then wondered where her vehement tone had come from.

"And that's what's so insidious about love, or the deprivation of love, used as political weapon: it doesn't even have to be about a 'real' threat. The mere fear of losing love–slash–never being loved–slash–being loved less is enough to psychologically and even physically stunt people." Saraswati looked each student, one after the other, deep in the eyes. Several minutes passed before she continued, but nobody noticed, because they were all too busy reflecting on their own lack of received love. The girl who had just complained about the lecture not focusing enough on racism cried a single, sharply visible tear and made zero effort to hide it.

Throughout her relationship with Simon, Nivedita repeatedly returned to scan her notes from this very first seminar with Saraswati and thought: *Fuuuuuuuck!*

But in this very moment her only thought was: *Wooooooow!*

After establishing eye contact with every single student, Saraswati grabbed her book-laden leather briefcase and whipped out her best seller at exactly the same moment as its cover image flashed onto the oversized screen. "Decolonization means we have to decolonize not just business and politics, not just our theories and practices, but our own souls, too," she said while writing *Decolonize Your Soul* on the blackboard. "We can only behave with esteem toward other people of color once we've internalized a sense of self-esteem. Before we can love our enemies, we first have to behave better with, and relate better to, our friends."

IN THE BATHROOM closest to the lecture hall, someone had scrawled "breasts not bombs" on the wall, and someone else had added "Viva la Vul-valation!" Nivedita took a selfie and thought about how she could put what had just happened into words. Maybe: *Discovering Saraswati feels like being at a party thrown solely for us*?

But even without her blog, her Twitter, and her Instagram, word about Saraswati spread like wildfire through all the secret channels that somehow always ensured that all the right people got all the right info. Over the following few weeks, more and more students of color joined them, finding their way from other departments, even other universities. Saraswati was the only prof. with a nose ring. Saraswati was the only prof. who was Saraswati. Identity politics was huge, and Nivedita's understanding of it was scant. And everyone was having a blast.

The only thing Nivedita knew was that, suddenly, she was someone—a person with a past and, consequently, perhaps even a future. She was no longer an absence, a blank page, a void within a space where childhood and adolescence were only conceivable in and envisioned for "*German* German" families. Suddenly she was anecdotes and recollections and body memory, because suddenly her anecdotes and recollections had meaning—not to mention her body memory!

And that's why Nivedita got busy, determined to collect as many new corporeal sensations and experiences as possible. Meaning: For the first time in her life, she got busy with men of color.

Although she and they had always cautiously circled one another and then courteously avoided one another, each turning to *white* sex partners—be it out of fear they'd infect one another with their otherness, or out of fear they'd only discover they weren't as special as they'd always been treated—now an entirely new buffet of sexual possibilities opened up: Are you homo, hetero, inter- or intraracial?

For Nivedita, sex with other POCs meant putting herself on the market for the first time without her unique selling point. It was the first time she was really naked. It all came to a head when she fell in love with Anish, whose parents were both from Kerala—not like hers, who came from West Bengal and Poland and wherever. She was awaiting the inevitable moment he was bound to say: "You're not really a real Indian."

Instead, he said: "Sometimes I wonder what my parents see when they look at me. A potato?"

They were lying on the mattress in his room, the window wide open. The autumnal scent of asters wafted in, as did the dismayed cries of his roommate, whose partner was closing the door on their relationship while literally leaving the window open for their breakup fight to be heard by all. As they lobbed insults at one another, Anish pressed his body against Nivedita's as if she were the only one capable of saving him from the abyss of his own existence.

The fact that Anish viewed sex with Nivedita as proof that he was who he thought he was acted as a powerful aphrodisiac. *But am I who I think I am?* she wondered.

2

"You're a coconut," someone had told Nivedita the first time she visited Birmingham, and she didn't understand. Well, technically speaking, she understood every single word—but she didn't get what that was supposed to mean. She didn't even know which kid had said it first, but suddenly they were all saying it: Coconut! Coconut!

She was eight and it was summer—shimmering and glitzy as Art Stuff Glitter Lotion, bright as turmeric rice, perfumed as the scented colored pencils she and her cousin Priti, who was thirteen months older, kept sharpening until only stubs remained, just to keep sniffing their synthetic smell. The shavings drifted down like ribbons onto the sidewalk behind the courtyard out back, accumulating on top of the hopscotch court drawn in chalk. The alley was dotted by a pile of pallets, a disemboweled old freezer chest whose tangled wires were hanging out, and a beat-up shopping cart. All these random surfaces were crowned by kids sitting or squatting atop them—kids who all looked like Nivedita.

"The kids there look like you," her mother had promised while packing a suitcase for their visit to the daughter of her dad's oldest sister. There was a word for how they were related, something involving degrees, but Nivedita didn't know what it was. All she knew was that dad's oldest sister was Didi—but that was her *title*, not her *name*, which was Purna—and her daughter was Leela . . . Nivedita still couldn't really understand how the gorgeous, haughty woman in a flame-colored sari who'd picked her up at the airport could be her cousin, even though she was old enough to be her mother, and that she had a daughter about the same age as Nivedita: Priti. So many names, so many intertwining family ties.

Auntie Leela, who was actually Cousin Leela, drove a mini car, but not an actual Mini, just a Vauxhall Nova. She was a doctor, but she wasn't rich, because she worked for the National Health Service, and they lived in Birmingham, but Leela and Priti called it Balsall Heath. Or sometimes Balti Heath, because only Indian families lived there, and all these families had kids. It was like the whole world had suddenly turned brown.

"We're going home," Nivedita had told her classmates, not because she'd actually mistaken Birmingham for Bombay, let alone Kolkata, but because she, too, wanted to "go home" for once, just like all her Turkish and Polish friends.

But in the snapshots her mother took of her and Priti and Priti's little brother Aarul in Birmingham, it actually did look like they were in India. At least that's how Nivedita always pictured India, chockablock with sofas and wall hangings decorated with so many little mirrored bits that they looked like someone had liberally spread them with the glittery lotion she so adored. The first time she saw the pictures on her mother's digital camera, she felt something expanding inside her, spreading out from her stomach, but she couldn't quite name it—it was like a combination of warmth and something totally new to her, something unfamiliar, something like an almost triumphant feeling of belonging.

And so it was as if the voices coming from the alley lined by those pallets and the freezer chest, the voices whispering *coconut*, took that feeling and smushed it up into a tiny, seething-hot ball of shame.

"Priti called me coconut," Nivedita said that night at dinner, although she said it in German for her mother's sake—and to keep Priti from understanding. "What's that mean?"

Her mother, Birgit, shot a quick glance across the dining-room table at Priti, who calmly continued tearing her chapatis, indifferent. Birgit was wearing the blue sari Leela had given her, and looked a bit like the Virgin Mary—if Mary were ever to have inadvertently wandered into the *Mahabharata*—and for the first time, Nivedita noticed that her mother was *white*.

"Oh, it doesn't mean anything, sweetie," her mother brushed it off with a silly high-pitched giggle.

Nivedita thought about it a little while, and then disagreed: "If it didn't mean anything, she wouldn't have said it."

Again, that silly giggle. Once Nivedita hit puberty, that giggle would fill her with a white-hot rage, making her so livid she wanted to knock it right out of her mother, no matter what it took. But on that particular vacation evening, as the setting sun cast its wistful rays through the window and then became one with the saffron-yellow walls, Nivedita hadn't yet loaded her mother's little laugh with any baggage—namely, years of conflict avoidance and evasion. That night, it just made Nivedita impatient.

"What does coconut mean?" she insisted. This time her voice wasn't any louder, but it was more penetratingly shrill, and Priti looked up.

"Maybe it's because coconuts are hairy, and you have such long, beautiful hair?" her mother ventured nervously, and Nivedita immediately became aware of her eyebrows, which were furrowing together over the top of her nose, as if to underscore why she'd never be chosen to play Maria in *West Side Story*, Baby in *Dirty Dancing*, or Elsa in *Frozen* for the school musical. Those roles were reserved for girls like her classmate Lilli, whose delicate, always-arched-in-surprise eyebrows made her look like a younger version of Lotte: Me? As Maria/Baby/Every-other-female-lead-you-could-ever-dream-of? For real?

FOURTEEN YEARS LATER, when Nivedita was finally studying with Saraswati, she sometimes gave herself a monobrow with makeup, à la Frieda Kahlo, brow-penciling her way into the #unibrowmovement. But that was later—back then, in Auntie Leela's dining room, the best Birgit could do was quickly pull herself together and stare sternly at Priti, who gazed right back at her nefariously. It was a nefarious gaze because Priti clearly resented her overly friendly, overly frantic, overly loud, broken-English-speaking German aunt, but still, all she did was beam an overly cheerful smile across the table. German women were silly fools, Priti concluded, although Nivedita only heard that from her much later. In any case, they were nothing like in the movie *Run Lola Run*. Franka Potente had given her the impression they were strong and sexy and, well, *potent*, but apparently they weren't. The rumors she'd heard about German women's armpit hair were true, but that was all—it was so weird.

After dinner, Priti took Nivedita aside. "You want to know what it means?" she asked almost tenderly, and from that very second up to the moment Nivedita remembered cradling a little shard of paisley-like, perfectly fish-shaped glass in the palm of her hand, her memory was a complete blank. She didn't remember leaving the house with Priti, or climbing up onto the freezer chest together, or the other kids forming a circle around them. Every time she tried to reconstruct the scene later on, their whispered chanting of *coconut, coconut, coconut* blurred into a dialect she only partially understood, but the ultimate verdict was: *You aren't authentic.* And like an indelible stamp, it made an impression on Nivedita's entire being. Over the following years, whenever anyone was disappointed that she didn't know how to cook traditional Indian dishes, or perform classical Indian dance, or play the sitar, she heard: *Coconut.* And the most coconutty thing about her was that she didn't speak a single one of India's 121 languages (or 19,569 languages, depending on which census you chose to believe).

Aside from English, that is. But of course English didn't count.

Then again, Hindi didn't count, either. Because Nivedita's perfect-A classmate Lilli went on to study yoga during several extended stays at various ashrams after which she spoke perfect Hindi. Nevertheless, because of her henna-red hair and milk-white complexion, nobody ever took Lilli for Indian. But then nobody ever took Nivedita for Indian either, despite her hair and skin color.

She had always assumed that was because of her *white* mother—who (per Priti's TV- and movie-fueled insider knowledge) she now saw as an inferior, incomplete version of the *typische Deutsche Frau*, with the exception of her armpit hair, which was the only part of her that measured up—but then one day Lotte finally got to the crux of it: "You just never really bothered to be Indian."

Nivedita was taken aback by the unusual degree of wisdom in her roommate's words. For people like Nivedita, *being* wasn't really something you *were*, it was something you *did*. In her case, that meant striving after a cliché of what it meant to be an Indian woman. But the problem with clichés was that they were always based on the most conservative aspects of the most traditional iterations: meaning an archetypal, Sita-esque Indian ultrafemininity, rather than a quirkier, Kali-esque Indian Queerness. ("Sita, Rama's wife, not *sitar,* the musical instrument," Nivedita explained to Lotte, whereupon Lotte asked, "Rama, like the margarine?" But of course this Rama had nothing to do with the margarine brand you find in virtually every German household, which had originally been called Rahma like *Rahm,* meaning "cream," but German dairy famers protested because it wasn't a real dairy product, so, voilá, extract the *h* and your imitation butter might now seem to be named after a legendary mega-masculine prince-turned-god. So then Nivedita did her best to summarize the plot of the *Ramayana*: "Okay, so Rama's a god and Sita is a goddess, and she was abducted by the demon king Ravana. Rama tried to free her with the help of Hanuman—a god who is also a monkey, who can also fly, and move mountains and all that, because that's how a god should be, right? Anyway, a god certainly shouldn't be like Rama, who first frees Sita but then also accuses her of cheating on him with Ravana, talk about total victim blaming. And then, on top of that, he expects her to undergo trial by fire, because everybody knows that abstaining from sex makes you fireproof. So then what does Sita do? Pathetically, she forgives the creep! Can you imagine Kali ever doing such a thing?" "What, move mountains?" Lotte asked, obviously a bit lost.)

Nivedita had long thought that the lurking feeling that she had no right to her Indian roots lay in the fact that India was just so far away. Then, at some point, she decided this distance was more of an emotional issue than a geographic one—meaning: it stemmed from colonialism. The first guy she fell in love with was "mixed" like her, which might well have been *why* she fell in love with him. But even though he didn't learn French until high school, he was still *fièrement français.* Ultimately, being French was something anyone could envision because everyone had seen all the French films full of talking incessantly and smoking even more. *And all of us have smoked at least once in our lives, or definitely at least talked.*

After Lotte had told Nivedita how to really be Indian, she fished a white T-shirt from the bag of old clothes destined for the donation bin, got a textile marker, and wrote *This is what an Indian looks like!* on it. A second later, she crossed out *looks* and wrote *feels. In case identities are something you feel. In case identities are even a thing.*

That was the problem: As soon as you start thinking about identity, reality starts compartmentalizing itself in so many damn dimensions and directions that you run out of words for them all. And then along came Saraswati, saying that it didn't matter, and that you can't live a precolonial life in postcolonial times, so instead it was just a matter of playing with the constructed nature of authenticity and beyond-authenticity, and not letting anyone assign you a fixed role amid the ruins of all the various empires. *Party like there's no yesterday!*

3

But Nivedita didn't know any of that on the day she sat atop that old freezer chest back in Balti Heath, the soles of her sandals drumming on the deep-sounding, hollow metal behind the white enamel surface. The blue sky was so spotless it looked scrubbed clean. The air smelled of gasoline and dust. The shard of glass she held was green as a reed, with bits of yellow sprinkled throughout, and slightly curved, as if it were a real fish you'd spot in the sea, sunlight glistening on its scales. But it was motionless and real in her hand—and sharp and oh-so-real when she dragged it across her brown arm. Outside brown, inside . . . "I'm not *white* inside, I'm red! Look!"

And, for a moment, all the kids were indeed looking at her. She had everyone's undivided attention and, sure, something you might even call respect.

"And who's red? Indians!" she exclaimed triumphantly, as if it were A-OK to replace one form of racism with another. "I'm an Indian!"

"Yeah, maybe American Indian," a girl with dreadlocks shot back scornfully.

Nivedita wanted to mount a counterargument, but couldn't find the words. Finally "Anglo Indian" sprang to mind, and everyone burst into boisterous laughter. The cut started to burn, and she felt the urge to pee, and then she felt even more of an urge to cry, when suddenly she felt a hand on her shoulder. Someone was patting her on the back. She thought the only place anyone ever patted a kid on the back was in Enid Blyton books. But now, undeniably, one of the older, cooler kids was patting her on the back, his hand as steady and warm as a caress: "Good for you, coconut!"

She now realized it was the very same voice that had started the whole coconut thing.

"Coconuts aren't nuts, you know. They're fruit," was Priti's retort as she jumped down off the freezer chest. And with that leap, in Nivedita's eyes, Priti ceased being merely her cousin. By the time her feet landed on the gravel below, she had become her friend.

AT LEAST SOMETIMES she was. Because from then on, Nivedita noticed that Priti had the power, at whim, to either bestow or deny her a sense of belonging. And the power worked in one direction only, because Priti had something Nivedita didn't—namely, a mom who wore saris all the time, not just when visiting family—so Nivedita always felt like a cheap imitation of Priti, like a cover version of a classic song, like a watered-down well drink compared to top-shelf single malt. Nivedita's problem wasn't that she didn't have a clearly delineated identity, her problem was that she felt like identities were something for everyone but her. Like she had no right to one because she fell through the cracks, somewhere between the categories. Even most theories about racism didn't seem to apply to people like her. Instead, they seemed intended for people who were more . . . unambiguous. For people who, sure, were still denied the right to a *here*, but nevertheless carried a *there* in their hearts, a heritage, some kind of background, or at least roots inherited from their parents. Anything but the confusing, impossible mishmash of backgrounds and supposed senses of belonging she felt, for which there was no clear model, no structure, just a chaotic mess of nested cocoons, a snarled skein of stories and histories that made no sense whatsoever and about which she knew hardly anything.

Nivedita had never felt represented anywhere—until the day Saraswati strode in for that first seminar. In that sense, Saraswati was more like family to her than her real family—with her overly empathetic-to-the-point-of-suffering mother and her utterly silent father. He didn't know how to tell his story to anyone—not even himself, and certainly not his anti-racist daughter, whose rage against the system was only exceeded by her rage against him, but only because he didn't display enough rage himself. Nivedita needed Saraswati to discover who she was.

BUT AT THE time Priti dropped that bomb, Nivedita didn't even know who Saraswati was.

DOWN ON ME

1

Priti started to cry on the other end of the line: "I'm so, so sorry!"

"Sorry about what, exactly? What did you do?" Nivedita asked in a whisper. The last light of day drained from the room like someone had pulled the plug on the sun, leaving her stranded in the dark on her bed, now illuminated solely by her laptop and the images of Saraswati sans any recognizable attributes. And, along with her mentor, Nivedita's piles of clothes, wine-crate bookshelves, and the utensil drawer she'd salvaged while dumpster-diving and used to transform the kitchen table into a writing desk had all lost their recognizable features and had turned into something else, something unknown. But Priti stayed true to herself: "I've gotta go, Niv!"

"Wait!" Nivedita yelled despite all previous experience with her cousin, who of course had already hung up and wouldn't answer a callback. Loneliness pounced in the form of a panic attack, and she scrolled back through all her missed calls: Priti. Lotte. Priti. Her roommate Barbara. Priti. Her mother. Lotte. Various classmates. Priti. Verena from this morning at Radio New . . . Verena?

But when she tried calling her back, it went straight to voice mail. The daylight seemed to have taken all warmth away with it, and Nivedita wrapped her blanket around her shoulders. It didn't really make her any warmer, but it did make the bits of her body that weren't under the blanket feel colder. Cold, *white* Saraswati stared at her from the screen, lips pursed.

"Hello, Kali? Are you there?" she whispered into the empty room.

I'm always here, the shadows answered.

ANISH HAD BEEN the first man Nivedita didn't feel like an alien around— or at least she didn't feel like the only alien in their relationship—but he also had depressive tendencies whereas she, despite her general dereliction, was chronically content. So the countdown clock was ticking, even though they didn't really hear it, until one day at lunch in the college cafeteria Anish announced that he was going to India to find himself.

"But you can't go to India to find yourself—you're Indian," she said, horrified.

"Exactly," he replied, as if that said it all.

"But what about me . . . ?" In a panic, Nivedita played out what would happen if she just up and left Saraswati's seminar, her blog, and her apartment for an undisclosed span of time in order to explore India with Anish. To her dismay, nothing seriously stood in the way: she could sublet her room, Saraswati had long been encouraging her to go to Shantiniketan and spend a semester or two studying at Visva-Bharati University, and as for her blog . . . wholly unbidden, a vision popped up in her mind's eye: the blog would get a new header, in flame-yellow type, her Instagram would fill with gorgeous images, and on Twitter all she'd need to post was *Identitti Presents: A Passage to India Redux*. But Anish simply stared at her with an abysmally sad look in his eyes, and it dawned on her that she had absolutely no role to play in his self-discovery.

Of course she did have a role, it was just a negative one—she would appear *in absentia*, you might say.

"If you and I stayed together, I'd always and forever be trying to be the man you need," he said with a note of melancholy so deep that it was all-encompassing, leaving no room for her pain. Anish began reaching across the table to cradle her hands in his and comfort her, but got lost on the way, and ended up sketching an *om* sign on the tabletop with a stray drop of salad dressing. Nivedita stared at his fingers, which seemed too long and lanky for his otherwise pudgy-palmed hands, and tried in vain to commit every line and dimple to memory.

And what's so bad about being the man I need? she thought—without saying it. Instead, she blurted out, "When're you coming back?" As she did, she realized it didn't matter.

But Anish loved her too much to spell it out.

And Nivedita loved him too much to spell out the absurdity of his whole sometimes-an-Indian-guy's-gotta-do-what-an-Indian-guy's-gotta-do philosophy, so her response to the ensuing silence was a straightforward, "I get it."

And it was true, she understood him. That was the problem with Anish: she always understood him, although that in no way meant things would work out between the two of them.

It was only when Anish came up during office hours with Saraswati that she grasped the full implications of his plan. Nivedita had always cried like a *desi* girl, loud and luxuriously lachrymose. Nobody had to teach her that crying was something best done with one's entire body. So she ran across campus convulsing as if possessed by an evil spirit, so shaken that even her teeth chattered. Then, as if offering a solution to all her problems, a hand reached out through the tidal wave of pain, held her fast, and Simon's voice asked: "Where you coming from and where're you off to in such a rush?"

Nivedita knew Simon from student government and various protests, where his phone number was circulated as the emergency contact for anyone who got arrested, because he was studying law—even if he always gave the impression that his number was wasted on students of color like her, since identity politics wasn't *real politics*. So, with as much pride as she could muster while her nose ran like a faucet, she shot right back: "Brace yourself: I'm from here—just like you—and where I'm headed is none of your business."

"No, I mean, where you coming from *just now*? I thought I saw you in the cafeteria," Simon said without loosening his grip. "Are you okay?" *Good question. What's the right answer here? Er, uh, I mean: What's your number?* she thought. Catching a whiff of his cashmere-and-silk sweater, plus the sandalwood scent of his skin, Nivedita suddenly had the feeling that maybe there was a deeper meaning underlying life's chance encounters.

Being with Simon was magical at first. Nivedita spent half her time supporting Anish and his long goodbye, the other half in Simon's powder-blue Clio on equally long drives through the autumnal landscape of the Lower Rhein region, and the third half on significantly shorter essays for Saraswati's seminar—she took a pic of every paper before turning it in so that, after it was graded, she could then post it with nary a change on her blog.

For the first time, really, life made sense. Simon seemed to be the only one who could decode it, gleaning meaning from the plowed fields and the crows cavorting on high-voltage power lines. They'd pull over to take in the view and, their hair waving in the breeze as they drank tea from his stainless-steel thermos, he'd eye the corvids and confess: "I'd never have thought I could feel like this about anyone ever again." Nivedita inhaled the intoxicating scent of lanolin from his fleece jacket—which was surprisingly lovely for loden—and felt the tea's warmth spreading through her chest. What *like this* meant, well, he didn't say. He was exactly like Anish, only even more desperate and *white*, a detail which meant Nivedita could be fairly certain he wouldn't just up and pack his bags and take off for some unknown homeland. She had no way of knowing that Simon was perfectly capable of just up and packing his bags for no reason whatsoever.

AND BECAUSE THE mere thought of Simon was so deliciously distressing, Nivedita opened his Facebook profile. He never posted his relationship status, so nothing had changed there, and she couldn't draw any conclusions. That said, since his Last Call (capital *L*, capital *C*), he had posted a picture of an orange garbage truck with ACAB graffitied on it, and before that a picture of his hand holding a drink of the same color, and before that an oh-so-wise aphorism that read *People who ask whether the glass is half full or half empty haven't yet realized that you can refill the glass.*

While Nivedita was still staring at the picture Simon had posted, some-one named Marina added a comment with a string of emojis, which clearly struck a chord with the click-happy masses because the comment immediately sprang as many heads as an Indian goddess, and every single head was laughing so hard it was crying. Nivedita clicked on Marina's name and discovered she liked Marie Kondo—or, if not exactly liked, she surmised from the countless critical articles Marina had shared, many of which actually panned her, that she nevertheless had a keen interest in being tidy. Practically the only thing Marina never posted were pictures of herself Nivedita could compare herself to.

The overture of "L'Internationale" welled up from her Messenger app: "Did you see Saraswati has her own hashtag now?!!!" Lotte wrote.

NO WAY!!!, Nivedita almost wrote, before opting for the more level-headed: "Nah, what is it?"

Instead of answering, Lotte wrote back: "Whaddya make of that call to give her the boost?" But by then Nivedita had found the hashtag—or, rather, *hashtags*:

> » **Call me Zadie @OutsideSisters** *New world record for cultural appropriation #SaraswatiShame*
>
> » **Fatma Aydemir @fatma_morgana** *that's not exactly how "POC is self-identification" was intended #SarasWhitey*
>
> » **Sibel Schick @sibelschick** *Jerrys really want to be racially oppressed, but they can't, so instead they just dye their skin a few shades darker like some sad Black Pete on Shrove Monday #SaraswatiShame*
>
> » **Nexotism @GauguinIsDead** *Potato = wannabe Chappati #SaraswatiShame #SaraswatiNeverAgain*
>
> » **Derya X @BrownLikeMe** *WTF?!? #SarasWhitey*
>
> » **Sausage Dawg @EffOffMissy** *#Saraswatishame that's not racism, it's just repugnant*
>
> » **Thorben Rackel @DrDr** *Islam doesn't belong in Germany!*

"Give her the boost?" Nivedita wrote to Lotte, scratching her head.

"Sorry, typo! Whaddya make of that call to give her the BOOT?!!!"

» Valerie Solanas II @AntiJaneEyre *When will D.U. finally grow a pair?*
  #SaraswatiRaus
» Call me Zadie @OutsideSisters *Saraswati told us what to think for so*
  long, now it's time for us to tell her what not to think #SaraswatiRaus
» Fatma Aydemir @fatma_morgana *white privilege at its best: when*
  there's money and fame to be had, suddenly they wanna be like us
  #SarasWhitey
» Minh Thu Tran (Trần Võ Minh Thư) @tran_vominhthu *You know why*
  #Saraswati really makes me mad? I didn't ask to look the way I do. As a
  POC, I had to take a stand against racism and deal with it. She "chose"
  to identify as a racialized person so she could seem "more credible."
  How absurd.
» D.U. POC Dept. @POC_StudentCouncil *Name a word with two is in a*
  row? Easy: ProfiIndian #Saraswatigate
» Karen Heimann @ARoseByAnyOtherName *Protest starting noon*
  tomorrow, meet at D.U. student union #SaraswatiRaus #Racism
  #Düsseldorf
» The Hessian @TheHessian *Islam doesn't belong in Germany!*
  #fireSaraswati

It was all so far beyond comprehension that, for one wild moment, Nivedita was thrilled to not have to think about Simon, as the throbbing vein of tweets flowed like a veritable river, following her meandering path deeper into the labyrinth. But no matter how many livid twists and turns she scrolled through, it seemed the Monster was always waiting right around the corner, just out of view, and she felt its breath take the form of her own panic.

At some point her eyes began to burn—maybe because her laptop was now the only light source, or maybe because of the vitriol gushing forth onscreen, or maybe both—and there was no way she could cross the chasm between the bed and the light switch. The only sound capable of breaking the spell would be that of a key turning in the locked door.

As if on cue, her roommate Barbara called out from the hallway, right before opening the door to her room: "Allow me to introduce you to our Asian cleaning lady—say 'namaste' to Nivedita! It's a foreign word, it means 'hello,' because Nivedita doesn't speak much German."

"*Ich kann nicht so viel Deutsch,*" Nivedita, parroting Barbara, said to the older man standing behind her, embarrassed (*since when is everybody screwing older guys?*), and instead of saying hello—or even namaste— he simply gestured, tilting his bottle of Monkey Shoulder triple malt in her direction.

"I *just* taught her that sentence," laughed Barbara, who looked like she'd *just* had sex in a taxi, which may well have been the case.

"She *just* taught me that sentence," Nivedita smiled, and noticed that she wasn't feeling as fatalistic as she had earlier. Barbara's presence always had that effect on her. Also, she'd turned on the light in the hallway.

"Have you already eaten?" Barbara asked. "We got bibimbap."

Nivedita shed her blanket and followed the two of them into the kitchen, where Barbara lit some candles and instructed her awkwardly shy guy to set the table. Nivedita, who would've been fine eating right out of the plastic take-out containers, felt the apartment coming back to life. It sucked that Barbara wasn't there very often.

"Have you seen the allegations against Saraswati . . . ?" Nivedita began asking. She was surprised to hear Barbara's companion pipe up first.

"Yeah, shocking, isn't it?"

"Bullshit," Barbara interjected dismissively while using the weight of her entire body to press the empty takeout containers into the overflowing garbage can. "I think it's totally punk."

"Punk?" he replied, perplexed.

"Paul and Saraswati are colleagues," Barbara clarified before planting a juicy kiss on his lips. "He's just pretending to be miffed to camouflage the fact that he's just committed a criminal act with a student."

"Criminal?" Paul echoed. "Punk?"

"Uh, yeah, duh—can you think of anything more radical?"

Right then, even Nivedita could have kissed Barbara.

Paul was rather less thrilled. "We already have enough problems at D.U. with 'Miss Jean Brodie,'" he grumbled.

"That's an amazing movie about an any-resemblance-to-actual-people-we-all-know-is-entirely-coincidental Superstar Professor. You totally have to watch it," Barbara filled Nivedita in.

"Book—it's an amazing book," Paul corrected her, plucked a flyer that read *Fuck Patriarchy! Feminism Rules! The Cunt is Queen!* from the fridge, turned it over, and wrote *Muriel Spark* on the back, but then Barbara snatched it from his hands.

"Movie! The book is boring," she added.

Nivedita tried answering all the W-questions—was it really criminal to have consensual sex with a student? (no); what did the term "colleague" mean if she'd never run into Paul in the postcolonial studies program? (As would later become clear, he was a professor of clinical psychology, and, much like Priti, Barbara liked fucking people of a higher social status); what was the book title again? (*The Prime of Miss Jean Brodie*)—solely so she could ignore the looming S-question: What did Saraswati's superhoax mean for Nivedita's studies, not to mention—*shit*—her entire life?

"Never ponder your problems on an empty stomach," Barbara interrupted her musings, "No ruminating! And if you absolutely must ponder your problems on an empty stomach, well, be sure to eat first." Barbara had huge eyes, a massive rack, and luscious, ironically inflected lips that looked as if they were capable of enjoying more delicacies than any other mouth on Earth. Even though Barbara was blonder and—if such a thing were even possible—fairer-skinned than Lotte, it never would've occurred to Nivedita to call her *white*.

2

Not long after they had moved into their shared apartment, Barbara and Nivedita sat down together in the kitchen instead of going to class. Barbara grabbed a kohlrabi from the fridge and peeled it, creating a perfect spiral of skin, as Nivedita explained to her: "Racism doesn't mean that other people think you don't belong—er, I mean, that's not all it means. Racism means that you yourself feel you don't belong."

"Wait a sec, back up—that's exactly how *I* feel," Barbara said. Her father was a hairdresser in Krefeld, and just like for Nivedita, the idea of pursuing an intellectual career after college entailed successfully navigating a vast rift and finding her way through a series of glass ceilings and invisible walls. But, unlike Nivedita, Barbara had concluded those ceilings and walls were there precisely so she could bulldoze through them.

"You and my Cousin Priti would really hit it off," Nivedita said, handing Barbara the highest compliment she could think of.

Barbara, utterly unfazed, sprinkled salt on the slices of kohlrabi. "Huh, maybe . . . but, y'know, I don't really ever hit it off with women."

Nivedita still found it hard to believe Barbara wasn't a feminist. All her friends were feminists—many were even second-generation feminists. Lotte's mother was an equal-rights representative in Worpswede, and Lotte could talk for hours on end about the structural discrimination women had to face, without seeming discriminated against in the least. At least she didn't seem to have suffered any disadvantages, not that Nivedita saw—although Nivedita also sensed a problem creeping up when it came to communicating with Lotte. She was always amazed at how easily Lotte would call the landlord whenever something in their apartment needed fixing, or how easily she could hail a cab from the train station when she'd missed her connection and found herself stranded in Cologne at night. But the kind of amazement Nivedita felt toward Lotte was like the amazement you'd feel toward a majestic mountain or waterfall, and her way of communicating with such phenomena was pretty limited: Wow, you're so impressive, but no matter what I do or how hard I try, I'll never be like you!

Which was unfair, because even waterfalls—oops (ahem), *whites!* (all these *w*-words . . .)—had feelings just like non-*whites* because they, too, bled if you pricked them, as Shakespeare so eloquently wrote. Although it's also worth noting that Nivedita was convinced Shakespeare had actually been a Black Jewish woman (namely, Emilia Bassano Lanier), not a *white* man (Shakespeare or Marlowe), and certainly not a *privileged white* man (Sir Francis Bacon or Edward de Vere, the 17th Earl of Oxford).

IDENTITTI

(TRIGGER WARNING: THE FOLLOWING TEXT IS A POEM.)

The first time
that I noticed my mother is **white**
that I noticed my mother is a **white** *woman*
I didn't notice
I didn't notice the color of my skin
just the distance between her & me
the distance between her womb, her mother's body
and my wound, my daughter's body
body to body
and blood?
The one-drop rule
Interbreeding
Mestiza
Mischling
Masala
How could I ever have been inside a white woman?
How could I ever have been a **white** *woman?*

Nivedita remembered the precise moment she began saying *white*, to pass judgment: *white* people with dreads, *white* blues, a *white* audience. (She would've been hard pressed to delineate exactly what she meant by it, although that never really came up.) It had been Priti—who else?—who introduced Nivedita to the concept of *whiteness*. Back in her senior year as an undergrad, while she completed her bachelor's degree in gender studies at Ruhr University in Bochum and was also starting to toy with the idea of pursuing a master's in intercultural studies/postcolonial theory in Düsseldorf, her cousin had sent her a YouTube link.

This'll blow yr mind, Priti wrote. *Paul Chowdhry.* She seemed to slap this same disclaimer onto every Indian English and/or Pakistani English comedian she shared but, annoyingly, she was also almost always right. So Nivedita went right ahead and watched it, even though she was still in class and—as usual—had forgotten to turn her phone off. The following twenty-three seconds changed her life.

While Nivedita nonchalantly stroked her hair forward so it fell across one side of her face and slipped an earbud in that ear, unbeknownst to all, Paul paced back and forth across her phone screen. His steps across the stage were slow and measured as he sized up the audience, then grabbed the mic, and said in a perfect Cockney: "What's happening, *white* people?"

It was like a punch to the gut, but in reverse. A dull, ancient pain suddenly let go, and all the air that had never quite sufficed to fill her lungs, all the wind that had been knocked out of her, abruptly rushed in. At once, all those old slights vanished into thin air. All those times people had told her how much they just love ayurveda. All those times people had told her how much they just hate that Indian women are considered unclean during their period. ("No!!! There are over a billion of us Indians! Do you seriously think that when, like, blood is gushing out of every other one of us, that we actually believe the devil has possessed them? You're confusing India with *The Exorcist!*") All those times people had told her how they're going to spend their summer vacation at an ashram . . .

Hallo weiße Leute, wie geht's?, she typed, translating Chowdhry's tagline into German. She had waited until leaving class, ran for the closest bathroom, took a selfie in whiteface (Nivea), and then braced herself against the sink so as not to pass out as the air poured into her lungs, taking deep breaths, and those words virtually manifested themselves on her screen. That was her very first post as *50 Shades of Beige*, long before she rebranded as *Identitti*.

AND NOW, ON top of everything, apparently even Saraswati was *white*.

What's happening, Saraswati? Nivedita tried typing under that same old selfie, but she didn't post it, because there were too many Twitterati already dumping their fury out into the Twitterverse about Saraswati.

Barbara cracked an egg, dripped the yolk over a bunch of beansprouts, and sighed: "Ah, soul food!"

"Comfort food," Nivedita automatically corrected her.

"See, what'd I tell you?" Barbara said to Paul. "Even in the midst of a crisis, she's still PC."

"What's un-PC about soul food?" Paul asked Barbara, whereupon Barbara asked Nivedita: "Exactly! Well, what *is* un-PC about soul food, huh?"

"Nothing, but only if you're using it to refer to African American food and African American culture. Haven't you read Amiri Baraka's essay on soul food?"

Barbara wrinkled her already-ironic lips into an even more ironic smile: "What do you think?"

"Sorry, I didn't mean to . . ." said Nivedita rather awkwardly.

"Pontificate?" Barbara filled in the blank.

"Lecture," Nivedita said. "It's just that the term *soul food* has its own very specific significance, and when we just use it for anything yummy, that's *cultural appropriation* . . ." and of course Nivedita deployed the English loan-word for this phenomenon, as everyone else did in Saraswati's class.

"What?" Paul asked.

"*Kulturelle Aneignung*," Barbara translated for him, "I told you she can't speak much German."

"Which brings us full circle, back to the subject!" Paul added. "Has the AfD hopped on the bandwagon yet?"

And oh, had they!

» **The AfD True Virtue @DieAfDEchteWerte** *It's come this far: German Prof. dresses up as n*****bitch so she can teach gender-BS-gaga #fireSaraswati*

» **Bernd Höcke @BerndHoecke** *The German education system is destroying the German Homeland #fireSaraswati*

» **Trotsky in Exile @DefendTheIndefensible** *Saraswati plays right into the hands of the far right #SaraswatiShame*

Paul—not Paul Chowdhry—continued: "Now, once again, the university's going to get a tsunami of complaints." Barbara grabbed a bunch of yellow rice with her hand and shoved it into his mouth to shut him up. "But it's true!" he lamented, barely opening his now-stuffed mouth. "Now we're all going to have to explain this away."

"Oh, somehow I overlooked the fact that all this is actually about you," Barbara retorted, casting an exasperated glance at Nivedita. But Paul had spent too long indefatigably arguing his points during endless faculty meetings, and was simply too used to having to articulate how his own position differed amid the doggedness imposed by group dynamics, to be even slightly irked or even affected by Nivedita's feelings—hurt or otherwise. "This is about not endangering the constructive work all the rest of us at the university carry out. The AfD is just waiting for an excuse to fire us all and abolish higher education."

"They can do that even without Saraswati," Nivedita said softly.

"But she's giving them a reason, and handing it to them on a silver platter."

Nivedita stared at Paul's cheeks—which bulged out each time he bit down—and tried her best not to be angry at him, because she was really only angry at Saraswati.

3

Sleep was utopia. Reality was hurling Saraswati's books against the wall (but, curiously, not ripping them to bits) and checking her phone for messages from Priti and Simon.

IDENTITTI

**Brothers and sisters of the night, dear somnambulists, fellow
sleepwalkers, night owls, and open-eyed dreamers, you who have**

certainly also been denied sleep by the sheer immensity of the recent news: let us spend the hours from now until dawn together as we try to discover what's really going on here. Up until now, my life centered on three core truths:

1. Kapitalism kills
2. Books can save your soul
3. Saraswati is one of us

Don't ask me why these truths seem truthier in English, but that's how I hear them, so pardon me for not writing these capital-*T* Truths *auf Deutsch*. And yeah, I know Kali has a whole theory about that—something to do with cultural imperialism . . .

"It's not a theory, it's an analysis, an analytical fact," Kali corrects me.

An analytical fact that just might be right.

"Just might be?"

Okay, okay, you're right, Kali. But we're not really talking about cultural imperialism here, instead . . .

"We're not?"

Yeah, dammit, even in this, regrettably, Kali's right. Because if what we've learned about Saraswati in the last few hours is true, then I seriously need to start giving some thought to cultural dominance and imperialism and all that—but conversely, or upside down, and . . . and now my head's about to explode, because my brain simply doesn't want to start imagining all the implications.

But let's have a closer look at these three core truths my life is centered on. (Er, well, at least two of them—as for the one about capitalism being lethal, I still swear by that one, or Kali herself can strike me dead.) What's most astounding about all these revelations regarding Saraswati is that no one has even questioned their veracity, or whether she really even is *white*. I mean, where are all the conspiracy theorists when you need them? What was unthinkable even yesterday is accepted without question today. Why? Because it just sounds in*comprehensible*, but not un*true*?

Because it gets at a dormant doubt lurking somewhere within us, a doubt that's been shaken awake by these revelations, and that is now shouting at the top of its lungs: I KNEW IT ALL ALONG!?

Which brings us back to the books—the books that saved my soul, or maybe just my psyche, or maybe just saved me from going crazy in a world that denied my every perception, my very existence, a world where at every turn I was told: You aren't real, your problems aren't real, and your story isn't relevant.

Now that Saraswati isn't real, does that mean the books she wrote, which were so vital to my existence, also aren't real? One of her suggestions for us was always: Read aloud! Sigh while you're at it! Swear! Slap the pages! Kiss your book! Reading takes place not in your mind, but in your body!

So here are a few tips for further reading, in case you want to try slapping—or even punching, go for it—some pages for yourself:

Saraswati, *Decolonize Your Soul, p. 7*
"They're all just stories.
Race is a story we tell ourselves."
Saraswati, *Decolonize Your Soul, p. 39*
"That's the Stewart Hall Paradox: That we know race is a construct,
but nevertheless our eyes perceive differences in skin color and
hair type."
Saraswati, *Exorcize Race(ism), p. 145ff*
"Race isn't real, race is a sociopolitical construct. Class is a sociopolitical construct. Gender is a sociopolitical construct. Yet at the same time,
all three are all too real, because out in the world they relate to realities
that have become truths, but in and of themselves *they are not* real.
These incarnated realities *can* have a major influence on us, indeed
they *do* have a major influence on us, but the ways in which they do are
different for each of us—*because their foundational realities are, in
and of themselves, equally* un*real*. Which means, above all: They are
not unchangeable."

Have you all ever screamed at a pile of books? It isn't so easy. Books full of Post-its and with dog-eared pages, books I wrote more in than I ever did in any diary, hell, books that are way more *intimate* than your most private diary and are nevertheless just lying there on the floor, and even if I trip over them, well, they're still there, just off to the side a bit, books that aren't anything like a direct phone line to Saraswati, or some secret communication channel where I can hear her voice and she can hear mine—no matter how loud I scream, none of my words will reach Saraswati's ears.

What's happened here shakes the foundation of my relationship to Saraswati, it shakes the foundation of my relationship to *myself*; my ability to access knowledge and histories and stories and understanding. In a world where Saraswati is *white*, I no longer understand myself.

NIVEDITA WAS TWELVE and Priti was thirteen the year Priti came to Essen-Frillendorf to study German. Several weeks before her arrival, Birgit had run around their 850-square-foot apartment like a chicken with its head cut off, as if hoping for a guest room to magically appear. The ability to completely ignore reality and its restrictions was one of Birgit's defining character traits, but eventually even she had to capitulate to the architecture she inhabited. And so she gave Nivedita a futon nearly as wide as her entire bedroom as an "early birthday present"—the kind of present she'd need to fold up into a sofa every morning, which from day one she understandably forgot to do, opting instead to spend the rest of her waking hours lying around on the mussed-up blanket and piled-up pillows. Priti's imminent visit loomed—it was as if some enemy takeover of her private realm were about to occur—and instead of looking forward to summer break, Nivedita dreaded it. The enthusiasm she had felt toward Priti after her visit to Birmingham had waned over the last few years. But the moment Priti tossed her backpack into the sole remaining corner not occupied by the futon and exclaimed "What the fuck's *that?*" it became one of the most magical summers Nivedita could ever remember.

All Nivedita's friends thought Priti was actually her secret, wholly imaginary alter ego, so when she introduced her very real cousin to them, they were all duly impressed. Priti, on the other hand, was duly unimpressed by "Lilli & Co.," as she dismissively labeled them. What did impress her, though, were Essen's yellow tramcars. As soon as she discovered that her student-rate summer ticket was unlimited, she spent entire days riding the lines from end to end, with Nivedita. The tram became their stage, and their fellow riders their more or less voluntary spectators.

"Simon is super-smitten with you," was just one example of Priti's opening lines, whereupon it was up to Nivedita to continue the thread.

"Oh, that was nothing compared to Tom, Priti. He couldn't take his eyes off you, like when you. . . ."

In retrospect, Nivedita was amazed to realize that even back then there had been a Simon in her life. But that was actually just Priti's compromise— she'd made one futile attempt at pronouncing *Jürgen*, the name of the guy Nivedita actually had a crush on, and thereafter just randomly went with Simon—deeming it easier to pronounce.

"*Ja, Tom ist süß*, Niv, but in bed he's so . . . well . . . *Deutsch*. Simon, on the other hand . . . what was it he did with turmeric? C'mon, girrrl, do tell!"

"*Turmerik*?" Nivedita asked, unsure whether it was some kind of solvent or a sex toy.

"C'mon, you know, it's yellow . . ." Priti explained, rather unhelpfully.

"*Auf deutsch* it's *Gelbwürz*," a guy with a gray ponytail sitting across from them surprisingly offered. He was clearly an ex-hippie who'd chosen a front-row seat to this particular show, all the better to size up the actresses. "Aka *Kurkuma*."

"He was totally a science teacher," Nivedita said after he got out two stops later.

"*Ja,* he sure looked like one," Priti agreed. They soon learned that everyone seated near them either devoted their undivided attention to eavesdropping on their conversations, or immediately switched seats. Those were the only two reactions.

Just like there were only two storylines. While Priti came up with more or less improbable sex scenes and then just fantasized out loud, Nivedita mainly made up Hindu rituals they'd both supposedly taken part in—and then dressed them up with ever-more-shameless details, which is how she discovered that Priti was as clueless about Hinduism as she was. But here, too, whenever the next line failed to pop into her mind, she could always loop back to turmeric: "If only you'd remembered to draw a circle with *Kurkuma*, that never would have happened!"

SARASWATI REALLY WAS right when she said race was a story. Like a story being told by two girls, one Indian-German and one Indian-British, on a tram in Essen, sometime in the early aughts—or the early noughties, as Priti liked to say. But now, at the dawn of the evil-roaring twenties, Priti wasn't at Nivedita's side to give the story of Saraswati's debunking an extra flourish of spicy, sex-driven subplots or equally spicy spices. Instead, Priti and her own piquant subplot with *Saraswati's brother*—of all people!—was in some unspeakable way responsible for the entire situation.

Nighttime was a sea into which Nivedita now drifted, rudderless. The farther she got from the Bay of Certainty (where Saraswati was Saraswati, and Saraswati's words held water), the bigger the sea grew. Finally, so as not to drown in her own dismay and self-pity even as she remained buried under the mess of blankets on her bed, Nivedita googled *The Prime of Miss Jean Brodie* and watched the whole movie in order to find out whether Saraswati actually was like Jean Brodie, and what really happened to her. Then she kept bingeing, streaming Professor McGonagall's top cinematic scenes from the Harry Potter series, followed by the Dowager Countess of Grantham's most biting bon mots from *Downton Abbey*, followed by—Saraswati's best onstage appearances, both domestic and international.

SARASWATI'S MOST UNFORGETTABLE public appearance was at the Hay Festival in Wales, where she'd been invited to appear alongside the brilliant psychologist—or extremely dangerous men's-rights activist, depending on which camp you're in—Jordan Peterson. Their event was titled "The Myth of Racism," and their brief was to debate . . . myths and racism.

Rewatching it, a painful memory resurfaced. Nivedita recalled how she and Simon had set a date at the student union to watch the debate together, live, as part of the Saraswati Fan Club public viewing, but then the day before, totally out of the blue, he'd up and left her again, for the second time. So then she'd just watched the BBC livestream from her apartment with Barbara and Lotte, plus special guest Oluchi (the girl with yellow-rimmed glasses who'd still be Nivedita's college BFF if it weren't for the fact that, way earlier, meaning at least a half-year before she herself and Simon were an item, Oluchi had had a fling with him, and their undeclared, unresolved intimacy remained, weighing on the women's friendship like a secrecy-soaked wet blanket, making all communication between them more difficult, and as a result Nivedita didn't say a word about the breakup for the entire evening—even though she had entrusted Barbara with the bad news but simultaneously made her swear to stay silent about it). Barbara had prepared a platter of cheese and grapes for the occasion, and took the extra effort of stabbing each morsel with its own little toothpick emblazoned with a tiny Indian flag. "From the last World Cup," she said, laughing at the incredulous expression on Nivedita's face.

"India's never even made it to the World Cup!"

"Aren't *you* a stickler . . ."

Before the televised duel of the minds began, Nivedita ran back to her room and swathed herself in a red dupatta à la Saraswati. But that night Saraswati had donned a silver dupatta, which made her look dazzlingly royal as she strode out in front of the stage's blue backdrop.

The entire concept behind the event was to bring together two intellectuals with polarizing, diametrically opposed convictions, let them have at it, and see how long it would take for them to tear into one another.

"Your book *12 Rules for Life*," the moderator addressed Jordan Peterson, "is about the battle between chaos and order," and then, rapt, repeated, "battle, chaos, order," as if he were trying to give his guests a heavy-handed hint at what was expected of them—although, taking a closer look at the grinning guy in a suit with slicked-back silver hair and the smiling sari-wearer whose dupatta matched her opponent's hair, such an outcome seemed rather unlikely. "One of the reasons your lectures often spark protests," the moderator went on, this time casting a provocative look at the live audience, "is that you attribute gender to the concepts of order and chaos."

"No," Peterson replied calmly.

It wasn't entirely clear what the moderator was getting at—a contradiction or the fuzziness of no such contradiction. "But you do *gender* order and chaos, do you not?"

"Not in the least. I merely reflect their traditionally ascribed gender attributes. And, traditionally, mother nature has always represented chaos, whereas order and logic, since the beginning of time, have symbolically been seen as masculine . . ."

"Saraswati," Saraswati interrupted.

"I beg your pardon?" said the moderator.

"My name is Saraswati."

Nivedita noticed she could read the moderator's mind: *That's it, femininity really is chaos, and this lady proves it—no meaning, no rhyme or reason, just a bunch of barely strung-together words: me, me, me.*

Saraswati waited until the audience had also heard his unuttered words, and then clarified: "And Saraswati is the Goddess of Knowledge—of all learning and logic."

The entire pavilion was so quiet that you could hear her seat squeak as she leaned back. And since that statement required no qualification, she gave none. Saraswati was good at recognizing when she'd made a point. Even back in the apartment, watching onscreen, Nivedita held her breath. Only Lotte dared make a peep: "*Touché*, amiright?"

"Shhh!" Oluchi snipped back.

Nevertheless, Peterson wasn't irritated by Saraswati: "I'm quite certain that Hindu mythology also has a masculine God of Logic."

"Of course," replied Saraswati, "we're not sexists."

The moderator perked back up. "Are you implying that Jordan Peterson is sexist?"

"In no way. I'm saying that the Eurocentric tradition of Western Antiquity shaping his thought is sexist." Again, you could hear her chair squeak. This time the audience was so spellbound that you could almost hear Saraswati smile, and even Lotte shut her trap.

The rest of the debate had vanished from Nivedita's memory—mainly because Saraswati and Peterson had both implicitly refused to deliver the anticipated spectacle-cum-debacle, perhaps because their mutual aversion to the moderator outweighed their differences of opinion—but then there was *this* clip: Peterson strode up to the edge of the stage to give his closing statement, head bowed as if he were deep in thought, as his hands pulled these words straight out of the air, the audience sizzling with excitement: "What is happening right now at universities, and rapidly spreading to society at large, is a collective narrative I find extremely dangerous. To be clear, we are all members of various groups, and collective narratives can be useful, but the current collective narrative—better yet, allow me to call it what it is: the *politically correct* narrative—is simply a cheap carbon copy of postmodernism- meets-postcolonialism."

Saraswati tossed her silver dupatta over her head, which Nivedita recognized as the clear signal she was getting ready to strike back. But the gesture seemed lost on Peterson, whose eyes were half-closed, as if he were reading from some internal teleprompter: "The main point of this ideology claims that the correct way of viewing the world is as a battlefield upon which different groups or races are waging war. And that negates not only the possibility of the self-sufficient, independent individual, but also the notion of individual responsibility. Take a good look at yourself"—he jerked his head high, turned his gaze to Saraswati, who was listening with a bemused expression, and directly addressed her for the first time—"with your endowed professorship at a German university and your countless appearances in the international media. Aren't you yourself, and your renown, clear proof that we're well past the point of always needing to talk about racism and white privilege?"

While about half the audience applauded and the other half booed, Saraswati gazed right past Peterson and straight into the camera from under her heavy eyelids—soon thereafter, *How to get bedroom eyes like Saraswati* became a popular meme—and with perfectly clear enunciation said, slowing down for extra emphasis: "You have just confused racism with fascism. The fact that in Germany, people like me are two times more likely to live below the poverty line than *white* people are is structural racism. The fact that our academic achievements are undervalued, and that we have greater difficulty getting a job, an apartment, or even adequate medical care, is structural racism. The fact that it's harder for us to work toward our life goals, let alone even develop any in the first place, is structural racism. Now, if all of those things were made *entirely impossible* for *all* of us, that would be fascism. But have no fear, that's precisely why I'm here—to explain such distinctions to people like you." And then slowly, deliberately, she delicately ran the tip of her tongue along her upper lip.

The clip went viral.

4

Of course Nivedita shared it on Facebook, Twitter, and Instagram, too, adding only the comment *Say it like Saraswati.*

Since the news had broken that Saraswati was neither Indian nor a person of color, it was only logical that this same video was making the rounds once again, accompanied by rather different comments:

> Whoever says "Fascist" first wins?
> You're the reason so few women of color get tenure, because you've already stolen all the spots!!!
> At least Peterson believes what he says—she only believes her own propaganda.
> One example of white privilege? Saraswati!

Nivedita read this steady stream of spite with reluctant intrigue. In her experience, sooner or later—usually sooner—people who picked a fight with

Saraswati were roundly defeated. But now it looked like the entire world was siding against her, or at least the entire World Wide Web.

IN A STROKE OF cosmic irony, the forecast thunderstorm never came. The night grew lighter and bluer, and the early birds were already singing by the time Nivedita's fits of sleep turned into real, deep sleep—only to be interrupted almost immediately by her phone's piercing ringtone. She felt around her bed, her eyes barely cracked open, and finally found her phone chillaxing on top of the special edition of Saraswati's book *Being Brown for Beginners*. She was so convinced that it had to be Simon, finally calling to check in and see how she was doing, that she answered before looking at who it was.

"How *are* you?" her mother asked in her usual super-sympathetic tone.

"You already heard?" Nivedita asked, touched.

"Heard what?" Birgit inquired, her tone now more sorrowful, such that Nivedita realized the sympathy she'd detected was merely the fundamental, melancholic empathy her mother directed toward the whole of earthly existence. Birgit was a social worker, and Nivedita had always felt sorry for her clients. She figured they were just unlucky, since their cases were being managed by someone who clearly felt the suffering of all humanity so thoroughly that she never had any empathy left for the actual people sitting right in front of her, but to Nivedita's never-ending surprise, all Birgit's clients adored her.

"My professor . . ." Nivedita tried to explain the inexplicable. "It's . . . on every channel."

As if a switch had flipped, Birgit's tone went from dismay to enthusiasm: "That's a good thing, right?"

In such situations, Barbara had always advised Nivedita to say the first thing that popped into her head. So she said: "Simon dumped me."

Once again her mother's tone did a one-eighty, this time from excited to offended. "What? Again!? And so soon?"

"Yeah, *again*," Nivedita confirmed.

"I thought he'd finally quit it. Have you spoken to him about it?"

Oh, that never occurred to me! thought Nivedita indignantly. Then she thought: *How am I supposed to have a conversation about our relationship with Simon if I can't even have a normal conversation with my own mother?*

The unwritten rules clearly stated that she was not to call Simon. She'd just have to wait for him to call her, whenever that might be. These were the same rules that said she could call Priti as often as she wanted, leaving as many panic-stricken messages as she felt like—the results were the same. Communication wasn't something that lay in Nivedita's hands, rather, it was something that happened to her—it was others' mouths that spoke to her, and others' fingers that typed texts to her, granting her a crumb of attention as if it were a gift whose duration and conditions she had no say in whatsoever. And just as most people took their minds off their own problems by focusing on others' issues, Nivedita was irresistibly sucked back into the social-media soap opera surrounding Saraswati:

» **AfD Legion @afd_verband** *Do-gooder lady encourages us all to paint ourselves brown so as not to upset the immigrants. What PC BS comes next? #BanPostcolonialStudies #BanFakeStudies*

» **Call me Zadie @OutsideSisters** *No room for racism here, neither from the AfD nor from Saraswati.*

» **Prada Loth @habibitus** *because im sometimes overcome by my own selfhatred, or maybe just the burning desire to see the world on fire, today i watched some videos of saraswati, and all i saw was a white cosplayin' as a poc #saraswatigate*

» **Patrick Bahners @Pbahners** *Friedrich Rückert once noted that August Wilhelm Schlegel managed to translate an Indian epic into German hexameter "without having to worry about being accused of travesty." One wishes the same degree of forbearance were granted the poetic rendering of an academic cv in the other direction.*

» **Fatima Khan @khanthefatima** *Saraswati is the epitome of the white savior complex. People want to save the "Other" so badly that they end up absorbing and assimilating them, just so they, too, can finally be a victim.*

Lars Weisbrod didn't tweet about Saraswati, but he did post three tweets about economic theory that he almost immediately deleted.

> » **Madita Oeming @MsOeming** *I am not responsible for the words and deeds of everyone I share an identity group with. I do not need to excuse or apologize for my fellow white people. Nor must I be ashamed of my own whiteness. But in this case I feel I must do all of the above. SOMEBODY PLS TELL ME, WTF IS UP WITH US?!*

After not sleeping all night, Nivedita was so beat she felt like she was growing porous around the edges, so the entire world could easily intrude upon her, and all the tweets felt like virus particles whose devastating effects were yet to unfold. Witnessing the utter horror of everything surrounding Saraswati, which she still couldn't fully grasp, Nivedita herself felt personally hurt by the shitstorm's sheer malice, and even more so by the fact that a not insignificant portion of the comments were coming from Saraswati's own students. @OutsideSisters was none other than Oluchi Schneider, she of the mustard-yellow glasses, who'd always go on the attack, then withdraw, then attack again, and run her fingers through her crown of black hair. The gesture was such an integral part of her communicative style that she'd even made a gif of it, a bonus of sorts, a way of emphasizing her words as more eloquent than everyone else's with nothing more than an animated emoji. Nivedita couldn't shake the suspicion that, like she herself, her almost-best-friend Oluchi felt less frustrated by the fact that Saraswati had wanted to be like her, and rather more frustrated that she had wanted to be like Saraswati.

"THE PROBLEM WITH anti-racism is that it really is asking too much," Saraswati had said in her last lecture of the semester. A stray strand of hair had fallen over her forehead as she said it, which she then nonchalantly brushed off with the back of her hand. She was one of those people who schlepped some kind of invisible wind tunnel everywhere they went—her hair was always blowing in front of her face so she'd have to make that shampoo-ad move with her head in order to see again, and in lieu of a billowing cape she had that omnipresent dupatta, which she was always tossing over her shoulder like a feather boa.

"Effective anti-racism would mean that everyone is always awake, aware, and woke, so nobody ever resorts to stereotypes. And even then we could never be completely sure that we aren't inadvertently sticking a label on someone, or putting them into one categorical box or another. Or, even worse, *not* communicating with people out of a fear of making a mistake. So we don't pay *any*one *any* compliments, we *don't* ask *any* questions, *don't* let *any* curiosities pop up, solely in an attempt to avoid falling into the trap of being racist. You guessed it: I'm talking about the typical, oh-so-predictable *where're-you-from* trap. And here I'd like to be very clear, so I must add: staying silent is worse! I repeat: *not* asking is just so much worse." As if to underline her point, Saraswati remained silent, and Nivedita—who had learned to recognize her tics and schticks by now—counted the seconds in her head: 24 . . . 25 . . . 26 . . . 27! "And why is this supposedly racism-avoiding silence worse? Because it robs us of any chance to grow closer, make real contact, experience true empathy!"

In retrospect, these words struck Nivedita as a secret message of sorts, a message in a bottle cast into the future, one she couldn't quite uncork yet. A hunger for leftovers and chitchat drew her into the kitchen, but the only traces of yesterday's meal were three unwashed plates and one serving of super-spicy kimchi. Barbara and Paul were either still asleep or already gone, so Lotte was the only one sitting at the table, which nipped Nivedita's hopes for good conversation in the bud.

Meanwhile, the international media had jumped on the bandwagon, as the headlines kept pinging in:

"**Blackface Scandal at German University**" (*The Independent*)
"**Saraswati Actually SarasWHITEy**" (*Washington Post*)
"**Prof. neither POC nor PC**" (*The Guardian*)
"**Human Stain at Heinrich Heine University, Germany**" (*The New Yorker*)

"Did you see? Like, the entire international media have jumped on the band-wagon now, too," Lotte said, twisting open a bottle of blue nail polish and huffing the fumes, entranced. Nivedita wasn't exactly in a position to blame Lotte for being such a slut for scandal, but that didn't stop her from doing so anyway. In order to stave off all possible attempts at further conversation, she turned on the radio: "*The case of the professor who passed herself off as a person of color continues to make waves. Countless organizations, including . . .*"

"Well well well, Saraswati's made the news," Lotte babbled on.

"Shhh!"

" *. . . are now calling for her resignation. After all, a professor now accused of racism is hardly a fitting representative, and certainly not the person you want teaching anti-racism. And yet there are also those coming to her defense.*"

For just a moment—despite her rage, despite her disappointment, despite the sinking feeling of having been fooled, despite the open question of who her thesis advisor would now be, despite the three years of her life that had suddenly just imploded and that she'd never, ever get back—Nivedita's heart softened. She was so happy to hear that somebody, somewhere in the whole wide world, was sticking up for Saraswati. But then the radio played a clip of none other than her own voice: "*Nowadays nobody's a serious intellectual until they've sat at the eye of a shitstorm.*"

"OMG—that's you!" Lotte needlessly piped up.

"*The people who accuse Saraswati of being racist,*" Nivedita had said less than twenty-four hours before to cheerful Verena and melancholic Mona in the national radio headquarters, "*just don't get her. Above all, they don't get what* being white *means to her.*"

IF I HAD A HAMMER

1

The last time Nivedita had seen Saraswati was toward the end of the semester. The star prof. had been lounging on the lawn outside the university library, drinking a glass of wine—perhaps in homage to Heinrich Heine, whose bronze likeness was hanging out just a few feet away, musing. Whenever Nivedita and Simon walked by that monument together, they'd take turns guessing what he was thinking:

"*Denk ich an Deutschland in der Nacht, dann bin ich um den Schlaf gebracht.*" ("When, Germany, I think of thee, at night, all slumber flies from me." Nivedita)

"*Ihr habt den Rhein, wascht euch!*" ("The Rhein's right here, wash up!" Simon)

"*Du willst mich nicht mehr lieben, aber . . . irgendwas, irgendwas . . . man schreibt nicht so ausführlich, wenn man den Abschied gibt.*" ("No longer wilt thou love me, thy letter, though, is long—something, something—in giving a refusal, far otherwise we act." Nivedita)

"Oh c'mon, that's one of his worst poems." (Simon)

But that day on the lawn—had it really only been a week ago?—Nivedita was rather more interested in what Saraswati was thinking. Clearly something was going on behind those gold-brown eyes all aflicker in the evening sun, reflecting its light like two Indian mirror-work medallions, but she found her professor's eyes so much harder to read than the empty eyes of the dead poet nearby. Saraswati was reclining on her side, stretched out across the picnic blanket, and she raised her glass toward the crowd of students milling about, chitchatting, and flirting all around her: "Isn't reality just such a marvelous metaphor, *mein Schätzchen*?"

It seemed the metaphor had suddenly caught up to her.

And now it was catching up to Nivedita.

"Woah, listen to thi—" said Lotte, but Nivedita had already run from the room. As the radio spat her own words back at her and nonstop notifications blew up her phone, she slammed the bedroom door behind her. The sheer force of self-hatred kept her phone glued to her hand, and her eyes glued to her phone.

> » Nele Breimer @ReadMyLips *Yet again @Identitti knows best, even on national radio. It's not SarasWhitey's fault, instead she blames the POCs who feel offended by her #SaraswatiShame*
>
> » Freeperiods Slayunicorns @WhereHaveAllTheGoodGirlsGone *Are we supposed to kiss the hand that hits us? #SaraswatiRaus #SaraswatiShame*
>
> » College Policy Dept. Düsseldorf @ColPolDept_DU *Racism isn't racism if people we admire are racist? Wake up, @Identitti!*
>
> » DU Student Union @StuU_DU *@Identitti's statements in the #GermanNationalRadioInterview do not reflect the student union's position.*
>
> » Felix Dachsel @xileff *Now can we get back to debating Jakob Augstein's bombshell tax-evasion reportage? @Saraswati*

The thing about the Internet is that every follower who loved Nivedita was followed by a follower who hated her, and proudly proclaimed as much. So a sense of solidarity led more people to follow her, but then the reverse sense of solidarity led more people to curse her and call her out, too. Up until now she'd always been loved by all the right people—meaning the people whose work and vibes she loved back—and hated by all the right people: *Thank Kali you don't like what I write. If my enemies are reactionaries, I'm revolutionary. Ish.* That's why Nivedita had always found it empowering to be publicly put-upon: her digital community was on her side.

Was.

» **Roxy Tafari @BlackLikeMe** *Make fun of your own people! I know where my solidarity lies #SaraswatiShame #IdentittiTame*

» **Brown Germans Movement @BGM** *Saraswati wants to be Black. Identitti wants to be white. And we're not supposed to make a fuss?*

» **Call me Zadie @OutsideSisters** *Heads-up, #thread: It's no surprise @Identitti is defending #SaraswatiShame. If @Identitti were white, she'd be in blackface, too. 1/5*

  » **@OutsideSisters** *After all, she's already proven she can't really resist blackface. You know her poem "The first time that I noticed my mother is white"? 2/5*

  » **@OutsideSisters** *In it, she writes about her life as a "Mischling" and mentions the "one-drop rule." That rule states that, if a person has even one drop of "Black blood," in the USA, they're considered Black. 3/5*

  » **@OutsideSisters** *"Black blood" means at least one ancestor of sub-Saharan African descent. The one-drop rule refers ONLY TO BLACK PEOPLE!!! 4/5*

  » **@OutsideSisters** *It would NEVER be used to refer to people of Indian descent!!!!!!!! @Identitti is well aware of that, so it's a conscious decision: she wants to look Blacker than she is #blackface 5/5*

People whom Nivedita considered members of her digital tribe were suddenly and ragefully repudiating her, and she found that fact even scarier than all the death threats and rape threats and death-by-rape threats she'd received in the past . . . the not-so-long-ago past. Even people she saw as friends, like

Oluchi, were sounding off. And they now saw her—*she herself*, not anything she'd said or done or written, but her very Niveditaness—as a racist threat.

"Nivedita?" Lotte called through the door to her bedroom, although she was too good-mannered to open a closed door. The Venn-diagram intersection between well-behaved daughters and demons seemed to be thresholds: neither could cross them without explicit invitation. "Nivedita? Nivedita?" Lotte repeated.

Nivedita threw herself onto the bed she'd built out of a bunch of bulk tea shipping crates and lay still and silent, waiting for the sky to fall, or for Lotte to give up and go back to devoting her attention to all the Lotte-style stuff she filled her days with—whatever that might be.

"Nivedita?"

Breathe in.

Ignore it.

Breathe out.

Kali came and went, and then came back with a beanbag so she could watch the whole Nivedita Show in comfort. *Did you know that all forms of life consist of vibrations?*

"Oh really?" Nivedita muttered through gnashed teeth. The intensely contrasting pattern on Kali's beanbag—blue elephants with intertwined trunks on top of a fire-engine red background—created a flickering that hurt her already frayed optic nerves.

And the main difference between us all is whether our vibrations' wavelengths are long or short—in short, it's our vibes. . . . Kali laid the warm heel of four of her hands atop Nivedita's eye sockets and gently pressed on them, which made her feel better for a bit, which then allowed the enormity of the situation to exert even greater pressure on her, as if the sky would fall sooner rather than later, which then made her tense up again, just to hold it all in place.

If our wavelengths are long, even the slightest attack goes straight through us, Kali dreamily continued.

"Nivedita?" Lotte called again from behind the door, less vehemently this time.

See? Goes straight through us, said Kali.

Lotte gave up, paced up and down the hall outside her door a couple of times, and finally left the apartment.

See? Kali repeated.

Nivedita tried to nod, mainly out of boredom from doing nothing for so long, and as a result her pillow fell to the floor and her head dangled over the edge of the bed at the exact same height as Kali's beanbag.

"Wait a sec . . . that's the suspension railway!" What Nivedita had seen as intertwining trunks were actually rails making psychedelic loops across the red fabric, punctuated at regular intervals by a blue elephant popping its head out of a train car. "And that's Tuffi!" The very thought of that particular elephant—an Indian elephant cow whose image was co-opted for a 1950s public transit ad campaign in which she was shoved into the Wuppertal monorail but was so startled by the ride that she burst through a window and jumped into the Wupper River—filled Nivedita with such a belated and out-size rage that she suddenly sat up from her super-uncomfortable position. "How's it possible that the most famous creature of color from my childhood was an elephant?" she asked Kali, appalled.

See? Kali said yet again, *It's so easy to just think about something else*, and then the beanbag vanished into thin air.

Nivedita grabbed her phone, which had also fallen off the bed, and checked the time. Three minutes! She'd lain motionless for hours, but only three minutes had gone by?! Her phone vibrated in her hand. Once again, it wasn't Simon. But the words she read were precisely the ones she'd yearned to receive from him:

"Come over, we need to talk."

Saraswati!

2

Kali opened the window and the sweet scent of linden blossoms burst into the room like a flood of pure joy, a feeling Nivedita found utterly out of place but then eagerly soaked up. *Interesting*, she thought, then shut her laptop, tossed it and its charger into her bag, and left a note on the table for Barbara:

Miss Jean Brodie (she of the fab flick but boring book) reached out!
I'm on my way to her place!!
Keep yr fingers crossed for me!!!
Niv

She wrote it not because Barbara would really care or even notice her absence, but because she simply had to share this major development with someone *stat*.

The euphoria propelled her halfway across Düsseldorf-Oberbilk until it occurred to her that she shouldn't arrive emptyhanded, and decided to bring Saraswati some kind of offering—something that could give a glimmer of making amends the way you might bring flowers when visiting someone who's sick. But Kölner Straße was one big One-Euro shop, a several-kilometer strip of discount shops full of nothing Nivedita would dare present to her professor, no matter how far she may have fallen. So she ended up forcing her way through a construction site fence across from Saraswati's building and picking a couple stalks of wildflowers from a broom shrub.

Saraswati lived on the top floor of one of the ugliest buildings on a street lined with hideous-looking apartment houses. That was part of her mystique: she lived "down in the 'hood." Local lore—or was it urban legend?—was full of tales spun by people who'd made the pilgrimage to Saraswati's house: beforehand, they had no idea how a world-famous public intellectual could live at such an address; afterward, they wondered how she'd ever found such a gem of a home. Even Nivedita, who'd already visited during a couple of intensive seminar sessions, was wowed by the sun-filled rooms and ample balcony winding around the entire place, offering a Mary Poppins–type panorama overlooking the rooftops of the entire neighborhood. The only thing missing were the dancing chimney sweeps in blackface and the admiral next door charging his second-in-command to fire the canon at the "savages." This was no mere apartment—this was a penthouse.

AND NOW THAT she found herself standing once again in front of Saraswati's door, she was suddenly at a total loss. What now? Her vivid powers of imagination had been enough to get her here, up to this moment, as her finger pushed the button that completed the electrical circuit that would in turn sound the bell, ringing in a new chapter in her relationship to Saraswati. As soon as she walked through this door, everything would change. Actually, everything already had changed. But now it would be official.

She had to look her demons in the face, and her demon was Saraswati. And with the word demon, *her hand, as if directed by remote control, hit the buzzer,* Nivedita's internal monologue ran on. Until she had started her blog, she'd found it impossible to say or write *me* or *I* and actually mean it to indicate herself. When she was a kid, *I* meant *white* little girls and, much more often, *white* little boys—basically everything she wasn't. And sometimes a child with her same skin tone would lose their way and show up in one of the children's books she read. Like Gustavus, the sissy prince from some ostensibly eastern land, whom the plucky British kids had to save in *The Circus of Adventure*. Or like Parvati Patil from *Harry Potter*, who only ends up attending the Yule Ball with Harry because he didn't have the courage to ask the girl he actually wanted to—bee tee dubs, he then doesn't even deign to dance with Parvati. Or like Andschana from Käthe von Roeder-Gnadeberg's *Andschana: Die Geschichte eines indischen Mädchens*, an "educational story for children age 10 and up" that Birgit had gone out of her way to buy so that her daughter would finally have a heroine she could identify with. But then Andschana turned out to be so unassuming and modest that Nivedita preferred Gustavus, because at least he threw terrific tantrums. But even then, none of them were really *me*. They were *he*, *her*, and *her*, and so even in her own head Nivedita became just another *she*.

IDENTITTI

Okay. Here's the truth, the whole truth, and nothing but the truth.

I always feel like I'm lying when I say or write the words *I* or *me*. Even when it has to do with things that've actually happened to me. Actually, above all when it comes to things that've happened to me. Because I always find I have to do it following the formulas and examples set by other authors—authors whose lives are part of Real Life simply because they're imaginable, and whose voices are part of the canon.

And so when I write *I*, I feel like I'm lying not about what happened or didn't happen, but rather about my place in the fabric of reality. I lay claim to an existence and relevance I'm not entitled to, and speak in a disguised voice, like I'm putting on airs.

And why is that? Because people like me simply do not exist in the world of literature. At least not as we know it. As the writer Zadie Smith recalled from her own childhood, "Practically the only star I had to steer by was that old, worn-out, paper-thin character the 'tragic mulatto.'"

Boy, can I relate to that, and I especially remember the tragic mulattas.

If we ever even made it into a story, it was always only a matter of time until our illegal existence was brought to an end, either by suicide or some other grisly plot twist. After all, what *shouldn't* be just *couldn't* be, right? Let's call it death by unimaginability.

The first book with a mixed-race narrator was Hanif Kureishi's *The Buddha of Suburbia,* which I encountered in Bernhard Robben's translation as *Der Buddha aus der Vorstadt*. That was 1990! Let that just roll off your tongue: nineteen-ninety! Meaning before I was born, but just barely before my birth. And before then, we only existed as slipups, accidents, human stains. Don't get me wrong, *The Buddha of Suburbia* saved my life. The only catch was that that novel and all the ones that followed in its wake were set in the UK or US, and their narrators resembled my cousin Priti to a T (hiya Prit, if you're out there reading this!). As a result, for me, Priti has always seemed much more real to me than I myself do. She's clearly more *I* than I am.

And that's why it's easier for me to write about Kali than about capital-M Me Myself. Kali has the sound and fury and severity I need to conquer the chasm that separates me from my ability to tell a story.

The door of the apartment that had separated her from Saraswati flew open, and Nivedita was shocked that her professor looked exactly as she remembered, down to the dupatta.

"Ah, Nivedita, come on in," Saraswati said before immediately turning her back on her.

Nivedita, who'd been expecting a deep, soulful look in the eye, followed her, stunned. "How're you doing?" she asked her professor in a muted voice, as if speaking to an invalid.

"How do you think?" Saraswati shot back, holding up the issue of *BILD* with her face on the cover. She stared straight at the viewer with an unusually haughty expression, and the headline emblazoned above her in bright-red type read: *Professor Who Kicked White Students Out of Seminar Is HERSELF WHITE!*

"Wowie, they learned a new color," Saraswati harrumphed. "If you fed me alphabet soup, I could shit out better titles than that."

Nivedita had expected to encounter a timid or despairing or at least sheepish Saraswati, only to find her livid. She was cursing like a sailor, storming through the veritable cathedral of light that was her window-lined penthouse, aping other people's voices: "*Who am I? And if so, What Race?* Is that the level of discourse we've stooped to?" Nivedita nearly laughed at how she'd twisted the title of Richard David Precht's best seller, as if to prove her alphabet soup remark.

Nivedita followed her through the still-oh-so-impressively styled living space and tried to pick up all the stuff her mentor's vengeful hands sent crashing to the floor as she passed: the *BILD* with the offending cover; a little red bowl holding a bunch of keys and loose change; a yellow bowl of dried goji berries; a pile of paper that would later turn out to be the uncorrected galleys of Saraswati's next book; and a Mason jar acting as a vase for a bunch of wildflowers, to which Nivedita added her blossoming broom stalks. A phone rang in the kitchen, but nobody paid any attention.

"Yeah—but is it true, Saraswati? Is it true?"

Saraswati stopped so suddenly in her tracks that Nivedita ran right into her.

"What kind of question is that? Did you learn nothing from me?"

Reality began to waver and the floor below Nivedita's feet started to give way, turning into quicksand. Her reflexes kicked in, she grabbed onto Saraswati's shoulders, and suddenly felt a need to shake some sense into her: "We're not in your seminar anymore, we're in the real world . . ."

"Oh, so now we're keeping that old dichotomy alive, too? What's next? Enough already, cut it out with all your dividing lines and categories . . ."

Meanwhile, the impulse to shake Saraswati's smugness right out of her had grown so strong that Nivedita's arms began trembling. "Is it true?" she repeated, and noticed her voice was trembling, too.

Saraswati wrested her shoulders from Nivedita's hands with an enormous shrug. "Truth, the way in which *they* define it, does not exist," she replied, and huffed off again, pacing through the apartment.

Maybe that was the moment Nivedita should've left. But she was so used to other people—Priti, Simon, her mother—setting the rules of interaction that, as if in a daze, she just kept following Saraswati, who yet again came to a halt, spun a one-eighty on her heels, and appeared to only now be noticing Nivedita's actual presence.

"*Schätzchen*, how sweet of you to rush over to see me so early in the morning—and what wonderful flowers!" she gushed, gesturing toward the tattered yellow petals. "Where did you learn that broom symbolizes humanity, humility, and tenacity?"

The abrupt pivot from criticizing print media to analyzing ethnobotanical traditions made Nivedita dizzy. She hadn't figured out yet how to handle people unable of giving anything their undivided attention. Other peoples' carelessness caused her acute physical pain. She was unable to dismiss it as yet another intellectual and emotional limitation all living beings have. As a result, she was incapable of inflicting that kind of pain on others. Saraswati, on the other hand, could turn her charm on and off at will—although her sheer munificence usually dictated that it be kept on at all times. So whenever she actually did listen closely to someone, it was with the conscious knowledge of having chosen to grant them the gift of her precious time and attention. The recipients of this lavish gesture then felt uplifted—honored that someone as special as Saraswati deemed them worthy of her presence, *win-win, bla-bling, cha-ching*.

And now she decided to direct her warm-and-fuzzy spotlight at Nivedita.

"Have you eaten breakfast, *mein Liebchen*? Of course you haven't. You must be famished, Nivedita. Let me make you some eggs."

The diligent student followed her professor yet again, this time to the kitchen, where she let Saraswati press her onto a wicker chair and even procure a footstool, as if she were the one who needed caring for, not the other way around.

"You want tea or coffee? Tea, of course! Soy or almond milk?" Without waiting for an answer, Saraswati set a red jug down in front of her pupil. It was decorated with white dots that reminded her of the toadstools in the picture book Priti's mother, Leela, had given her during that first visit to Birmingham. Children lounged on the mushrooms and peeked out from behind giant flowers, looking like teensy Victorian orphans, only with wings, and they wore flower petals for clothes. The book was Cicely Mary Barker's *Flower Fairies*. Birgit had been far too rapt by the illustrations, and kept pointing to the Hazelnut Elf in a hat made of brown felt, exclaiming that this particular elf looked *exactly like* her daughter. Nivedita found it unbearable because when she saw that image she thought not of some little Indian kid, but of the folksong "*Schwarzbraun ist die Haselnuss,*" which had been co-opted by the army and turned into a wartime oompah tune—it must've been the mention of hazelnut, and the chorus repeatedly talking about black and brown, that brought the song to mind . . . and she was too old for picture books anyway. Even more embarrassing was the fact that Priti's only reaction was to eagerly ask which elf looked *exactly like* her.

Then, like some picture-book *hausfrau*, Saraswati simultaneously put a kettle on the stove, cracked a bunch of eggs into an enameled cast-iron skillet and stirred them into an omelet, diced up an avocado, a tomato, and some basil—all while continuing her inner-turned-outer monologue.

"I expect nothing less from the illustrious *BILD*, but have you read what some of my esteemed colleagues are saying?"

Nivedita opened her mouth in an attempt to confirm that she had indeed read what the world had to say about Saraswati, but then Saraswati herself had enough to say about it that no one could possibly get a word in edgewise.

"Isn't it clear to them that their arguments oversimplify everything? People of Color is a political subject, not a racist one! Following the only successful uprising of enslaved peoples that we know of . . ." Saraswati grabbed the kettle and pointed its steaming spout toward Nivedita with a nod.

"The Haitian Revolution, seventeen ninety-one to eighteen-oh-four," she automatically recited.

"Corrrrrect, A-student!"

In another universe, such an evaluation would've fulfilled Nivedita's every dream. Even now she couldn't help feeling an ashamed twinge of pride. Saraswati presented her a mug as if it were a reward, gingerly setting it on the table and fishing out the tea bag with her fingers.

"Following the only successful uprising of enslaved peoples that we know of—which became the Haitian Revolution and significantly influenced subsequent rebellions against oppression—in eighteen hundred and four. the independent Black government officially declared the Poles and Germans Black because they had fought on the side of the rebels. It was even included in the constitution."

The tea smelled of tannin, warmth, and security, but those sensations were fleeting. Saraswati's sheer Saraswatiness enveloped Nivedita in a spreading haze of contradictions until she cynically pierced it, raising an objection that flickered like a will-o'-the-wisp within the dissipating fuzziness.

"So you're basically claiming that, by extension, you yourself took part in an uprising of enslaved peoples and can therefore now declare yourself Black?"

"Figuratively, yes," Saraswati replied, as if it were self-evident, as if Nivedita had asked whether she'd ever won a major academic award or received a standing ovation for a superb speech. "Incidentally, slavery was immediately outlawed in Haiti, a full thirty years before the Brits even began considering the idea. But you already know all that. My favorite part is how the free republic of Haiti explicitly forbid racism in its constitution." Off in the corner, a phone rang—a phone so retro it was orange, with rotary dial, and Nivedita immediately recognized it as a model produced exclusively by the BRD postal service.

The round, wrung-out tea bag on Nivedita's saucer looked like a whole-grain organic cookie, and she felt the urge to take a bite. Nothing was as it seemed. Whenever Saraswati was near, reality became distorted and truth began to melt. If you tried getting ahold of anything concrete, it all started slipping through your fingers. Just as Saraswati's seminars promised: instead of complete, cold-as-steel truths, she gave them undeveloped, breathing facts and acts that required a lot of TLC in order to grow. But then, as of yesterday, she'd broken that promise, and all those warm, fuzzy, embryonic Saraswati-thoughts were now replaced by a bunch of colossal lies.

"But . . . what should I call you, then, if you aren't Saraswati?" Nivedita asked with reproach.

"Don't be silly, of course I'm Saraswati," Saraswati replied.

And since no retort come to mind, Nivedita bit into her fake cookie. The black tea leaves felt like crumbs on her tongue. Radical acts always have a way of boomeranging.

3

The *Say-it-like-Saraswati* moment hadn't been the end of the showdown between Jordan Peterson and Saraswati at the Hay Festival. After, it was Saraswati's turn to give her closing statement—and, as before, the moderator tossed the theme her way like an extra-hot potato.

"Professor Peterson laid out, quite impressively, why he isn't against equal rights—or equity, as many are now calling it—for people of different heritages, so long as that means they're given equal chances, equal opportunity. What he's against is the presumption of equal outcomes. He illustrates his point using the Caucus race scene from *Alice in Wonderland*, in which everyone is declared a winner and everyone is given the same prize, despite their different levels of performance. You, on the other hand, describe the concept of equal opportunity as equal *pulling-the-wool-over-people's-eyes*. Could you elaborate on that, please?" the moderator asked, making sure to milk the very last drop of conflict out of the confrontation.

Saraswati gave him her (in)famous Saraswati-smile, which always contained equal parts promise and admonition, as she strode up to the front of the stage.

"My goal is for everyone to have an equal opportunity *to find out* where they're from. To find out what varied influences, constellations, and configurations shape them—thereby affecting not only what direction they head in, but also and above all, what direction they *want* to head in, as well as who and what they *want* to *be*." She cast another deep glance at the camera. Early in her career she'd learned to develop an almost erotic relationship to any and every camera lens, and the skill had paid handsome returns. "And so my goal is *not* for everyone to have the same chance—and that's it. Since Professor Peterson mentioned Lewis Carroll's *Alice in Wonderland*, allow me to contrast that scene with a cartoon by the German caricaturist Hans Traxler: it depicts a monkey, a stork, an elephant, a goldfish, a seal, and a poodle standing before a teacher who explains, 'In order for us to achieve a fair selection, you shall all be given the same test: climb this tree.' *That's* equal opportunity. The monkeys always win. Equal opportunity, and the very notion that anyone has an equal chance at anything, is a lethal lie. What's worse, because of that lie, those who aren't conditioned for the task are also ashamed they can't climb the tree fast enough. We're essentially telling the different ones, 'Everything was completely equal, so it must be your fault if you're left behind.' Whereby we're also denying that there *really are* differing preconditions. Now, you might be thinking, 'Sure, all that might be true, but are we then supposed to carry the goldfish up the tree?' Of course not! My goal is for everyone to be fostered *in whatever way they need* to realize their full potential as best they can and, more broadly, contribute to the happiness, good fortune, and spiritual well-being of this society," Saraswati concluded, her tone exuding both warmth and arrogance.

"Saraswati's voice is so mellifluous, it virtually hands you a pen so you can take notes," Barbara observed, stabbing the last grape with her mini Indian-flag toothpick.

At some point later that night, Simon suddenly materialized in Nivedita's room. Lotte must've let him in while Nivedita and Priti, who had tuned in from London, dissected the entire match, play by play. "Gotta go," Niv said into her phone, thoroughly satisfied to have finally turned the tables—until, of course, Priti cut her off, "No, *I've* got to go!"

"Are you feeling as rotten as I am?" Simon asked. Nivedita figured that was a euphemism since he looked like he'd neither eaten nor slept since the last time they'd seen each other. But then that also might've just been a projection, since she'd found those two things equally hard, and felt so thin-skinned that Simon's steady stare pierced right through her, reducing her to a massive jumble of raw nerves. He gingerly reached out for her shoulders, but she pulled back. "May I take you into my arms, Nivedita?" he said in his huskiest voice.

She opened her mouth to let him know he could fuck off, but since he was already pressing his trembling body against her, she closed it again.

"Why do I do this?" he wondered aloud, and Nivedita held his head as he bawled. "This," Nivedita discovered soon thereafter, meant breaking up out of the blue, like cutting a cord—a cord he could, mere days or weeks later, pick right back up again, without even trying to patch things up. And since Nivedita forgave him for a second time, again without any objections, a pattern was established whereby each time he broke up with her, they'd make up again even quicker. *Fuuuck.*

But first, for once, they celebrated their nearly lost and therefore now-so-much-more-precious relationship. They spent the next few days together in bed, and then the next few days after that camping out on the dunes of Domburg. A week later, as Nivedita came home with sweat-soaked clothes and half the sand from the North Sea's beaches under her heavy eyelids, she saw a girl that looked a bit like her cousin Priti sitting on a backpack at the end of her street.

"Hey Niv," the girl said. It really was Priti.

"What're you doing here?" Nivedita asked.

As would soon become clear, she was staying. Priti had come to Germany to study postcolonial theory. With Saraswati.

"Where can I crash?" Priti asked, heaving her huge backpack onto her shoulders. Big as the bag was, she still hadn't brought enough clothes, so the first thing Nivedita had to do was loan her a clean pair of underwear.

The next morning Priti strolled into the kitchen wearing ankle-length leggings (also Nivedita's) and a cropped T-shirt (her own). Barbara and Lotte were clearing the breakfast table of all the jars of Marmite and boxes of tea she'd left as an offering in lieu of rent, tidily storing them in the cupboard over the sink.

"Nice ass," Lotte remarked.

"Nice cunt," Barbara rejoined.

PRITI MOVED FIRST into Nivedita's bed, and then into Lotte's room, after Lotte took off for a three-month Erasmus exchange in Florence. Then a room opened up in Oluchi's apartment so Priti moved there, just as easily as she'd waltzed into the local Berlitz and landed a job within the hour that paid for her entire stay in Germany, covering all her expenses and then some.

Saraswati granted Priti an appointment during office hours the way a pope might grant a special audience, and then allowed the newcomer a place in her closest circle of advisees, albeit not before summoning Nivedita to conduct due diligence.

"Is this what you want?"

"Of course, she *is* my cousin," Nivedita replied, surprised she'd even ask such a thing.

Saraswati sighed and signed the paperwork for Priti's mid-semester change of major, effective immediately.

It wasn't until she and Priti were seated next to one another in the lecture hall that Nivedita caught on to what Saraswati was getting at. Suddenly a weird sort of double consciousness arose. Before, Saraswati's every word had been a secret message aimed directly at her—it was as if Saraswati's thoughts were engaging in erotic acts in the convolutions of her gray matter, giving birth to new, ultrapersonal ideas. But now her reactions to these intimate messages were being observed and judged by another person.

And yet her obvious kinship to someone like Priti also granted her a degree of authenticity she'd never have been able to attain all by herself.

"I was the absolute worst thing an Indian girl could be," Priti said with gusto, "too thin, too black, too clever." This invariably cued the male chorus in Saraswati's seminar to recite a string of affirmations, "You can never be too clever," or, rather creepier, "You can never be too thin."

The women chimed in more softly, and every now and then Nivedita even heard a mumbled, "Uhh, it's not like she's *that* thin." But no one ever once said anything that touched on that first bit, "too black."

Except Lotte. "Well, I'd actually like to be browner. So I don't really know what you're going for," she said in her high-pitched, breathless voice while Priti was holding court at the kitchen table one day.

"You couldn't possibly understand," Priti imperiously replied, "it's different for *Desi* girls like me and Nivedita."

"Why do you call yourselves *Desi*, anyway?" Lotte asked Nivedita, since Priti had turned to focus all her attention on Barbara. And Nivedita, who'd just written an essay on precisely this topic for Saraswati, automatically replied, "Because I find it better than *hapa*."

Lotte stared at her like she'd just spoken Hawaiian—which, in a sense, she had—but it took the two of them a little while to uncross their wires and finally clarify that *hapa* came from the Hawaiian term for "half," as in half Asian and half European, although over time it shifted to mean "part." And no, it had nothing to do with the half-and-half you might put in your coffee, or the part you put in your hair. While *Desi*, on the other hand, basically meant the exact opposite: it was an all-encompassing word for people in South Asia and the South Asian diaspora, granting a unified identity across borders and nations. It even crossed boundaries such as species. Anything could be *Desi*— chapatis and samosas, rice dishes and dance moves, books and podcasts, musical traditions and sex positions.

Saraswati gave Nivedita a vocabulary and language for her own life. And not just hers. The select circle of Saraswati's students communicated among themselves using a fantastic code of academic abbreviations in which entire enormous concepts and philosophies were distilled into shorthand: *Desi, hapa, subaltern. Imagined communities, critical race theory, intersectionality.* Whenever these terms were uttered, they all nodded knowingly. And each time such a word was pronounced—be it two syllables, three syllables, or just a couple deft twists of the tongue—it gave rise to an unnatural, heretofore unknown feeling of togetherness and belonging. Never mind the fact that most of the students had only the vaguest notion of what an imagined community might be, and wouldn't have recognized a subaltern if it were garnished with parsley and served to them on a silver platter. Although that last part might be chalked up to the fact that they were also convinced that they themselves were the subalterns. That made Saraswati so furious that she showed them all a lecture on YouTube by Gayatri Chakravorty Spivak—who had made Gramsci's term famous—but then even Spivak herself never really said exactly who the subaltern might be. Basically, there were people who were more subaltern than others, but at the end of the day it seemed like *subalternity* as a concept came down to a question of heart—something on par with goodness or purity of mind—that melted away the closer you got. But from afar, it shone like a lighthouse. With its help, and in the fabulously illuminating lights flashing from all the other lighthouses built of new words and concepts popping up all around her, she charted her course and navigated into new waters.

Priti was the uncrowned queen of the Diaspora Girls. Or, as Saraswati called them, the Third World Diva Girls. That was a bell hooks reference, although Nivedita didn't know that yet. Just like she didn't know that the thin/black/clever line was a quote from Arundhati Roy.

"Does *anybody* think original thoughts anymore?! Or are we all just quoting one another back at ourselves in some kind of sick funhouse hall of mirrors with no escape, where every mirror is framed by identity?" she griped to Kali after she finally came upon that quote from bell hooks's paper in the library.

But Kali, whose facial features increasingly resembled Saraswati's, just calmly remarked: *Always steal from the best!*

4

"You know damn well it's pretty racist that my skin color makes a difference to you," Saraswati said with relish, as if she were enjoying every word the way Nivedita was savoring every bit of her scrumptious omelet.

Nivedita froze. *Don't fuck me up with your so-called facts*, she thought. *Don't you mess with me* . . . The sun seemed to have followed them through the apartment and now shone directly into the kitchen. Of all the herbs on

Saraswati's windowsill, the dill was strongest, and its sharp, intense, lemony scent cut through Nivedita's increasing weariness like smelling salts—like something anachronistic, like an old memory woven from folktales full of ghosts and dangerous tasks that only a purehearted maiden could successfully pull off.

"It's not about your skin color . . . I mean, it wouldn't be about your skin color . . . ," she grasped for words. "What I mean to say is, it wouldn't have made any difference back when I met you, but—"

"But what? Now we know each other well enough that you're allowed to be just a little bit racist?" Saraswati asked, clearly amused. The orange telephone rang again, and Saraswati ignored it again.

From one minute to the next, Nivedita felt more and more disoriented. Why wasn't Saraswati responding the way a normal person would? What did Priti have to do with Saraswati's . . . debunking . . . unveiling, or unmasking as *white*? And how was Saraswati's supposedly long-lost brother involved? The one with whom Priti had . . . well, done just what, exactly? And why was it getting harder and harder for Nivedita to formulate a clear thought? *Kali, where are you when I need you?* she hollered into the hollow echo chamber of her own head, and Kali replied, *You don't need me.*

"Uh, yeah! I mean, no. But you're . . ." Nivedita wanted to say *so important to me* to Saraswati, but she bit her tongue, out of shyness or maybe out of a petty desire to deprive Saraswati of any such gratification. Instead, she said, "You're *you* because of everything you've taught me."

"And I still taught you all those things, regardless of whatever *race* I am." Saraswati again flashed that ironic grin as if this whole thing were one gigantic joke.

"Yeah, sure, but they don't *mean* the same thing anymore!" Nivedita sniveled, surprised to discover that a simple sob garnered her more attention than any argument in the whole wide world. Saraswati was still smiling over some pun only she understood, but she lifted her hands to cradle Nivedita's cheeks and take a much closer look into her eyes.

"Do you mean to say that you wouldn't have absorbed such superb scholarship if the person who'd been teaching it was *white*?"

Nivedita felt the warmth of her professor's palms on her face and a totally unrelated thought came to mind: *Three days, it's been three whole days since the last time Simon slept with me.*

"It does make a difference," she firmly said.

"Exactly *what* difference?" Saraswati asked. "And think carefully before you speak, since any answer you give will be just as much about you as it is about me."

Nivedita tried to return Saraswati's piercing gaze, but then noticed that her eyes began to burn the moment she tried to focus on anything. "Obviously, since I'm actually listening to you—not like all those people outside, who couldn't care less what you think!"

See, you don't need me, Kali extolled.

"Touché," Saraswati applauded, parroting Kali's tone perfectly.

Don't make fun of Kali! Nivedita yelled in her head, which had gone from mere echo chamber to full-on rattling noisemaker, now distorting her words and lobbing them right back at her.

"Why did you lie to me?" she asked out loud, suddenly realizing—despite all the racket in her mind—that this was the real reason for her presence here. She hadn't come to find out why Saraswati had lied to the university or to the entire world, but rather to *her.* This was personal.

But of course Saraswati was back to following her own line of reasoning.

"If I taught you anything at all, it's that *race* is a construct."

"Yeah, *race*, as a concept—but not yours . . ."

"Say it calmly: race. *Mein Schatz*, people can be divided into different races just as well as water and light can be divided into different sexes. People aren't dogs. What is it you want—me, or the image you've conjured of me?"

Nivedita yanked her head away from Saraswati's hands—"You must mean the image *you yourself* conjured?"—and immediately regretted it. The sudden movement felt like something had struck her skull, causing each and every bone to vibrate, making her head ring like a bell—although not like those chiming Indian bells of all different sizes and sounds that hung from the walls of her parents' home, looking like musical rosaries. No, more like the heavy boom of those super-thick Catholic church bells, the kind heralding the Last Judgment. On top of all that, she already missed the warmth of Saraswati's hands.

But her punctilious professor remained unfazed.

"What is it you want?"

Nivedita tried to avoid making eye contact, but Saraswati stared straight at her.

Help me, Nivedita implored, with an internal prayer louder than all the Angeluses ringing in her head, *Kaliii!*

You don't need me, Kali repeated.

And that was exactly when the lack of sleep, state of shock, lovesickness, and draining debate overwhelmed Nivedita, and her head tipped toward the tabletop.

Kali rolled her eyes like billiard balls. *Okay, fine, if this is what it takes . . .* She pointed to the pocket in Nivedita's skirt and the phone inside started ringing. *Arise, ye wretched of the Earth!*

"Umm, so, there's this man here who really needs to talk to you . . ." as usual, Lotte sounded out of breath.

"A man?" Nivedita asked, somewhat dazed.

"A man," Lotte reconfirmed.

"What kind of man?" asked Nivedita.

"What kind of man?" Saraswati prodded.

"He didn't say," Lotte said.

"Well then *ask* him!" Nivedita yelled—although not too loudly, since by now her whole body had a headache. She heard voices in the distance, some rattling sounds, voices even farther in the distance. Then suddenly Lotte was back.

"He said he'll come back."

"What did he want?"

"To talk to you."

Nivedita considered hurling her phone against the wall.

"About what?"

"About Saraswati."

How's that for divine intervention? Kali asked, as Saraswati gently swept Nivedita's hair from her forehead and issued a declaration.

"First, let's let you get some sleep. Then we can take it from there."

BANG BANG BANG BANG

1

The phone rang again right away. Nivedita tried to decline Lotte's call only to discover it wasn't her phone ringing.

"Ignore them," Saraswati said, "they've been trying all day."

"*Them?* Who?" Nivedita inquired.

"Yeah, readers of *Halle Speaks, Philosophia Universalis, Alternative für Thüringen* . . ." Saraswati was counting with her fingers, but she wasn't naming one website per finger starting with her thumb, like a German would. Instead, she started with her pinkie finger, and named one website per *joint* on *each finger*, tapping one knuckle crease after another with her thumb. Nivedita was too exhausted to get upset that Saraswati was counting like an Indian. Unpredictable as ever, Saraswati then stretched out one of her temple dancer–like arms and lifted the orange receiver to her ear.

"Hello? How did you ge—? *Click.*"

"*Halle*-wha?" Nivedita asked, puzzled.

"*Halle Speaks*, the so-called news for the other twenty percent, *mein Schätzchen.*"

Nivedita shut her eyes, but Saraswati had already flashed the phone screen at her face, and the image was burned into her brain like hellfire. It showed a stock photo of Saraswati with an extra-arrogant look on her face. "GOODY-TWO-SHOES says Whiteness is a CANCER—and that Germans should be FORCED to dye their skin STARTING IN KINDERGARTEN!" Underneath were Saraswati's email address and phone number. Maybe that's what had rung the bell tucked away in Nivedita's head: the Last Judgment was coming to Crazytown.

The phone rang again, or kept ringing—by now, what difference did it make? Unbelievably, Saraswati picked up yet again.

"Saraswati here," she said into the receiver, whereupon an unintelligible yet unmistakably furious squall of invective gushed forth. Then, in a voice mellow as milk and honey, she followed up, "Would you mind repeating that? I just hit 'record' . . . *Click.* Again."

Rrrrring!

"Hello . . . Yes, this is she . . . Could you please spell your na . . . *Didn't see that coming, either.*"

Rrrrring!

"Düsseldorf Police Headquarters—your call has been forwarded to us under suspicion of crimina . . . *Coward!*"

Rrrrring!

The calls were incessant, and seemed to fill Saraswati with an almost electric charge. The whole situation was so nightmarish, and at the same time absurd, that Nivedita was convinced Saraswati would give off sparks if she touched her. But before she could even try, the annoyance had pushed Saraswati past her own admittedly low tolerance threshold, and she pulled the plug from the ISDN box.

The absence of ringing filled the room with an audible, almost palpable silence. It was as if someone had turned on an old radio tuned to a station that no longer existed and then cranked the volume up to the max. Nivedita took a few deep breaths before the Wednesday-morning hubbub floating up from the street below began to assault her ears again. Kölner Straße was Oberbilk's main drag, lined with street vendors, and the buyers' and sellers' haggling voices grew louder as midday approached. The sun bore down, and everything had to go. Fingers of sunshine reached across the vegetable displays, and warm gusts of air pushed their way into the curtains shielding the balcony doors—they were in for a steamy afternoon.

"Now, what're we going to do with you?" Saraswati said to Nivedita, looking her over.

"With me?" Nivedita replied, surprised.

"If I'm seeing what I think I'm seeing, you didn't come here to hold my hand. You came to stay."

"No! I . . ."

With a mere hand gesture, Saraswati effectively shushed her.

"It might not be clear to you, but that's the real reason you came here."

"Saraswati, I came here because you called me!"

"Right—I did, didn't I? C'mon, you're beat, let me show you your room," Saraswati extended her hand.

Nivedita stared at it, stunned. The correct response would've been to give Saraswati the cold shoulder and head home—back to her apartment, back to Simon's silence, back to all Priti's missed calls, to all Birgit's beleaguered sighs, to all Lotte's *ohhh*s. Like someone about to drown, Nivedita grabbed Saraswati's hand. There was a faint spark.

SIX SEMESTERS AGO, the first time she'd visited Saraswati's house, Nivedita had briefly paused in front of her professor's bedroom while on her way to the bathroom. The door had been left slightly ajar, so she tried to catch a glimpse of something, anything. The only thing she'd been able to see was floor-to-ceiling white shelves, like the kind you'd see in a mom-and-pop corner store, but instead of groceries and laundry detergent, they were stocked with books. On the floor in front of them was something she couldn't quite make out, something that looked like a heap of feathers. Back then, since she hadn't dared push the door open and actually invade Saraswati's inner sanctum, she had to make do with inspecting the bathroom's contents.

Tubes and jars of all types crowded the shelves and every other available surface, lined up like so many brownies and fairies. Nivedita had gingerly twisted off their caps and taken a whiff. There were tons of tinctures that must've touched every inch of Saraswati's skin—eye creams, hair oils, homeopathic substances whose effects remained mysterious, unlabeled little bottles of colorful liquids, labeled little bottles of colorless liquids, witch hazel, *Sangre de Drago*, DMSO, vulnerary powder . . . vulnerary? Saraswati's entire house was unmistakably steeped in her strong personality, but Nivedita wasn't in a position to interpret all these signs.

The mere thought that she now had permission to venture into the dark underbelly of her (former?) professor's personal space filled her with an excitement that was almost sexual. The fact that Saraswati had been outed still turned her off, but now she felt both turned off *and* turned on. Then she sank into Saraswati's guest bed as if it were an embrace, and the scrumptious sensation of serene safety swept through every fiber of her being, drowning out all other feelings. The sleep that had eluded her all night now cuddled up with her, and she just wanted to close her eyes and let her thoughts wander. Her plan was to stay that way until the phone stopped ringing, until everyone stopped shouting, until posts of adorable little kitties (hers included) crowded out all the bile online, until Saraswati was brown again.

As if on cue, the hysterical pinging of incoming emails in the room next door came to an abrupt halt, probably only because Saraswati had set her phone to silent. But Nivedita could still hear the artificial clicking sound of the smartphone keyboard, and had to wonder how thin the walls were, since every keystroke was audible. Or was it just because Saraswati was typing with such brute force? Or was she just typing to save her own skin? And why was Nivedita worrying about her after Saraswati had clearly given up the right to be worthy of anyone's concern? She'd gambled and lost, but to whom? The devil? If so, did that mean all Nivedita's worrying now belonged to the devil?

To her surprise, the only thing Nivedita wasn't thinking about was Simon. Saraswati still had such an effect on her that everything else—people, thoughts, problems—faded away. It was as if Saraswati was surrounded by an invisible force field that overpowered everything. Nivedita pressed her face into the linens. They smelled like chlorophyll and sundried tomatoes—a far cry from the sheets back in her apartment, which reeked of period blood and Simon's semen.

Nivedita dreamed that her child stood before her.

"I believe in your god. Who is your god?" her child said.

"I believe in many gods and goddesses," she replied, noncommittal, still thinking about blood and semen. But she couldn't expect her kid to believe that.

"What god did you believe in when you were my age?" her child asked.

Good question, exactly how old are you? But the child wasn't any specific child, it was just a stand-in, symbolizing a generic prepubescent member of the human species. So Nivedita's answer was equally unspecific, although she delivered it in her best talking-to-a-kid voice.

"I believe in the Dear Lord," as if *Dear* were a first name.

What about me? rejoined Kali, bemused, from the wings.

"I don't have to believe in you—after all, I talk to you every day."

"Then I'll go with the Dear, too," her child decided.

"Wait, hang on!" Nivedita yelled in desperation. "My one and only goddess is Kali!"

"Too late. You blew it," her child said, and Nivedita awoke in a fluster, wondering whether it really was too late for her. *Too late for what?* Too late, just too late.

You're twenty-six, seriously, Kali reminded her. *Don't take yourself so damn seriously.*

> » **Call me Zadie @OutsideSisters** *Don't take yourself so damn seriously,* *@Identitti #IdentittiIsntTheCenterOfTheUniverse*
>
> » **Niv You Pussy @littleBird** *A little birdie told me @Identitti ran straight to Saraswati.*
>
> » **I looove The Stones' 'Brown Sugar' @Nicole777** *Wherever Saraswati is, @Identitti can't be far. Don't take yourself so damn seriously, @Identitti #DonTakeYrslfSoDamnSriouslyIdentitti*

By the time she actually woke up, it was already two in the afternoon. The sun was smack-dab in the middle of the penthouse's impressive wall of windows, shining through a slit in the curtains, making specks of dust look like glitter. Nivedita felt all sticky and dehydrated, but also energized for the first time since Priti's call. Groping around the side of the bed, she discovered a cup of tea that Saraswati must've brought in while she was sleeping. It matched Nivedita's body temperature so precisely that she only realized what it was when she pulled her hand up and noticed her fingers were wet.

Unlike Nivedita, the whole Saraswati-Saga hadn't slept. Indeed, it hadn't taken even the tiniest break. Glancing at her phone, she discovered that the plot (fraud, brownface) and cast (outed prof., cuz Priti) had gained a new character: Saraswati's brother, Konstantin T., a psychologist and social worker doing outreach with juvenile offenders in Southall, aka London's Little India. The headlines poured in. "Go figure. After all, his juvenile sister had gotten into identity theft early on" (*Express*). As for whose identity the young Saraswati had stolen, well, the illustrious *Express* didn't say. But clearly, judging from the media coverage, there was something deceitful about the skills she had (mis)appropriated: "Saraswati's Shame" (*The Daily Mail*), "cultural theft" (*Washington Post*), "racist masquerade" (the *New Statesman*). Konstantin T. had spent thirty years looking for the sister who had "vanished" (*Frankfurter Allgemeine Zeitung*), "gone underground" (*Die Welt*), "slid downhill into an underworld of fuzzy fake identities" (*Cicero*). He'd only turned to the media once he had incontestable proof that Saraswati . . .

Nivedita searched for a picture where she could see the guy who brought about Saraswati's downfall and look him in the eyes. But aside from that snapshot from the late eighties, with the piano in the southern German living room, nary a photo of him could be found online—and in that one, he wasn't even looking at the camera. Instead, he was looking at Saraswati, or rather the person who would one day become Saraswati. Konstantin T. wanted to remain anonymous. A voice in her head said that that made him seem more serious, which, in turn, made Nivedita even more furious, she just didn't know at whom.

Also unlike Nivedita, the Internet itself never slept. Saraswati was still #1 on Germany's Most Hated list, but Nivedita wasn't far behind. She'd even been given a new hashtag, #OnkelTomtitti, which swiftly entered the Anglosphere as #UncleTomtitti. Only twenty tweets into it, she stopped reading and started skimming for keywords, like the call to boycott her blog, to boycott her, to not believe anything she had written, was writing, or might ever write. Why hadn't they just gone straight to #CancelIdentitti? The DMs were, as always, even worse. Except for one:

> Hi Identitti,
> I've been following your account for a year now, and always read your
> blog. Would you be interested in writing a piece for us about
> #Saraswatigate? It can be as personal as you want. 1,000 words.
> Unfortunately the pay isn't great, but it would make an excellent
> feature. Shall we discuss by phone?
>   Best,
> Peter
> —
>
> Peter Weissenburger
> taz–Die Tageszeitung
> Editor
> Society/Media

2

The third time Simon up and left Nivedita was six months after the Hay Festival. He'd just passed his first round of law exams, they were at a party with a bunch of classmates, and he introduced his best friend to her. Richard was one of those guys who you could just see wearing jeans and a ponytail his entire life, adding a touch of spice with a bit of ethnic jewelry.

"Nivedita? That's an Indian name, right?" he said, beaming. "*Kannst du Deutsch*, or shall we speak English?"

Since she'd already had four semesters with Saraswati by then, her answer came easily.

"*Lieber Englisch.*"

And that was that.

She and Simon left the party, walking out quicker than they'd walked in.

"Why didn't you intervene?" she asked Simon when they got to Jürgensplatz. The square was like a stage set. Behind them, a series of Wilhelminian-era neoclassical facades formed a backdrop, and inside the buildings' warmly lit windows a bunch of law students sipped champagne from curvaceous flutes. In front of the soon-to-be-former couple, the facade of Düsseldorf Police HQ formed a curtain of sorts, complete with the imperial eagle now partially covered over by a triangular cast-iron plaque added in 1984 that read *Vor dem Gesetz sind alle Menschen Gleich*—All People are Equal before the Law.

"Why are you always so harsh?" Simon shot back.

"Why am *I*?" Nivedita was stunned. "*I'm harsh*? You really don't you get it, do you?"

"No, actually, I *do* get it. I totally get how, right after I introduce you to someone who hasn't done a damn thing to you, you dress him down in front of everybody."

"Saraswati . . ."

"Unlike your Saraswati, Richard's a good egg."

And then that really was that.

As usual, all her rage came spewing out—gushing like water from a jug with a hole in it, like rusty water from an old metal jug with bullet holes in it, like blood from a mortally wounded body—as Simon just turned away and shot his last words at her like three silver bullets: "It" and "is" and "over." Clink, clank, clunk—kerplunk.

That's not a real spell, Kali cut him to the quick. She never did understand why Nivedita froze each time Simon told her to get lost. *Anyway, he'll be back.*

"And what do I do if he doesn't come back?"

If only!

Along with Nivedita's rage, the last bit of warmth had also gushed from her veins, so she decided to take a taxi home, even though she put taxis in the same category as domestic flights or Gwyneth Paltrow's €80 This Smells Like My Vagina candle.

"There's no need to cry," the cabbie said with a fatherly tone, taking a pouch of pocket tissues from the passenger seat and handing it to her in the back seat. "You can keep the pack."

Nivedita didn't really know what she was supposed to do with the tissues. Dab away her tears? What for? But his gesture comforted her. Why couldn't Simon act like that when she felt hurt? Light from the street lamps hit her face intermittently, making her feel as if she'd landed in a road trip movie whose melancholic heroine was unattached—in the best sense of the word— destined to drive down endless highways, deep into the heart of night. *And miles to go before I sleep, and miles to go before I sleep.*

The driver held out a bulging bag full of roasted, salted pumpkin seeds, catapulting her back into the not-exactly-cinematic taxi.

"Here, they're good for your heart. Where're you from?"

Of course. Because it wasn't just *white* Germans who asked where she was from. She also got that question from . . . other people who were themselves constantly being asked that same question, so they turned around and used it in an attempt, however artificial or forced, to establish some kind of common ground. The flip side of Nivedita's inability to pass was that she actually could fit in pretty much everywhere, as long as melanin was present. And that's why Turks, Kurds, Egyptians, Algerians, Mexicans, Moroccans, Spaniards, Iranians, Sinti, Romani, Algerians, Brazilians, Afghans, Pakistanis, Bangladeshis, and sometimes even Indians took her for one of them.

"Where're you from?" repeated Mehdi Ziaar, as she learned from his prominently displayed driver ID. But because these kinds of conversations usually ended with the driver touting his son's suitability as a future husband, Nivedita took a different tack.

"Poland," she said dryly.

"You're from Poland?" Mehdi asked back.

"Yup, Poland," Nivedita confirmed.

"And where's your mother from?"

"Poland."

"From Poland?"

"Yup, Poland."

The taxi continued along Hütten Straße and soon emerged from the underpass below the train tracks. Now they were in Oberbilk, and she was home.

"And your father?"

"He's from India," she capitulated.

"That's an original mixture."

She doubted that had played a role in her parents' decision to have a kid. She just couldn't picture them saying, *We'd just love to make the most original mixture ever.* And anyway, the vast majority of people in the Ruhr Valley had Polish roots somewhere in their family tree. Birgit's maiden name had been Schimanski. As a kid, Nivedita had found that especially ironic, since her mother, Birgit Anand, bore zero resemblance to Horst Schimanski, the superstar homicide detective from the TV show *Tatort.* But the older Nivedita got—it finally clicked when she had her own first boyfriend—the more she realized that that baby-blue-eyed, beige trench coat–clad, trenchant-remark-making investigator was precisely the kind of man she found attractive: he was a smoker (like Simon), a drinker (not so much like Simon), and *German* (like Simon). And the TV show helped Nivedita solve the puzzle of how Birgit Schimanski and Jagdish Anand had gotten together.

Because in Birgit's eyes, *Tatort* detective Schimanski wasn't German.

"I still remember exactly when I first saw him on TV. It was nineteen seventy-nine. No, wait, 'eighty-one." For her, *exactly* was a relative term. "A Polish police detective! You can't even imagine how prejudiced people were against Poles back then. How many Poles does it take to change a lightbulb? While you're busy placing your bets, someone'll swipe the lightbulb. The idea that a Pole could be the detective chief inspector instead of just the criminal, I mean . . . my gosh! We experienced real racism back then. It's so great things aren't like that anymore."

Every time Birgit told this story—and it was often—Nivedita wondered whether she should go for the jugular.

Of course her father was also fond of telling her that *he* had experienced *real* racism. He'd had such a hard time finding anyone who'd rent an apartment to him that he ended up living in students' quarters until he married Birgit, even though he hated such arrangements. But at least he didn't lie about racism still being *a thing*. He just thought it was *racism lite*. So every time he heard the word *microaggressions*, he usually responded with macroaggressions.

"What's your problem with that roommate of yours? Lotte, right? So she wears a bindi, huh? What's wrong with that? Her purchases support an Indian bindi-maker and an Indian bindi-exporter, did you ever stop to think about that, huh? We went around afraid they'd beat us up in the streets. Back then there was real racism, not like the shiny-happy racism there is today."

Nivedita looked at him and thought about all the things he had no language to express, and she had no language to explain it to him.

So she tried to explain it to Priti one day while they were waiting for Saraswati to show up, late as usual to her own seminar.

"I wish I could've grown up as an Indian girl in England. At least there, there's a community and a modicum of cultural awareness of . . . us. Whereas here . . ." But she stopped short when Priti slammed her three-ring binder on the desk.

"Ach, all you *Deutsche* and your cuddly cute racism! You don't know what racism is until you've come to Fashi-England. Take one guess at why I left. *Germanistan* is a walk in the park compared to where I'm from."

"What about the NSU? Germany has an actual, active National Socialist Underground. And what about Oury Jalloh?" Nivedita replied somewhat cautiously. She'd grown up with *The Avengers*—Emma Peel with her catsuits and John Steed with his umbrellas—but tried to temper it and keep herself in check.

"Like I said, all that's a walk in the park compared to what we have to put up with every day in the UK," Priti said, although her tone implied she hadn't had to tolerate too much, nor did she sound very traumatized—nor did she seem to have a clue who Oury Jalloh or the NSU were.

FAQS

Q: You write about racism a lot. What do actually mean when you say/ write *Racism*?

A: Really? I do? I thought I was just writing about myself. But then again, there's very little in my life that isn't affected by racism in some way, shape, or form. So, where should I start? Okay, let's start with a definition:

We still think that we've always thought people would naturally distinguish one another according to skin color, but it turns out this idea is relatively new. By *new* I mean the eighteenth century—in other words, the period we mistakenly refer to as the *Enlightenment*. Before then, of course, people were still discriminated against and divided into an *us* and a *them*, but the distinction wasn't chalked up to their supposed "race," rather it was attributed to—wait for it!—the weather! Less sun = more diligent, resourceful, tougher people, because they had to eke out a living under inhospitable conditions. More sun = the exact opposite. I'm simplifying a bit here, but not nearly as much as they did back then!

(Race and ethnicity, incidentally, are often confused and used interchangeably, but since even I often confuse the two, I won't write a thing about that here, for once.)

The word *race* was first used in France, and had nothing to do with skin or hair or nose shape, but referred instead to blood. To put it more precisely, it referred to bloodlines—I'm talking about the fourteenth and fifteenth centuries here, when they were negotiating what constituted "true" nobility: ahh, race *sweet* race.

The first homework assignment Saraswati had given her class was to keep a "race diary" from that day until their next meeting. That meant jotting down all the situations in which *race* played a role or had some effect on them.

"Our . . . *race*?" Oluchi was skeptical.

"Just give it a try, you'll see what I'm getting at," was Saraswati's imperious reply. Then she gave a brusque wave, shooing them from the room.

"Just *one week*?" Nivedita asked Oluchi once they were out in the hallway.

"We'll see what she's getting at," Oluchi parroted their professor. She was shockingly good at imitating other people's voices. "For now, I need coffee."

"Me too," Nivedita echoed enthusiastically, even though she couldn't stand coffee. She hadn't even been at college a week yet and she'd already made a friend—a friend who wasn't *white*!

Like most people, Nivedita had assumed racism was when someone came up to her in the street and said, 'I'm gonna insult/hurt/offend/belittle/clobber you because of your skin color.' And so she found it rather difficult to decide for sure whether any given statement/treatment/omission was actually racism or not. And she found it even harder to make the case when relating any given incident to other people.

Like Simon, for instance.

Richard was the only one who didn't take umbrage at the idea—meaning he really was a fundamentally good egg.

"Oh, so it's, like, racist when I ask you if you speak German?" he asked her the next time their paths crossed.

The fact that he'd given it even the slightest thought afterward made such an impression on Nivedita that she forgave him for wearing an om pendant.

"Obviously, because it implies that people who look like me aren't from here."

"Nivedita takes this all very, very seriously," Simon added, addressing Richard, by way of explanation. And then he turned to Nivedita. "Richard meant well. He was just trying to be nice."

"Really?" Richard ignored him, thereby proving his niceness.

"Well, yeah, otherwise the question of whether I speak German or not would be totally superfluous."

"Wow, right—that hadn't even occurred to me," Richard said. So the next question that came out of his mouth was a real shame. "Have you ever experienced racism, Nivedita?"

In fact, thanks to her race diary, Nivedita was only just realizing how often racism cropped up in her life on any given day. Going for coffee with Oluchi at Ex Libris Café that day turned into her first entry in her race diary.

"I don't really like studying that much—every text has the N-word in it, at least once, if not more," Oluchi had confessed to Nivedita.

At the next table over, two guys—who later showed up as fellow students in Saraswati's next class—were discussing soccer.

"No joke, this dude from the Socialist Party actually called Özil *a goat-fucker*!" the cuter guy said to the other guy. They'd later learn the cute one was named Iqbal.

"And the Football Association doesn't do a damn thing! The league's leadership doesn't say a word—can you imagine, bro?" the other guy added, indignant.

Nivedita glanced at the issue of *BILD* that just happened to be on the table—it was as ubiquitous on campus as everywhere else—and saw the cover had a picture of Horst Seehofer, the CSU pol currently serving as minister of the interior, building and community. Underneath his face the headline read: *Islam doesn't belong in Germany*. Then her eyes wandered over to one of the demitasses on the counter. They all bore a logo of a roly-poly, grinning, totally stereotypical N-word, whereupon Nivedita began to suspect Saraswati's homework assignment could be a whole lot of work.

"The problem with racism is that we always act as if it's an individual issue instead of a systemic one. That turns the fight against racism into a fight against bad people, which is a significantly more heroic endeavor than structural change," Saraswati triumphantly began their second class. "If every instance of racism were conscious, individual, and intentional, it'd be just grand. Because then people could just stop. But most racism takes place on the unconscious level because it's internalized. Furthermore, it's virtually impossible for *anyone* to *avoid* internalizing *any* racist stereotypes! It doesn't matter what side of the race divide you're on: racism is the air we breathe. Consequently, experiences with racism are also, primarily, issues having to do with individuation and self-realization."

· · ·

THE TRAM-AS-THEATRICAL-STAGE summer was also the summer of Nivedita's coming out as Indian. She felt good—so good that she even decided to don the sari Priti had brought from Birmingham.

"A gift from my mum."

The mauve swath of silk cloth was longer than her bedroom and embroidered with golden threads. Never, in her entire life as a radical feminist Antifa, would Nivedita have even dreamed of wearing anything so appallingly pink. Now, in her new life as an out-and-proud POC, there was only one thing holding her back.

"So, uhh, how do I tie it?"

"How should I know?" said Priti, helpful as ever.

A few short online tutorials later, Nivedita paraded alongside Priti down Kettwiger Straße with a bag of french fries in her hand and a whole new world of possible identities in her heart—until a sharp, white-hot pain cut through her swagger. Out of the corner of her eye, she saw a guy walking away. He'd stubbed his cigarette out on her arm with such a natural, of-course-this-is-totally-normal nonchalance that she almost doubted her own senses. Her memory then stored this experience, but without any details about the guy who did it, so he became just a rough silhouette cut out from the crowd of people on the sidewalk that day. In the hole he left behind, her golden french fries lay strewn across the gray pavement. She hadn't had the chance to eat even one.

3

When Nivedita got up, Saraswati was nowhere in sight, but the penthouse didn't feel empty. She'd only been here a couple of hours—had she already developed a sixth sense for detecting Saraswati's presence? Then she saw a pot of water vivaciously boiling on the stove, and decided it was time for some answers.

She finally found Saraswati in her home office, almost entirely hidden inside her Arne Jacobsen Egg chair. Nivedita would only find out who Arne

Jacobsen was later—Saraswati's place was full of high-design Scandinavian furniture, not a single piece of it from Ikea—but the chair's name made immediate sense to her. What other name would anyone give a chair that looked exactly like a giant, leather-upholstered egg, cracked open at an angle, its contents swiftly scooped out? Instead of the yolk, there sat Saraswati, smack in the middle of the empty shell, legs tucked under, eyes glued to her laptop. Nivedita reached out and rotated the chair around so they were facing one another, and still her professor didn't bat an eyelash. Above the desk hung a portrait of Saraswati by Moshtari Hilal: blunt strokes of super black India ink showed the framed subject head on, unsparing and unsmiling, holding a tuft of cowslips in one hand and a book in the other. Of the book's title only one word was legible: *Decolonize*, a clear reference to her first big book. The actual Saraswati in the egg chair was also unsmiling. In fact, her face was so expressionless it seemed her lifetime quota of emotions was already completely spent. Nivedita could hardly stand looking at her, and glanced back to her portrait, whereupon she noticed that Saraswati herself had stuck a quote onto the frame. It was the very same quote she'd also prominently posted on the door to her office on campus: "As long as you think that you are white, there is no hope for you."—James Baldwin, *Notes of a Native Son*

Nivedita thought about how often she had read and reread those words while waiting to ask Saraswati all the questions she couldn't find answers to anywhere else. Each time, the phrase struck her as the very height of all possible forms of rhetoric: As soon as you place yourself above others, you cut yourself off from your own humanity, thereby dooming yourself for all eternity.

And now, with this single sentence, Baldwin—James Baldwin—was giving the argument a new spin. Nivedita's eyes followed the portrait subject's eyes, as if propelled by remote control, and she realized the phrase was now focused not on the *white* world out there, but rather on the brown/*white* woman now seated before her, crouching in the chair like a prematurely hatched chick: Saraswati—whoever "Saraswati" actually was.

"Who *are* you?" Nivedita instinctively asked.

Right before her eyes, the frightened little chick transformed back into Saraswati, Mistress of This and Every Other Situation.

"What's *that* supposed to mean?" came her domineering answer-in-the-form-of-a-question.

Hey, I'm the one asking the questions here, Nivedita thought, *and that was MY question. What's ALL THIS supposed to mean?* And since she wasn't sure whether Saraswati could hear her thoughts or not, she reiterated them aloud.

"Who—okay, fine, I'll go there—*what* are you, if you aren't . . . Indian?"

"Define *being Indian*," Saraswati demanded, acting as if the laptop perched atop her lap weren't pinging nonstop with notifications, none of them the least bit concerned with any academic discourse on the metaphysical nature of being. "Oh, right, I forgot—that's only The Question your entire life revolves around."

These words were like a direct punch to Nivedita's solar plexus. Whatever happened to *Racism is the air we breathe. Consequently, experiences with racism are also, primarily, issues having to do with individuation and self-realization*? Perversely, it now seemed that Saraswati actually could hear Nivedita's thoughts, because she carried right on.

"And that's also the question *my* life revolves around," she added, speaking a tad softer. "After all, I could've gotten Indian citizenship back when I was studying at Shantiniketan."

"This is not about citizenship!" Nivedita yelled.

"Ah, but what is this about, then? Even if I had been born in India—like, say, Joanna Lumley, the *Absolutely Fabulous* Joanna Lumley—in your eyes, I still wouldn't be Indian enough. And then I have to ask myself, or, better, I have to ask you: How is this reasoning any different than the AfD's?"

"The *AfD's*?" Nivedita was aghast.

"You heard me. The AfD's," Saraswati confirmed, "the line of reasoning that, in one of your oh-so-lovely little missives, led you to accuse that group of calling you a *Passdeutsche*, as if the only German thing about you were your passport, or as if you existed solely on paper. But you're not a fictitious German, you're a real German—those are your words, *mein Schatz*, not mine.

And so why can't I be Indian then? Last I checked, *Indian* isn't some kind of fundamental philosophical category."

How on earth had Saraswati managed to swing that? Now, all of a sudden, Nivedita was the one who had to justify herself? In order to keep Saraswati from noticing her uncertainty, Nivedita made a point of replying ASAP.

"Maybe *Indian* isn't, but *color* certainly is a category. Namely, a category used for oppression. You can't just take your pick."

"Apparently you can," Saraswati countered, closing her laptop. Then she seemed to realize she wasn't on some talk show—*and might not be invited to one ever again*—and reached out for Nivedita's hand.

"*Schätzchen*, I could take a DNA test, and I'm a hundred percent positive I'd find Indian ancestors somewhere in my lineage." She traced the lifeline on Nivedita's palm with her long, thin index finger. "The last time we looked, there were a billion of us. Being Indian isn't especially exclusive. Everyone's connected to everyone. *No man is an island*. And *no woman is . . .*"

"A subcontinent?" Nivedita ironically chimed in.

"Correct," Saraswati concurred unironically. "Identity is a necessary lie, but a lie nonetheless."

Nivedita knew Saraswati was quoting from one of her own books, as she had also been fond of bringing this one up in class. She just didn't know exactly which book. That almost never happened to her. She always mentally jotted down all Saraswati's sayings, as if they were clues that would help her solve the greatest existential mysteries, but now suddenly she was forgetting key points of reference within the Saraswati Universe. Had it really come to this?

"Sure, but most people don't lie about their identities as much as you do. And no, I don't mean that as a compliment."

"They don't? How can you be so sure?"

"Saraswati, you know as well as I, that you obviously . . ."

"As Althusser . . ."

Nivedita had to pause and think for a second. *Althusser? Isn't that the guy who strangled his wife?* Then she thought, *What does Althusser have to do with anything?* And then she found out what he had to do, or rather didn't have to do, with all this.

"As Althusser so succinctly put it, obviousness is a fundamental charac-teristic of ideology. The moment something seems obvious or apparent, we know we've entered the realm of ideology."

"Saraswati!" Nivedita yelled, yanking her hand away, although the tingling sensation of Saraswati's fingers on her skin remained. "But you obviously did something. I might not have the right words to describe it, but you consciously *did* something!"

"Well then, find the right words," Saraswati ordered her.

"Why don't *you* find them? After all, *you're* the one who can twist words until they mean whatever you want."

"I won't do this for you because learning how to describe the harm you've endured is an important step toward self-empowerment."

Right. *Right!* Fuck. Saraswati's class had, in fact, resulted in Nivedita dis-covering she was suddenly able to talk about parts and aspects of herself and her life in a way she'd never been able to before. She had noticed them, sure— but they were like ghost notions, like some vague phantom pain. As a direct result of Saraswati's seminars, Nivedita had begun to post not just fun facts about nipples on her blog, but fun facts about nipples and racism, about the wonderland of identity politics, and what it meant to lose yourself in that world and no longer be able to find yourself again.

One time Lilli had asked Nivedita why she hadn't chosen to go to college in a city where history had happened. *Because in Düsseldorf—what?—time had just gone by?* A city that would've been easier for Nivedita to love, Lilli clarified, because other people had already poured *their* love for it into poems and pamphlets and novels. Since they'd already expressed it, Nivedita could just line up behind them. Of course Lilli was deliberately forgetting the fact that, even though she'd since gone on to study at the Sorbonne, before that she'd gotten her bachelor's degree alongside Nivedita at Ruhr University in Bochum. But hey, who'd ever notice a little detail like that, right? Not to men-tion the fact that Lilli had long been considering going to Ravi Shankar's ashram—not *that* Ravi Shankar, but Sri Sri Ravi Shankar.

"Why don't you go study in London, like your cousin? Or at least Berlin?" Nivedita asked her.

But it was precisely because so many people had already painted, sung the praises of, and filmed the streets of Paris and London and Berlin that Nivedita felt it would be tantamount to a voyeuristic act of hubris to insert herself in their great ranks. As for Düsseldorf, she couldn't think of a single novel or ballad about it, aside from a vague memory involving Heinrich Heine, from German class: "The city of Düsseldorf is very beautiful, and if you think of it when you are far away, and also happen to have been born there, a strange feeling comes over the soul. I was born there, and even now feel as if I must go straight home." But Nivedita was neither born there nor had spent much time far away from it since having moved there, so she didn't feel obligated to concur. She didn't really see anything particularly marvelous or breathtaking about the place except the Rhine, and even that wasn't unique to Düsseldorf—the river passed through many other, more remarkable places on its way to the North Sea. There was nothing of any import in Düsseldorf to constantly remind her of her own unimportance, her absence from the history of this and every other place, which is precisely what made it possible for her to live here.

And then, after only the second session of class, Saraswati loaned her Zadie Smith's novel *Zähne zeigen*—aka *White Teeth*, as translated by Ulrike Wasel and Klaus Timmermann—and it was like a light bulb went on in her head. A light bulb she hadn't even known was there. And, ever since, every chance she got, she'd quote phrases like, "There was England, a gigantic mirror, and there was Irie, without reflection."

And it was while she was waiting outside Saraswati's office to return the book that she first read the quotation: "As long as you think you're white, you're irrelevant." As she later discovered, Baldwin had written a ton about whiteness, and Saraswati frequently swapped out the quote on her office door to see if anyone would notice. Later that week, it became "The people who think of themselves as White have the choice of becoming human or irrelevant. Or—as they are, indeed, already, in all but actual fact: obsolete." But here, after yet another switch, the quote was back to "irrelevant." Saraswati had opened the door and gave Nivedita her famous smile. Nivedita always smiled at people with the hope that they'd smile back. Saraswati smiled at people with perfect awareness of the fact that, in so doing, she was bestowing a gift upon them. Her smile was warm and generous and clearly conscious of its own generosity.

"Come on in, Nivedita." That was another thing that set her apart—she always addressed her students informally and had memorized all their names after the very first class, so everyone felt special and especially seen and heard. "Honey or lemon?"

Is that a fundamental question, whose answer reveals your approach to life? Nivedita had thought it over, and then spotted the square, yellow Scandic tea tin on the coffee table. Her grandmother in Duisburg had the same exact one, except hers was green, and they even had the same teapot. Saraswati's office looked altogether more like a living room than a professor's office. There was a sofa and a pouf chair and even a box of Kleenex next to the tea tin because, sooner or later, students were inclined to cry. Here, they'd let out all the tears that otherwise had no place to flow at this university.

The same was true of Nivedita but, much to her own surprise, it was neither racism nor othering that triggered her tears. The topic that ultimately did it was her father: Jagdish Anand, born in Calcutta (nowadays Kolkata), math teacher at the local public high school on Wächtler Straße in Essen Südostviertel (literally the "southeast quarter," the least-inspired neighborhood name ever), married to Birgit Anand (née Schimanski), no hobbies (unless math counts?), and already she was bawling into the steaming cup of tea Saraswati had just handed her.

"We lived under the same roof for *twenty* years, and we have *nothing* in common."

Maybe she actually was a *Kuckuckskind*, born not of her purported parents, but instead hatched from an egg that some cuckoo stranger had snuck into their nest. The underlying suspicion that the man who raised her wasn't her real father, and that she was a foreigner within her own family of origin, was another thing she had in common with Oluchi. Only Oluchi's father had left Germany before she was born, because his visa had expired and he had to go back to Nigeria, whereas Nivedita saw her father every single day, but almost never really communicated with him. Birgit had taken on that role, since she was so good at talking about emotions, showing emotions, and having emotions. The overflowing cornucopia of her friendliness left little room for any other conversations or feelings. As a result, both Nivedita and Oluchi felt their own skin as an absence where there should have been a presence—an emptiness, a void, an exceedingly visible nothingness. Of course she knew and shared all the "Privilege of a white parent" memes, understood the privilege of Birgit's skin color, and especially appreciated it when she showed up for parent-teacher conferences or any other interactions with authority figures. But sometimes Nivedita yearned for nothing more than the privilege of a brown mother. Meaning sometimes she yearned for nothing more than the privilege of someone like Saraswati as her mother.

But the fact that one of her parents was *white* meant that her heritage was even less clear, the ties that bound them were even looser, and her place in the fabric of reality was even more tenuous. She was perpetually in search of acceptance from both camps—*white* and Black, *white* and Brown—only to end up being not good enough for anybody. She was deemed too deviant from all directions, not native enough for any homeland, not sufficiently discriminated against to claim any such descent.

"I have nothing in common with my father," Nivedita repeated. She was seated on Saraswati's office sofa, sobbing, sniffing up the warm scent of ginger and sweetgrass from the hot cup she was cradling in her hands.

"Like most students your age, I'd say," Saraswati noted.

"Yeah, but he's the only link connecting me to India. If I can't even begin to relate to him, then the same goes for India . . ." She stopped short and held her breath, because the thought was too horrific to even articulate.

"Time," Saraswati sighed.

"What?"

"That will change with time—your relationship, as well as your perception of it. You're too young to even imagine it, because you haven't yet experienced time as a sort of library whose stacks you can consult whenever you're bored, or as a blanket that keeps you warm during your long journey through the ages. Nothing is as it always was, and nothing stays the same forever. In India, not even death is final or eternal."

Nivedita vowed to use every single one of these phrases in her blog, but didn't dare dig out a pen to jot them down, for fear that such a gesture would make Saraswati stop talking.

"If your father were your best friend, right *now*, well, that would be cause for concern."

"Lotte says her mom is her role model." Nivedita wasn't sure why she countered with that. After all, she had never held Lotte up as any kind of example except maybe for how *not* to be.

"What a crock of contemporary bullshit," Saraswati shot back with just the right amount of shock. "In any case, it would be just as much cause for concern if, over the coming decades—in the time that you and your father will have together, to come to terms with one another—some common ground can't be found."

"I really doubt it," Nivedita sighed.

"And that, there, proves you're a healthy twentysomething."

"But what about India?"

"What *about* India?" Saraswati echoed.

"How am I supposed to feel closer to India if I . . ."

"Right—I'll tell you how. The same way you feel closer to anything else: read a book!" Saraswati said, plopping Amartya Sen's *The Argumentative Indian* down on the table.

"A *book*?" Nivedita was incredulous.

"Okay, well, a whole pile of books." Priyamvada Gopal's *Insurgent Empire* swiftly joined the Sen, followed by Amitava Kumar's *Am Beispiel des Affen*—aka *Immigrant, Montana*, as translated by Nikolaus Stingl—and then Githa Hariharan's *In Times of Siege*. That would do for the stack next to the sofa, so then Saraswati started staring at her other shelves, hunting for books the way a raptor scans the terrain for prey, suddenly jumping up to snatch the best ones. "That's the way someone like you approaches the world. Through words. And you, especially, feel closer to things through language. So why should it be any different with India?"

Nivedita put the books into her backpack without another word, until it was so stuffed not even an ad flyer would have fit. And then Saraswati shoved one last book into her hands: *Das Haus auf meinen Schultern* by Dieter Forte. *What's* 'The House on My Shoulders' *even supposed to mean?* she thought as she examined the author photo, which showed a very *white* old man.

"A guy named Dieter is going to teach me about India?"

"This guy named Dieter is going to teach you about Polish families in Düsseldorf's Oberbilk neighborhood. Maybe one of these days you'll finally take an interest in your invisible family history."

Apparently there already was a novel or two about Düsseldorf.

Nivedita left Saraswati's office bewildered. Up until this very second, she actually had assumed that India was something you absorbed through your mother's milk. Consequently, for everything she lacked or was missing out on, she figured that the train—or, in her case, the milk cart—had already left the station, as it were.

"ART AND LITERATURE are always instruments for finding and forging identity," Saraswati said, lounging in her home office, a mere six semesters and one outrageous scandal later, as if seamlessly picking up where she'd left off so long ago.

"I thought identity didn't exist," Nivedita said with spite.

"Of course the backdrop before which these instruments always operate is, as you so beautifully put it, the fundamental truth that identity does not, per se, exist," extolled Saraswati.

Nivedita was so accustomed to Saraswati explaining the world to her, thereby making her feel both smarter and better, that Saraswati's words had become the water she needed to grow. And she'd grown so dependent on them that she now had to actively stop herself from saying *thanks*. Instead, she said something else entirely.

"Did it really never occur to you that what you did might, just *might*, be racist?"

Clearly it hadn't.

"Do you know who first used the word *race* for Hindus?" Saraswati asked, as if she'd just been waiting to hear the keyword. And Nivedita knew she'd regret asking.

"Who?"

"Golwalkar."

She knew it. Saying "Golwalkar" was like saying "Björn Höcke" or "Stephen Miller," only worse. Madhav Sadashiv Golwalkar was one of the leading ideologues of the Hindutva movement. To this day the experts argue over whether this predominant form of Hindu nationalism is best described as an extreme form of conservatism, or ethnic absolutism, or, as most claim, fascism. And whoever says *fascist* first, wins.

"Do you seriously mean to say that anyone who complains that you lied to them about your . . . about your . . . ethnic heritage are actually Nazis? Are you seriously implying that anyone who doesn't agree with you is a fascist?"

Saraswati looked at Nivedita with her Saraswatieyes. #bedroomeyes.

"Fascinating."

"I give up."

"What?"

"You!" yelled Nivedita. "I give up on even trying to talk to you! No matter what I say, it just pours fuel on the bonfire of your unbelievable arrogance."

"Oh really?" said Saraswati, evidently amused.

"See! That's it!" Nivedita ran out of the room and tried to slam the door behind her, but there was so much drag that it wasn't even audible. Then she didn't know what to do next, so she ran back in. "And one more thing . . ."

"What?" Saraswati repeated with the same rapt amusement, before suddenly pivoting to focus her empathy on Nivedita. "What's going on with you? You look so pale . . ."

This shift in perspective was so jarring that Nivedita felt the room begin to spin. When her vision finally came back into focus, she was seated in the egg chair. Saraswati knelt before her, and wrapped an arm around her.

"You're mad at me, Nivedita. What can I do?"

"You can tell me the truth," Nivedita immediately said, before Saraswati changed her mind.

"Okay, first you have to define what 'the truth' is," came the automatic reply, albeit without extra emphasis.

"Let's start with your passport," Nivedita's tone was severe. "I'll presume you have one. What name is listed in your passport?"

"Saraswati."

"Since when?"

"Ah," she was caught.

"And what was there before?" Nivedita felt Saraswati's arms slide away, like Kaa releasing Mowgli's body after Bagheera had planted a punch square on the snake's slippery serpent chin. "Well?"

Silence.

"Well?" Nivedita insisted.

This time the ensuing silence lasted so long that Nivedita was about to give up any hope of getting an answer when Saraswati opened her mouth.

"Sarah," she whispered.

"What?" Nivedita was surprised.

"Vera," Saraswati softly said.

"Sarah or Vera?"

"Sarah Vera."

"Sarah Vera?"

"Sarah Vera Thielmann."

The letters melted into one another right before Nivedita's eyes: SaraVeraT. *Saraswati didn't even have to change her signature much!*

"You can't be serious. For real?"

"You want to see my birth certificate?" Saraswati's voice was normal again.

"Sarah Vera Thielmann?"

"Sarah with an *h*."

"As opposed to . . . ?"

"Sara without an *h*."

"Who names their kid Sarah Vera?"

"That's what I used to say!" Saraswati replied, triumphant.

Nivedita was stunned. And then it hit her.

"Did you just ask if I wanted to see your birth certificate?"

She felt Saraswati's gaze, and it felt exactly like her mother's gaze had back in Birmingham. During the summer they spent there, once Nivedita and Priti had become friends, her cousin rewarded her by telling her the *facts of life*. Okay, they were more like the *facts of sex*. But Nivedita still didn't get what a pussy had to do with *you-know-what*, so she asked her mother. Who just looked at her, gave a little laugh, and asked if she wanted to watch them, just once.

"Watch who?" Nivedita couldn't hide her surprise.

"Y'know, Daddy and me."

Nivedita declined, disgusted, of course. After all, she was only an eight-year-old who didn't yet trust her own instincts and therefore tended to overtheorize everything. And so, after she'd given the matter careful consideration and returned to the original offer, she of course realized that it never really was an actual offer. Instead, it was just her mother's way of avoiding having to give a real answer. Just like Saraswati's birth certificate offer now—it wasn't really an actual offer. Just like Simon's promise that, this month, he wouldn't leave her.

Still, Saraswati kept staring at Nivedita as if she were the twisted one, the one coming up with such perverse ideas—like watching her own parents have sex, or like asking such absurd, invasive questions. Questions like, *What's your name?*

"Sure, I'll show it to you," Saraswati spat out as she stood up.

"Forget it," said Nivedita.

"What?" asked Saraswati, and Nivedita realized she'd fallen for it yet again. Hoping for answers from Saraswati was like playing one of those infamous Indian board games. Whenever she managed to move her piece forward, it was inevitably gobbled by a snake and she'd have to go back to square one.

"Sarah Vera," Nivedita repeated, if only to preserve her tiny bit of progress.

"Call me Saraswati," Saraswati said.

On the wall above her desk, in addition to the oh-so-serious black-and-white portrait, hung just one other picture. It was a mockup of the cover of Robin Norwood's best seller, but with two words added to the title: *Women Who Love Their Work Too Much.*

"I CAN'T GET through to her," Nivedita told Kali.

You haven't been trying long enough, Kali countered.

"I'll never get through to her on my own. She's just too . . . too *Saraswati.*"

Aren't we all?

"Aren't we all *what*?"

Aren't we all too much ourselves?

"I need your help, please."

Kali sighed and the doorbell—the one Saraswati had disconnected—began buzzing like mad. Mail for Saraswati, signature required.

4

The letter was short and to the point, although that's not to say it was clear:

> *Dear Sarah, dear little Sarah Vera,*
> *It's all your fault, but I forgive you, and I'm ready to help you.*
> *Your loving Brother*

For the first time ever, Saraswati no longer looked as if she had everything and everyone under control. She turned the letter over in her hands, as if hoping that the letters would detach and move around to compose new words. Her vulnerability made Nivedita's anger fizzle on the spot, and she cautiously ventured another question.

"What's *up* with . . . ?"

"Konstantin," Saraswati filled in the blank.

"What's up with Konstantin? What's he after?"

Much to Nivedita's surprise, after pausing to fold the letter up into ever smaller squares, Saraswati actually gave a real answer.

"He wants . . . he needs . . . he . . . Konstantin is like Dracula. He can't cross the threshold until you invite him in."

Nivedita had just heard about vampires needing to be invited in for the first time recently—but *where*?

"Okay, so now what are you going to do?" she asked. *Meaning how're you going to protect yourself from him? Call the police? Sue him for libel?*

"I'm going to invite him in. What else can I do?"

PART II:
POP-
POSTCOLONIALISM

WOMAN, NATIVE, OTHER

NIVEDITA'S CLASS NOTES:

"Once you go Asian you'll never go Caucasian."—TEZ ILYAS

"The personal is not intrinsically political; something constructive and transformative has to be done to make it political."
—MICHELE M. MOODY-ADAMS

"I'm honored to be known for: to not be understood widely."
—HOMI BHABHA

IDENTITTI

This is the best blog you'll ever read, in this and/or in any/all your lives. #Reincarnation #Hinduism

Just kidding! This isn't about religion. That's the #2 biggest advantage of Hinduism: I don't *have* to write about religion. If my father were Muslim instead of Hindu—after all, India has the largest Muslim population worldwide, after Indonesia—I'd constantly be asked about my stance toward Islam, what Islam's stance is toward everything, and why I don't wear a headscarf. Okay, I get asked why I don't wear a headscarf all the time anyway, but that's just because people confuse skin color and religion.

The #2 biggest advantage of Hinduism is that nothing is permanent, not even death, and not even gender/sex, only . . .

"*Race?*" That's Kali again, the #3 biggest advantage.

"I was actually going to write *Caste.*"

"But what about *race*?" Kali doubles down.

That's what this blog is about, and if you read on long enough, I'll tell you the answer. But for now, give this a try:

Quiz

How brown are you?

—How do you interpret the above question?

    a) Brown, Black, or BIPOC, *duh.*

    b) You mean like Black and Tans or Blackshirts or National
       Socialists?

    c) No clue.

—You're riding your bike and a police patrol passes you, turns around, and starts following you. What's your first thought?

    a) Not again!

    b) Whatevs.

    c) Obvs the police need my help. #Sherlock

—You have a €500-Euro bill. What do you do?

    a) I take a *white* friend with me to the bank and exchange it for
       smaller bills.

    b) I pay with it the next time I go shopping.

    c) Nothing, €500s aren't printed anymore. Where've you been, in
       prison?

—Your child is having problems in school and you're asked to come in for a parent-teacher conference. What do you do?

    a) I introduce myself as *Dr. So-and-So* so the teacher doesn't think
       we're an uneducated household.

    b) I'm happy the teacher is giving my child individual attention.

    c) I tell the teacher how to improve the curriculum and syllabus.

    d) I sleep in.

—How often are you asked about your thoughts on liberal democracy?

    a) Once or twice—per week.

    b) When I'm sworn in as a civil servant.

    c) Are you recording this?

—Vacation in your parents' homeland is . . .

    a) not a vacation.

    b) beautiful.

    c) Define *homeland*.

—Do you know the names of all your uncles and aunts?

    a) No.

    b) Yes.

    c) Yes, and I've met them all.

—Who is your favorite musician?

    a) Beyoncé.

    b) Beethoven.

    c) The Beatles.

    d) Beyoncé.

—Chapati or Injera?

    a) Chapati.

    b) Injera.

    c) Huh?

—How many languages do you speak?

    a) German, English, Latin.

    b) One.

    c) Two.

    d) Three.

    e) Four.

    f) Five.

    g) More.

—On a scale of 0 to 10, how entitled are you?

    a) 5.

    b) Entitled?

    c) 42.

—How woke are you?

    a) I know what *entitled* means.

    b) Entitled?

    c) I'd tell you, but then I'd have to kill you.

Answer Key

Mostly *A* answers:

Congratulations, you're a Kinder Surprise egg! You're worried you might be brown on the outside and *white* on the inside, but have no fear—it's all chocolate.

Mostly *B* answers:

Congratulations, you're a Kinder Surprise egg! Made and marketed in Germany. But even you have immigrant roots: the Kinder Surprise brand is owned by Italian confectionary conglomerate Ferrero SpA.

Mostly *C* answers:

Congratulations, you're a Kinder Surprise egg! Nothing could be sweeter and more surprising than you.

Mostly other answers:

Congratulations, you're a Kinder Surprise egg! As for why, we'll let you fill in the blank—but you didn't actually read to the end, did you?

PEAU NOIRE, MASQUES BLANCS

NIVEDITA'S CLASS NOTES:

"Don't expect to see any explosions today. It's too early . . . or too late.
I'm not the bearer of absolute truths.
No fundamental inspiration has flashed across my mind. I honestly
think, however, it's time some things were said. Things I'm going to
say, not shout.
I've long given up shouting.
A long time ago . . .
Why am I writing this book? Nobody asked me to.
Especially not those for whom it is intended.
So? So in all serenity my answer is that there are too many idiots on
earth. And now that I've said it, I have to prove it."

—Frantz Fanon (translated by Richard Philcox)

1

48 HOURS POST-SARASWATI

"Nivedita?" said Fatih, the chillest chef in the whole wide gastronomic world—especially when you consider that, in German, *Chef* comes from *chief* and actually means *boss*. He had taken over an old inn called Gauguin and single-handedly transformed it from a traditional pub into a joint teeming with scenesters, solely by plastering all the walls and even the ceiling with posters from art exhibitions and movies. The whole thing read like a scrapbook of all his über-authentic cultural references—which, of course, it wasn't, because then it'd be all indie rock posters. But Fatih's fandom was a secondary characteristic. He was, first and foremost, a businessman. As such, he was great at nailing his target clientele and serving up the stuff they'd love to consider "culture" well before they were even conscious of any such aspiration. And it worked. Customers came and immediately felt like they were in a sixties-era French film set in twenties-era Montparnasse. The place was hopping.

"Nivedita?" Fatih repeated.

"I was just at table five, they don't want anything else."

But, uncharacteristically, this time Fatih didn't have any tips for how she might improve her performance as a waitress.

"Someone came by yesterday and asked for you," he went on.

"For me?" She was alarmed.

"I told him to come back today."

"Am I paranoid to suspect this was the same guy who just dropped by my apartment?" Nivedita asked Beanie, who staffed the bar. Fatih was old school: boys poured the beer, girls brought it to the tables. Beanie's eyes followed Fatih until he disappeared into the kitchen to hover behind the cook.

"Just because you're paranoid doesn't mean they're not out to get you."

Nivedita took the full tray (latte, cappuccino, barraquito, latte, cortado) and kept it balanced as she made her way between tables of totally blasé afternoon customers. After thirty-four nonstop hours of Saraswati, the rest of reality looked as if the color dial could be cranked up a few notches: it seemed to be lacking in light, contrast, volume, saturation, Saraswatiness. At the Gauguin there were still people who hadn't even heard about the scandal, let alone gotten all hot and bothered about it. Nivedita assumed she should be relieved about that, but instead she was disappointed. Who was it who once said, *If you're not outraged, you're not paying attention!*?

But right then the door flew open and *Outrage* stormed in, in the form of Oluchi.

"I know what you're up to!" She stood before Nivedita, tall, proud, and angry and surrounded by a bunch of friends Nivedita had never seen before. "I thought you were a *Sista*!"

I am, every fiber of Nivedita's being wanted to scream—but the problem with Afro-Americanisms like *Sista* was that others could call you that, but you couldn't call yourself that, so her reply was rather blander.

"Hi, Oluchi."

"I heard you on the radio. How's it feel to be the only person sticking up for Saraswati?" She parroted Nivedita's voice, *"Nowadays nobody's a serious intellectual until they've sat at the eye of a shitstorm*—my ass!"

"That was taken out of context." Nivedita was desperate.

"In what context is your phrase '*The people who accuse Saraswati of being racist just don't get her. Above all, they don't get what* being white *means to her*' anything other than a highfalutin act of kiss ass?"

"That interview was recorded *before* . . . When I said that, I didn't yet know . . . anything about . . . *about all this*." Nivedita searched Oluchi's face for even the slightest sign of understanding. "I'm just as shocked as you are about *all of it*."

Oluchi sized her (former?) "sister" up just as urgently, her natural hair expanding from her head like a black halo.

"Oh yeah? Then why were you the first to sprint straight over to Saraswati's place yesterday?"

If Nivedita had been paranoid before this, now it escalated to active panic.

"Where'd you hear that?"

"I have my sources."

Lotte, Nivedita said to herself, *it must've been Lotte.* But her gut had already made up its mind: *Konstantin!* The mysterious, secretive, invisible Konstantin—he of the snapshot from the late eighties, with the piano in the southern German living room—was pulling every last thread to make it all unravel.

"C'mon, let's go," said the most eye-catching of Oluchi's friends. "I refuse to drink in any establishment that employs people like *her*."

"Good idea," Nivedita snarled. Just a moment before, she'd found him sexy. "Go ahead and boycott me, even if you have no clue who I am."

"Oh, I *know* who you are, Uncle Tomtitti," he retorted, running a hand through his 'fro. Taken together, his coif and gesture made for a look that just screamed *I'm with Oluchi*. "And I'm not boycotting you, I'm boycotting this establishment, because it employs racist waitresses." Casting a contemptuous gaze at the poster for *Guess Who's Coming to Dinner?*—ACADEMY AWARD WINNER! it trumpeted in red atop a yellow background, complete with a black-and-white (of course) picture of Sidney Poitier and Katharine Houghton—he turned to leave. The others followed. Only Oluchi hesitated.

"You need to decide what side you're on, Nivedita."

"Oh yeah?" Nivedita was getting riled up. The brass band in her head riffed on *Which side are you on?* and struck up a tune: *Which side on you on, girls? They say in North Rhine-Westphalia, there are no neutrals there!* "What's so alluring about being on a side so quick to cancel anyone that might disagree with them?"

Oluchi's eyes shone as she looked at Nivedita.

"I thought you at least . . . *had integrity*. But no, in reality, you're just a *white chick* with brown skin."

If she hadn't said those words, Nivedita would've reacted to the audible hurt in Oluchi's voice by saying something more sensitive. Instead, her sensitivity went out the window.

"Not like you, right? Or what? You only defend your own Blackness so vehemently because you aren't really sure you're actually Black." She knew she'd crossed an invisible line, the *color line*—the line that implied that it was fine for any POC to deny their own POCness, but that Nivedita could never ever *ever* deny others' POCness, especially not when those others were Black, because Black people bore the brunt of the most extreme racism in Germany. On top of that, unlike Saraswati, they had zero hope of ever passing. Nivedita's awareness of all that made her transgression against Oluchi that much more powerful and unforgivable. It was like saying *cunt* for the first time when previously you'd only ever said *pussy*—even when referring to annoying people instead of that particular part of the female anatomy. And so she doubled down and put the cherry on top by adding, "you *cunt*."

Oluchi shrugged and followed her new friends out the door, when suddenly Fatih popped up out of nowhere, right next to Nivedita.

"What did you call my customer?"

"That wasn't your customer—that was just Oluchi."

"I think that's the end of your shift," he declared, and vanished back into thin air. Nivedita pictured herself dumping several poorly pulled glasses of everyone's favorite local swill over Fatih's head. But the person she really wanted to douse was Oluchi. Or Oluchi's hot, woke guy friend. Or Saraswati. Or herself.

Beanie put a hand on her shoulder.

"Go home, Nivedita. You can apologize to him tomorrow, and then it won't be such a big deal."

But Nivedita had had it with reality. She called Barbara, asked her to cover her shifts for the rest of the week, and only stopped by the apartment to pick up a few more things.

"He came by again!" came Lotte's bubbly greeting.

"Who?" asked Nivedita.

"You know—him!"

Nivedita stormed into her room and, just to bypass any more BS, decided to guess.

"My father?"

"Nope."

"Simon?" A glimmer of hope was audible in her voice.

"I haven't seen him since yester . . . no, the day before yester . . . no—wait, how long's it been since I saw him? Are you guys fighting again?"

Great, just great. "Who was it?" Nivedita asked as she shoved a toothbrush and undies into her backpack.

"Y'know, that guy." Lotte's ability to play the fool always proved to Nivedita which camp she herself was in. (The other one.) Just like Priti always knew which group she belonged to, at least more or less.

"*Which* guy, Lotte?"

"The one who already came by once this morning," Lotte oh-so-unhelpfully replied.

Nivedita was dumbfounded. *He must've raped her. That must be why Saraswati ran off—off to the ends of the earth, off into an entirely different skin!* But even as she was thinking that, she knew that the only place rape could ever explain the inexplicable was on TV shows like *Tatort*.

"Are you taking off because of . . . all the stuff going on?" Lotte asked with an air of intrigue as one of her fingers wiped a bit of dust off Nivedita's bookshelves. Why were Lotte's shelves always so much cleaner?

"Uhh . . ." Nivedita wasn't sure whether Lotte was referring to the shit-storm or the guy or what.

"Oh," said Lotte, "are you moving in with Simon?"

"No."

"What's going *on* with him?"

"Nothing." Nivedita hoisted her backpack onto her shoulders and wondered how she'd ever manage to ride a bike under such a load. As usual, her keys had vanished at the last minute, only to surface a few minutes later in a spot she'd already checked multiple times. Just as she was about to leave their shared apartment for an indefinite amount of time, she was overcome by a sudden need she'd never felt before, and turned around in the doorway.

"Lotte?"

"Yeah?"

"Thanks . . . for . . . well—just *thanks*."

Lotte beamed as if she'd just won the Best Roommate of All Time award.

"You're going to Saraswati's, aren't you?"

SARASWATI'S PLACE SMELLED of basmati rice and togetherness, even if this particular togetherness consisted mainly in the fact that here was a person who remained present, who didn't run away. Even when Nivedita tried to pick a fight, this person was simply thrilled by her indignation and wanted more of it, as if it were some special form of attention and awareness—sheer *outrage* turned into an impassioned pastime.

"You're early," Saraswati said, standing over the kitchen sink and cleaning beans as her laptop continued to spew fire and brimstone from its spot on a side table near the window. Of course, in order to ensure nobody lost interest, the varieties of fire and brimstone continuously evolved. "Look, I've even gained a new hashtag!" #transracial

» Ugly Duckling @WhatIf *If you accept Laverne Cox and Chelsea Manning as #transgender then you've got to accept Saraswati as #transracial.*

» Imperator Nadias Best Account Ever @shehadistan *I see trans-racial as being in the same league as trans-entitled or trans-famous: if it doesn't exist, it doesn't exist! People like Saraswati need to immediately stop mocking trans folx by appropriating certain terminology and applying it to their own super-fraught constructs of identity!*

» Julius Eisenhauer @BismarcksMuskrat *This is what you get when you start just letting people pick a new gender from one day to the next. #transracial*

» Joerg Scheller @joergscheller1 *"Is this the dawn of the 'Transracial' Era?" The answer's simple: People have never been anything but "transracial." Clearly delineated identities, races, and ethnicities have always been utter fiction.*

» Noel Pasaran! @RightsNotTheRight *Gender and race are not the same thing! #transracial*

» Christian Surfer @D_Walter397 *What Saraswati has done goes against the Creator and against all of creation. #GodIsNotTrans*

» Felicia Ewert @redhidinghood *Racism and anti-trans-ism all in one. Must be nice to serve up multiple kinds of discrimination all in one go. #transracial*

» Ms. Manners Stan Account @TellingItLikeItIs *Where do we draw the line? What's next, someone self-identifying as a dog? Or as a helicopter? #transracial*

» Auenland Suffragette @Genderbender replying to @TellingItLikeItIs *You clearly self-identify as an asshole. #NoAttackHelicopterIsIllegal #transracialIsNotAThing*

» Dr. Nö @WhatWillItBeNext *You're all hypocrites, guys. Or should I make that gender-neutral? You're all hypocrites, peeps. Y'all wanna be female, but nobody can wanna be Black? #transracial*

» MagdalenaM @MagdalenaM *fuck trans*
    » Possible World @BetterWorld replying to @MagdalenaM *fuck AfD*

"At least now they're going after each other," Saraswati observed.

"Was this your idea?" Nivedita asked, sinking down into the nearest designer chair.

"Was what my idea?"

"Hashtag-trans-you-know-what."

"Does that sound like something I would do?"

"Actually, that sounds *exactly* like something you would do."

» Antje Schrupp @antjeschrupp *A white person who masquerades as a "POC" openly displays the constructed nature of "race." But in this case, unlike with trans women, such self-representation is utterly banal, because "race" is and always has been nothing but a construct. 1/4*
    » @antjeschrupp *It isn't possible to be born into the "wrong" skin color because skin color in and of itself is completely irrelevant in terms of humans' ability to live with one another. Skin color is only and solely relevant as an expression of power dynamics 2/4*
    » @antjeschrupp *or a political struggle against such "ruler-vs-ruled" relationships. Hence it is completely legitimate for people who experience discrimination based on this characteristic to attempt passing for "white," but not vice versa. 3/4*
    » @antjeschrupp *Because to deny one's own position as a white person is also, invariably, to deny one's own responsibility as a white person. Okay, that's as far as I've thought it through, but I'm sure more reflections will come. Therefore, discuss! 4/4*
    » Jacinta Nandi @JacintaNandi *Couldn't sleep last night thinking about Saraswati, you know the German Rachel Dolezal. I wonder*

*if she actually did actual brownfacing like wore darker foundation
or something—does anyone know? #indianface #brownface*

Saraswati poured Nivedita more tea—leaves taken from a tin that looked like the taller, thinner sister of the one in her office—and mused dreamily.

"D'you think *Transracial* would make a good book title?"

"Pshaw," Nivedita replied. She could never be sure whether Saraswati was joking or dead serious. "Are you suffering from race dysphoria?" The tea tasted green and like it had been harvested by hand. The scent suddenly reminded her of afternoons spent on Oluchi's balcony, when they'd pick fresh herbs from her planters, rub the leaves between their fingers, and debate the many questions that had come up in Saraswati's seminar while surrounded by a cloud of melissa and cilantro. And, as if she'd somehow heard Nivedita's thoughts, Oluchi again took to Twitter.

» **Call me Zadie @OutsideSisters** *If only Saraswati had chosen to be
Black . . . But no: dress-up Indian that she is, she's instead opted into the
most comfortable variant of racism. #transracialIsNotAThing*
  » **Simone Dede Ayivi @simoneayivi replying to @OutsideSisters**
  *They're all too happy to take our coolness, as long as they can leave
  us the pain. #saraswatishame #culturalappropriation*

"What now?" Saraswati sniffed as she put her laptop to sleep. "Am I being accused of blackface, or of not-black-enough face?"

Nivedita secretly agreed with Oluchi. In Germany, being Indian was like drawing the joker from the immigration deck, if your imagination were twisted enough to be able to think of ID cards as playing cards whenever someone said *"Ausweis, bitte."* And Nivedita had never been discriminated against as an Indian—at least, not nearly as much as Priti had in England. In Germany, it wasn't just the ex-hippies and *Siddhartha* fans of all ages who'd get all teary-eyed the moment they heard the word *India*. Even the Christian Democratic Union's megaracist *"Kinder-statt-Inder"* campaign slogan back in 2000—a German cousin of the chant "You will not replace us . . ." encouraging Germans to have more children of their own instead of letting more Indians immigrate, stoking a populist bonfire—had projected a nervous undertone, implying that Indians were such good computer programmers and mathematicians (like Nivedita's father) that Germany had better hurry up and bolster its humanism-heavy education system. Indians were superduper-foreigners. They had a Festival of Colors so fabulous it might as well have been invented by Instagram, they pretty much held the copyright on spirituality, they embraced an earthy kind of poverty instead of pennypinching to buy into unfettered capitalism, they had a growing women's rights movement protesting gang rape, and they had scrumptiously leavened, airy bread before every meal. Of course there was discrimination, but when Nivedita experienced it, it was because she was perceived as non-German, non-*white*, or because people assumed she was Muslim—in any case, it never targeted her as an Indian. Germans loved Indians, perhaps also, ultimately, because they saw them as fellow Aryans. But instead of saying any of that, Nivedita took a different tack.

"You know that @*OutsideSisters* is Oluchi, don't you?"

"Of *course* I do," Saraswati retorted.

"Oluchi came by the Gauguin yesterday."

"Oh."

"And I don't think I'll ever set foot there again."

"Ohh," Saraswati drew the syllable out this time, and swept her hair out of her face.

Suddenly it struck Nivedita where she'd first seen that gesture. It reminded her of when Uma Thurman fixed her hair after the fight scenes in *Kill Bill*—she'd seen the movie three times, even though she'd come to despise Tarantino in the meantime. The gesture was a combo of hand-swish and nothingness, merely to emphasize that not a single hair was out of place. But now, instead, such demonstrative imperviousness on Saraswati's part just came across as fragility.

"You can ignore me, and you can ignore the whole world, but you ignore Oluchi at your own peril." As she said this, Nivedita was fully conscious of the fact that not even thirty minutes had passed since she herself had done just that.

"Okaaay," Saraswati said, as if, from now on, she'd decided to sound out how strange every single word might taste on her tongue. "Sooo, Oluchi's offended."

"Aren't *you* observant."

"Offended that I didn't choose *her* color?"

Nivedita was stunned.

"You really don't have even the slightest clue what this is about, do you—or exactly how this is so offensive? It's not a competition, no one's vying to be ripped off by you. It's about . . . let me put it this way: Back in the nineties, every good leftie made a pilgrimage to India, so all you had to do was tag along. What would you do if you were twenty today, wear a hijab?"

Saraswati looked at her (former?) student as if she'd just given an especially good answer to an exam question, and Nivedita felt exposed. *Of course Saraswati knew what Oluchi meant, she was just trying to suss out whether Nivedita did, too. Nothing had changed. Saraswati led, and Nivedita followed her onto thin ice.*

Saraswati's expert hands skillfully slipped the rubber band off a bunch of green onions and stuffed it into a honey jar already filled to the brim with other rubber bands. As she held the onions under the faucet, she answered Nivedita's pointed question.

"Why not? Right now, wearing a hijab would almost certainly be an effective political action."

"And, voilà, see? You're no better than the average yoga teacher who calls herself maharani!"

Saraswati had to stifle a snicker.

"*You're* the one who took yoga classes—until you came to *my* class!"

UNFORTUNATELY, THAT WASN'T even remotely true. Nivedita had only started taking yoga classes *after* she'd spent four full semesters studying with Saraswati. Decolonizing was *hot shit*, and Priti had decided it was high time they decolonized not only their psyches and imaginations, but their physical bodies, too. With that lofty goal in mind, what could be better than yoga?

It made no difference that Priti had only a basic familiarity with yoga, and Nivedita had none whatsoever. After all, if there was one thing they'd learned from Saraswati, it was that books were an equally valid way of gaining experience. So they borrowed Tara Stiles's *Slim Calm Sexy Yoga* from the school library and met up once a week with fellow BIPOCs to practice "moves that get your glow on" right there on campus.

Saraswati fumed the moment she found out.

"Decolonize your bodies as much as you want, just don't call *that* 'yoga'!" she raged. "Call it *performance art*, or *a happening*, or *an experiment*, whatever, but for heavens' sake, don't call it *yoga*! Didn't you know that ninety percent of what's passed off as yoga is actually Swedish calisthenics?"

"Ninety percent?" Nivedita marveled.

"Okay, maybe I exaggerated, but the vast majority of it is."

"So yoga's bad, then?"

"No, it's just yet another word that's been used so often it's lost all meaning."

Priti stood up from compass position and straightened out her yoga top, whose multiple, overlapping straps made it look like some kind of spiderweb.

"Oh yeah? So you're saying words are only meaningful when nobody uses them?"

"Don't be silly," Saraswati dismissed her, turning away.

Looking back at it now, Nivedita realized that was what had sparked the tension between Priti and Saraswati.

THE SPEED WITH which Saraswati chopped the onions into hair-thin slices was only exceeded by the speed with which her fingers withdrew before the blade, holding the green stalks down as she cut.

"Maya Angelou," she said, one syllable per slice, "Ma-ya-an-ge-lou."

"What?"

"Maya said: 'When someone shows you who they are, believe them the first time.'"

Leave Maya Angelou out of this! Nivedita's head screamed, although, as usual, her mouth wasn't onboard.

"Sure, and if *Doctor* Maya Angelou were here right now, she'd be the first to tell you she meant something entirely different when she said that."

"Would she?"

Nivedita opened her mouth to answer, but instead of her own voice, Oluchi's rang forth.

"After all, you think only *white* women can really be *brown*. Free of the formative and deformative forces colonialization exerts on the soul. Even *color* is now something *white* people do better than we do. What do you even need us for, then? Aside from as an audience?"

"That's absurd."

"Who here is absurd?"

"Race is obviously more nuanced than . . ."

"Oh, spare me all your nuances. For the last three years, I've done nothing but follow you into the thicket of all those nuances, all those ambivalent terms and concepts. You were my moral compass, and now it turns out you don't have a moral bone in your entire body!" Nivedita felt Oluchi's incensed breath exiting her lungs, and for a moment she felt empty and alone. So to return to herself, she continued—this time in her own voice.

"And anyway, nuance and ambivalence always work in favor of those who hold the power." *Put that in your pipe and smoke it, Sarah Vera!*

Saraswati looked as if she'd never once, in her entire life, thought about the morality of her actions. She'd almost certainly considered the effects they might have on concrete individuals, but she'd definitely not given any thought to it on a more abstract moral level. Mainly, her reflections in this regard had all centered on her, and *her*self.

"Feminist and anti-racist theory addresses precisely that—how to achieve the right to define yourself. So how can *all of you* deny *me* the right to define myself?"

What would you say, Kali?

Apparently nothing. *Kali?*

Something rang. Nivedita automatically reached for her phone, but it was the doorbell.

"Everything you say is right," she called after Saraswati, "but what you did is still wrong."

"We'll make a hermenaut of you yet," Saraswati called back.

Heart pounding, Nivedita scrolled back through all the calls she'd missed in the last half hour. No Simon. But Priti's name popped up, at the precise moment when she absolutely could not call her back. *Kali?* Nivedita called out, peering around Saraswati's kitchen. *Kali? What now?*

Instead of Kali, Saraswati answered—an altogether different Saraswati than had been there just moments before. This Saraswati held yet another piece of registered mail in her hand.

"Sooo . . ."

"Is that another letter from Konstantin?" Nivedita asked, gingerly taking it from her hands as if it were a bomb. And it was—but not from Konstantin.

"One sec . . ." Saraswati said, dialing the phone. "Simone, you there?" ("My friend Simone's a lawyer," she whispered to Nivedita.) "I'm putting you on speakerphone. Okay, go!" With a nod, she signaled Nivedita to open the letter. "Well?"

Nivedita scanned the few, highly disingenuous, extremely courteously worded lines on the single page, in which the word *regrettable* appeared no fewer than four times.

"It's from the university's legal team."

"Of course it is," Saraswati said with a huff, "they must've sent it immediately, no later than Wednesday at least."

"The dean requests that you issue a public apology to all students of color," Nivedita continued, giving a start as Saraswati smacked the orange receiver against its cradle.

"Why on earth should I apologize to anyone for having made a decision regarding *my own* life? I'd just as soon step down from my endowed professorship."

"Oh, I'd wait 'til they dismiss you," Simone's dry voice came from the other end of the line, somehow miraculously still connected.

"That's your other option," Nivedita said, taking a nervous gulp of tea and watching as all color drained from Saraswati's face, which turned first a pale white, then flushed red. The tea now tasted of wet bricks, or clay, or maybe a mouthful of dirt. "They're giving you fourteen business days to respond."

And still, not a word from Kali.

IDENTITTI

You all remember how, during sex, Kali's always on top, right? Whether she's lying, sitting, crouching, or magically standing with her legs twisted behind her head, whatever—basically anything *but* the missionary position—she's always on top.

Don't worry, I'm not obsessed with Kali's sex life—but you know who *was*? The Brits, back when they came to India, the richest country in the world at the time, to do their missionary work and colonize the place. They simply couldn't fathom how Kali could possibly sit on top of Shiva during sex, lasciviously rubbing her li'l cockscomb-clit up against his stomach. No wonder that, for the Europeans, Kali was the very embodiment of the extreme far East (they'd have said Orient), the most otherly other, the *Darkest Heart of India.*

The English home front got to know Kali through novels like *In 80 Tagen um die Welt*—which some of you might know as Jules Verne's *Around the World in Eighty Days (as translated by George Makepeace Towle)* or, in the *authentic* original French, *Le tour du monde en quatre-vingts jours* (the first German translators weren't credited)—where she was portrayed as a savage goddess whose offspring trampled on every last taboo with their filthy bare feet. Translation: she had wild orgies where she wildly dispatched countless human sacrifices. Which is just the kind of thing that happens once people start satisfying themselves. (Click here to read my earlier post, *Cum Better with Kali.*)

Kali became the justification for why so many people and so many unscrupulous goddesses (after all, it wasn't just Kali—there was also Durga, who rode a lioness, and the Gopis, who had group sex with

Krishna, and . . .) had to be so urgently domesticated. Colonization as *white man's burden to civilize.*

So far, so good—I know you know all this. What's less well known is that the Bengalis (Kali is the tutelary goddess of the Indian state of Bengal, where both the Bengal tiger and my father are from) elevated Kali into a symbol of anticolonial resistance against the Brits.

"Because of course there was a resistance movement!" Kali adds, for one.

And the call for freedom in the colonies also influenced the critiques of empire coming from within Britain, too.

"Because of course the very heart of the empire had a resistance, too!" Kali adds, secondly.

But above all it was influenced by the Western concept of . . . freedom! What we currently conceive of as freedom was originally formulated, in large part, in the colonies.

"Meaning, by me!" Kali adds, thirdly.

And *that's* what I'm actually obsessed with right now. *That's* what I want to learn from Kali.

"Uhh, you want to learn what, exactly?"

"How should I know? If I knew, I wouldn't need to learn it from you, Kali. Oh, and I'm always open to picking up a few sex tips on the side, y'know."

2

"*Fucking Empire,*" Priti said two weeks after the yoga-related hullabaloo, in an apparent attempt to earn Saraswati's approval. But their prof. just kept packing up her papers.

"In Germany, imperialism was different from how it was in England," she remarked evasively. But Priti wasn't one to be evaded.

"Oh yeah? Why, because Germany didn't have any colonies?"

"No," said Saraswati, letting her eyes wander around the classroom, "Germany also had colonies, and a colonial history, but . . ."

"But what? It was just really short?"

"No . . ." Saraswati repeated.

"Ah, I see! So it wasn't short—instead, it was long and glorious?" Priti cut her off again. Nivedita knew that Priti was only trying to cover up her own embarrassment. After all, *Fucking Empire*—or had she said *Fucking Imperialism*? Was there a difference, and if so, did it matter?—it was just Priti's attempt at a peace offering. But to everyone else's eyes, it just looked like an angry young woman telling a more established, older woman what was what.

Saraswati smiled patiently and went back to her papers, which of course just made everything worse.

"Is that all?" Priti yelled, her voice turning more threatening. "So then, was Germany also an *international player* or what?"

"There's no point talking to you when you won't listen to me." The way Nivedita remembered it, the second Saraswati said that, Priti leaped up onto the desk with both feet, causing a loud stomp, but maybe she'd just slapped her palm down.

"*Ach ja?!* Well then, it makes no sense to learn from you when you don't take us seriously!"

And, as with any challenge, Saraswati accepted this one with relish.

"Okay, everyone back in their seats! Class isn't over yet. Everybody—tell me everything you know about German colonialism." Amid the general shuffling of feet and chairs, the fact that even the students who already had a foot out the door returned to their seats was a testament to Saraswati's authority.

"It lasted from the eighteen-eighties up through the end of World War I," Oluchi said somewhat tentatively, putting her mustard-yellow glasses back on.

"Can any of you name a few German colonies?"

"The Kingdom of Rwanda," said Oluchi.

"Tanzania," said Saida.

"Back then it was Taganyika and Zanzibar," Oluchi elaborated.

"Burundi—I mean, the Kingdom of Burundi," added Saida.

"Namibia," said Oluchi, uncertain of its precolonial name.

"Cameroon," said Enrico. "Togo."

"Nigeria," said Oluchi. A grim look came over her face as she added, "if the Brits hadn't snatched it, ditto for Cameroon."

"You're all so *PC*," Saraswati complimented them, "not a single one of you has used a colonial name. Now, how about in the Pacific?"

"Samoa," said Iqbal, the one with radiant eyes and pouty lips—the one Priti always referred to as *Sexbal*. "And . . . Nauru?"

"Okay, nice work—I'll give you the Marshall, the Caroline, and the Northern Mariana Islands, plus Palau. And Jiaozhou, in eastern China. That's all right, and all wrong!" Saraswati summed up imperiously. She put on her glasses, which she reserved for special occasions, when she wanted to get a closer look at people's reactions to her. "In Germany, if we even talk about colonialism, at best we talk about all these colonies. The Canadian historian Robert L. Nelson refers to this as the so-called *Salt-Water Thesis:* The motherland is here, the colonies are way over there, and in between there's just a ton of water—everything's neatly separated. And yet it's also true that the relationships between Germany and Poland, Southern Europe, and above all Turkey, aka the Ottoman Empire, could just as accurately be called *colonial*. Of course no one ever does use that term since it's so dirty. So, now: What are the characteristics of colonialism? Anyone? Anyone?"

"Attempts at economic and cultural dominance," Nivedita called out.

"Correct! Go on . . ."

"Expropriation of a significant portion of the colonized culture's heritage to the country of the colonizers," added Iqbal.

"Correct again! Also military intervention, and economic migration from the colonized countries . . ."

"And, I mean, is there a point to what you're saying?" Priti asked, although her attempt at a yawn morphed into a sneer.

"As I just said, there's no point talking to you when you won't listen to me." Nivedita could feel the tense energy emanating from her cousin. It felt like a million needles pricking her skin, or like air charged with static electricity just before a thunderstorm.

"Why don't you get to the point then?"

Aaand *boom*, right on cue, the storm delivered its thunder.

"That *is* my point!" Saraswati's voice ripped through the air as her hands tore her lecture notes to shreds. "All your knowledge about colonialism is not only imported, but—as a rule—it's imported from North America! Is that clear enough for you?" The storm broke, but Saraswati's thundering voice continued to echo as the bits of paper she'd torn up and tossed into the air rained down around her. "Just like your fixation on skin color! Which is also imported from the USA! To keep it plain and simple: over there, color means something different than it does here. The meaning of POC does, too. In the great melting pot that is the United States of America, all Europeans get fused into one single *white* super-race. But here in Europe . . . but who'm I saying all this to?" Saraswati stretched out an arm and gestured toward Enrico, who did his best to hide behind his binder. "Here, in no way can you make the case that all *whites* are equal—you can't even claim they're all equally *white*."

Priti knew when she lost, but she never knew when it was time to give up.

"Oh yeah? Are you really trying to say that here in *Deutschland über alles* there's no racism, because all you Germans are too refined to use a word like *race*—ahem, *entschüldigung—Rasse*?"

"Nicely done," Saraswati lauded. As usual, her thunderclouds had parted, again revealing a sunny magnanimity. "What I'm saying is that we Germans, for comprehensible historical reasons—and yes, I'm talking about fascism!— have a real fear of getting anywhere near the word *race*. We shrink back in horror, not only when it comes to admitting to ourselves *that* we *do* racialize, but also *how* we racialize. You can see it in countless evasive, fuzzy German terms, such as the oh-so-beloved word *Ausländer*. I am not a foreigner, nor am I an alien, and neither are most of you. But we get called that simply because people want to avoid any terminology involving race. The more lefty a newspaper is, the fonder its editors are of writing *Migrationshintergrund* instead—'people with an immigrant background,' as if nobody could see through *that* veil, *ha*. And sometimes it's even correct—I, for example, come from an immigrant background. My friend Jeanie also has an immigrant background, you might even say she has an immigrant foreground, since she only moved from Edinburgh to Berlin six years ago. But when we say

Mimimi—our adorable abbreviation of *Mitbürger mit Migrationshintergrund*, 'fellow citizens with immigrant backgrounds'—we don't normally picture someone like Jeanie from Scotland. No, we picture someone like Enrico, whose parents came here from Naples, back in the eighties. Or someone like my friend Maragrita from Greece. Even though in America both of them would be *white and nothing but white*."

"WOW, SHE'S PRETTY crazy, isn't she? For real." Priti said on the way to the cafeteria. A rumor was going around that Heinrich Heine University had won an architecture prize, and the winning building was supposed to look like a ship on waves, but to Nivedita it looked more like a bunch of unfinished parking garages. For a moment she wished she'd enrolled at a better-looking school, like Oxford or Cambridge or even Cologne, at least. But then she returned to her mantra, reminding herself that she'd feel excluded and invisible in places like that, while here she was *Notorious Nivedita*: Saraswati's student, Oluchi's friend, Priti's cousin.

"Who's crazy?" asked Lotte, who she sat down to join them, fresh out of her Neuroscience Psychology 101 class.

"Saras-high-and-mighty," quipped Priti.

"Aren't we all?" Nivedita snapped back, feeling quick-witted. Priti turned and gave her a forced grin while staring at her intensely.

"Of course, *natürlich*, Niveswati."

"Don't call me that!"

"What should I call you, then?" Priti's provocation immediately lit up a bulb over Nivedita's head.

"How 'bout Nivekananda?" After the Indian philosopher and mystic Vivekananda.

"Hold your horses, sister," Priti said, unable to stifle a rather more good-natured grin.

Oluchi smiled, too, and again parroted Saraswati's haughty voice.

"And what are you, my child—POC or PC?" Whereupon another bulb lit up over Nivedita's head.

"I'm PIO!"

PIO was the acronym for Person of Indian Origin, and PIO cards were a passport of sorts for the Indian diaspora until they were superseded in 2005 by the OCI, which stood for Overseas Citizen of India—but that acronym always made Nivedita think of OCD, and she was already uncertain enough about whether India was in effect a kind of obsessive-compulsive disorder unique to her.

"Race is one of the major human experiments ever conceived of," Lotte chimed in, surprisingly.

"What about sex?" asked Priti.

THE SECOND TIME Priti came to Essen to polish up her German, Nivedita was fifteen. By then Nivedita was no longer so smitten by Jürgen—now she had her eyes on the much more fascinating Yannik. And then Priti decided it was time for them to not just talk about sex, but to lose their virginity. Together.

The trick, it turned out, was to go up to a guy and talk to him. Nivedita had spent her entire sophomore year of high school silently yearning for Yannik's cherry-red lips. Priti, meanwhile, just strode over to him.

"We want to talk to you."

"Ah," Yannik answered.

"Good," said Priti.

So the following night they rang the doorbell of a drab duplex in Essen-Kettwig. Yannik had procured beer, and they'd brought beer, so nothing stood in the way of an orgy—until Yannik's expression turned suggestive and he finally spoke up.

"I've always wanted to sleep with two women at once."

"You mean you've always, *one* day, wanted to sleep with *one* woman," Priti corrected him. Her German really was getting *sehr gut*.

Yannik looked as if he'd just been scared by his own courage—as well as Priti—so Nivedita piped up.

"Me, too."

"What?" he asked, bewildered.

"I've also always wanted to . . ." Nivedita clarified, "sleep with a woman."

"Let's play strip poker!" Priti cut in.

While Yannik pimped up a margherita pizza with onions and dolphin-safe tuna, Priti scanned through his parents' CD collection. Since none of the names said much to her, she chose the sole album that she recognized, one that her mother, Leela, had at home back in Balsall Heath: *The Black Saint and the Sinner Lady*.

Yannik raised a knowing eyebrow.

"You listen to jazz?"

"Yeah," Priti lied, taking in the cover photo of Charles Mingus in front of a wall with white tiles. "But only Black and Indian jazz."

"*Indian* jazz?" Yannik asked.

"Yup," Priti ended it there since she had nothing more to add on the subject. Although he was a grade above them in school, Nivedita knew he'd played the cello for years already, and had chosen various music classes for all his electives. So she understood how urgent it was that she find a way to change the subject.

"Where are your parents?"

"Out," Yannik said, with an arm gesture so broad it encompassed Mingus, Nivedita, Priti, the whole open-plan kitchen and long living room—which were only separated by a counter—and even the now-dark backyard, visible through the reflective glass doors.

"And when are they coming back?"

"Not until tomorrow night."

"Let's play strip poker," Priti repeated.

Priti wedged a beer bottle into her underwear, which was rather unattractive.

"Want a sip?" she offered Yannik, thrusting her narrow hips toward him.

Nivedita was so busy eyeing her cousin with a combination of anger and wonder that Yannik's answer totally failed to register. The alcohol and the neon-green Fatboy beanbag she was lounging in made it feel like someone had turned the gravity knob up a few notches. All the while, Priti's movements were so quick and springy she was virtually aglow. Her white undershirt flashed as she danced in front of a lamp whose translucent paper shade looked like some movie-backdrop moon perched atop a tripod, casting Yannik into shadows that groped him all over. Much to Nivedita's surprise, he seemed to have declined Priti's offer, because she'd grown tired of the bottle, extracted it from her undies, and set it down on one of the speakers. Then she went over to the bookcase covering most of the wall and ran an index finger across all the spines.

"Ooh," she said knowingly, pulling one book from the shelf, "what have we here?" But Yannik was more interested in picking out the next album. ("I doubt that dude can even read," Priti griped to Nivedita the next morning.) And so she began reading to him aloud.

"In Oriental lands, by night, the flat rooftops are a favorite spot . . ." she gazed over the top of the book and paused dramatically before continuing, "*to have sex.*"

Nivedita had once had a shopping cart race with Jürgen and Lilli (and another friend of theirs) on the flat rooftop of the local Kaufhof mall. It involved a lot of pushing and body contact, so the "favorite spot" mentioned in the book struck her as a perfectly good idea. But Priti was incensed.

"*Aber*—I mean, c'mon, 'Oriental lands'?! Do you all really say shit like *Orientalische Länder* here in Germany?"

That was the other thing Nivedita really envied about her already sixteen-year-old cousin from England: Priti was up on (anti)racism. Her education on that front came mostly through comedians like Nish Kumar and Lilly Singh, and classics like *Goodness Gracious Me*, but Nivedita wasn't in on any of that yet. The way she imagined it, all British Asian kids met up once a week at temple—kind of like how she went to her Antifa group—and strategized about the activism they'd carry out over the next seven days.

"Wow!" Priti interrupted her reverie. "They really even put the *n-word* in here!"

"What word?" asked Yannik.

"The n-word. As in n*****."

"As in what?" he was confused.

"You know," Priti insisted, "n*****."

"N . . . nnnn?"

"N*****!"

"The word you cannot and must not say aloud," Nivedita interjected, glad she knew what Priti was talking about.

"Y'mean 'You-Know-Who,' 'He-Who-Must-Not-Be-Named'? Like, Voldemort?"

"Yeahhh . . . but, like, referring to Black people."

"Oh, you mean *n******!"

"Would it really kill you to *not* say that?" Nivedita shrieked.

"You two started it," said Yannik.

"Ugh, that is sooo . . ." Priti checked the copyright page of the book she was holding, "nineteen seventy-two. They even spell the word out in full, and don't bother skimping on the clichés. Like here: '*N-style: from behind. She kneels, hands clasped behind her neck, breasts and face on the bed. He kneels behind.*'" Yannik, meanwhile, was totally disoriented, but at least Priti finally had his undivided attention. So she kept going. "*He puts a hand on each of her shoulder-blades and presses down. Very deep position—apt to pump her full of air which escapes later in a disconcerting manner—otherwise excellent.*" Nivedita tried to sit up from the beanbag and prop herself up.

"What the hell are you reading?"

"Oh, just a book that happens to be not only *racist* but also *sexist*," Priti replied without actually answering. "Get a load of this: '*Shoe leather "pre-serves" the fatty acids found in both foot sweat and in the vagina—the same fatty acids that trigger sexual arousal in apes and anthropoid apes. Although they*' . . . meaning the fatty acids, not the apes, '*have a rather rancid odor, they likely stimulate the male on a subliminal level.*'"

"You're making that up," Nivedita protested, despite knowing better.

Priti pointed her chin at Nivedita's feet. As if hypnotized, Yannik crawled across the cream-colored, wall-to-wall carpet toward Nivedita.

"*Now—Jetzt!*" Priti commanded like a sorceress, and Yannik's fingers began hovering over Nivedita's toes. Priti set the book down next to her long-forgotten beer bottle and with just two strides stood behind her cousin. She sat down behind her cousin so that Nivedita's head could rest on her stomach.

"Do they smell like her vagina?" she whispered. "Yann? . . . You wanna sniff her vagina?" He nodded without lifting his head. Somehow Nivedita managed to spread her legs. The leather upholstery squeaked and made farting noises with every movement, but she didn't find it funny. Or were they queefing noises? Nivedita could feel Priti's breath going in and out of her warm abdomen, and Yannik's breath warmed the crotch of her jeans. Then Priti's hands wandered down her shoulders as Yannik's slid up her legs, the lips of her vulva began to pulse, and her breasts grew eager eyes.

"SO, WHICH ONE of us was better?" Priti asked.

Nivedita hadn't thought it possible to go from complete relaxation to total tension with a mere seven words. As Yannik held his breath and Priti appeared to have choked on her own question, Nivedita's razor-sharp intuition saved them all.

"It's against the rules to ask that!"

Priti stumbled to her feet and put the book back on the shelf between Günter Ament's *Sexfront* and Nobuyoshi Araki's *Love Hotel*, but didn't protest.

"For real, what book was that?" Nivedita asked.

"*The Joy of Sex*, from the seventies."

"But that was supposed to be such a . . . *progressive* book, I was told."

"Clearly not when it comes to race," Priti dryly replied, heading straight back over to Yannik, and directing her next words at him. "We have something like that, too. But ours is called the *Kamasutra*, and it's waaay more ancient."

"It's called *Tantra*," Nivedita corrected her.

"Yeah, I guess you could say that's the sequel."

WHEREVER THEY WENT, it was always the same. Whenever she had Priti by her side, people took her more seriously. It was like the mere fact that they were together lent them an aura of life experience and street cred. For a while she thought that, if only she and her cousin spent enough time together, then the rest of their patchwork identity would just fill itself in, and eventually click into something recognizable. After all, their evening at Yannik's made it feel like all the tall tales and crazy yarns they'd spun together riding the tram three years before just might accumulate and add up to *one real* epic saga. When she introduced herself and her cousin, she did it as if they were Kali, melded into one figure with four arms instead of two, symbolizing their superhuman powers. Privedita held both pairs of arms up, palms facing forward, so that you could clearly see what was in each hand: a flower, a sickle, a bowl holding flames, and the severed head of a man, blood oozing from his neck.

3

"I helped you get major cultural capital," Saraswati said, eleven years later, as they lounged on her terrace.

"You?" Nivedita asked, amazed. "You helped *us* . . . ?" The sun—whose light encompassed the entire rainbow spectrum, as long as that spectrum was red, red, or red—had long since disappeared behind the surrounding buildings. But the air remained so warm that Nivedita stretched her arms out to catch the nearly imperceptible breeze, and Saraswati's dupatta lay nearby, coiled up like a slumbering serpent.

"Maybe not just me, singlehandedly," Saraswati conceded. "But, thanks to me, you all have gained real pop culture currency."

"While you were busy shedding all scruples to enrich yourself through our cultural capital, you mean?!" Nivedita shouted while casting a guilty glance back through the terrace door at the Eero Saarinen Tulip table atop which the university administration's letter lay ticking like a time bomb. After all, Saraswati had enough problems as it was, so Nivedita really should be a bit more patient with her. Instead, turning the tables yet again, Saraswati displayed great patience with her.

"Cultural capital isn't a limited resource," she said, her tone much milder.

Nivedita stared at Saraswati and wondered how she ever could've thought she looked Indian. But that wasn't the real problem—the real problem was that, just the previous night, she'd looked into the mirror and wondered exactly how she could be so certain she *herself* looked Indian. That's what Saraswati had done to her. *She hadn't only lied about herself, she'd lied about me, too.*

"You've certainly taught me what *cultural appropriation* is."

"I taught you what the *concept* of *cultural appropriation* is," Saraswati corrected her. "And, as with any concept, the idea of the critique of cultural appropriation contains a broad range of possibilities, spanning from highly useful to extremely destructive."

"And I suppose you're the one who decides exactly where on that 'broad range of possibilities' you stand, right?" Nivedita was cynical.

Saraswati shrugged.

"And why not? After all, even Barack Obama was given the right to choose to be Black."

"Barack *who*?"

"Obama. Forty-fourth president of the United States. But that was before your time."

"Ha-ha."

Saraswati's fingers twitched as if she were about to grab her dupatta, which Nivedita had come to recognize as a sign she was about to launch into a lecture.

"His mother was *white*, he grew up in a *white* family. He attended an elite *white* university. He even lived in the goddamn *White House*, for Chrissake. What more does one have to do to be *white*?"

"But he's . . . he looks Black," Nivedita protested.

"QED." Saraswati's fingers budded open, as if blossoming.

"QED? Are you fucking kidding me?"

"Why? How? And where's the difference?"

"He didn't need to resort to some wacky herbal skin treatment to look the way he looks!"

"Ah, herbal treatments . . ." Saraswati effused dreamily.

"Ugh, I don't even want to know . . ." Nivedita cut her off.

"What *do* you want to know, then?"

"Why you . . ."

"*Why* can never be separated from *how*. And since we've now wandered into the territory of appropriateness and inappropriateness . . ." Saraswati pulled her phone out from under her dupatta and brandished it at Nivedita like a pistol.

Nivedita took it and felt a burning sensation. It started at the roots of her hair, and then spread out, slowly and inexorably, over her entire body as she read:

» Second Enlightenment @TheEarthIsFlat *Let's put it this way: If all the people Saraswati had mocked over the last few years all got together, we wouldn't even need one stone per person.*

» Susanne Hersel @Susanne_herself *You, my dear, should be ashamed of yourself. I hope a whole swarm of filthy n****** comes and rapes the sh*t out of you until your f*cked-up head stops producing such BS. Then you'll see what they really want.*

» God @GodIsInDaHaus *I know how I can make your skin black permanently. I'll just come on over with a match.*

» Abolish Delish Dish @Dima_Nadim *Doesn't the fact you think everything is BS mean that you're full of it?*

» Hockeymom Speyer @LaLaLand *Don't feed the trolls.*

» Shaparak Khorsandi @ShappiKhorsandi *If you find me feeding the trolls, you know it's because I have a deadline and I'm procrastinating. You're right. You're right. I'm going x*

The doorbell pierced the silence and Nivedita nearly dropped the phone.

"Who do you think that could be?" she whispered, even though it was obvious that nobody down on the street below could possibly hear anything being said way up there on the sixth-floor penthouse terrace. "Wait!" she said somewhat louder, as Saraswati stood up.

"Why?" she asked with audible surprise.

"It might . . . it could be GodIsInDaHaus."

"At this hour?"

"Uh, yeah! Who else would come by so late?"

"It must be *so* exciting to live in your world of imminent danger and perpetual paranoia," Saraswati dismissed her, gently removing Nivedita's hand from her forearm.

Nivedita curled her arms around herself in a self-protective hug and wondered just how cynical such an answer was in a country where her own acquaintances—okay, just some people she followed on Twitter and Instagram—had long since learned to live under (more German-sounding) pseudonyms, even and especially on their door-buzzer labels, out of fear of neo-Nazis and straight-up Nazis. Then she wondered whether she should start hyperventilating, and then she wondered how hyperventilating even worked. It seemed like an eternity passed before she finally heard footsteps in the hallway.

"Saraswati!" was the next thing she heard, from an unfamiliar voice. And then she heard something that sounded suspiciously like a long, steamy French kiss. She lifted her head, eager for more information, just as Saraswati strode back onto the terrace alongside a person with the absolute lightest hair color Nivedita had ever seen.

"This is Nivedita, the one I've told you so much about," she said, as if she were the grande dame at some gala dinner. "And this is Toni." *The one you've told me absolutely nothing about!*

Nivedita sized Toni up, scanning for any clues about their gender.

"Toni what?" she asked before she was able to stop herself.

"Toni Cade Bambara," Saraswati laughed.

"Toni who?" Toni themself asked, perplexed.

"An African American writer, *darling*—it's got nothing to do with you, it's not something you'd be interested in."

"Then why didn't you say Toni Morrison?" Nivedita asked before she was able to stop herself.

"I *told* you she was my star student," Saraswati effused.

Toni bowed to Nivedita and held out her hand. From closer up, Toni no longer looked like an androgynandroid straight out of an art-house movie, and more like a woman in her midthirties with a light case of albinism.

"Hi, Nivedita—she's always so patronizing, but you get used to it." With that, she vanished back into the bowels of Saraswati's condo, and Nivedita tried her best not to stare as she went.

"Are Toni and you . . . have you two . . . are you two . . . ?"

"Of course—obviously." Saraswati was amused by the question, and Nivedita was glad to have a skin color that didn't make it totally obvious when she blushed.

"So, why's . . . Toni just coming over now?" she asked brusquely.

"She lives in Berlin."

"So? There are trains from Berlin every hour, on the hour—aren't there?"

"That's what I so adore about you—your loyalty," Saraswati said as she lit a candle. The sound of a shower being turned on in the bathroom echoed down the hallway, and suddenly they were back in a time loop, returning to their discussion about Barack Obama and *white* privilege.

"But you grew up with all the benefits of *white* privilege," Nivedita said, as if a few paces away there weren't a naked woman with a pigmentation disorder standing under the shower, separated from them solely by a milky-*white* pane of semi-opaque glass.

"Boy oh boy, are you ever overestimating *whiteness*, baby," said Saraswati, slinking back down onto her lounger.

"Boy oh boy, are you ever . . ." and since Nivedita couldn't come up with the right noun form of POC, she switched gears, "underestimating what it's like to grow up in this country as a non-*white* kid."

"You aren't the only one who's experienced exclusion here."

"Yeah, well, just for the time being . . ." The candle flickered and flared, hissing like a cat, and then calmed back down.

"It's like a ghost just walked by," said Saraswati. *The ghost of years past, in Saraswati's classes*, thought Nivedita. But then she realized it was Kali. Kali had finally come back and was now crouching on the end of her lounger, following this endless debate between Nivedita and Not-Nivedita.

"You simply didn't have the same experience, as a kid, knowing that you were never, ever included, always excluded." Nivedita was growing more determined. "You don't know what it's like when none of the cultural messaging is meant for you or *anyone like you*. You don't know what it's like to never be in the system, to always be on the outside, looking in."

"Oh, baby," Saraswati said—and those two words sounded less like they meant *oh, little one* and more like they meant *oh, you newborn* or, maybe slightly less weirdly, *oh, you really were born yesterday*—"you don't seriously believe that the experience of being excluded is limited to a set skin-color palette, do you? Of course I was never included! People like me, who are born into a skin that doesn't match the one they feel is theirs, are never included because people like me aren't supposed to exist."

Nivedita was taken aback. But still she had to speak up.

"It's not the same."

"No two experiences ever are the same."

Well? asked Kali. *What're you going to say to that?*

Yeah, what should I say to that? Nivedita asked Kali back.

Kali raised her hands up, and suddenly Nivedita knew exactly what she wanted to say.

"That's all well and good for you as a private individual, but not as a professor and public figure. How is it that you could *only* teach postcolonial studies?"

In a perfect imitation of Kali's gesture, Saraswati raised *her* hands up.

"Because, although no two experiences are ever exactly the same, we can nevertheless learn from other people's experiences. It's a magical phenomenon known as *empathy*."

Nivedita knew there was a mistake somewhere in there, she just didn't know exactly where.

"Stop *qualifying* everything! Not *everything* is relative."

"And why shouldn't you have some empathy for my position, huh? After all, I sure feel a whole lot of empathy for you."

"Saraswati, you don't know what you're talking about when you talk about empathy. You aren't capable of empathizing with anyone, except maybe your own books," Toni said, sitting down next to her. By candlelight, her hair was the same color as the white hand towel with which she was rubbing it dry. Nivedita opened her mouth in order to counter Saraswati's last remark, but something else entirely came out.

"Simon dumped me."

"I had a sneaking suspicion you weren't here for purely altruistic reasons," Saraswati purred.

Altruism is one of the most misunderstood concepts, Kali noted.

Except race, said Nivedita.

Except race, right, Kali concurred.

Except gender, Toni's *white* silhouette seemed to add.

Except Saraswati, who always needed to make an exception for herself.

"But the pain you're feeling from the breakup has nothing to do with Simon. Simon is just the trigger. The pain is older, and deeper."

"What fortune cookie did you lift that one from?" Nivedita was stunned at how easily she kept being stunned. "So, if I'd had a happy childhood, I wouldn't feel hurt that he left me?"

"No, because in that case you wouldn't ever have been with him in the first place."

"Saraswati, did you hear what I said? He dumped me. He is *no longer with* me."

"*He* might not be, but *you* still are."

"She's right," Toni casually chimed in. "I'm taking her side, because she's so goddamn smart."

"Toni! Did you get the memo on what a total mess she's made of her life?" Nivedita countered. "And of her career?" She added that last bit out of spite since Saraswati had hurt her.

"Why are you madder at me than you are at Simon?" Saraswati was rapt as she awaited the answer.

"Because I trusted you," Nivedita howled, thinking: *It's true, the reason I'm so mad at her is because I actually trusted her.*

"Maybe it's high time you trusted your life partner, too."

"Wouldn't *that* be a laugh . . ."

"That's precisely my point!"

And then Saraswati got up from her lounger and hugged Nivedita with four arms. Saraswati's body was soft and still warm from the heat of day, but also already cool in the night air. Her body was like a bridge between this exact summer and all the summers that had gone before—all the summers Nivedita had experienced in her entire lifetime, as well as all the summers she had never experienced, but that had nevertheless made her who she was. All those invisible, parallel-plane-of-existence summers that had still given her the vitamins and nutrients she needed in order to grow. They had become her very bones, and had also created the political fault lines and forces that had compelled her ancestors to leave their various countries of origin and head elsewhere in search of home, education, work, love, and recognition of their specific individuality as human beings on this planet.

And then Nivedita noticed that two of Saraswati's arms were brown as cedarwood, while the other two were oh-so-Snow White and still damp from the shower.

"What Simon did isn't racist, but the fact that it got so completely under your skin has a whole lot to do with racism," the very brown Saraswati said.

In the lingering heat of day now morphing into a tropical night, Nivedita could almost understand what that meant.

ORIENTALISM

"Trouble with the Engenglish is that their hiss hiss history happened overseas, so they dodo don't know what it means."—WHISKY SISODIA

"Europe is literally a creation of the Third World."—FRANTZ FANON

"The mythologies of empire are dangerous not just for the colonized but also for the colonizer."—C. L. R. JAMES

1

Just to get it out of the way: This Is the Post with the Orgasm.

That was how the blog entry "Cum Better with Kali" started, and it got the most clicks of all Nivedita's posts—until, that is, she posted her statement about the interview she'd given on national radio. Because of course she *had* to write a statement.

During her first night at Saraswati's.

After her first fight with Saraswati.

If you could even call it a fight when she was the only one getting upset, while Saraswati just took each point she made and spun it around for so long that Nivedita herself didn't even know what POC meant anymore.

"Why are you—you and Oluchi and your whole mob of trolls—suddenly investigating my ancestry?" Saraswati's voice trickled, slow as honey, into the dark living room where they'd taken refuge from the mosquitos outside.

Fury had grabbed Nivedita and yanked her up out of the fiberglass Eero Aarnio Ball chair, because Saraswati's words were so right and yet so wrong! Or did she mean so wrong and yet so right?

"Why are you all of a sudden pretending everything's so arbitrary?" she shouted. Then she started pacing back and forth across the room, until her extremities—which she clearly had no control of by now—began hurling objects every which way.

Saraswati's eyelids slowly lowered, acquiring the same disapproving expression visible in the almondine eyes of Indian girls in Mughal-era miniatures.

"Just because things aren't the way they always were doesn't mean they're arbitrary. Once you've made a decision, it changes you. We *are* our decisions."

Nivedita stopped dead in her tracks and thought about her (for lack of a better term) ex-partner Simon, who wasn't thinking about her. She hadn't merely made the decision to be in a relationship with him, she *was* that decision—like a disease, she became that decision in flesh and blood.

But that still wasn't the issue here. The issue at hand was: *Does Saraswati's decision make her more Indian than me? Does she, therefore, deserve to be Indian more than I deserve to be?*

Kali's ironic voice replied: *Some are born POC, some achieve POCness, and some have POCness thrust upon them.*

What's that you're quoting? Nivedita asked, indignantly.

That—as you so perfectly put it, in appropriately ungendered terms—is Shakespeare.

And what does he/she/they mean by it?

That there are more things in heaven and earth than your philosophy has ever even dreamt of.

"Don't give me that nonsense," Nivedita said, without knowing whether she was addressing Kali or Saraswati or both of them.

Saraswati stood up.

"That's precisely what I'm giving you!"

And then she took off.

NIVEDITA STAYED, AND now she had the shadow-filled living room with the smoking candle on the coffee table all to herself. She grabbed the bottle of wine and refilled her glass. She caught a glimpse of her own reflection in the black-as-night windowpane and wondered who it reminded her of, aside from her mother. Aside from her mother!

You're drunk, she said to her reflection.

But her reflection was just as quick to hurl the accusation back at her: *No, you're drunk*. She *was* drunk, and furious, and if Saraswati came back, Nivedita decided she'd jump up and thrust her bare-naked loins in her face. A shiver of excitement flowed through her whole body. She whispered to her reflection: *You mean your ass, not your loins—dumbass.*

Loins, her reflection insisted.

And then Nivedita realized she was drunk enough and confused enough that it was the perfect time to make a public statement on how she got wrapped up in the whole Saraswati Affair.

———

IDENTITTI

You all know what I said on national radio about Saraswati's unmasking. None of you know what I said on national radio about Saraswati's unmasking. Because I said *nothing* about it!

Because that interview was recorded *before*. Saraswati's debunking only happened *after*.

That's how little any of us can trust our ears.

You get what I mean? No, I don't either—because I still don't have enough information about Saraswati's actions and motivations and what effect she and they have had on all of us.

I promise to do everything I can to get the necessary info and to try and understand what it all means, what happened.

I'll be back. Love you all.

Until then:

Don't believe the hype.

Believe the hype.

Be the hype.

Don't be the hype.

But above all: be gentle!

And while she was still taking screenshots of that post—and posting them to Instagram, at which point she noticed the typos, which she then corrected in the comments of the already-published post—the first reactions began popping up on Twitter.

» Maciej Jaśkowiak @MyManMattes @*Identitti answered the question! How many words does it take to say exactly nothing? #UncleTomtitti*

» Call me Zadie @OutsideSisters *You have to think about where your loyalties lie, @Identitti. Fence-sitting is white privilege.*

» Berit Glanz @beritmiriam *1. I'm trying to follow the whole Saraswati debate, but now I'm totally confused. Does anybody have a link to a good, more substantial post?*

    » Berit Glanz @beritmiriam *2. Has the university already taken a position on this whole Saraswati Thing, or are they just sitting it out?*

    » Berit Glanz @beritmiriam *3. Was @Identitti's statement deleted or was her account taken down?*

    » Berit Glanz @beritmiriam *4. The hottest hot takes on this whole Saraswati Thing are of course behind a paywall. I'm sure people already rubbing their hands at the prospect of such clickbait.*

And amid all the other Twittering there was even a tweet from Anish, all the way from India:

> » Anish Kapoor @DAnishDelight *Nivedita, you know that up until now*
> *philosophers have only tried to understand the world, but that every-*
> *thing depends on changing it.*

Nivedita sent him a DM: *Thanks for nothing, Anish!*

And then she immediately regretted having hit *send*. The candle flickered one last time, then went out. Nivedita cautiously made her way through the obstacle course that was Saraswati's living room, navigating solely by the bluish light of the notifications now lighting up the screen as the venom poured forth. Little tables and chests dotted the room, piled high with books, waiting in ambush to collide with her shins. The floor felt warm under her feet as long as she was inside, but once she crossed the threshold and strode out onto the terrace, she noticed the concrete outside had cooled much faster than the white-varnished floorboards inside. She took in the woodruff-lemon-vanilla scent of the large tufts of sweetgrass growing in Saraswati's planters and then instinctively thought of her grandma who, every year, used to give her braided sweetgrass as a present, "to ward off evil spirits." But not nearly enough sweetgrass could grow on Saraswati's terrace to ward off all the demons now descending upon her. The darkness of night burst with scent and softly buzzed as if none of that were any of its business. Nivedita wished she smoked, or could do something, anything, to make the world look a little less enchanting. The night's sheer fullness only made her broken heart hurt more, but at the same time her more practical-minded side insisted that each and every beauty must be enjoyed, and not to do so would constitute a momentous waste. She was inundated with sensations—from her dull, piercing, throbbing, screaming pain, as well as the humming, sizzling sound of life all around her—and despairingly hoped for distraction. Right then and there, distraction walked out onto the terrace.

"I'm preparing overnight oats. Shall I make some for you, too?"

"Overnight oats? Have we already grown so intimate?" Nivedita asked.

"I don't know, what do you think?" Saraswati replied dryly.

"Don't tell me I need to define *overnight* and *oats* and *intimate* for you . . ." Nivedita shot back.

"Do you want some or not?"

"Yes, please."

But instead of vanishing back into the dark gullet of the terrace door, Saraswati's silhouette walked over to Nivedita and laid her dupatta over her shoulders. Nivedita posed no resistance, and let Saraswati pull her down onto the hammock, where they swayed together as if they'd plopped down onto a very narrow, very intimate canopy swing. In the cocoon of Saraswati's care, Nivedita began to suspect that deception and admiration, loyalty, and betrayal, all blended together like Kali's yoni and Shiva's lingam. She felt Saraswati's breath flowing through her body, and then the vibration of her words, soft and dark as a caress.

"The hardest part was the hair."

"The hair?" Nivedita repeated, bewildered.

"Don't tell me it's never occurred to you that your . . ." Saraswati raised her hand and Nivedita froze. Touching someone's hair was not just a no-no, it was a blaring no-go, even worse than the where're-you-from/do-you-speak-German questions. But at the same time Nivedita just loved it when people played with her hair, so she was disappointed when Saraswati lowered her hand without touching a thing.

Of course Nivedita knew why her hair was the way it was. She knew it because she'd endured years of torture before she finally, in an unassuming little store in Düsseldorf, found a hairbrush that wouldn't tear out a veritable bird's nest of tangled hair with every stroke. That brush had become her savior, and she kept it on her at all times, like some treasured relic. Of course that induced the constant fear she might lose it and never be able to replace it, and then her only option would be to grow dreadlocks—that skillfully felted, somehow maximalist coif that fascinated her. But of course she also knew that even on her, that style would be cultural appropriation, although the earliest written records mentioning dreadlocks came from India (as did the oldest images: they showed Shiva wearing dreadlocks, and what he did with them . . .). Indeed, Nivedita was beginning to suspect that everything could be traced back to India if only she dug deep enough.

2

The second night was different than the first, because it was no longer just the two of them and Saraswati wasn't lounging on the terrace with Nivedita. Instead, she and Toni lay in her queen bed, behind that heap-of-feathers thing on the abraded spot on the floorboards, onto which Nivedita had projected her wildest fantasies after her first visit. (Was it a sex toy? Or some ritual implement?) It turned out to be yet another work of art, titled *Feathers Without Blood for Ana Mendieta*, which fired Nivedita's fantasies right back up.

Nivedita had always been able to hear people having sex in the apartments she lived in. In the last few years, it had usually been Barbara, sometimes Lotte's girlfriends, never Lotte herself. And now it was Saraswati and Toni.

Since she couldn't sleep anyway, at some point Nivedita began rummaging around the guest room. Had this been the plot of a mystery, or an episode of *Tatort*, at some point she would've found Saraswati's diary, or a water stain where there normally wouldn't one, or a tiny model train set with a conductor dressed in the wrong uniform, something that would give her the clue to solve the whole riddle. If, that is, she'd written herself into the plot, played a starring role, and therefore knew the convoluted explanation already, and if, of course, Saraswati's motives had been logical or comprehensible in the slightest. But that was a lot of *if*s. Instead, Saraswati's guest room was as full of promise and empty of redemption as Saraswati herself. First and foremost there were the books, which seemed to thrust their colorful spines at Nivedita while issuing immoral provocations: Touch us, feel our pages rustle between your fingers, open us, ohhh, open us! She viewed books as mason jars of sorts, primarily for preserving scents and feelings, and only second-arily for preserving stories and thoughts. All the books on the wine-crate shelves back in her apartment overpowered her anew with sensory input, each and every time she opened them. That was especially true of the books Saraswati had written, which she'd read as if they were holy scripture, books of miracles, or herbaria in which she'd pressed wondrous daisy and calendula blossoms, or—in the case of *Decolonize Your Soul*—reverently redone the cover of by carefully pasting a postcard reproduction of Amrita Sher-Gil's *Bride's Toilet* on top of it. She stared at Saraswati's shelves with the same degree of concentration, wondering what vertiginous bursts of color and light they might've held for their owner. As if to prove the point that no one is ever alone when they have a good book in hand, Nivedita's phone sounded the opening notes of "L'Internationale" from the bed.

"You're *where*?" Priti asked, her envy audible.

"At Saraswati's," Nivedita whispered back, deciding it was time to change her ringtone.

"What're you doing *there*?"

"Sorting out your chaos."

"Should I come over?"

No! every fiber of Nivedita's being screamed. *This is my adventure.* And, simultaneously: *You're a bad person if you begrudge your best cousin some time with the woman you currently hate more than any other.*

"Not yet," she finally whispered, "Saraswati's still pissed . . . I'll tell you when it's time."

Much to Nivedita's surprise, Priti didn't protest. Countless unanswered questions floated in the air between them, like softly humming radio waves, but at least this time Nivedita wasn't the only one yearning for an explana-tion, some more context, and above all a cohesive storyline. In the drawn-out silence that followed, she succumbed to temptation and pulled Ibram X. Ken-di's *How to Be an Antiracist* off the shelves. Below the official dedication, *to survival*, was a personal dedication, the letters so energetically rounded they could've been written with a spirograph: *to Saraswati*. A slip of paper fell out of the book—a grocery list, which Nivedita picked up and read like a poem:

Cherries

Arugula

buttercups

Cilantro

Simone, Simone!

Findi alternatives

Eyebright

Orange (the color or the fruit, *Nivedita wondered)*

Cornflower honey

And then she *really* found something, in a sandalwood box with a Kali yantra carved on its lid.

THAT SUMMER ELEVEN years ago with Yannik had been just as endlessly hot and perfidious as this one, the summer of Saraswati's downfall. For Nivedita, lies still smelled like asphalt and scorched fields, and her palms began to tingle, recalling the sensation she had all those years ago when she'd stick her arms out and run them along the hedges as she biked past, heading off to Kettwig the second Priti's German class started. Yannik and Nivedita spent those stolen hours almost exclusively in his bed. Sex with Yannik was a revelation, an epiphany. But even though everything he did constituted a mind-expanding experience for her, she'd still have liked an instruction manual for the male member. Not Yannik's specifically—she still had no idea of what extreme variation there was among penises—but in general, some kind of one-size-fits-all guidebook, something that could answer her burning question: how can I give the best hand job?

In search of both inspiration and stimulation back home, she perused Birgit's books and came across *The Joy of Sex*. Apparently everyone's parents had nabbed *their* parents' copy. Nivedita decided to break with tradition and instead pilfered Cynthia Heimel's *Sex Tips für Girls*—for some reason, the translator remained anonymous—and hid in the bathroom as she read it. After all, neither Priti nor Yannik nor Birgit could find out. Although the book delivered on its titular promise—"How to perform oral sex—Take the penis into your mouth and suck on it."—many of the chapters were aimed at Birgit's generation, so were of little practical use to Nivedita. What could she do with "Zen and the Art of Diaphragm Insertion"? Nothing. But then there was this one tip, which she'd have loved to underline in red, but refrained from doing so as not to divulge any intimate details about herself in a book she technically shouldn't even have been reading—"People with their clothes off tend to take things rather personally . . . The Golden Rule, for example (which, in case it slipped your minds, requires doing unto others as you would have them do unto you), should be closely observed."

The very fact that she got naked with Yannik meant she was breaking the golden rule, at least with regard to Priti. On the angled ceiling above Yannik's bed in his attic bedroom, he'd hung a poster of a gorgeous indigenous woman, with a saying printed in bold, socialist-red type: *Solidarity is the tenderness of the People.*—Ernesto Cardenal. During their first and only night as a threesome, Priti had adapted it: "Solidarity is the *Gruppensex* of the *Völker.*" Whenever Nivedita gazed into the guerilla's eyes, she felt simultaneously aroused and contrite.

"Now you're a chocolate lollipop," Yannik declared as he thrust into her, and she immediately came. She'd never felt as Indian as she did in that moment, but that moment turned out to be unrepeatable.

"Your rack is even hotter than Pretty Titti's," Yannik (aka Mr. Coitus Interruptus) exclaimed as he came all over her boobs.

"Than *whose*?"

"Y'know, your cousin."

Never had anyone given Priti such a wacky nickname, but Yannik made it sound like a mutually agreed-upon term of endearment. Nivedita wondered how many times he'd called Priti that, and how the devil Priti had managed to hide her ongoing rendezvous from Nivedita just as well as Nivedita had hidden hers from Priti.

Saraswati also had a copy of *Sex Tips für Girls*. She even had a diaphragm, which looked like a movie-prop flying-saucer from some sixties-era sci-fi flick, especially since she stored it in a silver-colored silk pouch. And then there was the sandalwood box with a Kali yantra carved on its lid and a vibrator inside. Nivedita reverentially fingered the bright-pink silicone shaft ringed by a collar made of something resembling nonpareils. Were it not for the little bottle of ethyl alcohol also in the box, she might've taken the pink penis for a kitschy, ironic work of art. Nivedita tried pushing the button with the symbolic 0 on it, which morphed into a symbolic 1 as the head began to vibrate. She pushed the button again, and the studded collar began a clockwise rotation. On the other side of the sheetrock wall, Saraswati—or was it Toni?—moaned, and before Nivedita could make a conscious decision, she found herself disinfecting the sex toy with a tissue soaked in alcohol, thinking about how it must be eco-friendly, fair trade silicone presumably produced by a woman-owned small business with an eye for high design. The scent of the swiftly evaporating alcohol intensified the feeling she'd done something extraordinary—and extraordinarily forbidden. Normally she needed a sexual fantasy with at least minimal plot and action, but the idea of plunging Saraswati's schlong deep inside—without Saraswati's consent, sure, but she'd worry about that later—turned her on. While Saraswati and Toni went at it in the room next door, and she listened, she became so aroused she was afraid she'd come without warning. She hastily looked for something, anything to delay her orgasm, and the image of Simon and Marina appeared in her mind's eye, even though she had no idea what Marina looked like, or whether Marina and Simon were even . . . had even . . . but that didn't help damper her excitement in the least. To the contrary, it filled her with a pressing, painful degree of lust, exactly like what she'd felt back when she found out about Yannik and Priti . . .

Priti was already home by the time Nivedita returned from Yannik's. For some obscure reason Nivedita never figured out, her cousin had pulled half her hair into an updo but had left the rest, so her head itself resembled a hairbrush that had suffered a stroke.

"That's how I feel, too," Priti concurred. Nivedita regretted that their secret bond of friendship and family ties was about to come undone forever, and it overcame her like a tidal wave, robbing her of breath for several seconds.

On their way to his place shortly thereafter, they stormed right past Yannik's mother and pounded on the closed door of his bedroom.

"I just can't choose between the two of you," he said by way of greeting, grinning as he looked at one, then the other, and back again, as if he'd just said something unbelievably clever. "It must be my karma."

"Nuh-uh," said Stroke-Stricken Half-Hairbrush, flashing a smile that vanished a millisecond later. "I'd say *this* is your *coma*," and without further ado kicked him good and hard in the balls.

For a moment Nivedita couldn't be sure whether Priti had actually done it, or if she'd just projected her own perverse desire onto the situation. A split second later, she grabbed Priti's hand and yanked her out of Yannik's room, down the carpeted stairs, and they burst into laughter before they even got out the door and slammed it behind them forever. They felt like they were suffocating, but in reverse.

That had been the most heroic memory of Nivedita's entire life until the day she went to see Saraswati during office hours and recounted the entire episode.

"Just imagine if the tables had been turned. Imagine you'd secretly been seeing two guys, and at some point they both caught on. How would you have felt if they'd come straight over and clobbered you?"

"But it's different," Nivedita said, irritated that Saraswati wasn't seeing what an exception this situation was for her.

"Is it, really?"

And, as always when Saraswati corrected her, all of a sudden Nivedita was no longer sure. But one thing she *was* sure of was that it really meant something that Priti had chosen her. Sure, it wasn't so heroic when you considered that, a mere two days later, Priti was set to fly back to Birmingham, and Nivedita's relationship with Yannik was effectively nipped in the bud. But Nivedita would've broken up with him sooner or later, whereas Priti would always be her cousin, and the fact that both of them had chosen their own friendship over their sexual competition for a guy had to count for something.

And, at that very moment—in Saraswati's guest room, with Saraswati's vibrator—Nivedita had the most intense orgasm she'd had in months.

3

Nivedita woke up to the smell of burnt toast. It was the first time she'd slept through the night since #Saraswatigate. She felt almost dizzyingly optimistic and reflexively reached for her phone.

Still no calls from Simon, Kali burst her bubble. And, as usual, Kali was right. Instead, Priti had sent a flurry of increasingly panicky texts from Oluchi's apartment on Höhen Straße. *Being your cousin makes me a persona non grata here.* And, *I can't stay with Oluchi, no no no.* Then, finally, and most cryptically, the emojis *storm clouds* and *a pint of beer.*

And then there was voice mail—a nice sophisticated touch—from an unknown number.

"Hi Identitti, my name is Steffi Lohaus and I'm from the editorial team of *10 nach 8*, published through *ZEIT* online. I've been a big fan of your blog for a long time now, and was wondering whether you'd like to write a piece for us. Theme: 'Saraswati and Me.' Please give me a call . . ."

The sweet scent of charred bread trapped in the toaster and sending out smoke signals in hopes of being freed from its cage transported Nivedita back in time. She pictured Simon's kitchen, where, perhaps at this very moment, he might be performing an almost identical ritual—scraping black crumbs off his burnt toast, leaving a trail of fine dust on top of his garbage can, until he paused and poured half-and-half into his tea. In retrospect, Nivedita realized how that garbage can, plain on the outside but divided into multiple sections inside, complete with specific compartments for corks and jar lids, was a total red flag. She'd also always wondered how someone simultaneously more politically engaged than the average citizen and more of a gourmet than the average student—although it's also true he was an unrepentant meat-eater, and had once bought real wild boar salami—could go for dairy that was so eco-unfriendly, totally not organic, and ultra-pasteurized, to boot. He bought it by the truckload, and stacked it on the kitchen shelves with the doors made of chicken wire fence.

"I built that myself," he'd said the first time he had her over for dinner or, more accurately, sex. "Chicken wire is great for building things. If you'd like, I can make you one like that, too."

Nivedita had never even drilled a hole in the wall, and she usually ended up just stacking boxes on top of each other, rather than neatly on her bedroom shelves. Then she'd tie them together with twine to make them more stable—even though they were still wobbly. So, at the time, Simon's handyman skills enchanted her. But somehow he never followed through.

And now, at Saraswati's, Toni was the one happily chowing down on the crispy toast, looking as if she, too, not only knew how to build her own kitchen shelves but would also have no problem actually going through with it if she had promised her girlfriend she would.

"Is that true?" Nivedita asked, pointing at Toni's T-shirt, which proclaimed, *My pronouns haven't even been invented yet.*

"How nice of you to ask," Toni grinned. It seemed like she really did find it nice, and so Nivedita—who liked people who liked her—liked Toni twice as much. "My pronouns are actually pretty banal: she/her/hers. Friends gave me the shirt. But I like to make people unsure, simply," she swept her arms out wide, "because I can."

Asking Toni questions was as easy as it was hard to get answers from Saraswati. So Nivedita went on to pose a question that had been weighing on her since Toni's surprising arrival.

"You must be wondering why I'm here." *You must be wondering whether I'm interested in Saraswati, sexually speaking.*

"Not really," Toni said.

Nivedita was surprised, but Toni's answer surprised her less than her own did.

"To be honest, I myself don't exactly know why."

Toni gave her a super-warm smile.

"You're here because Saraswati wants you here."

Saraswati was busily clicking around on the Internet when Nivedita walked into the living room.

"What are you up to?" Nivedita asked.

"I'm trying to buy back my childhood," Saraswati replied, hastily closing a browser tab. "Not exactly the way it was, of course—I want the designer version."

But Nivedita got the feeling Saraswati had been looking at something else entirely. She'd spotted the word *adoption* in large type, and as far as Nivedita knew, you still couldn't buy kids on Amazon. Or maybe Saraswati's next strategic self-defense move would be to claim she was adopted, so even though Konstantin was legally her brother, he wasn't actually her brother biologically? Surely not even Saraswati could be so crass. *I was adopted* was the intellectually dressed-up version of, *In a previous life, I was Marie Antoinette.* Total BS.

Nivedita looked into Saraswati's glassy eyes—*too much sex, drugs, and ragas?*—and reflexively said, "Is what you said about Obama true?"

"What?"

"That he had a *white* mother?" Nivedita thought that was just a bunch of Trumpist propaganda: *See, everybody? The black guy isn't even really black, he just wants to play the race card.*

"Haven't you googled it yet?" Saraswati tossed back her hair before standing up, and the gesture struck Nivedita as unbearably camp. "What I find even more interesting is that, by US standards, his father wasn't Black enough."

"I thought he was Kenyan?"

"So you *have* googled him!"

Nivedita felt the invisible red of her blushing cheeks begin to rise, and quickly added, "Well, I'd say he's Black enough."

"Indisputably—but what he's missing is the specific experience of being Black in the US."

"Specifically . . . ?"

"Slavery."

"You know slavery's been abolished."

"Of course, but most Black people in the US have at least one enslaved person in their ancestral line—and not very far back, either."

"And Obama?"

"That's the best part of the story!"

"What?" Nivedita asked. She figured that, since none of Obama Sr.'s ancestors had been enslaved, that was the end of the story.

"They subsequently ran some DNA tests on his *white* mother—meaning the autosomal test, you know the difference, right?—and discovered that *she* most likely had an enslaved ancestor in *her* lineage. One John Punch, back in the seventeenth century. That means that, according to American criteria, Barack Obama needs his *white* mother in order to be considered Black because, over there, Black isn't an objective matter—instead, it's a whole social classification system," Saraswati concluded, triumphant.

"Saraswati, why do you always have to spoil all the best stories with your know-it-all attitude?"

"That's precisely why you love me."

Was it? Purely for the sake of disagreement, Nivedita said, "You're starting to sound like the people who say, 'I don't see skin color.'"

"Ah!" Saraswati said—but not *Ah* as in *Ah, you caught me,* but *Ah* as in *A-ha! I found an error in your line of reasoning.* "Quite the opposite! I see skin color so clearly that I can even change it. What I do is . . . *racial drag.*"

Whereupon Nivedita inhaled so sharply, she was afraid the incoming air might slice her right open.

AND, RIGHT ABOUT the same time, the Internet began seeing that parallel in critical light.

» Regula Staempfli @laStaempfli *The Ego has landed #RacialDrag*
» Carolin Amlinger @Camlinger *#saraswati is not making a conscious gesture of solidarity. Nor is she a radical example of #whiteguilt. Instead, she embodies the desperate reaction of the privileged, who've had to forfeit a tiny bit of their power #transracial*

» Soul Seifert @ZerosAndOnes *By claiming that identity is something you can just choose for yourself, she's threatening our hard-won rights. That's the narrative of TERFs and neocons, neoliberal right-wingers. That trans people would just wake up and think, every day: What gender do I feel like being today?*

» Meredith Haaf @MeredithHaaf *Setting aside the question of who or what #saraswati is or isn't, the question remains: what's going on with the political and cultural left if such a deception can basically guarantee success? And isn't it a huge political loss that it's now become virtually impossible to say "us" or refer to any agreed-upon "we"?*

» Female Period @TransAsTransCan *The difference between Saraswati and me is that Saraswati has chosen to be POC and I am a woman. Transwomen are women. #RacialDrag*

"Oh, so it's okay to transcend your gender, but a category as obviously made-up as *race* should be more fixed and inflexible than *sex*?" Saraswati asked Nivedita.

AND THE INTERNET answered:

» Rogers Brubaker @wrbucla *The individual may be understood, in the prevailing language of individual liberalism, as owning her body, but she does not own her ancestry. #transracial #TheTransOfBetween #TheTransOfBeyond*

"What's *that* supposed to mean?" Nivedita asked.

"That your sex and gender don't depend on the sex and gender of your ancestors. Just because all your mothers were women, doesn't mean that you also have to be a woman," said Saraswati.

"But if your mother is *white* . . ." Nivedita said, suddenly getting it. For one fleeting moment she saw the whole situation from Saraswati's point of view, and heard all the cacophonous voices from the Internet through her ears, and everything sounded like one thing: *Essentialism! Please! Where are*

you from, Saraswati? No, where are you from from? No, where are you from
from from?

"Correct!" confirmed Saraswati, adept as she was at tearing her oppo-
nents' worldview to shreds and then diving straight into the gaps. "Except,
your mother is *white*, too."

"You sure about that? Maybe she self-identifies as blue," Nivedita shot
back with a hysterical laugh.

"Like Krishna . . ." Saraswati said in her dreamiest tone, and Nivedita got
serious again. So Saraswati slowly got back to it. "The question isn't, 'So, if all
of us can be anyone or anything, where does that leave us?' Instead, it's,
'Who am *I*? Myself, as an individual. Write *that* down!"

"No," said Nivedita, appalled. "*You* can write it down yourself."

"But you could use it in the article you're writing about me."

"How do you kno . . . Did you . . . my phone?" Nivedita froze.

"Of course not, *mein Schatz*. Nor do I have any idea who's reached out to
you. But I do know it's going to be more than a blog post on Medium."

4

4 DAYS POST-SARASWATI

Since Toni appeared, Nivedita's list of things she hadn't known about her
ex-professor grew exponentially.

Starting, of course, with Saraswati and Toni's relationship (even if Nivedita still couldn't say precisely what kind of relationship it was).

But, to be more precise, the list *actually* had to start with the fact that
Saraswati did yoga.

"But just face yoga, to prevent wrinkles," Toni cheerfully added.

"*Yoga?!*" Nivedita repeated.

"It works," Toni conceded, "especially around the lips."

Nivedita was stunned. She'd always considered Saraswati living proof
that intelligence was enough to make you beautiful—you know, *mens sana*
in corpore sano.

"Why are you so shocked?" Toni laughed, holding her amber-colored glass of beer up to the sun. "After all, it's not like Saraswati's skin turned brown all by itself, either. And I know she had at least one eyelid operation."

"*Operation?!*" Nivedita replied, even more shocked.

"Well, what did you expect?"

In truth, Nivedita had deliberately avoided thinking about how Saraswati's body had been transformed—even as the extent to which her history had been oh-so-craftily crafted was growing increasingly clear. Absurdly, the news that even Saraswati's confident Saraswati-voice was the result of diligent voice lessons hit Nivedita even harder than the more concrete, physical details ("You didn't know that? It's right there, on her official CV, for all to see!"). That fabricated voice and those words had worked their way into Nivedita as deeply as Simon's, giving her such confidence that she almost felt anything was possible, as long as Saraswati verbalized it. But now it seemed this voice was less a force of magic, and more a force of sheer discipline.

And that was the next item on the list of heretofore-unknown things about her professor: much as she loved to invoke free-spirited transgression, she herself followed a frightfully rigid diet. With the occasional exception of some basmati rice, she ate zero carbs and completely avoided sugar. "Her fave two things to read are doorstopper philosophical treatises and diet books." Toni didn't mince words. "Saraswati loooves Dr. Anne Fleck, an anorexic *white* cis chick with an MD, whose books promise to save not only your body, but your psyche, too."

Saraswati, who up until now had been basking in Toni and Nivedita's attention, raised her head and flashed her forbearing Saraswati-smile. Except now that smile enraged Nivedita nearly as much as her mother's martyr-like smile. "You're still too young to relate to such a problem."

"I thought you could never be too young to have a problem," she said, her fury only slightly overblown.

"Obviously, but it's not the same thing, it doesn't *feel* the same. It's like a set of curves that are all in the same family, but not all equal—not every variable parameter results in the same curve."

"Is it just me, or is it getting a bit nerdy?" Toni asked, and then whispered to Nivedita, "She also coats her entire body with Blue Nectar Ayurvedic Slimming and Anti-Cellulite Massage Oil every night."

But no matter how steadily Nivedita's list of surprising Saraswati-facts grew, it still didn't give her any clues as to what had driven Saraswati to become Saraswati.

5 DAYS POST-SARASWATI

Nivedita pushed open the door to the tobacco shop that now doubled as a post office, since so many post offices had closed and so few people bought tobacco anymore. Packages yet to be picked up and packages yet to go out took up most of the room, and the line for post office services seemed as if it were mocking the total lack of customers at the tobacco counter, as if to say: See? Just look—everybody, in every socioeconomic class, wants box-shaped consumer goods, but smoking was a thing of the eighties, and under the new health-care guidelines, who in the underinsured middle class can afford it?

This was the first time Nivedita had set foot outside Saraswati's place in four days, even though there was no logical reason she'd limited her own movement like that. No right-wing mobs were waiting in ambush outside the front door, wielding baseball bats manufactured in foreign sweatshops and blue, biodegradable-in-spite-of-themselves balloons emblazoned with the AfD logo. Not a single crowd of woke students was patrolling the streets of Oberbilk, and nobody was brandishing a loudspeaker, shouting for Saraswati to show herself. Although #transracial was still trending, even on social media there were only a few isolated accounts defending it. Like on Facebook:

> » **Hilal Sezgin** *The opinions I'm seeing tagged #transracial seem to be*
> *seesawing toward a mob mentality, and—people!—I'll totally*
> *understand if you pillory me for this, but I've just got to get it off my chest:*
> *over the last decade we've learned that there are more than two sexes,*
> *and that the presumption of heteronormative secondary sex attributes is*
> *overly restrictive, or can be. We've also argued against racists for*
> *decades, stating that nothing like "race" actually exists, and that all*

people are in some sense related to all other people. And now we're accusing someone—a person who doesn't feel they belong to the exact "race" their family tree would suggest—for opting out of one self-chosen category and opting into another?

» **Abdourahime Bah** *No, I'm not accusing Saraswati because of the category she's chosen within the private sphere. What I'm accusing her of is inventing an identity that she then used for political reasons in the professional, public sphere—that's the part you can't just choose!*

» **Hilal Sezgin replied** *That doesn't strike me as entirely right (or left). Maybe we can concede here that "identity" is just an extremely complex and difficult issue, that identities can change, and that they develop within specific dialogues and social networks. And that when we try to pin people down to one specific identity or way of being, significant suffering ensues.*

» **Anahita Das replied** *That's like yelling "all lives matter" when Black people are killed. Sure, identities can change, but to appropriate an identity, ignore the protestation of members of that very community, and then essentially tell that community "I don't give a damn about your opinion" is NOT anti-racist.*

Meanwhile, in the parallel realm of the Twitterverse:

» **Ruprecht Polenz @polenz_r** *This is just like @Bild's reaction to Günter Wallraff back in the day. The people who've been unmasked get all hot and bothered about the masks and the people who fell for them instead of dealing with their own behaviors and actions. #stopdiscriminating*

» **Mary quite contrary @MaryaDiallo** *Saraswati can choose whatever skin color floats her boat. Those of us born into brown and black bodies cannot. We can't just up and peel our own skin off even if we wanted to. #Saraswatigate #racism*

» **Justin E. H. Smith @jehsmith** *Since when is there a moral duty to remain faithful to the accidents of your birth and to accurately report your*

vital-statistical information to the whole world? I don't give two shits
what my ancestors say about who I "really" am. We all have a right to
reinvent ourselves.

» Lars Weisbrod @larsweisbrod *Can't we please discuss money and*
economic theory instead?

» Call me Zadie @OutsideSisters *What about whiteness as commodity?*
What Saraswati's up to is racial capitalism: being POC as product.
#transracialIsNotAThing

» Ralph Tharayil @RalphTJames1 *i was a kid in the 90s. that was the era*
when x. naidoo and s. setlur and i myself all sold ourselves as black.
while f. mercury always did so as white. now i'm older and #saraswati is
#sarahvera—where does that come from? that comes from here.
#whereIendandYoubegin

» The Real Ibram X. Kendi @therealIbramXKendi* *Our world is suffering*
from metastatic cancer. Stage 4. Racism has spread to nearly every part
of the body politic; spurring mass shootings, arms races, and
demagogues who polarize nations, shutting down essential organs
of democracy.

» René Aguigah @aguigah *#Racism is a relationship power dynamic*
(not a delusion, not a virus, not a cancer).

» Sarah Fartuun Heinze @sa_fa_he *#Saraswatigate indeed: racism,*
transphobia, people wielding their privilege and dropping hefty
#decolonize-discourse . . . what a heady cocktail. To be honest, I've
kinda lost track at this point. And I'm kinda dizzy. Here, there,
and everywhere . . .

In the line for packages at this Kinder Surprise version of a post office, complete with teensy play stamps, Nivedita thought back to the expression on
Saraswati's face as she slapped her laptop shut before Nivedita had a
chance to read the remaining 136 tweets—or was it 631? Who knows? Every
moment that passed, more popped up. "Okay, solely to preserve our sanity,
we need to make a decision. Do we want to get sucked into the maelstrom of
anger, or limit our time online?"

Nivedita, who hadn't assumed that was an actual question, nodded and Saraswati rewarded her with a surprisingly wistful smile. "The real racenauts—like astronauts rocketing toward our future understanding of *race*—are people like you, Nivedita."

"Like me?" For a moment Nivedita thought her fear of transgression, like Saraswati's passing, were the same as the fear tied to her earliest memories of when she'd become conscious of her parents' biracial marriage. That fear had led people to find their union strange, to ridicule it, and try to hinder it even though it was already a done deal—with the subsequent, pernicious side effect that that also meant wanting to hinder *Nivedita herself* even though *she* already existed. At some point it became clear to her that the people who said her parents had made the most original mixture ever when they mingled their own ostensibly separate and pure races to produce Nivedita were actually saying it was the mere act of mixing, in and of itself, that they found original—meaning *unusual* . . . meaning *abnormal*. They'd have said exactly the same thing about any other mixture that wasn't as *white/white* as English+German or Swedish+Dutch or Magdeburg+Hamm. Also because then it wouldn't be called a *mixture*, it'd be called a *combo*, and would therefore immediately sound less radical. Combinations complete one another without giving up their individual properties; mixtures, on the other hand, undergo a fundamental change of character: there was no longer yellow *and* blue, they became green. And when you mix long enough, at some point, everything becomes brown.

BACK IN SARASWATI'S seminars Nivedita had learned that, in order to prevent such colorful mixtures from proliferating at the end of the nineteenth century, the German Reich had sent hundreds of German girls off to its colonies, to ensure the colonizing German men also had suitable sex partners and, above all, suitable offspring. "Suitable" = *white*. But, foolishly, the German men lusted after and loved and married Brown and Black women anyway, in such great numbers that in 1912 a *Mischendebatte* arose: the debate surrounding this mixing came home to the Reichstag, even though by that point such "mixing" had been illegal for over a decade already.

"Eurocentric knowledge obtained through violence is the foundation of all our institutions, including universities," Saraswati had proclaimed in one session. "So, what are you all doing here?"

"What are *you* doing here?" Priti shot back.

"*Excellent* answer!" Saraswati enthused.

Up in her penthouse, the crown jewel of Oberbilk, Saraswati repeated her earlier phrase. "The real racenauts are people like you, Nivedita. People like . . . ," and she didn't say *me*, she just briefly held her breath, "like *you all* can only realize your full potential if you're aware of that. That's why *I* went to university."

And with that, in a certain way, Nivedita became something she'd always dreamed of: Saraswati's intellectual offspring, a spiritual daughter of sorts. Consequently, Nivedita's relationship to Saraswati became—what else?—a ballad, set to the rhythm of Goethe's "Erlkönig." *Who rides there so fast through the night dark and drear? The mother it is, with her child so dear* . . . then something about *tightly clasp'd in her arm . . . safe . . . warm.* Except, of course, you'd have to overlook the fact that, by the end of the ballad, the child was dead.

"Did you know the term *transracial* is even older than *transgender*?" Nivedita heard Saraswati's voice as if from far off, like wind rustling through dry leaves.

"I didn't, but I'm sure you'll explain it to me ASAP."

Saraswati seemed to lose a bit of her glow, and Nivedita wondered whether that dig had hurt her more than anticipated. She wondered whether maybe, just maybe, all of it—the whole situation—was worse for Saraswati than it was for her. "The term *transracial* comes from the world of adoption, when kids are adopted . . ." Saraswati shrouded herself in her dupatta as if it were a feather boa made of fog instead of feathers, "from other countries . . . *visibly* other countries. Which sensitized us to the idea that such adoptions could be . . . problematic."

At that very moment, Toni walked in and tossed a small stack of attempted-delivery slips onto the coffee table. "Poor li'l part-time, full-time-asshole mail carriers! We've been home this entire time! Apparently they aren't paid enough to even ring . . ."

So now Nivedita was in line waiting for the POC employee—who was not only younger than her, but also super chatty with every single customer—to find Saraswati's not-quite-attempted deliveries in the mountain of incoming and outgoing packages stacked up next to the newspaper display. In contrast, her utterly indifferent elder coworker stood behind the tobacco counter as if he were just waiting for the ghosts of all smokers past, from the dawn of time until the present day, to bust down the door. And then, suddenly, a deep flash of sunflower yellow shone through the shop window, looking a whole lot like one of the wax-print turbans Oluchi loved to wear. Nivedita instinctively ducked behind the greeting card display rack, so she could get a better look across the street without being seen. It actually, absolutely was Oluchi— staring straight up at Saraswati's place. In any other situation, Nivedita would've run out and asked her what she was doing there—but, then again, the very nature of the current situation was that it decidedly *was not* any other situation.

"Found 'em!" the cheerful mail attendant finally called out, scanning Nivedita's pickup authorization form and every single parcel as the scan gun beeped the all-clear. Across the street, Oluchi still hadn't moved an inch. Nivedita decided it would be cowardly not to talk to her, and walked out the door with conviction. That very moment, Oluchi turned around and disappeared into the crowd of passersby. Nivedita was certain she'd been spotted.

Oluchi and Nivedita had been Saraswati's star students from the very start. And that didn't change two years later when Priti joined the class—her inability to idolize anyone but herself made her ineligible to join the closest ranks of Saraswati's inner circle. Their shared, illustrious insider status forged a particularly tight bond between Nivedita and Oluchi. In the heat of the first few semesters, they even used code names for one another: Nivedita called Oluchi *Zadie* (as in Smith), and Oluchi called Nivedita *Mahasweta* (as in Devi). So they took it as a sign when they discovered that their mothers not only had the same job titles—both were social workers, toiling away deep in the boiler room of human history—but even the same name. Well, almost, since

Oluchi's mother was named Brigitte. And what could tear such outrageously tight ties asunder?

The answer to that vexing question was S-I-M-O-N, although they didn't dare say so in any direct way. When he waltzed into Nivedita's life that third semester, everything changed. Nivedita knew she'd eventually need to talk to Oluchi about the widening chasm of weirdness between the two of them, but she also knew she'd much rather punch herself in the face. Keeping her mouth shut, however, would mean giving up the secret-society-type bond of friendship she'd established with the most spectacular women in her entire life aside from Priti—and aside from Saraswati, of course, although she was obviously in a class by herself.

So one day, after the class lecture on Amartya Sen's capability approach, she asked Oluchi if she'd like to get another coffee at the Ex Libris.

"I can't, I've gotta go straight to . . ." Oluchi didn't say where she had to rush off to, probably because she herself didn't know.

"No worries, in that case, let me walk to the train station with you."

Oluchi scrutinized Nivedita though her yellow-rimmed glasses, then gave in.

"Sure, let's go."

Nivedita hurried alongside Oluchi, down an endless hallway that felt like some kind of allegory—one closed door after another, ad infinitum—and was seriously considering letting the whole thing slide until she felt a sharp jab. Kali's finger dug into her ribs.

Don't chicken out now!

Why not? Obviously Oluchi doesn't give a shit about me, Nivedita spat back.

Obviously she does, otherwise she wouldn't be running away so fast!

Nivedita found that pretty convincing, so she finally spoke up.

"Hey—Oluchi?"

"Yeah?"

"I'm in a bit of a bind."

"Oh really?" Oluchi's tone wasn't exactly inviting.

Nivedita had rehearsed the rest of the conversation so many times with Kali that she now saw her cue.

"Yeah, really. I'm kinda falling in love with Simon, but before that happens, I need to know if . . . if that's okay with you."

Oluchi turned around, looking not surprised, as Nivedita half expected, but furious. "You seriously think that I'd still be grieving, pining away for that . . . that . . . pale imitation of a human being?"

Pale imitation of a human being? "I didn't mean *grieving* or *pining*," Nivedita wavered. "But maybe . . ."

"Maybe *what*?" Oluchi pressed.

"I thought maybe . . . maybe you weren't finished with him, er, over . . ." Nivedita clumsily concluded.

"I *am totally over* him! And I'd suggest you . . ."

But then Oluchi just stormed off, and Nivedita stood there as the undelivered suggestion dissipated into thin air.

Nivedita didn't see Oluchi until a week later, back in Saraswati's class, where she was unusually quiet. Saraswati, on the other hand, was in high spirits.

"SEX! And now that I have your attention, I'd like to talk about identity—or, better yet, identities." There was a loud groan from the back row. She continued, "About *sexual* identities. But wait, there's more! Because, in the case of India, that's a tall order. Not because we supposedly didn't have any sex beyond the missionary position. Quite the contrary: there are even prehistoric cave paintings in India depicting women having oral sex with one another. But what we in the Western world consider sexual identities—homosexuality, heterosexuality, bisexuality, and so on and so forth—for many centuries, didn't have specific names in India. The parallel with Michel Foucault's discourse analysis regarding homosexuality springs to mind. He refers to the 'birth' of homosexuality in the nineteenth century—when people who'd previously done and loved countless things in countless ways, including what was termed the 'crime of sodomy,' suddenly became 'homosexuals,' meaning people whose singular nature led them to sleep with people of the same sex. More specifically, he mentions eighteen-seventy, when the term *homosexual* first officially came into use. In India, there was no such specific turning point. In the religious, literary, and performative history of India, desire was described solely as *that which lay outside one's control.* The *Kamasutra* insists that passions know no order or ranking."

"But what's up with homosexuality?" asked a new student who might as well have had the word *straight* tattooed on his forehead.

"Yes, what *is* up with homosexuality?" Saraswati asked back, pinning him down with her strongest Kaa stare.

Seriously? You really have to bring that shifty snake from The Jungle Book *up again?* Kali asked Nivedita.

Hey, it isn't my fault I grew up with so few Indian points of reference, Nivedita said in self-defense.

Meanwhile, Mr. Eurocentrism continued to writhe under Saraswati's gaze and, as expected, couldn't manage to wrest his way out. "But homosexuality is strictly forbidden in India . . . because Hinduism . . . ," he stammered, as she beamed with satisfaction.

"*Was.*"

"What?"

"Same-sex marriage was legalized in India in twenty-eighteen, the same year as it was in Germany. Any more questions?"

But the new guy was so pitifully shaken by this that he couldn't stop, and just kept digging himself an even deeper hole.

"Sure, twenty-eighteen. But . . . before then?"

"You heard correctly!" Saraswati's mood shifted faster than the weather, and suddenly she displayed warmth and interest. "I'm glad you brought this topic up. The legal prohibition of homosexuality, incidentally, was introduced by the Brits—by our old friend Thomas Babington Macaulay, in eighteen-sixty-one. So it didn't stem from some supposedly genuine Indian homophobia, it stemmed from a genuinely British homophobia. Nevertheless, we do of course share responsibility for the fact that it took us until twenty-eighteen to expunge that from the penal code."

The new kid was so relieved by Saraswati's apparent praise that he didn't even realize he was speaking his thoughts out loud: "But it's really Islam, above all, that's the homophobic religion . . ."

"Oh really? In all the other so-called Oriental countries, the situation was basically the same, insofar as any laws restricting homosexuality were instituted by the colonial administrations. But, certainly, there are statements condemning homosexuality throughout the Quran," Saraswati conceded. "That said, throughout the entire Ottoman Empire—which lasted over five hundred years—*not a single person* was convicted for consensual homosexual acts. People were convicted for *raping* men, but not for *loving*."

Throughout the entire class Nivedita had tried to make eye contact with Oluchi, but she didn't even seem to be listening to Saraswati. So Nivedita was all the more surprised when Oluchi tapped her on the shoulder as they left the lecture hall.

"Listen up, Mahasweta."

"Yeah?"

"I think I might not have made myself clear last time."

You can say that again!

"I have nothing against you and Simon . . . I mean, I don't have anything against it because *I* . . . with him . . . what I mean is, I'm against it because *you* . . ."

Oh yeah, that's way clearer.

"I," Oluchi tried again, "just want to warn you."

"Warn me?" Nivedita echoed, taken aback. "About what?"

Oluchi shrugged her shoulders, which seemed weighed down by something. "Simon isn't . . . safe."

Nivedita, who knew Simon had never really loved Oluchi, looked at her with a compassion bordering on pity. "Thanks for . . . the heads-up."

Oluchi reeled backward as if Nivedita had punched her. "Forget it!"

"No, really, I appreciate it."

"Forget I ever said anything!" Oluchi nearly shouted.

"Wait!" Nivedita desperately called after her.

But Oluchi had already run halfway down the hall before turning around one last time. "I wasn't even in love with him!"

"You weren't?" Nivedita's surprise was audible.

"And still, when I was with him, I felt *so small*—like I'd shrunk to under two centimeters tall."

But at this moment Nivedita felt like she was over two meters tall, if only because Simon had chosen her over a superheroine like Oluchi.

So she wasn't surprised when, six months later, Oluchi and Priti decided to direct and produce a feminist porn flick—and decided not to invite Nivedita along for the ride. Curiously enough, Lotte, who'd never even enjoyed recounting any of her own amusing sexual exploits, was invited. Their working title: *Kinky Tantra*.

She wasn't surprised, but she still felt excluded every time Priti updated her on their latest script-related research: "Did you know that the Koovagam Festival started in the third century *before the common era*?"

"Yeah." Nivedita had actually never heard of it until then, and doubted Priti had known about it much longer. The next words out of Priti's mouth confirmed her suspicion, since—as she discovered while reading up on it a mere ninety minutes later—they were basically a summary of the Wikipedia entry: "It's a celebration of the wedding of Krishna and Aravan (aka Iravan), for which Krishna became a woman—he transitioned, baby! That's why it's the most important trans festival in India. *Und* what we want to do *ist* a kind of Koovagam *für Deutschland*."

"I thought you were making a porn film . . ."

"*In* the porn, stupid—as a frame, within which we'll present many different kinds of desire."

Nivedita was impressed, hurt, and therefore silent.

"We're not just the better Germans," Priti said in her über-thick British-German *akzent*, tilting a thermos-top cup on which she'd scrawled *White Tears* in permanent marker, "we're also the sexier Germans."

Saraswati, running ten minutes late to her own class as usual, gestured to Priti's cup.

"What's that?"

"White tears," Priti proudly declared, "I'm drinking *white* . . ."

"I know what it says—I can read, after all." Saraswati retorted. "But do *you* know what it says? No dehumanization, of any sort, is allowed in my class—got it? I will not tolerate anyone dehumanizing any of you, nor will I tolerate any of you . . ." then came a pause, which in retrospect Nivedita realized was extremely significant, "dehumanizing *white* people. *White* people are not the enemy, they simply occupy a different position in the network of power and disempowerment that we call racism. You, too, might find it difficult to be humane if you had to be *white*."

"Am I supposed to cry about *white people* now?" Priti decried, just to hide her embarrassment.

"Maybe it would do the world some good if all of us had a little more empathy for one another," Saraswati said. Then she smiled her special Saraswati-smile, showering Priti in the golden sunlight of all Asia. "Of course you don't need to cry about *white* people. You have every right to your anger. It's just that anger doesn't do any good. Hatred can't change a thing. That's why, next semester, I'm going to offer a seminar in Whiteness Studies. What do people have to give up in order to become *white*?"

"To become?" Priti was skeptical.

"*White* is not a concrete condition, just as Black isn't. Race must be manufactured. It's performative: *doing* race. So, how is *whiteness* manufactured, what does *being white* entail? What is *white* socialization? How is *whiteness* prepared and polished?" And then Saraswati couldn't resist the temptation of giving them a little lecture about her conceptual teaching principles. "Cherry-picking the most pigheaded opinions of the opposing side and then making fun of them is the easiest thing in the world. And it's even easier when you take them out of context. What I demand of you all is that you not only understand the other side's line of reasoning—that, too!—but, much more importantly, that you also understand the underlying motivations that led them to those views. And by that I don't mean you need to try and read their minds, nor do I mean to imply they always have bad intentions. What I want is for you to find out—*really* find out—what brings people to hold convictions that are diametrically opposed to your own convictions. You don't need to share those convictions afterward. But I really believe that you'll have earned the right to *not* share those convictions only *after* you've tried this, instead of just unthinkingly rejecting them. Only that degree of understanding will make it possible for you to speak to the other person in a new way. Indeed, it will even make it possible for you to speak *with* them, rather than just talk *about* them. Yes, Priti?"

Priti, who up until that moment had been anxiously drumming her fingers on her desk, suddenly stopped—and then spent the rest of the class so wide-eyed that everyone could see the white surrounding her pupils and irises.

"But, sorry, everything you're saying is precisely what James Baldwin means when he talks about the language of oppression," she sighed, then held up Baldwin's essay "Stranger in the Village," and read aloud: "In so far as I reacted at all, I reacted by trying to be pleasant—it being a great part of the American Negro's education (long before he goes to school) that he must make people 'like' him. This smile-and-the-world-smiles-with-you routine worked about as well in this situation as it had in the situation for which it was designated, which is to say that it did not work at all." And with that, Priti raised her fist in the Black Power salute.

6 DAYS POST-SARASWATI

That's why it was a breathtakingly audacious and breathtakingly aggressive move for Priti to suddenly pop up at Saraswati's door and proclaim, "I'm here to request asylum."

THE LOCATION OF CULTURE

NIVEDITA'S CLASS NOTES:

"Knowledge never was, and never will be, an innocent endeavor, but was, and is, utterly sullied."—Aziz Al-Azmeh

"Where there is power, there is resistance."—Michel Foucault

"Where there is resistance, there is power."—Nikita Dhawan

1

"Come again?" Nivedita snorted. "*Asylum*?"

"You took the words right out of my mouth, *Schatzi*," Saraswati said as she eyed Priti, who was standing halfway down the top flight of stairs. Her expression was a combination of Desperado and Please-don't-hit-me as she sought in vain to hide her hope-filled backpack behind her bare, brown legs. It was the selfsame backpack she'd been sitting on at the end of the street the year before, when she'd shown up at Nivedita's. But, in Saraswati's case, simply showing up at the door wasn't enough.

"You have exactly thirty seconds to give me a good reason why I should even listen to you before I shut the door."

Priti answered with such velocity that each semi-utterance took on a life of its own, sweeping the next one along with it. "I'm serious . . . I'm . . . I've . . . Nivedita! I reminded Oluchi that you're my cousin . . . and that she shouldn't treat you . . . or talk about you like that . . . in these circumstances . . . *Ich* . . . I just can't stay under the same roof as her . . ."

"Okay—*auf Wiedersehen*!" Saraswati said, slamming the door.

Nivedita stared at the front door to Saraswati's apartment and could've sworn she could still see Priti's silhouette partway down the stairs, the perspective making her look a little hunched, as if she were a paper cut-out casting a shadow on Nivedita's retina. But Priti had already sprinted up the last few steps, and was holding her finger on the doorbell until Saraswati finally opened the door again.

"All right! I'm here to say I'm sorry!"

"Fine," Saraswati said, deciding to be gracious about it.

"Sorry for what?" Toni asked.

"It's a long story," Nivedita said.

"That's my favorite kind of story," Toni replied.

"As you can see, Priti, you have an audience waiting with bated breath, hanging on your every word. So, go on—let's hear it," Saraswati nudged her. Nivedita wondered whether Saraswati was aware of the role Priti had played, with Konstantin, in publicly exposing her. But then she realized she herself wasn't fully aware of what had actually gone down. She had a whole knotted-up mess of theories, but she'd only gleaned them from the muddled hints Priti had dropped here and there.

"*Ich war es*!" Priti stepped forward as if she were about to dive off a twenty-five-foot-high platform and wasn't sure the pool below was deep enough. "It was me. I'm the one who . . . found the photos in your office . . . and stole them."

"Oh really?" Saraswati's skepticism sharpened her tone. "Tell me something I don't already know."

"But he told me he only wanted them in order to . . . to *help* you," Priti sobbed.

"Who's *he*?" Toni interrupted.

"Konstantin," Saraswati replied impatiently.

"Is this guy Konstantin really your brother?" Nivedita couldn't hold back this last, absurd hope.

"That's an intensely philosophical question," Saraswati said, "but if you're asking whether he's my brother, *legally* speaking—well then, yes."

"Oh," said Nivedita, hurt.

"He swore he just wanted to help you," Priti repeated, turning to Saraswati. Nivedita saw that she actually had tears in her eyes.

"Undoubtedly," Saraswati said dryly.

"And you *believed* him?" Nivedita yelled, uncertain who the brunt of her anger was aimed at—Saraswati's brother, who she pictured being like some Bond movie Bad Guy, or Undercover Agent Priti, or Saraswati/Sarah Vera.

"Oh, you'd better believe Konstantin when he says stuff like that," Saraswati cut in. "Stan always just wants what's best, for you and from you. I just don't know if I want to give him my best."

"So, is she coming in, or what?" Toni asked.

"Good question—Nivedita!" Saraswati commanded, and Nivedita followed her into the kitchen as Toni draped an arm over Priti's shoulder—it was less a friendly gesture, and more like she was unfurling the long arm of the law—and led her into the living room.

"SHE DOESN'T REALLY mean to apologize, she just doesn't want anything bad to happen to her," Nivedita grumbled as Saraswati, on autopilot, turned on the kettle and took a few cups down from the galvanized-steel rack that looked like one of Duchamp's readymades.

"So that's how you see it? It's all just so exciting over here, all fun and games, that's what you two think? You came to watch *The Rise and Fall of Saraswati T.*?" Saraswati said, exasperated, as she slammed the cups down on the counter.

"Yeah, it's exciting," Nivedita snapped back, "I'd even go so far as to say it's alarming as hell. Because it's not like this only affects your life, it totally affects mine, too!" Apparently it didn't matter who she was mad at, as long as she could dump her anger onto somebody.

Saraswati's eyes flickered, and her next words were a surprise.

"You want to share your bed with her?"

"Under no circumstances," Nivedita confessed.

"Okay, then I'll send her back to Oluchi's."

"That's not what I meant!" Nivedita was shocked. "What I meant was: I don't *want* to share my bed with Priti, but of course I *will* if necessary."

"Yeah," Saraswati smirked, "I figured you'd say that."

"The more interesting question is why *you're* letting her stay," Toni said, pulling the kitchen door closed behind her. "What are you plotting, hmm?"

Saraswati kissed Toni on the mouth, and Nivedita tried not to watch, but couldn't help it.

"I'll never understand why you always presume I have some kind of ulterior motive. Okay, Nivedita, go tell Priti she can stay. *For the time being.*"

Nivedita nodded.

"Oh, one more thing."

"Yeah?"

"Let her sweat it out for a bit!"

WHEN NIVEDITA WALKED back into the living room, Kali was sitting cross-legged on the back of the sofa, her sweet, deep voice singing:

> *What grows in the dark*
> *And what grows in the light*
> *What gets eaten*
> *And what's left behind*
> *What binds us in friendship*
> *And what cuts us like wire*
> *What's meant for healing*
> *And what sparks desire?*

Priti looked at Nivedita, her eyes brimming with trepidation. Kali looked at them both with equal trepidation—but more as if they were some kind of chemistry experiment that might froth up and boil over at any moment. Nivedita knew she could decide Priti's fate with her next few words. For the first time in days, she had power—what's more, she had power over her mercurial cousin, who up until then had always had power over her. But, much to her surprise, this power just felt hollow, dizzying. What if she were to banish Priti? Would her cousin cease to exist, cease to think, cease to feel? No. She'd go on doing all those things, just somewhere where Nivedita couldn't witness it. So Nivedita just shrugged and grouchily said, "It's all right."

Priti was so visibly relieved that the druggy sensation of power resurged through Nivedita's veins. One minute the living room felt hot and sticky, a second later it radiated an inner symmetry, and Nivedita felt certain that, in the end, all her actions would add up into one perfect sum, providing the answer to Saraswati, the universe, and everything.

Priti was radiant as well, but with gratitude. "You're a genius! I could kiss you. I will kiss you. And as a token of thanks, I'll let you in on a secret: tomorrow at eleven a.m."

"Tomorrow at eleven a.m. *what*?"

"Uh, there you have me! I heard that part, but that's all I heard, because that's when Oluchi noticed I was still in the apartment. You can't imagine how tense it was getting . . ."

"She means the protest," Toni interrupted, bringing in a stack of bed linens and towels.

"No, that's no secret, everybody knows about that," said Priti.

"Uh, well, I didn't," Nivedita demurred.

"Well then? Spit it out," Toni said.

"That's what I didn't catch. I only got that it would happen at the protest," Priti said, reaching out to catch one of the towels as if it were a bride's bouquet.

7 DAYS POST-SARASWATI

At breakfast, they rolled breadcrumbs up into little balls (Toni), listlessly prodded their overnight oats (Saraswati and Nivedita), cut an apple into ever-smaller slices (Priti), and waited for what would come next, staring at the clock on the wall, whose perversely slow arms refused to move past 10:26.

The radiant sun of the past week had now given way to a metallic mugginess, and even the air smelled of metal.

"You just don't get it," Toni said, flicking one of her tiny bread balls at Saraswati.

"Oh, and since when do you suddenly 'get' postcolonial theory or have even the slightest interest in it?" Saraswati shot back with an uncharacteristically sharp tone. Normally she took Toni's ribbing as a tribute of sorts—as if she found Toni extra sexy simply because she didn't marvel at her with wide-open eyes and mouth—but today Saraswati's tone signaled that a bit more marveling and a lot less questioning was in order.

But Toni just wasn't cut out for marveling. "Since you're no longer all-knowing and can therefore leave a little space for me amid all your perfect theories, that's when."

Saraswati sighed.

"Now she'll do some breathing exercises to counteract the effects of too much oxygen in her lungs," Toni said, leaning in so close to Nivedita that she could smell her moisturizer, a mixture of sea breeze and coconut with a touch of something synthetic, like sunscreen.

"Really?" Nivedita asked, as dumbfounded as she had been at every other revelation Toni had shared. How could it be that she'd spent three years studying with Saraswati but still hadn't noticed what techniques she deployed for total self-control?

You were just too busy focusing on yourself, Kali observed.

Who asked you? Nivedita demanded.

You did, Kali said. Meanwhile, Saraswati explained.

"When you breathe in too much oxygen, you have less oxygen in your blood. It sounds paradoxical, but it's true. One purpose of breathing is to get rid of carbon dioxide. The deeper we breathe in, the more carbon dioxide is released from our blood. But the level of carbon dioxide in our blood also determines how much oxygen is sent on to our cells. More carbon dioxide, more oxygen. So when we breathe *less*, we have *more* oxygen in our blood. That's known as the Bohr effect. *Capeesh*?"

Priti, who normally would've used the Bohr/bore parallel to crack an off-color joke, instead silently grabbed the bright little bag of turmeric sitting on the table and held on to it like a talisman. She'd spent most of the night sitting up with Nivedita on the super-hygge softwood bed in Saraswati's guest room, chatting into the wee hours.

"ARE YOU IN love with Saraswati's brother?" Nivedita had asked, since that would've explained everything—or at least a few things, or at least would've offered the cliché of an explanation.

To which Priti's response was, "God, *no!*" as she tossed the bed linens aside for emphasis. "He's too . . . just too much like Saraswati for me to feel anything like that."

"Oh really?" Nivedita said, involuntarily intrigued by this absentee brother whose specter hovered over the whole Saraswati-saga like some evil twin—Konstantin Thielmann from Karlsruhe, about whom she knew nothing beyond the fact that he'd betrayed Sarah Vera.

"It'd be impossible for me to lie under such a monster," Priti said emphatically, kicking the bedspread off entirely and extracting one of Saraswati's saris from one of her closet shelves. Nivedita almost chided her, until deciding to do the same, since the night was still too warm to put anything more than thin silk on their bare skin.

"It's surprising, actually, how similar the two of them are," Priti looped back to the crux of it, shaking out both saris and draping them in such a way that they poufed up with air before gently, sensuously drifting down to cover them both. "When they say 'jump,' you jump."

"Did he force you to sleep with him?" Nivedita was alarmed.

"No, *that part* was gorgeous! But Niv, I swear, when he begged me to . . . get . . . those photos in order to help Saraswati, well, it struck me as the most logical thing in the world."

Nivedita wondered—not for the first time—exactly what was in those photos. In this era of "fake news" and "alternative facts," any reputable media outlet had to spend two to ten times as much energy fact-checking and veri-fying such sensational exposé-type stuff, so what could've made these pics so swiftly, indisputably convincing? It must've been more than just the pic-tures Nivedita had found while searching the Internet the previous week—or was it a previous life?

"*Logical*?"

"Well, yeah. The notion that a person who's acting like they belong to another *race* would need help—that's pretty obvious, isn't it?"

And when Priti put it like that, it struck Nivedita as logical, too.

BACK AT THE breakfast table it was still 10:26. Eleven o'clock was incredibly near and at the same time incredibly far off, and then it—what, exactly?—would happen.

"People have always trespassed supposed racial boundaries," Saras-wati said.

"Sure, but not in this direction," Nivedita countered, ignoring the soundtrack to "Soul Man" that started playing in her head. The air's muggi-ness coated her skin like an oil slick.

"In this, that, and every other direction, really," Saraswati said.

"No!" Nivedita insisted against better knowledge. She knew full well, as a rule, that Saraswati had all the facts at her fingertips. Sure, she could twist and bend these facts, but she'd never outright deny them once they'd come to light.

Toni leaned over the table—which was starting to look more and more like da Vinci's *Last Supper,* with Saraswati as both Jesus and Mary Magda-lene simultaneously—and asked, "What's the difference, really, between one direction and any other?"

Priti chewed on her little bits of apple with gusto, so as not to open her mouth and say something that could get her kicked out for good. That left Nivedita as the sole party able to answer.

"The difference is that people have always, perennially passed them-selves off as *white* in order to escape extermination, or to avoid being enslaved, or to get work, or even just to have a better life. The difference is that such people, unlike Saraswati, didn't greedily pretend to be something they weren't merely in order to get some of the few grants and scholarships that we . . . that others worked so hard to earn."

Saraswati let out a laugh like splintering glass.

"Discrimination isn't a limited resource," she said.

"No, but a tenured professorship in postcolonial studies sure as hell is!"

"*Schatzi*, do you seriously believe there would even be a postcolonial studies program in Düsseldorf if it weren't for me?"

Grammatically speaking, Nivedita had to agree: *if it weren't*, subjunctive mood, past tense—Saraswati was subjunctive, Saraswati was past.

"The university wanted me, and they wanted my best sellers, and they wouldn't have had anything against an orchid studies program with a hip name, as long as it guaranteed them the limelight in social and mainstream mass media. But that's just one example—I could've taught porn studies—if I'd wanted to."

"Well, I wouldn't say Düsseldorf University is *that* daring," Toni chimed in.

"Don't underestimate my market value." Now here was something Saraswati would never do. You could count on her to never, ever underestimate her own market value.

Dark, dense clouds gathered outside the kitchen window as if they, too, were just waiting for the clock to strike 11:00 so they could burst. But it was still only 10:26.

Saraswati began clearing the table and putting the leftovers in the fridge. Priti jumped up to help, but was swiftly shooed back to her seat.

"Why aren't you grateful? As a *white* person, it would've been easy for me to just ignore the issues of *race* and racism entirely and just take what I had coming to me. Instead, I chose to exit my comfort zone to find out what it felt like to exist outside what Tupoka Ogette calls the *white* Happyland. If that's not empathy, I don't know what is!" With that, she spread her arms as if she were about to try a cross on for size.

Nivedita sized up Saraswati or Sarah Vera or whoever this person was across from her, and thought about what her father might say about the whole thing. ("What a brave woman, you have no idea how bad racism was back then," or "Why is this German lady wearing a dupatta?") And then it struck her.

"Saraswati! Did you basically just *admit* that you're *white*?!"

And at that very moment, the clock's hands leaped into motion, whipping forward to 11:00.

2

"We . . ." a loudspeaker rasped out from the street below. The amplifier swallowed the rest of the sentence and spit it out as a piercing buzz.

Like the minute hand on the clock, Nivedita had also leaped up and was already out on the terrace, with no idea how she got there. Next to her, Saraswati leaned over the planters still in bloom. Nivedita wondered whether she was about to wave to the protesters down on the street like the queen or like Meghan—the Duchess of Sussex was Nivedita's guilty girl crush, "guilty" only because lefties aren't supposed to display any interest in royals, not even if they're biracial and quit the Firm—but Saraswati had entirely other icons in mind.

"You don't have to agree with me, but you can still love me," she called out, although her words were drowned out by a chorus of whistles from the street below.

"Is she going to start singing 'Don't Cry for Me Argentina'?" Priti whispered.

Nivedita nodded without uttering a word.

"Come out, Saraswati!" Oluchi's voice boomed through the crackling speakers. "Come out and face us!"

And the crowd chanted, "Come out, Saraswati! Come out!"

Saraswati, who seemed to have lost all connection to reality, turned around, her dupatta fluttering.

"Wait!" Nivedita shouted. "It's not like they've come to *speak* with you!"

But Saraswati was already halfway down the hall. She paused in front of the mirror, only to shove her glasses into her hair, ready for battle. "So what? *I* will speak with them!"

"You don't understand! The people down there . . ."

Saraswati paused in the doorway to provide clarification.

"The word 'understand'—*verstehen*—comes from Old High German, and it means 'to place oneself in the place of another, whom one wishes to understand, and to see through his, her, or their eyes.'"

"What's that supposed to mean?" asked Nivedita.

"Nothing," said Saraswati as she sashayed out the door.

Nivedita stood there for a moment as if she'd gone completely numb, and then ran after her.

"**HERE COMES IDENTITTI—AT** Saraswati's side as usual!" the soundwaves of Oluchi's amped-up voice met them as they stepped out the main door and onto the street together. Nivedita automatically took a step back and collided with Priti, who was right behind them.

"See what I mean?" gasped Priti. "Oluchi has completely lost it."

And Nivedita saw what she meant.

Oluchi stood, legs wide, on the back of the pickup truck repurposed as a mobile stage for the massive speakers. Much like Saraswati, she looked fired up by something larger than all their personal differences, larger than the seminar circle, larger than the protest itself, which consisted of a hundred or so extraordinarily good-looking, cool-vibe-emanating people. Nivedita saw more dreadlocks here than at the German Burning Man Fusion Festival, except that here none of them were blond.

"Welcome to Saraswati's cancelation!"

"Oh," said Saraswati in a tone that implied: *so it's come to this—my own students protesting against me, drawing their own raison d'être from the act of denying* me my *raison d'être.* Nivedita marveled at how Saraswati managed to pack so much punch into a mere two letters, one of which was silent. The grim-looking crowd of protesters mirrored the demographics of Saraswati's seminars exactly—70/30 BIPOC/*white* (white students are allowed to return to class after the first semester)—so as she spoke, she employed her best I'm-lecturing-here voice.

"How can you deny me the right to determine my own identity? The right to make decisions about my own life? *You*, of all people! You all know, better than anyone, what the opposite of such freedom feels like!"

Oluchi gripped the mic like a hand grenade and let her words do the detonating.

"This here, for once, is not about you, Saraswati! It's not about *your* decisions! It's not about *your* life! It's about how what *you* do, does something to *us*!"

"Oh really? And what's that?" Saraswati called back in her best I'm-posing-the-questions-here voice.

"Your cosplay makes a mockery of Black people and People of Color!"

"Think about what you just said there, Oluchi."

But Oluchi was well beyond even considering taking Saraswati's suggestions, especially regarding what, when, or how *she* should think.

"It's *our* skin you're misappropriating! *Our* history!"

The crowd grew, filling the sidewalk on the opposite side of the street. It blocked men from bringing their broken phones to any of the many repair shops lining the street, and got in the way of the other guys who just wanted a quick smoke outside the OTB. Only the mothers clad in headscarves with big shopping bags hanging from their strollers were able to weave their way through the crowd with no problem.

Nivedita spotted Enrico, who avoided eye contact with her—out of embarrassment?—and Iqbal, who winked at her from under his thick, dark eyelashes, eyelashes so thick that after all these semesters she still couldn't say what color his eyes were: Amber? Brown? Pantone Artichoke Green with Crayola Glitter Dots Sparkles? But most of the protesters weren't their classmates. They were new people, wearing serious expressions and holding up signs with messages like NO MORE LIES and HANDS OFF OUR LIVES! The signs looked like talismans designed to protect the crowd from Saraswati's evil eye, that Wicked Witch of the West.

"Where's Toni?" Nivedita murmured to Priti, without knowing exactly why. It was obvious that the honking cars now pushing back the groups of protesters who had colonized both lanes of the street would drown out her voice.

"She opted to stay up there and take in the show from her box seat," Priti shouted back at a more appropriate volume. For just the blink of an eye, Nivedita wished she, too, had kept a safe distance between herself and the tragedy now unfolding before them. Then the waves of rage coursing through the crowd like an electrical current swept her up as well, and she directed her fury at Toni the Traitor for not standing at Saraswati's side in solidarity, no matter what she might have done. Did Nivedita really mean that, though? Really, truly *no matter what* Saraswati had done?

"My child, you weren't even aware of the term *Black, Indigenous, People of Color* before coming to my class," Saraswati called over to Oluchi, and Nivedita immediately cursed herself for her misplaced solidarity. The only advantage to Saraswati's pugnacious, suicidal attitude was that it made Oluchi forget about Nivedita's presence, and perhaps even her very existence.

"Unless you've spent your entire life as a BIPOC, you have *no* right to define who *we* are!" Oluchi declared, mouth to mic.

"Race was and has always been unstable, conflicting, and wholly artificial."

"Sure, and maybe all those attributes apply to you, too—whatever! When it comes down to it, you are *not* a Person of Color!"

You could hear the exclamation point at the end of every sentence Oluchi barked, and Nivedita had to wonder whether that was just an effect of the mic and amps. Saraswati, on the other hand, didn't need a mic—she was exclamation personified as she strode out, head held high, and crossed Kölner Straße without paying the slightest attention to the cars honking their horns and screeching to halt all around her. "My God, even in South Africa, people were allowed to file requests for *racial reclassification*. Don't tell me you are even more intolerant than the apartheid regime."

One lone person in the crowd clapped, but was swiftly drowned out by boos and by people yelling, "You'll never know what it feels like to be us!" and "You can't just pick and choose—you can't just take what doesn't belong to you!"

Standing on the other side of the street, separated from the people who actually were her peers, cut off by Kölner Straße—which couldn't seem to decide whether it wanted to be an urban highway or a pedestrian zone and hence was an awkward combination of both—cast the extent of this catastrophe into sharp relief for Nivedita. In real life, she'd have been over there with everyone else, looking skeptically at Saraswati's hideous house, and then she and Oluchi would've sauntered across the parking lot and into Sonnen Park, where they'd have lain on the lawn enjoying a bag of chips while debating race and wrong. Instead, she was stuck in this upside-down world, where Saraswati wasn't Saraswati, and the crowd wasn't protesting alongside her, it was protesting against her. And threatening storm clouds loomed above it all, so stationary that they, too, seemed to be holding their breath.

"Identity is a social relationship, not some private characteristic or individually determined property!" Oluchi shouted as the crackling loudspeakers warped her words into a feedback loop. And suddenly it became clear to Nivedita that the anger Oluchi felt toward Saraswati was completely different from her own. Oluchi's rigor and refusal to compromise resembled Saraswati's life-sustaining delusion much more closely than it did Nivedita's deep lovesickness—she desired nothing more than to undo Saraswati's betrayal.

Meanwhile, in one swift, single bound Saraswati was up on the truck bed next to Oluchi, taking the mic from her (former?) student's hand as if she'd been saving it specially for her soon-to-be-ex-professor. "Yes, and our social relationship is obvious, as far as my identity goes, right, Oluchi?"

Oluchi tore the mic from her hand. "Not *anymore*!"

Whereupon her hot new friend, whose shirt was mustard yellow like Oluchi's glasses, chimed in: "That's right! You're a missionary *white* woman, Saraswati! Just another Karen, nothing more!"

Saraswati looked at him as if spotting a long-lost son down in the crowd. "*Bijan*, long time no see! What've you been up to?" And when he didn't answer, she continued, "If you all, like Bijan here, were or are my students, then you read Grace Halsell's book *Soul Sister* for my intro seminar. She was an investigative journalist who, back in 1968, took hormones to heighten her skin pigmentation, donned a wig, and went to Mississippi to work as a Black maid. Now, it might've pained you to read that book, but why did you read it? Why were you interested in the first place? She only spent *two days* there as a cleaning lady—whereas I *live nonstop* as a POC through and through! And what about musicians like Johnny Otis or Mezz Mezzrow, who described themselves with terms like *voluntary negro* and *ex-white*? How is that okay?"

"Now she wants our privileges, too!" shouted a woman with a perfectly shorn head and Grace Jones–esque profile. She was so lean, her taut skin looked as if it were stretched directly over her muscles—a person reduced to their very essence. Nivedita wondered what it would be like to have sex with her, but then quickly realized she'd only be able to reverentially explore her ultrafit physique with her hands—nothing more—just to see if there were any soft spots.

"A-*ha*! So you *do* have privileges!" Saraswati shouted.

Write it down, Kali whispered.

What? Nivedita asked, taken aback.

What you just thought, Kali replied. *You'll end up on your own blacklist if you don't write it down.*

That's a racist idiom, right? Nivedita wondered. *Why don't we—oh, wait, we do have* whitelist, *but that just makes it worse!*

You can worry about that later, Kali promised.

So Nivedita fished her phone from her skirt pocket and started typing up her initial, less-than-organized thoughts, which she later reworked into a post titled "Might and Melancholy."

IDENTITTI

Leave me alone, I don't need to hear you ramble on and on about your
racist grandma and the latest racist thing she said at your family reunion.

I have no beef with your racist grandma because your racist grandma has no power over me!

The problem with racism is that sentences that begin with "The problem with racism is . . ." are necessarily false.

So let's try this again: *One* of the many problems with racism is that racism disparages and devalues a part of our identity, our heritage, our connections, and relations. As the people directly affected by it, we have two options for how we respond. Spoiler alert: they're both wrong!

1) We can adapt, assimilate, integrate, whitewash ourselves. In which case—and I use that in the clinical sense, as in pathological cases—the best-case scenario is that we become *almost as good* as your Average *White* Joe. In the way I, you, and all of us learned about and internalized it, integration is based on the proverbial *concept of empty-handedness*, which implies that those who need to integrate have nothing to offer in return. They come with endless neediness and nothing else, and as for their roots and everything else that makes them who they are, they just have to give all that up like so many bad habits.

2) We can be proud of our [fill-in-the-blank-with-the-country-of-origin-of-your-non-*white*-parent] identity by casting it in bronze, carving it in marble, smoothing and polishing it until it sparkles like an eternally immutable diamond. But that's precisely what will prevent it from being truly vital, stifling its ability to grow with us and change over time.

We have so much racist knowledge that we can call it up at any time, but we have so little anti-racist knowledge.

But above all we have so little knowledge capable of thinking outside this little white box. In Germany people perpetually act as if all BIPOCs have the same ancestry, as if we all came from the same country, some place called *Foreignland*. Germanistan versus Whoknowswherestan.

But maybe the latter is less of a place than it is a feeling? A state of mind?

Does *diaspora* come from *desperate*?

Saraswati laid her hand over the hand with which Oluchi held the mic, and Oluchi jerked away like the contact had singed her. "Just because there isn't a standard operating procedure for changing one's race yet, just because there are no doctors and judges to give an expert opinion—the way they'd intrusively and paternalistically express their expert opinions if I were transgender—just because there's no entry for race in the birth registry and I can't change data that doesn't exist, just because I can't get a new passport or government-issued ID or any other official categorization, you all are saying that what I did cannot be done. But here I am. I exist, and people like me exist! It isn't my fault there isn't yet any social and organizational infrastructure that exists to name it." For a moment it seemed as if she were winning over the crowd, and even the clouds parted here and there, letting honey-colored rays of sunlight stream down through the milky morning sky. And so she continued. "Haven't you ever asked yourselves why the left has more qualms about opening up the boundary lines of race than those of gender?"

Good question—what's the answer, Saraswati?

"Because you're so very afraid that your hard-won victories in terms of gender and sex and trans and inter and nonbinary rights will be denied if, all of a sudden, other people demand the same rights in terms of race. You're afraid that the conservatives are just lying in wait, itching to jump in and cancel that third gender. They gave you a hand, and now you not only want the whole arm, you also want your true skin color. But you're no different from *them* when you dismiss our demands out of hand—out of fear, really. What you're doing is also boundary work—google it! No, try googling the name Thomas F. Gieryn. To say that the only real trans is transgender is tantamount to trying to separate the sciences from . . . other forms of knowledge acquisition. It's like distinguishing between high and low culture, or between art and craft."

"You really want to insist that you're transracial?" Oluchi asked, disgusted.

"I am *post*racial!" Saraswati replied with maximum dignity.

Oh Kali, sighed Nivedita.

"Skin color has absolutely nothing to do with race, and you all know it!" Saraswati continued. "The Aboriginal people of Australia aren't Black, but they're racialized as Black. The bloody modern age even managed to racialize Jews, so they had to wear specific clothes, be locked up in their own specific neighborhoods, and of course eventually sew yellow stars onto their jackets, because otherwise they wouldn't be recognizable."

"There are Black Jews, too," Bijan chimed in.

"You know what I mean."

And Nivedita knew what Saraswati meant, she just no longer knew what she herself meant.

"What's next—are you going to claim you're Aboriginal, since people can just switch everything up now?" Oluchi's friend in the yellow shirt sneered.

"Don't be silly! That's not what I'm saying. What I'm saying is: I'm a *race traitor*, in the sense of the movement historian Noel Ignatiev called for, as follows . . ." To Nivedita's surprise, Saraswati then pulled out a notebook, from which she read: "*I call upon all whites to cast off the protection their skin affords them, and to renounce their membership in the club of the white race!*" So she had come prepared. "*Treason to whiteness is loyalty to humanity.* See, y'all—I've burned my club card! *The more of us break away, the greater the consequences will be within the system of whiteness.* Shall I continue?"

"Please don't!" groaned Oluchi.

But Saraswati kept talking anyway: "Just like sex, race is something we *do*, not something we *possess*."

"Then why did you have to lie?" asked Oluchi, speaking right into the mic. This time the speakers, for a change, were crystal clear. "If it's all so simple, why couldn't you just do what you did as a *white* ally?" Without all the interference, Nivedita could now hear Oluchi's voice wavering, as if mowing down row after row of people standing between them, and she wondered what was really being dealt with here. "Why—did—you—have—to—LIE?"

"Lying can be one way of telling the truth. Sometimes you need to take the messiness of the world and clear it up a bit, so it can be understood," Saraswati said, almost tenderly.

Off in the distance, the first thunderbolt rumbled. Drops of sunlight fell from the surrounding leaves, forming puddles at Nivedita's feet. For a few fleeting moments she thought: *As soon as you establish an identity, it dissolves; it's impossible to prove something as insubstantial as smoke, as air, as gas—something that can be equally life-giving and lethal.* Then she thought: *Is there a less pathetic way of putting it?* And then, casting a glance at the deeply moved expressions on the faces across the street: *Nope. Apparently, when it comes to identity-based attacks, all nuance is lost, and there is no such thing as overstatement.*

Then Saraswati's clearly enunciated voice came through the loudspeakers, as if she aimed to speak straight to everyone's soul.

"Race is more than you as an individual. It's your history and your ancestors' histories. Race is the flesh and bones you're made of." The speakers crackled. "All that is true and relevant—and at the same time entirely wrong. Race isn't formed through blood and soil, nor is it somehow 'original' or 'authentic.' Race is a system, a way of fitting people into a framework, putting them into categories they're not supposed to be able to step out of. And under no circumstances are they to question the authority of the system itself. I am a race terrorist! I push the purported authenticity of the framework past the point of absurdity. I blow it up, and from its fragments I build a new world in which race is something we can enjoy, something we can play with, something that isn't deterministically set in stone by our supposed destinies."

The crowd was with her up to a point—or at least some of the protesters were—but then the notion of Saraswati as a messiah heralding a *new world* was a bit much.

"Identity isn't a commodity," Bijan roared.

"We're not identity-shopping here!"

And suddenly everybody was booing and shouting again. Nivedita felt the electric current in the air, exerting pressure on her temples. Sooner or later, something would have to give, but it wouldn't be Saraswati.

"Your intolerance is founded upon some supposedly higher moral principle! In fifty years we'll look back on today and wonder what we were so upset about, why we were so nervous about people like me wanting to change categories. Oh, what am I saying—fifty? Not even! In thirty—no—in ten years! What's going on right here and now isn't identity politics, it's identity McCarthyism!"

"No, this here is a reality check, Ex-Saraswati!" countered Oluchi, who seemed, much like her opponent, to have plugged into some invisible force field. "This here is about facts that go above and beyond the individual level. And no matter how hard you deny it, biogenetics *do play* a role, the history of enslavement and disenfranchisement *do play* a roll. Those constitute experiences we can feel, down to the cellular level—and that you *can't*!"

Nivedita looked at Oluchi with a mixture of envy and horror. How often had the two of them discussed how they'd experienced authenticity only as a limitation, as a corset restraining them, dictating what they could *not* do, like: no going out with *white* boys, no going out with brown boys, no going out with Black boys, because a good Indian girl wouldn't do any of that without first introducing the boy to her parents. And of course no sex, either, no matter what gender or skin color the other person might have, lest they themselves be taken for "typical" brown girls.

Nivedita had been raised on terrifying tales of Indian kids who preferred to play the electric guitar instead of the sitar, and who chugged enough Coca-Cola to completely drown out their parents' culture. So she made the great sacrifice of not drinking any cola whatsoever—okay, well, as little as possible—even though she found the taste extraordinary and, secretly, somehow extraordinarily Indian, and even though she'd never really cared about being a good Indian girl. Actually, what she wanted to be was a badass Indian girl, but in her pre-Saraswati years that hadn't really been an option—at least not anywhere outside her most daring dreams, meaning her constant conversations with Kali.

Back on the bed of the pickup truck, Oluchi seemed to have left that behind her. Authenticity was no longer a force used against them—now it became a weapon they could aim at Saraswati. "We could paint ourselves white, and we'd still feel the deprivation of basic human rights in our bones. But you, Ex-Saraswati, were *always* entitled."

Oluchi was unquestionably right about that. Saraswati had always been entitled, Nivedita had never once seen her frightened, intimidated, or unsure of whether she was actually allowed to be where she was, or even allowed *to be*, period—up until her unguarded moments over the last week. But Saraswati's arrogance, her certainty, her conviction that she was better, smarter, and *woker* than everyone else had enveloped Nivedita as well, promising her she, too, could be smarter, better, and happier, at least sometimes. Saraswati's aura made it seem as if people like Nivedita could feel the way she did—*she* being Saraswati herself, not just plain old Nivedita.

The first thundery squalls swept Saraswati's hair upward, fanning it out like the arms of her namesake Indian goddess. "If non-*whiteness* means experiencing discrimination and nothing more, then that also means that you all need to hold on tight to those experiences of discrimination," she declared. "Because only they have the power to define what you are, who you are, what you're made of. Letting go of them would mean letting go of your identity. I, on the other hand, offer you empowerment and self-determination—through both my seminars and my own life example."

"Saraswati, you sound like an American televangelist," Bijan sneered, although he did say "Saraswati" instead of "Ex-Saraswati" like before.

Oluchi scanned the crowd, nodded with gravitas, and then explained: "That is the very definition of white privilege—that a *white* woman tells us what racism is, that a *white* woman talking about racism gets more attention than Black people who talk about racism. That *she*'s invited on TV shows, while all the POC are left out—before, during, and after."

Saraswati let out a menacing laugh. "Do you seriously believe, Oluchi, that you all would get even one second more media coverage if I were never interviewed ever again?"

"Yes, I do! It's about time the voices of real BIPOCs were heard, and the voice of Ex-Saraswati never gets heard again!"

"Silencing me only means that these topics won't be discussed as much. It doesn't mean it'll be your turn. You're making the mistake of thinking that the goal here is to compete for a supposedly limited space within the public sphere. But the real goal is to expand that space, to change it! And above all . . ." Saraswati gave up trying to convince Oluchi, and turned to the crowd of protesters, which had long lost any unanimity it might've had to begin with. She turned to Iqbal, who had laid his sign ("Who betrayed us? Saraswati!") on the ground. She turned to the girl with a bedsheet that still clearly read "Cancel Saraswati!" as she draped the sheet around her shoulders like a dupatta. And went on: "Who gets to decide what POC means? Who are the gatekeepers? And what qualifies them for that role?" Saraswati then inhaled the uncertainty emanating from the crowd as if it were a waft of pheromones, and punctuated those rhetorical questions with an even more rhetorically intended provocation: "Please, come forward!"

A BROWN MAN stepped out of the crowd and walked up to the microphone. Like a gust of wind across a body of water, all heads turned in his direction as he jumped up onto the truck bed. Nivedita hadn't experienced such a pulse-quickening mood swing since the very first revelations about Saraswati had come to light—just a week ago, though it felt like a century. The faces in the crowd, which ranged from uncertain to angry to contemplative to even embarrassed a mere moment before, now shifted, from one second to the next, becoming sharp and resolute. Resolved regarding what, Nivedita couldn't say, because in the meantime her gaze, too—as if hypnotized—was drawn to this man. He was older than most people present, but moved among them with such natural ease that the crowd looked like one big peer group. They were the body, he was their head, and that head now began speaking without needing any mic. "We are all horrified by Saraswati's betrayal," he said in a voice like the warmth following a first sip of whiskey. "Horrified and shocked. *I* am shocked. But let us not condemn her before we've heard her explanation for why she committed this deception in the first place. Believe me, I know what I'm talking about—after all, I am her brother . . ." *Dammit!* thought Nivedita. *Saraswati's brother also brown-washed himself. Not him, too!*

". . . her adopted brother."

"I thought her brother was *white*," Nivedita hissed to Priti.

"Why'd you think *that*?" Priti hissed back.

"But, that picture . . ."

"Huh? What picture?"

Nivedita googled "Saraswati" and "Karlsruhe" and held the screen of her phone in Priti's face. Priti burst out laughing. "*Echt*? You really think I'd do *him*?"

"How should I know?"

"You should know I have better taste than that."

Nivedita glanced back at the stage the pickup truck bed had undeniably morphed into. If this protest had been announced, where were all the usually-so-solicitous police?

"Better taste, as in—him?"

"I *know*, hot, right?" Priti nodded.

"Cultural appropriation means you've stolen something from us," Konstantin elucidated, and Nivedita instinctively nodded. At that very moment, her eyes made contact with his, and he winked at her. She was taken aback at how stunning Saraswati's brother looked. His face was simultaneously tragic and ironic, with large, melancholy eyes that held an unspeakable pain as if it were a secret treasure. His chiseled chin gave him a determined look, and if he ever hit a dry spell with his social work on the streets of Southall, he could always use that chin to advertise high-end Indian craft gin.

"How can I steal something from you that had no value before I came along?" Saraswati inquired, unmoved. She seemed to be the only person there who wasn't in the least surprised by Konstantin's sudden arrival—as if she had been just waiting for him to appear.

Oluchi wiped the back of her hand across her mouth, as if trying to get rid of a bad aftertaste. "That's exactly what Elvis Presley said when he stole the blues!"

"Yes, but unlike Elvis, the people who directly and indirectly benefitted from my," and here Saraswati raised her hands to make emphatic air quotes, "'appropriation' were *you all*. Which makes it less 'appropriation' and more 'appreciation,' less 'acquisition' and more 'recognition,' wouldn't you say, my darlings?"

Nivedita caught her breath. But Konstantin went on, unflappable: "Your deception was in no way 'appreciative recognition'!"

"Well then, you tell me—just what might appreciative recognition look like, in practice?" Saraswati said, as pain enveloped Nivedita's heart.

"No tips for you! We're not your personal three-one-one information service! Go home and just leave us alone, for*ever*!" Oluchi said, bitter yet calm.

Saraswati straightened her already-straight-as-a-board posture and laid her hand on Oluchi's shoulder. "That's what the poet LeRoi Jones said after the Harlem riot of 1964, when he was asked what *whites* could do to help. He just phrased it a little more drastically: *You can help by dying. You are a cancer.* The interviewer continued, somewhat uneasily, and asked about the *white* civil rights activists the Ku Klux Klan had murdered. To which LeRoi Jones replied that those *white* kids merely wanted to assuage their drooling consciences." She then slowly laid her other hand on Konstantin's shoulder. "Ten years later, LeRoi Jones called himself Amiri Baraka, and explained, in an interview with the *New York Times*, that seeing whites as the enemy was a narrow ideology he, too, was guilty of, but had since left behind because it didn't get anyone anywhere. And that's exactly what all this, here, is about: Hate won't get us anywhere! Pitting ourselves against one another, as if *whites* were only *white* for want of character, doesn't get us anywhere."

But Saraswati had underestimated the situation and the crowd. This wasn't just another TV interview, there were no cameras to idolize her and her every observation, this wasn't a lecture or panel discussion where she could just overpower the audience through the sheer force of her magnetic personality.

"No. *You* are the problem," Konstantin said, sounding almost sad. He was about to add a second sentence, but then remained silent, as if choosing not to spoil the devastating elegance of his words with any further remarks.

"Saraswati go home! Saraswati go home!" the crowd began to chant. Even the sky chimed in, exploding with the first real burst of thunder and lightening.

And Saraswati jumped from the stage and went home.

3

When Anish had finally booked himself a flight more than two months after first telling Nivedita his plan, she and Simon drove him to the airport in Frankfurt. It was the first and last time she spent time with both of them together, and she was surprised by how dull the drive was. To the right and left of the highway, the trees' bare branches shivered under the gray November sky. Inside the car, the two most important men in her life had nothing to say to one another.

Before Anish even got through security, Simon disappeared to smoke a cigarette, leaving Nivedita and Anish standing in silence in front of the boarding-pass scanner.

"He seems nice. I'm glad you don't . . ." Anish finally started to say, whereupon Nivedita was overcome by the urge to kick him. Of the thousands of things she still wanted to say to him, only one came to mind.

"I hope you know what you're doing."

For the first time in weeks, he looked at her not with the feverish determination of a man on a mission, but with the vaguely ironic and uncertain expression of the adorable old Anish, and replied, "Of course I don't."

And then he crossed the line, out of the Schengen Area and into the transit area, and had already left the country, even though they could still see one another. Then he whirled around, as if he was about to run back to her, but only made the gesture and left it at that. One last time, Nivedita felt the deep and desperate love she'd always associated with Anish and was just as swiftly overcome with a sense of relief—everything they'd been through was now water under the bridge—and she set out to look for Simon.

On the way back, she asked Simon, "What's the deal with Oluchi?" After the heat of the airport, the car felt somehow cold, which only heightened the feeling that they were in a space shuttle of sorts, zooming through the cosmos—just the two of them, alone, in the boundlessness of infinity.

Simon adjusted the steering wheel with tiny, automatic movements, as if his hands were speaking a secret, wordless language of love with the material world around him. That sparked a feeling of affectionate tenderness in Nivedita, until he answered her question.

"She just couldn't come to terms with the fact that I'm not done yet with Marija."

"What do you mean, you're not done yet with Marija?"

Of course Nivedita knew who Marija was. Marija and Simon had been one of those couples that everybody in the philosophy department knew. They were larger than life, like a billboard ad for their own relationship, up until about a year or so ago when Marija moved to Utrecht to get her master's in clinical psychology. But, since then, Nivedita had only heard Simon mention her in passing, and even then, it was always in the past tense, so this plot twist took her aback. "What do you mean . . ."

"Yeah, I heard you the first time," he cut her off, curt.

"Well then just answer me," she replied, sounding more surprised than irritated.

But that irritated Simon.

"Okay, c'mon—it's not like you and Anish have totally broken up either, you know."

"Uhh, hello!? I just put Anish onto an airplane that's now hurtling away from me at over five hundred miles per hour!"

"Distance has no effect on true bonds."

But since for Nivedita distance had every effect on any bond, she let out a sound that perfectly echoed the noise Tuffi's feet made as he slogged his way out of the muddy Wupper River.

Simon stared straight ahead at the highway. "Are you actually jealous of Marija?"

"Do I have a reason to be jealous?"

Simon didn't answer.

"Well?" Nivedita prodded.

"I'm thinking about it," he replied, audibly miffed.

"Still?" she asked, a full five miles later.

Since they had gotten up at what Birgit would've called "an ungodly hour" in order to get to the airport in Frankfurt on time, it was only early afternoon when they got back to the southern edge of Düsseldorf. But Nivedita felt as if she'd spent days wandering the circles of hell and, just like Dante's, this hell was cold, and each circle got colder. And they were already on the beltway.

"Where should I drop you off?" Simon pierced the frosty silence.

They had planned to cook lunch together, but that was before—and there's no food in hell, so Nivedita just meekly said, "On campus."

But Saraswati wasn't in her office, and even if she had been, what would Nivedita have said to her? And so she ran, distraught, straight across campus—just as she had after Anish dropped his India-bomb on her, only now the temperatures had plummeted, and the school was virtually deserted. Hell, hell everywhere. But then suddenly Saraswati was standing before her, buying her a salad with miso-tahini dressing from the cafeteria.

"Don't you have seminar, like, right about now?" Nivedita sniveled.

"Seminar, schmeminar!" Saraswati replied, steering the plastic tray and Nivedita—after quickly eyeing the room—past the tables packed with students, through the wave of heat emanating from the philosophy department, and out toward the economics building, where a set of large wooden steps doubling as seats overlooked an artificial lake. Saraswati spread her woolen dupatta out on the ice-cold seats and magically pulled a thermos from her bag, plus, even more magically, *two* enamelware cups. "Here, you look like you could use something heartwarming."

Nivedita extracted her balled-up fists from her pockets, grabbed the steaming cup, held it to her chin, and waited for Saraswati to ask her what had happened. Not coincidentally, at that very moment she was asking herself what the hell had just happened.

But Saraswati had other plans. "You see that?" she said, as Nivedita looked across at the trees on the other side of the lake, stretching their naked branches up into the deserted sky.

"No, not the woods—I mean the earth and stones beneath the trees' roots. That is eternal. And you, just like them, live forever."

The wind got caught up in Nivedita's hair and for one wild moment she really did feel immortal. But then the pain caught up with her, and the breeze died down. "Simon can't say whether he's still in love with his ex-girlfriend," she whispered, and then marveled at how easy it was to say that unspeakable sentence out loud.

"Ah, a narcissist," Saraswati nodded.

"Yeah, but at least he knows it. That's why he's also in therapy."

"No, he's in therapy because narcissists love therapy."

Nivedita sipped her tea, but couldn't taste anything beyond a metallic burning in her mouth. And since that first unspeakable sentence was already out, the second came hot on its heels. "What if I never find anyone like him ever again?"

"You're twenty-four. It's highly unlikely that that will have been it for you," Saraswati said, unconcerned.

"But I'm afraid of being alone."

"Are you alone right now?"

"Not *at this moment*, not *here*."

"If you need people to trample your boundaries, sweetie, you can *always* find them, both in *and* outside a committed relationship."

That was easy for Saraswati to say, with her many books and all her students ready to give an arm and a leg for her—at least Nivedita would've gladly given up various limbs and appendages ever since that first day Saraswati had swept into class. Without having planned it, she suddenly posed the question that had been bugging her ever since that very first revolutionary seminar session. "Why didn't you just explicitly say *only for students of color* in the expanded course catalog?"

"What good would that have done? Then no *white* students would've shown up and, ultimately, I wanted you all to feel real Black or Brown privilege, for once."

Saraswati reached out and touched Nivedita's cold cheek with her warm hand, giving it one caress, then another. "You're very beautiful, you know."

You are, too! every fiber of Nivedita's being cried out. *You even more!*

"And anyway, that would've precluded the collective decision-making process. That initial, intense experience of being excluded from the very first seminar teaches many students more in one day than they'll learn in the entire rest of the semester. Including your friend . . ."

"Lotte," Nivedita helped her out. "But she's my roommate, not my fri . . ."

"Schüssler," Saraswati added, surprisingly.

"How do you know Lotte's last name?"

"Because I don't just dump all the students I kick out, of course," Saraswati replied, looking at Nivedita as if she still had a lot to learn—meaning, above all, what a brilliant professor Saraswati was. "There's aftercare."

"After . . . ?"

"Precisely!" Saraswati took a gulp of hot tea, and Nivedita decided she must be fireproof. "After getting kicked out, every single one of them receives an invitation to a one-on-one meeting with me, and most of them accept— like your Lotte. You can't seriously think I'd just dismiss them and leave them alone with such a rejection. That would be unethical."

Wow, Nivedita thought, and so she said, "Wow."

Saraswati tossed her hair back. "I'm just a damned good professor. And a damned overworked one, at that."

Ask her if anyone's ever filed a complaint, Kali suggested before Nivedita melted into a puddle of admiration at Saraswati's feet.

"Has anyone ever filed a complaint?" she asked.

"All the time. Every semester, like clockwork, there's at least one student who escalates their complaint all the way up to the dean. Usually it's some über-woke young guy, griping that I'm running some human experiment with him as the objectified subject. I have a standard answer: that teaching is always a form of human experiment. Especially for the wiseasses who want to sue their way into my seminar on the premise that otherwise they're being denied the right to learn. After all, I offer the same course content in a private, unannounced seminar for *white* students only."

Nivedita tried picturing Charismati Saraswati in that other seminar, and in her head it was a carbon copy of the seminar she'd taken, only it looked like the black-and-white version, instead of full Technicolor. *"When you, as* whites*, are in a room full of* white *people, you're experiencing the absolute height of racialization, but none of you notice it. Why is that?"* said the Saraswati in Nivedita's head, as her dupatta licked at her arm like so many flames. *"How can we talk about racism when the vast majority of you think it has nothing to do with you? How can we talk about racism when you* whites *think you don't even have a race?"*

Lotte was the only part of this scenario Nivedita couldn't imagine. When she tried, all she could picture was an empty chair, a Lotte-shaped hole in the lecture hall. Everything Lotte achieved in life, she achieved from a position of privilege, and when Nivedita performed at the same level, in her mind that meant she was more worthy, because she'd had to work harder for it. Nivedita always had to catch up to the head start Lotte was given through her parents and the household she came from, where she had flute lessons and a subscription to the feminist magazine *EMMA* and an authentic, limited-edition Niki de Saint Phalle centerpiece on the living room table. When Nivedita transposed these reflections onto the real-life Lotte she knew—who'd ditched the flute as soon as possible after giving it the prover-bial good try (as duty dictated, "Once you start something, you have to stick with it for at least a year"), and whose mother had spent years trying every possible treatment for her cancer, both standard Western medicine as well as every thinkable alternative treatment—they seemed utterly absurd. But, on the abstract level, that notion of being more worthy had been the de facto motto of Nivedita's entire life. Which is also why, up until now, she'd only ever really felt jealous of fellow POCs—meaning primarily Priti, first and foremost.

"Why didn't Lotte ever tell me about that?" she finally had to ask.

Saraswati shrugged her well-toned shoulders. "Out of shame, maybe?"

Nivedita tried squaring the concept of shame with the concrete person Lotte, and couldn't swing it. It's not that Lotte had lived a pain-free existence— quite the contrary—it's just that she'd lived an existence free of the things that triggered fear and shame in Nivedita. Like Lotte's ability to not only name all the legendary French film directors (plus Agnès Varda), but to pronounce their names correctly—stuff like that. Of course Lotte had also brought a whole bundle of her own obscure, shame-triggering baggage into their shared apartment. But it was always stuff Nivedita just never understood, like when they were hanging out in the Volksgarten and Lotte had to pee, she wouldn't just duck behind the bushes, she'd leave the park to look for the nearest café. Once, when Barbara suggested they clamber over the fence at Südstrand and sneak a nighttime swim in Unterbacher Lake under cover of darkness, Lotte refused. She sat cross-armed and pouting in Dinah's car—at the time, Dinah and Barbara were an item, and Dinah happened to not only be an editor at a major public broadcasting network, she was also friends with Saraswati— listening to Janelle Monáe for so long that the battery nearly died. Dinah, Barbara, and Nivedita had come back, dripping and all scratched up, but just in time for there to be enough juice left to start the car again.

Lotte was like tightly wound clockwork that always ran at double time. Standing next to her, Nivedita could almost feel the whir and hum of all her hopes, fears, and expectations. Presumably, being Lotte wasn't exactly easy, either. But that didn't stop Nivedita from incredulously saying, "Shame, really?"

"No—I swore her to silence."

The way Saraswati said it, it sounded obvious, like a matter of course: people hold conspiratorial, secret seminars, and the earth beneath the trees lives forever. This time not even Kali tried to dampen Nivedita's admiration, and Saraswati smiled with joy in the cold winter afternoon. "It's not like it's Lotte's fault she's *white*."

Just then, Nivedita felt so light she thought the wind might simply sweep her away, and she'd float off over the brutalist buildings and the whole campus, off over the red roofs of the university hospital, and ever farther north, over to Bilk, where she'd hover over the blue-and-white art nouveau building that housed Simon's little shoebox of an apartment, look down, and finally see how very small and unimportant it was—how meaningless his rejection was in comparison to Saraswati's fundamental acceptance. And then that lofty perspective left Nivedita dizzy.

· · ·

THAT WAS ALREADY a year and a half ago, and the Saraswati who now appeared in the doorway to let Nivedita and Priti back in—they'd followed her at a safe distance as she left the shouting crowd—didn't look like she could overrule the forces of gravity. Actually, for the first time ever, she looked fragile and mortal, not at all like some otherworldly being.

"Hello, Stan," she said, whereupon Nivedita turned around. Konstantin really was just a few steps behind her on the stairs, but it felt like he'd just materialized there.

"Hello, Sarah," he replied.

"Don't call me Sarah."

"Don't call me Stan."

"What should I call you, then?"

"Raji," he said, with the same exact hand gesture Saraswati used when making a particularly clever point in class.

"Raji? *Raji*?" she asked, genuinely appalled.

"*Saraswati*?" he asked, no less appalled.

"Sure, but *Raji*? For real?" And with that she whirled around and disappeared back into her penthouse. Priti followed close behind, so as not to arouse any suspicion that her just-barely-a-fortnight-before romp might mean she was still in the same camp (read: bed) as Konstantin/Raji.

Nivedita had never been any good at reading people's body language, but even she could see he had a battle raging within. Part of him wondered whether he should leave right then and there, doing an about-face to deny Saraswati the satisfaction of seeing him come running after her. The other part thought maybe he should push his way into her holy sanctuary and kick the image of the goddess off its altar. Then he gazed up the stairs and straight into her eyes. From up close, he looked even more like a Bollywood star, albeit not the dashing young lover—instead, he was the not-exactly-young-but-still-dashing lover returning from a long and difficult exile. The first few gray hairs glinted like stars amid his black-as-night curls, and nothing could be funny enough to explain all those laugh lines.

"So, you're Nivedita. Or Identitti, as the Internet would have it. I've been dying to meet you."

"Likewise," she said in all honesty—and honestly surprised by her own reply. He grabbed her hand, and she felt its warmth swiftly seep up her arm.

"Leave Nivedita alone!" Saraswati ordered from the doorway. It seemed both siblings had a knack for materializing out of thin air.

"Oh, right—she is, after all, *your* young lady." Raji grinned, strutting right past both of them and straight into Saraswati's kingdom. From behind, unlike from the front, he didn't seem to be the one holding the reins. Instead, it just looked as if every single muscle under his Nehru jacket was so tense it was on the verge of tearing the fabric. Saraswati took Nivedita's arm and walked after him, although they didn't get far. Raji's wake only carried them up to the door of the living room, where Toni and Priti sat on the yellow corduroy sofa—the former sizing up this new arrival with immense fascination, the latter inspecting her fingernails with equal fascination.

"Priti you know already," Saraswati dryly said. "And this is Toni. Toni, this is . . ."

"Raji," Raji said, leaping forward to give Toni his signature warm handshake.

"Raji," Saraswati repeated, trying out the feel of this new name on her tongue. "Raji is . . . my brother."

"Her *problem* brother," he specified. "The black sheep of the family."

"I was thinking more like the brown sheep of the family," Toni said in her tonitypically blasé way.

"That, too," Raji said, as his eyes sought out Nivedita, the most generous member of the audience in this particular room. "Before you stands the result of an experiment that failed. Namely: Can a heathen child be saved if he's taken in and offered all the advantages of a Western upbringing, or will his bad blood ultimately gain the upper hand?"

"Don't believe a word he says," Saraswati said calmly.

"Indeed, Josefa and Konstantin the First had no such altruistic motives. It was just easier to adopt a kid from India than it was to adopt a *white* baby, the wait lists were too long. Even for the well-heeled family of a dentist."

"Our parents were . . ."

"*Your* parents," Raji corrected her. Whereupon his Bollywood face looked like that of the not-exactly-young-but-still-dashing lover returning from a long and difficult exile *in order to take revenge.* "Jo and Ko Senior have long since washed the stench of my presence from their clothes and their lives, just as I have theirs from mine."

"Our parents were deeply engaged in social work," Saraswati soldiered on. "They figured that if they were going to adopt, at least they could do some good in the process . . ."—whereupon Raji gave a scornful huff—"and save a child from a 'third world' country . . ."—this time Raji's huff sounded more like a choking fit—"but they had no idea of the difficulties such an adoption would bring with it."

"Especially in retrospect, when they realized that all that effort hadn't even been necessary, from the moment they got pregnant with a baby of their very own. A little angel, in contrast to the swarthy Indian devil they'd picked up."

The tone of voice in which Raji and Saraswati conducted this exchange made it clear this wasn't the first time they'd rehearsed these lines. The whole scene felt a bit too studied and, despite all the bitterness, a bit too flat—like the Disney version of a transcultural childhood. But at least it answered one question: why had Saraswati chosen India, of all places? That's why!

Nivedita leaned into the doorframe, awaiting further revelations.

Like a shadow, Priti suavely slid over to her. "I told you he's *hot.*" And then, leaning closer, she whispered right into her ear, "Mad, bad, and dangerous— although maybe a bit too dangerous for my taste."

"But not too mad?" Nivedita whispered back.

"The jury is still out on that one," Priti replied.

Raji flicked a nonexistent bit of fluff from his jacket—which was either custom-tailored raw silk or 100 percent polyester, either too perfect or too vulgar—cast a sardonic glance at both whispering cousins, and in perfectly accent-free English said: "First Saraswati stole my place, and then she stole my race."

To which Saraswati coolly replied, "And just what have you been up to in life since the last time you accused me of that?"

"Oh, it's a long saga, full of tears and disfunction. If I told you, it would break your heart—if you had one."

"Always the same old story—you really can't change your tune, can you?"

"If you call the realization that babies adopted back in nineteen-sixties West Germany were *in no way* 'abandoned orphans,' but that we were actually *stolen* from our mothers—if you call that 'the same old story,' then yes: business as usual. Or, more accurately: big business as usual. And you—what have you made of your golden future? No, don't answer! After all, now the whole world knows you're a fraud."

While Nivedita might've been overwhelmed by Raji's individual pain and the collective trauma of their shared blood—*Did you seriously just think the words 'shared blood'?* Kali asked, rolling her eyes—she was now overcome by indignation: "And *why* does the whole world think it knows Saraswati's story? No matter what my sister might ever have done, I would never have compromised her in public the way you did!"

Raji looked at Nivedita as if he were disappointed that she would stab him in the back like that, and she felt her indignation melt away under his rueful gaze, morphing into pangs of remorse. She was relieved when Priti spoke up and concurred: "It's a question of honor!"

Raji gave a dramatic bow in Saraswati's direction: "You've trained your harem well."

Ironically, today of all days he looked more like Saraswati than . . . not. But that was backward, it was actually Saraswati who had pulled a reverse Michael Jackson to more closely resemble Raji. Even the architecture of her face looked as if it had been cast from the same mold as Raji's, the only difference was that her hair was long and straight whereas his was wavy. And now her nostrils flared in an eerie imitation of his expression. "Harem? Are you trying to imply that what I really need is to find the right man?"

"What I'm implying is that you're incapable of being alone," Raji said, crossing his arms. There was a sibling rivalry between them that went far deeper than any brotherly or sisterly love ever could.

4

"Hey, incidentally, the Internet is no longer a hundred percent against you," Toni broke the spell.

Although that didn't exactly make everything in any way better:

» Ralf Sotschek *I'm with the professor—of course she's a POC. Anyone and everyone is POC. Black and white are achromatic, and that goes for both of them. Scientifically speaking, they aren't even colors, because they either absorb all visible wavelengths of light (black) or reflect them (white). All this nonsense and all these constantly changing terms get on my nerves. And for the aforementioned reasons I consider POC an absolute low point. "People of color?" What's next, "Personen von Farbe"? That brings us frightfully close to the old terms "coloreds" and "coloureds" and "Farbigen." In Sweden, they banned* Pippi Longstocking in Taka-Tuka-Land, *aka* Pippi in the South Seas, *because of the n-word. In the new edition, Pippi's father is King of the South Seas, and he speaks Taka-Tuka. Is that any less racist? Shouldn't he actually be called the King of Persons of Color, and speak Persons-of-Colorese? But, according to the logic of the cleaned-up Pippi books, that would make POCs Taka-Tukas. Great.*

> » LawAndOrder replied *Astrid Lindgren isn't racist—it's whoever thinks she is that's racist!*
> » Peter Paulus replied *The Irish are the best people, so much soul!*

» Arne Hoffmann *I'm so over all this bickering about Saraswati/Sarah Vera. We shouldn't suppress her, we should respect her as the pioneer that she is. It's 2020, and the time for new concepts is now. Why should we still keep thinking in black-and-white terms? If there's such a thing as "genderfluid," why shouldn't there be such a thing as "racefluid"? A new kind of drag, if you will—trying on another identity? The only other thing we'd need is a nonbinary wiki for ethnicity. If there's "foggender" and "ilyagender" and so on, why don't we just make categories like, i.e.,*

POC-B (B for "born") and POC-C (C for "chosen"), and all the other
possibilities? On the other hand, though, even these distinctions could
create more ways to discriminate, in all different directions . . .

» Bilke Hauser replied *When the illustrious Herr Hoffmann, leader*
of the men's rights movement, comes out here on Facebook in favor
of Saraswati, that says it all. That shows where she stands, and
where we should leave her. It's high time we all forget about
Ex-Saraswati!

» Katharina She-Wolf replied *Saraswati, if, after all this, you still*
claim to be a feminist, you can't be surprised when all the feminists
laugh at you out loud: HAHAHAHAHAHAHAHAHAHAHAHA-
HAHHAHAHHAHAHAHAHAHAHAHAHAHAHHAHAHAAHHA-
HAHAHAHAHHAHAHAHAHAHHAHAHAHAHAHA

"Why are people attacking me so vehemently?" Saraswati asked, using the same tone of voice she'd use to say, "Analyze the stylistic methods deployed in Mahasweta Devi's short story 'Draupadi,'" only to then provide her own answer: "Because they believe I have power. To be more precise: they believe I have power *over them*." Saraswati loved speaking in italics. "Just imagine a three-year-old boy attacking Angela Merkel, babbling about how women can't lead entire countries. Would she then post a shocked tweet about it? Of course not! She'd just flash him a smile full of pity."

"Angela Merkel would probably flash a smile full of pity at anyone who'd talk such trash, because Angela Merkel doesn't believe anyone has power over her," Toni mockingly added.

Saraswati blew her a kiss. "QED!"

"QED?" Raji asked.

"Quod erat . . ."

"I know what QED means—but since when have you ever used Latin abbreviations? It's like you're performing a pastiche not just of me, but of Konstantin the First."

Saraswati flashed him a malicious smile. "That's exactly how I meant it: you really shouldn't have such a high opinion of Konstantin the First."

"And you really should bid farewell to the idea that everyone has such a high opinion of you," Raji ominously replied, and then began reading from his phone, aloud:

> » **Clubmate Lenin Kaviar @RudiRüssel** *The left is devouring itself #transracial #Saraswatigate*
> » **Justus Raichle @TruthFinder1** *If a bag of rice were to fall in India, it'd be more interesting than this non-event. #Saraswatigate*
> » **Frau Kunkel @TruthFinder2** *I LOOKED EVERYWHERE BUT I COULDN'T FIND FUCK #boring*
> » **Lands End @classwar** *#Saraswati speculates on skin color while the Amazon Basin burns #TheAmazonIsBurning*
> » **Joachim Stopp BDS Raichle @TruthFinder23** *What is this overblown scandal about an unknown professor intended to distract us from? #non-event #SaraswatiIsBoring*
> » **Amanda Thörnblad @TruthFinder42** *Does Saraswati even exist, or is she a deepfake invented by the left? Or a fake deepfake? #CancelSaraswati*

"I'm writing not for this generation, but for the next one," Saraswati said in her most dignified tone as the first drops of rain began spotting the concrete terrace floor with black dots just outside the door.

"You really believe that, don't you?" Nivedita whispered in the rapidly darkening living room. The storm was suddenly as close as the ghosts of the past, all of whom had also tried to write books about all of this, but only a few of whom had really succeeded: Toni Morrison and James Baldwin and Zora Neale Hurston and Kamala Das and Edward Said and . . . Saraswati?

"All good scholarship is a message in a bottle, sent into the future, in anticipation of what might be, in order to make it possible through the act of writing," Saraswati said, her voice oddly muted. "It's not about describing the world, it's about changing the world."

"That's Marx, right?" Nivedita flatly asked.

"Of course it's Marx," snarled Saraswati, "and I'm paraphrasing, not plagiarizing."

"For a change—how refreshing," Raji remarked laconically. In the dim living room, Nivedita could only make out his silhouette, a narrow-hipped apparition with youthfully lanky arms and legs, as if his body had been frozen in time, back when he and Saraswati lived under the same roof as Josefa and Konstantin in Karlsruhe.

"Speaking of change," Saraswati continued, "why did you come here?"

"Finally!" Toni said, turning the floor lamp next to the sofa on with a sharp *click*. "I thought you'd never ask him."

Raji ignored Toni and stared at Saraswati with his reproachful, dark eyes. It was a good day for raised eyebrows and knowing glances. "I came here to help you."

"Oh, fuck off!"

His smile spoke more clearly than any words ever could: See, *that's* what I want to help you with—you need to learn how to overcome your animosity, resentment, and hatred. He had a talent for mirroring any and every emotion without the slightest effort, and because Saraswati did, too, Nivedita wondered whether she had learned it from him as a child.

"You know where the door is, so I don't need to see you out," Saraswati said.

"And you know that I'll leave whenever you want, if that's really what you want," Raji said, winning that round.

"Are you also getting the feeling we've been relegated to the sidelines, as a captive audience, just here to applaud on cue?" Priti asked Nivedita. And since that was the exact feeling Priti had always instilled in Nivedita, her nod was only halfhearted.

"Oh *really*? First you move heaven and earth and hell and the mass media just so you can march in here—and then you'd just up and leave? You want a room here, or not?" Saraswati said, sounding not quite half as benevolent as usual.

"A room, a bed—whatever you can spare," Raji replied, only slightly irritated, perfectly parroting Saraswati's patronizing *the-world-belongs-to-me-and-if-I-bestow-even-a-bit-of-my-precious-attention-on-you-then-at-least-you-get-a-small-share-of-it* tone.

"Nivedita and Priti are sharing the guest room, Toni's sleeping with me, so I can clear the sofa for you."

"Sofa?" Raji said, looking askance at the yellow sofa in the middle of the living room with Toni sprawled out across it. For just one moment, Nivedita could hear the voice of the unloved son, who was always given the worst seat in the car and the smallest slice of cake.

"The sleeper sofa," Saraswati specified—as the thunder whined outside the windows like an abandoned puppy but then swiftly made itself scarce— "in my home office."

And Raji's face lit up like the sky.

CAN THE SUBALTERN SPEAK?

1

8-19 DAYS POST-SARASWATI

The next week and a half were a mess of fragments in Nivedita's memory. They didn't fit together, nor did they yield a coherent timeline, but they did all glitter brightly. No matter how often she tried to sort them out in her head, she could never be certain what had happened first and what next. But since she had to start somewhere, she decided that the first bit of shrapnel had lodged itself into her flesh on the only night—or, more precisely, the wee hours of morning—they'd spent as an odd constellation, all five strewn on every available bed throughout the penthouse, two pairs plus Raji, sleeping solo.

Nivedita had woken up with a sense of alarm, but couldn't quite put her finger on exactly what had triggered it. Next to her, Priti was sound asleep, her arms folded beneath her. Her skin was coated in a thin layer of sweat, looking so firm and healthy it might as well have been an ad for hyaluronic acid. Nivedita heard Priti breathing, heard the birds chirping out on the terrace, and then heard a rustling sound in the hall that propelled her onto her feet and caused her to wind the sari around her body like a super-long bath towel. She didn't know what to expect—Raji, semi-stealthily letting in a bunch of protesters in balaclavas?—but when she opened the door a crack she only saw Toni, presumably on her way to the Volksgarten for her morning run. Nivedita was about to close the door again, but then she noticed Toni had a big bag draped over her shoulder.

"Toni!"

Toni turned around, guiltily. "Nivedita—what are you doing up?"

"What're *you* doing?"

"I'm leaving," Toni said, pointing a thumb at her overstuffed courier bag. "There's too much DNA in this place."

Nivedita thought she'd heard wrong. "But you can't just leave Saraswati in the lurch, not right now."

"You're so sweet, Nivedita," Toni said, "but it was always clear I'd only stay for a few days. I'm flying to Nicaragua next month, and have a lot to take care of back in Berlin between now and then."

With just a few steps, Nivedita got right up close to her. "Flying *where*?"

"You know—a country in Latin America, the one that had a big revolution?"

"Why there?" Nivedita whispered, although that wasn't the question that was really nagging at her.

"Because I've never been," Toni said, rather amused. Toni's life consisted of projects: lifestyle projects, art projects, relationship projects, construction projects. She and a group of "folx" had bought the supposedly sole remaining abandoned farmstead in the Uckermark region and were in the process of renovating the whole thing, one barn at a time. But now that particular building project would be interrupted by this travel project.

Nivedita told herself she shouldn't really be surprised, but nevertheless she was. "Does Saraswati know?"

"What do you think? She's probably marveling at the fact that I didn't decamp ages ago." Toni, still visibly amused, opened the door. Early morning light cascaded through the stairwell, making her complexion look even lighter, turning her hair into an extremely close-cropped halo atop her smooth neck, and leaving Nivedita in the dark hallway.

"Do you love her?" Nivedita instinctively asked.

"Not as much as you love her," Toni replied.

"What do you mean by that?"

"Don't be like that," Toni smirked, whereupon Nivedita realized she'd miss her. It wasn't so much that she'd miss Toni for who Toni was—she knew too little about this shimmering, whiter-than-white, oh-so-unpredictable being—it was more because she realized no situation could get too melodramatic as long as Toni was there. In the presence of her über-casual comity, even Raji and Saraswati looked like two bickering siblings quarreling over some long-lost toy, rather than the hero and heroine (or did she mean protagonist and antagonist?) of some ancient, tragic, epic bloodbath. And then Nivedita noticed that she hadn't once thought of Simon since she'd woken up—almost a whole fifteen minutes ago—and she decided to consider that a victory.

"In case it means anything, I'm pretty sure Saraswati doesn't love me as much as she loves you, either," Toni freehandedly added.

"Why?" Nivedita whispered over her racing heart, which suddenly seemed to be beating in every last inch of her body.

"I'm too *white*, that's beyond clear," Toni said, her grin growing even wider, leaving Nivedita aghast. "Hey, now—it's not so grim. It's not like I've deluded myself into believing we'd still be together twenty years from now. Saraswati is married to her mission, she has no room for an all-encompassing love. But not every love story has to be *the* great, big, one-true-love story."

Nivedita, who could only conceive of love in *the* GREAT, BIG, ONE-TRUE-LOVE version—all or nothing, Saraswati or Not-Saraswati—repeated in shock, "Why?"

"Because she's Saraswati. Because it's just cool to be with someone of your own caliber."

Nivedita thought she'd heard wrong. "Because she's *famous*?"

"Never underestimate the power of fame. It's just super sexy to bed someone when everyone who's in the know, plus people who've just seen her on TV, also want a piece of her."

"Why are you telling me all this?" Nivedita asked, choking up a bit.

"Because it concerns you." Toni grabbed her shoes from the squat, white shoe rack out on the landing—the same rack next to the door of every hippie-dippy household that expected everyone to take their shoes off before entering, which almost never happened. Nivedita stared so intently at the back of her head you'd have thought she was trying to stop Toni in her tracks through her sheer force of will, but then she actually did pause and turn. "Okay, so you'll be more forbearing with her. She loves you. Maybe not the way you'd like her to—definitely not the way you'd like her to. But that doesn't mean it's not love. It absolutely is."

And then she left for real.

SARASWATI SAT UNDER the awning on the terrace, stoically typing something into her laptop. A text that few would read if anyone even read her ever again. Nivedita wanted to ask her about Toni, but then Raji's voice triumphantly burst through the open glass door:

Come fair, come foul,
I'll twine the rope and sing

(and then he appeared, cup of coffee in hand, and sang onward)

. . .

"WAGNER, I PRESUME?" Saraswati asked, unimpressed.

"The *Götterdämmerung*," Raji confirmed, "although, in your case, 'Twilight of the Gods' becomes 'Twilight of the Goddesses.'"

"Have you already used your wily ways to inform the press that you're now camped out in my harem? What does that make you . . . one of my eunuchs?" Saraswati asked dryly. Nivedita felt her phone grow heavier in her skirt pocket. Or, more accurately, she felt the mounting weight of all the incoming press requests she had yet to answer:

> *Dear Nivedita Anand,*
>
> *Enrico Ippolito here, critic with SPON, we met at a Seebrücke event some time ago and you gave me a statement on racism in Germany for my article—hi again!*
>
> *I'm back with another professional request: Would you like to write something for us on the accusations against Saraswati, if you have time? Esp. in light of the parallels with the Rachel Dolezal case in the USA a couple years ago?*
>
> *Why do whites want to be BIPOC all of a sudden?*
>
> *Happy to discuss at your convenience, whenever, wherever . . .*
>
> *Warm regards,*
>
> *Enrico*
>
> *Enrico Ippolito*
>
> *Culture Critic*
>
> *SPIEGEL Online GmbH*
>
> *A Division of SPIEGEL Media Group*

Meanwhile, Raji remarked: "I take back what I said about your harem. What you've got going here is a cult, a Saraswati cult, only it's not centered on spirituality, but on your very own brand of narcissism—a cult of personality, one might say . . ."

His sister grabbed the cup from his hand, took a gulp, and handed it right back to him. "Oh, don't be so modest. You know that when it comes to narcissism, I can't hold a candle to you."

Spending a night under the same roof hadn't softened their fervent, mutual hostility. Saraswati and Raji traded insults the way other people traded compliments, as proof of the severe claims each leveled against the other.

Nivedita tried to figure out who Raji reminded her of—someone of her mother's generation, a perennially all-too-perfectly dressed brown man who looked like he was mixed race, as if his body knew something his mind didn't, as if an unsuspected talent lay dormant, deep within. Prince?

"*Hexenzirkel*!" Raji suddenly cried out, "A coven of witches—that's the word I was looking for. The coven of Saraswatiites you've set up at Düsseldorf's Heinrich Heine University."

Saraswati stared at him and clapped her hands very, very slowly. "Wow, it's like Donald Trump is in the house: 'She's a witch.' Have you ever considered becoming a political consultant for the AfD? I see incredible career-growth opportunities for you there."

"I have the wrong skin color for that," Raji said, with such surprising bitterness that even the bees stopped buzzing about and collecting pollen in the hollyhocks.

"I don't think so," Saraswati replied softly.

Something lingered in the air for a second, pungent and cloying as camphor, like a festering wound, pulsing as it bursts, until Raji rashly added: "Is that why you decided to steal mine?"

Nivedita was certain he'd have said something entirely different had she not been there.

"Calm down," Saraswati said. "Being brown isn't a limited resource. According to the latest data, in a hundred years we'll all be brown."

"And you just didn't want to wait that long, or what?"

LATER—OR WAS it earlier?—Nivedita was in the kitchen with Saraswati. Priti was still sleeping, and Raji was nowhere to be found. Saraswati was processing Toni's departure by throwing herself into food preparation. Much as her shelves were filled with books, her kitchen was filled with bunches of beets, slices of lemon bulging up against the convex sides of mason jars, and shiny white and red onions surrounded by tiny yellow mustard seeds swimming in vinegary brine. Ever since her very first visit, Nivedita had wondered where Saraswati found the time to read all those books *and* cook all that food. Now she had at least a partial clue regarding the enigma that was her professor.

"My mother once tried to commit suicide by enamel," Saraswati said as she held a lit match to the stovetop range. The gas lit up with a soft *poof* and burned almost invisibly in the bright morning sun. Nivedita pondered whether it was possible she'd landed in some parallel universe where the word *enamel* meant something else—like arsenic or strychnine or, on the more exotic side, curare, the poisonous extract from South American vines—or whether Saraswati was just stringing together words without worrying about meaning: skin like gold and my teeth like diamonds yeah yeah *lorem ipsum dolor sit amet.*

But Saraswati actually did mean exactly what she'd said, for a change. "There was my mom, just five years old—Josefa, what a name. And her brother—named Walther, although everyone called him Harald—had warned her that enamel could rip up your guts." Saraswati stirred water boiling in a red enamelware pot with white dots. "So, in secret, Josefa scratched a couple fingernail-size shards of enamel from a milk jug, gulped them down, and hoped she'd bleed out from inside."

A wave of sadness swept over Nivedita. "Why?" she asked, sympathizing with the little girl.

"Yeah, you'd think my mother would've remembered that, at least. But she didn't remember whether she'd even gotten a stomachache from it. *Not even that!*" Saraswati stirred the whirling water into an eddy. "There was nothing my mother couldn't suppress." With a disdainful gesture she cracked two eggs with spotted shells and poured them into the pot, where they immediately turned white and moved around, looking a bit like jellyfish in the boiling water. "Stan had already made himself scarce—he had cleared out awhile before—but on that particular day, like on so many others, he'd sent a real, bona fide letter, because he needed money. And instead of talking to me about my dad or anything else, out slipped that story about her attempted suicide, which I had never heard a peep about before. I was finishing high school, preparing for my college entrance exams, and planned to study art history and religion. I hoped to eventually land a teaching post, just like Josefa had thirty years before, right in the middle of the postwar boom—just like *Josefa*!—but at that moment it was clear to me that under no circumstances would I take that route. Instead . . . well, you know where I went from there."

Nivedita didn't know where to direct her gaze, so she looked all around the kitchen and noticed that every single pot and pan Saraswati owned was enamelware.

Raji offered Nivedita poached eggs, too. She couldn't tell whether they were the same recipe, on a different day, or maybe the exact same eggs that same day. Maybe that was just the Thielmann tribe's favorite breakfast? As he served them up, he looked her deep in the eye and said, "We've earned it."

Have we? thought Nivedita, although she'd never actually mouth off like that. She took a wary sip of the coffee Raji had foamed up for her with butter and coconut oil in the mixer, and was surprised it didn't taste like pure fat. It wasn't some ancient Indian recipe—no, Saraswati's brother, just like Saraswati, followed a strict fitness regimen. In his case, it took the form of protein shakes and bulletproof coffee, and Nivedita could picture him offering his butter-coffee to the young BAMEs he worked with in London (she knew, since the Brits always require special treatment, they shunned the North American term BIPOC and insisted instead on BAME: Black, Asian, Minority Ethnic), saying: *Here, drink this, then you'll be able to do twice as many sit-ups.*

So in her case, of course, the equivalent was: *Here, drink this, then you'll be able to attack Saraswati twice as hard.*

Because, ever since Raji had shown up, everyone's focus had shifted toward confrontation.

"You're like me," he told Nivedita. "You, too, are here to finally get some answers." Nivedita didn't say a word, because he was absolutely right about that, but it would have struck her as disloyal to admit as much.

"That's one of your most admirable qualities," he said, as if he'd read her mind. The intimacy of sharing breakfast gave her the feeling that she could read his mind, too. Maybe he was right, maybe nobody but her really understood him.

"Hypnosis," Saraswati interrupted.

"Huh?" Nivedita shook her head, suddenly distraught upon realizing she hadn't noticed Saraswati sitting at the head of the table, scornfully spying on them both.

"What he's doing to you right now, Nivedita. That's hypnosis: 'neuro-linguistic programming,' voodoo, mindfuckery, whatever you want to call it."

"And what did *you* do to her, Saraswati? What did you do to all of them, if not hypnotize and manipulate them?" Raji prodded her. Internally, Nivedita frantically looked around for Priti, but apparently her own brain had already edited her cousin out of that particular memory.

"Tell her," Raji nudged Nivedita.

"What's she supposed to tell me?" Saraswati shot back. "And why don't you tell me yourself, Raji?"

The bright morning sun had led Raji to stretch his long limbs out lazily across the kitchen table and floorboards, but now, with an almost imperceptibly subtle movement, they tensed up. "Nivedita should tell you which taboo you broke, in her eyes, Sarah."

"Oh, spare me. But maybe you'll tell me just *how* I broke the taboo, huh? How, precisely?"

"That's exactly what I mean," he hissed. "Why should *I* have to explain to you what's racist about your behavior? Why don't you give that some thought—some of your oh-so-precious thought—for a change?"

"I have, and I do. In fact, I've thought about it so much that I even teach a . . ."

"Oh, Saraswati, it's not about what you did or didn't do," Nivedita cut in, despairing. "It's about how what you've done has discredited your own work."

"Have you slept with Saraswati?" Raji asked, out of the blue.

Nivedita nearly choked on her perfectly poached eggs. "Of course not!"

"Hmm, that's unusual. Normally, that's Sarah's preferred tactic for securing her alliances—undying loyalty through sexuality."

"Did *he* already ask you if you'd sleep with *him*?" Saraswati imitated Raji's tone with her lips, which looked like an imitation of his lips on her face, which itself looked like an imitation of his face. Nivedita wondered whether all the coffee grounds she'd downed along with everything else would soon land in her stomach and go on to transform every drop of liquid in her body into coffee, making her more and more awake, until the extreme coffee high landed her in the hospital.

Don't let these two turn you into their toy, Kali advised. *You aren't at their mercy—strike back.*

With what? Nivedita asked.

Whatever you've got, Kali replied.

And so Nivedita said the first thing that popped into her head: "Then why did you invite Raji to stay, Saraswati? After . . ." the caffeine rush petered out, and she ended with a whimper, "all?"

Saraswati stroked Raji's pinkie with her own pinkie, the stingiest sign of tenderness imaginable. "Because *he* isn't actually here to help *me*, but *I am* here to help *him*."

Raji tensed up even more than before, if that were even possible. "You really do believe all people are good—but really you mean *you*, first and foremost."

"And you really do believe all people are victims—but really you mean *you*, first and foremost."

Somehow Saraswati's words struck Nivedita to the core. "But you were the first person ever to give me a language with which I could talk about my experiences as a victim," Nivedita protested, her mouth filling with the butter's rancid aftertaste.

"Nonsense. I gave you a language with which you could transform your experiences as a victim!" Saraswati said dismissively. "So you could turn them into a weapon, instead of just wallowing in them for the rest of your life!"

The puddle that was Nivedita's heart shouted back: *And what am I supposed to do with the experiences that aren't transformed yet? What am I supposed to do with the ones that are still raw? With the ones that're still so pain-ful they want to scream? Should I just hit pause on all that and say: shut your trap until you're more enlightened?*

Raji laid an arm around Nivedita's shoulder and said to Saraswati: "Can't you see how dreadfully cynical it is of you to tell her how she should live her life after lying to her since the moment you met?" His voice floated around the kitchen like cigarette smoke, filling every last crack.

"He's right," Nivedita said, visibly moved. "I believed you. *We* believed you!"

"What's changed?"

"Everything's changed!"

"Nothing's changed, except that your vanity's been bruised," Saraswati said, correcting Nivedita or Raji or maybe even Priti, who had followed their raised voices into the kitchen. She had an unusual expression on her face, and was sizing up Saraswati, looking for her weak points, much as she had over the previous two semesters, except this time she wasn't compelled by helpless fury—instead, it was more like . . . pity?

Raji's presence did something to Saraswati. Cracks appeared in her facade, revealing . . . more Saraswati, except even bigger, even browner, and even haughtier. "You didn't study with me in order to make the world a more just place, or in order to learn more about racism, Nivedita. You studied with me in order to learn more *about yourself.* Instead of calling your course of study *postcolonial studies*, it would be more accurate to call it *Nivedita stud-ies*. Or *broken-heart studies*: *post-traumatic theory*."

White-hot wrath spread through Nivedita's body, as if diffusing from Raji's trembling arm and down over her entire being. Saraswati was the first person who had given Nivedita the feeling that she had the right to grapple with her own situation—to truly come to terms with herself. That she was rel-evant, with her special history, amid the special web of circumstances that make up the present day, and that her special history was political. That she didn't have to deny any part of herself, as she often had in so many situations with Lilli or Lotte or other *white* classmates—with the exception of Barbara—where the sole connection was their shared femininity, as if universal femininity were *white*. And then her professor had taken all that away, with one sentence, one gesture, one grand delusion. And now Saraswati deigned to add, coolly: "You aren't interested in Indian women in India, you're interested in Indian women here in Germany. You only want to save yourself." And the wrath ran its course, ebbing as quickly as it had flowed, leaving no major, illuminating truth in its wake—just an endless chill, as if all the ice melting away in the arctic were now collecting under her skin.

"Pff! And you?" Nivedita asked through her clenched yet jittering teeth.

"I really support others."

"Yeah—so much that you want to *be* them?" Raji softly snarled.

"I sound like a vampire when you put it like that," Saraswati said, baring a dangerous grin. For a moment she looked like a vampire, too—an Indian vampire, a chedipe. And chedipes only attack men.

Raji laid his head on Nivedita's shoulder and exposed his neck. Saraswati licked her teeth and asked, "Happy now, Raji?" and the kitchen turned back into the kitchen, and Saraswati was—well, whoever she was, but she no longer seemed to be some coldhearted, contemptuous being from another planet as she had a moment before. "You just love that even sweet Nivedita and I are at each other's throats, don't you?"

The warmth returned to Nivedita's limbs, but not just that: suddenly all the colors were bright again, the world was filled with scents and sounds again, and not all of them were pleasant, but at least they were there, and Nivedita was no longer left utterly alone in a bleak and hopeless universe. "*Nivedita studies*?" she asked, sounding uncertain.

"Why not? Know thyself," Saraswati said.

Raji, too, smiled, seeming a bit as if he'd been caught red-handed, adding, "That tiny bit of goading was nothing. Most adopted children become mass murderers."

"You've got time yet," quipped Saraswati.

"Is that true?" asked Nivedita.

Raji gently caressed her forehead with the same gesture she'd only ever seen come from Saraswati. "You have such a marvelously trusting nature, Nivedita."

And with that, he grabbed the shiny little yellow bag of turmeric and sprinkled a colorful cloud onto his egg, making the kitchen smell like Nivedita's parents' house back in Essen.

2

- » Ijoma Mangold @IjomaMangold *If skin color is just a construct, what's keeping us from all being POCs? Make identity politics universal!*
- » Jeff "Koons" Kühns @JeffKühns *Yeah, sure, and sex is also just a construct, which would make us all trans, or what? Make body politics universal?*
- » Obsessed over identity @WesleyMorris* *Rachel Dolezal, Caitlyn Jenner, and Saraswati have shown us how trans and bi and poly-ambi-omni we all are.*
- » JK_Rowling @jkrowling *If sex isn't real, there's no same-sex attraction. If sex isn't real, the lived reality of women globally is erased. I know and love trans people, but erasing the concept of sex removes the ability of many to meaningfully discuss their lives. It isn't hate to speak the truth.*
- » Boomergenerationfarts @LGBTABC *Homiez, if any of all y'all are still following Rowling, I'm unfollowing you, stat. Enough already!*
- » Rogers_Brubaker @the_wrbucla *Gender and race are of course 'different differences' #transracial*
- » Kai M Green @Kai_Mgreen *We are all responding to the question: Is she POC or nah? We have too easily answered this question with a resounding NAH! But I think that's the wrong question. The question we should be asking is: When was/is she POC?*

"What're you doing?" Nivedita asked. Apparently she was doomed to ask this same damn question every morning, just addressing different people. This particular morning it was Priti, who gave a suspiciously guilty start and then shoved a few very private-looking letters back into the stack of papers she was kneeling next to on the wooden floor of Saraswati's home office. Moshtari Hilal's portrait of Saraswati gazed down on her critically;

otherwise, there were no eyewitnesses. "Where's Raji?" was Nivedita's next question. The sleeper sofa had been meticulously folded up, and aside from his sand-colored, waxed-canvas carryall, nothing hinted at his presence in Saraswati's life.

"What, you can't bear to be without him?" Priti parried her cousin, looking up from her spot on the floor.

"Which of us was the one who stole compromising photos for him?" Nivedita shot back, stepping over a crooked little wall of books Priti had taken from the shelves.

"Don't make it a big deal, that's just what happens when Raji focuses his attention on you. And now, for the past few days, he's been focusing it on you like there's no tomorrow."

"Priti, *what* are you up to?" Nivedita repeated, so as not to venture right back into that labyrinth—she didn't want to have to discuss Raji and how he'd thrown Saraswati to the press, and the best reason he'd offered was that he didn't "want any more secrets," as if denouncing her were the only way to arrive at the truth. Raji, who obviously not only played his cards close to his chest, but played with an entirely different deck. Raji, who she nevertheless couldn't stop thinking about, as if he were a wound to the head that she constantly had to check on with the tongue of her thoughts.

"I'm looking for diaries, letters, *irgendetwas* that might explain what Saraswati, now as before, has refused to tell us," Priti said, as if she couldn't fathom how Nivedita hadn't yet had the same idea.

And Nivedita herself couldn't fathom how she hadn't yet had the same idea. "And?"

"And nothing, of course. Raji must've snatched it all already."

Nivedita crouched down next to Priti and began randomly flipping through books. It wasn't the first time she also found herself wondering what had happened to the attraction Priti and Raji had felt for one another. They both behaved courteously while also keeping one another at a distance, like two people trying to prevent a one-night stand from turning into one endless night, thereby completely overlooking the fact that the other party had that same exact goal.

"I give up," Priti groaned. "Every tidbit I find about Saraswati is just . . . a tidbit about Saraswati. Sarah Vera simply doesn't exist anywhere in this household."

"But then how did you find that . . . those photos?" Meaning the photos that were apparently so convincing they had won over the German press—a messy mass media that, after wallowing in Hitler's diaries (they were forged) and lavishing no fewer than nineteen journalism prizes on Claas Relotius (a "reporter" prone to fabrication), one would hope had learned to do at least a little critical due diligence—whereupon they felt the need to break the explosive news about Saraswati actually being Sarah Vera ASAP.

"The photos were just lying there," Priti pointed to Saraswati's desk. "As if she had laid them out for me."

Nivedita felt a shiver between her shoulder blades. "And what was in the photos?" she asked, almost holding her breath, as if asking such direct questions in this particular household were akin to driving while Black in the United States and getting pulled over by a cop.

Priti gave her a surprised look. "I thought you knew."

"If I did, would I be asking?"

As she soon discovered, after just one night with Raji, Priti had strolled into Saraswati's place under the pretext of returning a borrowed book and having a cup of tea with her. She then strolled out with full documentation of Saraswati's transformation: before pics, after pics, during pics, even pics from the operating room. It was like an illustrated version of *Becoming Brown for Beginners and Advanced Alike*. "There's no reason she would've held on to them if she hadn't wanted to be found out."

Flabbergasted, Nivedita let the book she'd been holding slide from her hand and sink into the orange-yellow, spiral-patterned, high-pile carpet. Then she looked at the cover design and noticed it had almost the same spiral pattern, only in black and white, as *Decolonize your Soul*. The answer was staring straight out of the dust jacket, right at her. The closest thing to Saraswati's *diaries* would be Saraswati's *books*! Nivedita picked the most influential book of her twenties back up and read the first page again—this time looking not to learn anything about her own soul and its entanglements in world history and power dynamics, but rather to learn about the entanglements its author had therein:

> We must write as if our minds, souls, and spirits already
> lived in that better world: the world we conjure every time we
> criticize contemporary power relationships—above all, when
> we criticize contemporary power relationships. Because change
> only becomes possible when at least some of us already live in the
> future, and the rest of us just need to follow. That is how we
> demonstrate that change is not only a worthwhile goal, but also
> eminently possible.

Nivedita had underlined that last word—twice!—back when she so zealously devoured this book along with every other book by Saraswati, because she wanted to *be* Saraswati. And avidly reading was the only way she could imagine of slipping into someone else's skin. *But I didn't really understand her back then. Not the way I understand her now, at least, with everything I know about her betrayal.* Or maybe it wasn't a form of betrayal at all, maybe it was just a radical form of "living in the future." Maybe Saraswati was not so much trans-race as she was beyond-race. Somewhere over the racebow?

"Okay, so an old man boards the tram and says to the conductor, 'I'd like a one-way ticket to Adolf-Hitler-Platz, please,'" Saraswati had said, welcoming her students to the second class of the semester, three years before. Nivedita was feverish with expectation.

"The conductor is as shocked as you all are. 'It's no longer called Adolf-Hitler-Platz,' he tells the old man. 'It's now called Graf-Adolf-Platz—as in Count Adolf.' Whereupon the old man says, 'Beg pardon? They made that Adolf guy a count already?'" Nivedita was so shocked she just had to laugh—especially when she pictured the difference between Adolf Hitler and Count Adolf VIII of Berg. Oluchi, in the seat next to her, was also trying to stifle a guffaw.

"No worries, you're allowed to laugh. This kind of cognitive dissonance is precisely what I'm getting at. For us, nowadays, the notion of living on a street named for Adolf Hitler is unthinkable, even repulsive. But what about other mass murderers who've shaped our history, our present day, and even the geography of our daily lives? And no, I in *no* way intend to imply that the crimes perpetrated by the Nazis compare to any other crimes against humanity in any way, Sebastian."

The arm Sebastian had angrily shot up into the air just a moment before now sunk back to his side.

"Why doesn't it strike us as strange, here in Düsseldorf, to live on Wissmann Straße?" Saraswati continued at her usual breathless clip. "After all, Hermann Wilhelm Leopold Ludwig von Wissmann played a crucial role in quashing the Wahehe resistance, resulting in the deaths of approximately seven hundred thousand people. The existence of Wissmann Straße only strikes us as *not* strange because we've never heard about the crimes he committed. And why haven't we been told anything about that? Because it wasn't taught, nor even mentioned in passing, in school."

That was followed by a slew of other jokes, but by then Nivedita's laughter was stuck in her throat. She wasn't yet aware that Saraswati didn't consider her lectures successful unless at least two or three people were sufficiently provoked to the point of totally losing it right there in class. Sure, Saraswati preached love, but her love was no cuddly-wuddly, we-all-agree-here-type love. No, hers was a confrontational, to-love-means-we-don't-avoid-any-conflicts-here-type love. "We must love our community, meaning not on an individual level—needless to say, it isn't possible to love every single person at every single moment—but on the collective level. What *white* people think about BIPOCs is not of primary importance. What *is* of primary importance is what *you all* think about BIPOCs. And we need to hold one another more, hug more—but we'll get to that later in the semester."

Nivedita scanned down the syllabus and saw that there actually was a class whose content was listed as *Radical Cuddling*. Not everyone was into it. Meaning, not everyone thought they should touch each other.

And—bull's-eye—once again, Professor Saraswati had reached her goal.

Saraswati's favorite quote was: "As Gustav Landauer says, 'The first revolutionary act is to treat the people we love well.'" Nivedita had never managed to find that phrase anywhere in Landauer's writings. And Saraswati's second-favorite quote was probably *The state is a relationship, a partnership between people, a way that people relate to one another; it is destroyed when one becomes involved in other relationships.*

Nivedita had always read that as a commentary on her relationship with Simon—as a call to look for a man who didn't only love her when she was out of reach.

Kneeling next to Priti among Saraswati's books, she realized it was also aimed at her in another way. It called on her to love others even when they were imperfect, or made decisions she didn't understand. That was the reason she moved into Saraswati's guest room, instead of heading to Oluchi's apartment to cook up conspiratorial plans against Saraswati. And then there was the fact that Landauer wasn't just any old guy, from any old place, who'd shared his wisdom about human relationships with people in any old town. No, Landauer had been a socialist, an anarchist, a pacifist, and a Düsseldorfer—or at least almost. He had lived and worked right here, and would have been appointed dramaturg at the Schauspielhaus Düsseldorf had the establishment of the short-lived Bavarian Soviet Republic not intervened. So Landauer and Nivedita were distant in time, but not in space. He had given lectures on Shakespeare in Düsseldorf, much as Saraswati had also given lectures on Shakespeare in Düsseldorf—the theory that Shakespeare was actually Emilia Lanier was a notion Nivedita had of course first heard from Saraswati—and that proximity gave his arguments additional resonance in her mind. His ideas echoed and reverberated through hers, filling her with a sense of possibility: he and she might well have shared *the same experiences*, which therefore also called for *the same solutions*. That's why his words touched her as if he were speaking directly to her. So when Landauer said she should treat the people she loved well—even if he did so through Saraswati's mouth—then Nivedita would do just that. And that's why she wasn't answering all the invitations the press and media were bombarding her phone with. That's why she tried to get answers *from* Saraswati before even hearing any answers other people gave her *about* Saraswati. Although she also had to admit that it probably would've been way easier to get answers from Landauer—who'd been tortured and then murdered a hundred years ago by fascist paramilitary gangs—than to pry any from her now ex-professor. That's why Nivedita was sticking it out in Saraswati's abode and Saraswati's world.

AND THAT'S WHY NIVEDITA was so intrigued by Raji, who appeared to be the answer incarnate to all her questions—at least she *hoped* that was the reason for her interest.

"Why did you come looking for me at the Gauguin and at my apartment back then?" she asked while Raji studied her palms, as if trying to memorize her lifeline.

Back then? asked Kali. *Is there now a distinction between pre-Raji and post-Raji? Ante Rajum novisti and anno Raji?*

Nivedita ignored her. Whereupon Kali began licking Raji's face with her long, red tongue.

"Is it just me, or is it hot in here?" Raji sighed, wiping Kali's saliva from his forehead as if it were covered in beads of sweat.

"Sure is," Nivedita agreed, attempting to keep the conversation with Raji going while simultaneously trying to signal to Kali that she should leave him alone. But Kali just waved at Nivedita with her tongue and kept at it.

"What were we just talking about?"

"My apartment. Why did you . . . go there?"

Unlike his sister, Raji loved nothing more than answering Nivedita's questions, although his answers never seemed to clarify anything either. "Because I wanted to meet you. Of course."

"And why did you . . . ?"

He gazed at her with his prophet-on-fire eyes. "When Priti showed me a picture of you on her phone, it became clear to me that you're going through the same battles I am."

She smelled the coconutty scent of his skin—Raji not only put coconut oil in his coffee, he also used it as a moisturizer—so she had to really focus before managing to say: "What battles?"

Kali lifted her skirt of amputated arms and flashed Raji, exposing the long and curly hairs that were now the only thing standing between him and the most glorious vulva on this as well as every other planet. But he only had eyes for Nivedita. "Your roommate was nice."

"Lotte?" Nivedita asked, surprised.

"She said really sweet things about you."

"Lotte?" Nivedita repeated, still surprised, but also distracted by Kali's vulva.

"Nivedita, the way to Saraswati's heart is through her mind," said Raji, changing the subject for the third time in as many minutes.

"Meaning?" she asked, obviously flummoxed.

Instead of answering, Raji laid his hand on her heart, and suddenly Nivedita's brain refocused on her breasts, to the exclusion of all else. "Here, where the pulse of your heart is beating against my fingertips—in Saraswati, there's nothing but words and more words."

Nivedita could only think about her breasts.

You gonna fuck him? Kali asked, with relish.

"I can't sleep with the man who . . . with my cousin . . ." Nivedita answered—only unfortunately she said it out loud, and her breasts veritably shrieked in silent protest as Raji withdrew his hand.

"You mean you can't sleep with the man who makes your golden Saraswati so angry," he said dryly before leaving the room.

At that very same moment, as if they were in some off-off-Broadway play, Priti rushed in through the same door and asked: "What did he want?"

"You know what he wanted . . . ," Nivedita vaguely replied.

"Sex?" asked Priti, sounding hurt in spite of the carefully cultivated distance she and Raji were maintaining.

Much to her own surprise, Nivedita snarled, "I bet Yannik called you a chocolate lollipop, too." She was horrified by her own outburst, but also curious to hear whether she was right.

"You were really in love with Yannik, weren't you?" Priti asked.

Nivedita nodded. She had loved Yannik, but also Priti. Priti above all. And she'd loved the whole situation that had allowed fifteen-year-old her to be a young Indian woman—the sexual-fantasy version of a young Indian woman, maybe, but still.

Priti grabbed a tiny spray bottle from one of the random little tables that, by night, made Saraswati's living room a kind of obstacle course, and spritzed an aethereal cloud of oil into the hot and humid air. "He never said anything that wacky to me."

Nivedita smelled lemon and Litsea, and felt like some invisible hand was scrubbing her soul squeaky clean. That Yannik had saved his racist remarks— or were they sexist? Or both?—solely for her was the very last thing she should be happy about. All of a sudden she yearned for Barbara. Barbara could've grounded the whole situation—she'd have twisted her ironic mouth up into a funny face, thereby bringing a steadying perspective to this otherwise chaotic M. C. Escher–esque Möbius strip of emotion. With Barbara, Nivedita never took herself as seriously as she did with Saraswati. But Barbara was half a mile away as the crow flies, way at the other end of Oberbilk. The only person here was Priti, who would never in her entire life choose to stay grounded when she had the option of being dramatic. And so Priti's next sentence caught Nivedita to the quick: "To be honest, I agree with Oluchi's take."

"Oluchi's *what*?"

"Take." Priti spritzed a fine mist onto her third eye and gave a jolt as the droplets created a connection with her first and second eyes. "Oluchi's right: Saraswati should have been an ally! Instead of just a weird, exoticist copy of an Indian woman."

"Was what she did exoticist?"

"You seriously have to ask?"

"And what would you have said about her before you knew that she . . .'" Nivedita still had a hard time saying it, "that she's *white*?"

"That she's crazy," Priti said without missing a beat. "I've been telling you the entire time. You yourself have seen how she teaches. It's like she thinks she's initiating us into the mysterious art of Saraswatism."

"Ugh, so now you're saying Raji's kind of right about her, too?"

This time Priti hesitated, but only briefly. "In a certain sense . . . yeah."

"Why are you even here, then?" Nivedita asked, startled.

"I thought it wasn't about having to say Saraswati was right about everything, regardless of what she did, but rather . . ."

"Rather *what*?" Nivedita pushed her.

Priti gave her the same strange, sympathetic look that she had when answering her questions about Yannik. "They might *be* right, but they don't *act* right. They're treating Saraswati as if she had no feelings. And I thought the same thing, in the beginning. But that was a logical error. People *only* do things *because* they have feelings, and . . ."

"Wow, who sounds just like Saraswati now?" Nivedita remarked, while also internally admitting that she'd paid Priti startlingly little attention over the last few days. Sure, she'd been distracted. She also got all churned up when Priti suddenly popped up, forcing Nivedita to share her unique position in Saraswati's household with her. But after that, the two of them had fallen back into their old patterns, following a rhythm that basically let them drift on autopilot—as long as they weren't competing over some dude or some professor—so Nivedita had hardly noticed Priti's uncharacteristic reserve. After all, Saraswati and Raji had demanded most of her attention.

And now Priti declared, after pondering, bossy as ever: "That's why there's only one!"

"One what?" Nivedita asked, and she knew she wouldn't like the answer.

OLUCHI'S APARTMENT DOOR had a poster of May Ayim on it. Nivedita had seen the poster a million times, but now found herself wondering, for the first time, why she had nicknamed Oluchi Zadie instead of May—clearly Oluchi considered May Ayim more important than Zadie Smith. She also found herself marveling at how easy it had been to escape the spell Saraswati's apartment had cast over her—although of course that didn't mean she had managed to escape the spell Saraswati's insanity had cast over her.

"You know you're trespassing," Oluchi said as Priti and Nivedita burst into her kitchen like a particularly unpleasant surprise.

"Hey, it's my apartment, too," Priti said.

"I'm not talking to you," Oluchi stared past Priti, straight at the scratchy blue carpet—as if merely looking at Priti would turn her to stone or into a pillar of salt. Suddenly it was clear to Nivedita that it wasn't just Priti's deep-seated desire for drama that had led her to seek refuge at Saraswati's place. The week in which Oluchi realized Priti was Nivedita's relative must have been pure hell, for both of them.

"Well, sucks for you," Nivedita took the reins, "'cause *we*'re here to talk to you."

Whereupon Oluchi raised her gaze and directed her anger at Nivedita. "And who are you, Saraswati's secret police?"

"No, because if I were, I'd have no problem convicting people without due process," Nivedita replied, returning Oluchi's steadfast gaze.

"Is it okay if I just pack up some of my things, or have you already tossed them to the curb?" Priti asked. When no answer came, she continued, "All right, then I'll just go to my room."

"Anna-Lena," Oluchi said.

"Come again?"

"Anna-Lena . . . is staying in your room now."

"Wow, you don't let the grass grow under your feet, do you?"

"*Temporarily* staying in your room."

"And when were you planning on telling me?"

For a moment Oluchi's eyes flickered at Priti, then she shrugged the same way she had the day Nivedita had tried to talk to her about Simon, and said, "Fine by me."

Nivedita had almost stumbled forward, into empty space, but then Oluchi's defensive remark captured every last bit of it. "*What*'s 'fine by me'?"

"Let's hold a trial. Bring her here! No, what am I saying? Of course Saraswati won't go to the mountain, the mountain will have to go to her."

Kali grinned and, against her will, Nivedita couldn't help but smile too. Oluchi turned, grabbed the jacket she really didn't need, given the temperature, and Priti chimed in: "So is Anna paying her share of my rent?"

SARASWATI INVITED THEM in like some official delegation—anti-racists of the world, unite?—and not just any delegation, but one she'd been expecting. The corn-yellow sofa that had previously been piled high with manuscript pages was now completely clear, and there was a carafe of iced tea with fresh mint sprigs and lemon wedges on the white tulip table.

"Nivedita forced me to come," Oluchi said, just for the record.

"Well, it was actually Priti's idea," Nivedita said, just for the record.

"Oluchi sublet my room," Priti said, just for the record.

"Now that you're here, why don't you all sit down?" Saraswati said, and Nivedita automatically plopped down on the sofa.

Priti slid down next to her and mumbled, "It's weird, Saraswati did some seriously shitty things, but it's not like that gives me the right to be shitty to her."

"What?" Nivedita whispered back.

"Shit for shit, and we all go brown."

Nivedita put her hand in Priti's. "I'm glad you've been here with me this whole time."

"Really?" Priti asked, surprised.

"Yeah," Nivedita said, equally surprised.

Oluchi was still standing, and now she was casting a disparaging glance around the room—at the corduroy sofa, the Eero Aarnio Ball chair, and the white wool carpet—as if to say: *so this is what you bought with all the money you made off our stories, our history.*

Saraswati's eyes were following Oluchi's, and she dryly remarked: "Any other professorship, I'd have earned so much more money . . ."

"Then why didn't you?" Oluchi cut her off.

Good question, thought Nivedita. And then she began to wonder what would have become of her had Saraswati not been Saraswati, and she gripped Priti's hand even tighter.

"Because I am responsible," Saraswati said grandiosely, strolling over to the panoramic window where, backlit by the sun's rays, she turned into a silhouette with a shining halo around her head.

"I knew talking to her wouldn't change anything," Oluchi said to Nivedita.

"Well it's not like you even tried yet," Priti hissed.

Saraswati straightened her swanlike neck. "I gave up my *whiteness* for you! I gave up *being white*! Isn't that what you all are always calling for? *Give up your privileges*. I clearly gave up the ultimate privilege."

Oluchi looked at her, making no effort to disguise her disdain. "But you didn't have to pay the price, Saraswati."

For the last ten days—or was it eleven? Or twelve? Or thirteen?—Nivedita had been trying to explain exactly that to Saraswati. Now that Oluchi had said it, even though Nivedita understood, she couldn't help but say, "What price?"

"For us, it's a matter of life or death," Oluchi emphatically said. "And for her, it's just a matter of a tenured professorship and a few TV appearances. Saraswati never really had to be afraid. If somebody said *'Ausländer raus'* to her, or 'Go back to where you came from,' deep down inside she knew that it wasn't her they meant—it was never really *her* they were talking about. She wants to be like us, but she hasn't had to pay the price for it. And she'll never have to pay it."

"Au contraire—you've got that backward." Saraswati stepped aside so that the sun fell directly on Oluchi, blinding her. *"Your* understanding of anti-racism *requires white people* to pay the price. In reality, it doesn't bother you in the least, Oluchi, that I haven't experienced enough discrimination—what bothers you is that, as a *white* liberal, my conscience isn't guilty enough."

"That's not fair," Priti protested, whereupon Saraswati's indignation was redirected toward her.

"Since when has this been about fairness?! Are you saying that you are being fair to me?!" But the tempest dissipated as quickly as it had risen. Saraswati turned to Oluchi and, in a much milder tone, said, "You have no idea the price I paid."

"Oh, but I do," Oluchi countered. "I know all about you and Raji . . ."

"Raji!" Saraswati shouted. "Did it ever occur to you that Raji just *might* be a pathological liar? It's not his fault, but that doesn't change the fact that he lies through his teeth, so convincingly that he'd get anyone to believe the sky is anything but blue. Every single one of his tall tales is as reliable as the weather!"

The ball chair swiveled around, bringing Raji's slender-limbed body into view like the corpse in a murder mystery, except he was holding a glass of iced tea in one hand. He gave Nivedita a conspiratorial wink.

Oluchi was the first to recover. "I'm in no position to judge that. What I can affirm, however, is that you—*you*, meaning *you personally*—are a liar, Saraswati! And not once have you apologized to us for a single one of your lies!"

And suddenly Nivedita realized that was precisely what she had been waiting for this whole time: for Saraswati to say a simple *I'm sorry*. Just as Priti had, back in the stairwell, upon arriving at Saraswati's house. And, just like Priti, it would be entirely possible that Saraswati would both very much mean it and at the same time not mean it at all—after all, there had be a reason each of them did what they had done. But Nivedita needed to hear Saraswati say *I'm sorry! Please forgive me!* Nivedita needed to feel the vibration of these words' soundwaves in her body, and then something would happen, and maybe then she could let go.

But the Saraswati she knew would never say these words. Never. Never, ever.

"I'm sorry," Saraswati said at that very moment, in a perverse twist of timing. "I'm sorry for all the pain and all the confusion I've caused. Nothing could have been further from my mind than hurting all of you—especially you three. But I'm not sorry for the work I've done or for my job and career or for the life I live—and my life includes my skin color. I cannot and will not apologize for who I *am*."

Oluchi managed to give the impression that she was about to stand up, even though she had never sat down in the first place. "And *that's* exactly why we will *never* agree."

"Why not?"

"Because your color is only skin deep!"

For just a moment, Nivedita was back in Birmingham, holding a shard of glass and trying to show her fellow Indian kids what lay underneath her skin. She felt her arm burn, and could hardly stifle the urge to slap Saraswati on the back and say *Good for you, coconut!* At the same time, she was back in the French class she had taken years later, where an overenthusiastic teacher had her read a passage from Flaubert's *L'Éducation sentimentale* aloud in class: *"Il connut la mélancolie . . ."* and all Nivedita could read it as was *the coconut of melancholy.* And that was the point: she *understood* Oluchi, and agreed with her, but she *felt* like Saraswati. She didn't sympathize *with* Saraswati, but she felt *like* her—within Saraswati's dilemma, she recognized a terrifically significant amount of her very own problem.

"Skin color, in and of itself, is superficial," Saraswati said, eyes ablaze, looking at Oluchi. "Underneath, we're all the same."

But Oluchi had learned to recognize this eye-to-eye-stigma-for-stigma gaze long ago. *They're arm wrestling with their eyes*, thought Nivedita, now an intrigued referee of sorts. Only this particular staring contest was more like a match of aura wrestling. Oluchi and Saraswati were not battling over different viewpoints. Instead, they were waging war over distinctions within the same level of meaning—a level that lay deeper than words, deeper even than feelings, and neither of them could give in because that would mean negating their very being, their own existence, and all of their own subcutaneous reactions to life.

"I will never—not for a day, not for a minute, not for even a second—have the opportunity to walk down the street and not be seen as a Black woman," Oluchi emphatically said. "But, at any moment, you can simply turn around and—*voilà!*—Saraswati is Sarah Vera again, and it's all good."

"Then try walking down a street in Lagos, where you will most certainly not be seen as a Black woman—you'll be seen as a *white* woman: a *white* German tourist."

Oluchi jerked backward, and Saraswati went on, in a more conciliatory tone: "If you can be German, why can't I be POC?"

"I never said that. But being a Person of Color isn't up to you. You can't just take it upon yourself. It must be bestowed upon you."

"Like an honorary doctorate?" asked Saraswati, who held an honorary doctorate from the University of Dhaka.

Oluchi clenched her fists. "Sure, why not?"

"Then why don't *you* grant me this honorary-POC-ness?"

Nivedita wondered why Saraswati—high-and-mighty Saraswati—was even asking for Oluchi's acceptance.

"Forget it," Raji sneered from his space-age seat, and there was Nivedita's answer.

<h1 style="text-align:center">3</h1>

"Well, that got us shit," Nivedita said a moment after Oluchi had turned and strode out like a queen with nary a glance at her opponent, leaving the rest of the delegation behind. (A queen who had cast an imperious gaze at Nivedita to imply she'd better go with her, and—when Nivedita did nothing but grimace—said only one word: "Coconut.")

"Nonsense. Oluchi just had to get that out of her system. It'll do her good," Saraswati reassured Nivedita, handing her a fresh glass of iced tea.

"Are we sticking with the shit metaphor?" Priti snickered. "Just *what* has she got out of her system?"

"The feeling that, even if Saraswati were on fire, she wouldn't deign to piss on her," Raji chimed in.

"The pain she feels knowing I am not her mother," Saraswati answered in a stately tone. "Oops, no, that's actually you, Nivedita," she concluded, clumsily.

"Leave Nivedita alone," said Raji.

"I just wanted to give you the chance to defend her," Saraswati reassured him. "And don't worry, Nivedita, I'm ready to be your mother at a moment's notice, meaning your *Doktormutter,* of course—don't you just love how we turn doctoral advisors into family members *auf Deutsch*? That is, if you ultimately decide to pursue a doctorate after finishing your master's."

"You mean *if* you're still at the university," Raji corrected her.

"Where else would I be?" Saraswati asked, and for just a moment Nivedita's disappointment in Saraswati was overshadowed by her concern for her.

» **Christian Baron @c_baronaldo** *Maybe the example set by #SarahVera gives us a chance to think about who is allowed to achieve and speak from privileged standpoints. Why would a professor ever become the*

> mouthpiece of POC? Racism and classism are tightly intertwined, and it's high time those #atthebottom were heard, too.

» Eni @OkBoomer *Because we only listen to the most image-obsessed people. Which are usually old white dudes like Saraswati.*

» Freckled Leafy Sunlight @HalliHallo *Don't harass the poor lady. What #Saraswati needs is therapy. #transracial*

» Buzz Checkers @YourBestFriend *Have you ever thought of getting therapy?* @Saraswati

» Melissa Harris Perry @MelHarrisPerry *The idea that passing to Black or POC is inherently crazy is something we need to question. The idea that 'OMG, only a crazy white woman would want to be BIPOC' should distress us. #Saraswati #RachelDolezal*

Saraswati reached behind her back and pulled open the terrace door to let in some not-yet-refreshingly cool evening air. "What I did was above and beyond just teaching—I *demonstrated*, in my very being, the fact that *not being white* has become a form of cultural capital. It's a sign of our success."

"*Our*?" asked Nivedita, stunned again.

Saraswati used her warmest, sunniest smile to make her doubt herself. "*Love Politics*, remember? That's what I did. I drew you all to my bosom and nourished you."

"Wow, you really think you're all-powerful, don't you?!" Nivedita exclaimed, simultaneously noticing that she spoke more bluntly with Saraswati than any other person on the planet, even her own mother—especially her own mother. Because Nivedita was always worried Birgit might collapse under the weight of her anger, and that she herself might then collapse under the weight of her guilt. So, with eyes registering all of the worry and preemptive guilt, Nivedita looked over at Saraswati, only to notice she looked neither particularly shaken nor particularly impressed. Instead, she looked rather satisfied, as if she were grading Nivedita's every word: this student displays independent, kill-your-idols thinking, *ergo*—mission accomplished. Whereupon Nivedita felt a whole new wave of anger surging within.

"Haven't you ever wondered why you all looked so pathetic when you first walked into my classroom?" Saraswati gleefully elaborated on her so-called Love-Politics project. "Every single one of you was wan, pale, pimply, and awkward. You wore your clothes as if you wanted to be someone else. All you needed was a healthy dose of attention and self-love. And then you all quickly started to shine from within."

"Me, too?" Priti asked.

"Especially you," Saraswati answered.

"Me, too?" Raji asked, and then preempted her answer: "Of course that's a rhetorical question, Sarah."

The humidity was so high they might as well have been swimming through the air. Verbal soundwaves were distorted by the time they reached Nivedita, so it almost seemed as if she were feeling Saraswati's next words more than hearing them.

"Have you ever noticed how people of color, in the few historic films they appear in, always look unbelievably gorgeous? Like brown versions of the *white* stars? Even the ones who weren't played by *white* actors in black-face? In real life, that of course wasn't and isn't the case. When the message you're given, every single day, is that your body doesn't fit in with that ideal form of body type, well then you try to make it fit in by deforming it. And I'm not even talking about skin-lightening creams and hair straighteners that leave chemical burns on your scalp. No, merely learning the lesson that you must be ashamed of the skin you live in is sufficient. Because then you won't feel good in your skin, and you won't wear it with pride. You have fewer blemishes than you did back during that first class, and just look at your hair. Do you really think that's a coincidence, Nivedita?"

Nivedita shuddered when she realized Saraswati actually expected to get a reaction to such utter hubris.

"I should market my lectures as beauty treatments, as self-care seminars! Look at you! Just *look* at you! Without me, you'd never look the way you do."

"Are you trying to say that you made me what I am?" Nivedita asked, sounding as if she were under water.

Well, what would you *say?* Kali asked, wagging her tongue in Nivedita's face.

Nivedita held her hands over her ears so as to shut out both Saraswati and Kali. But the questions kept echoing in her head: who was she without Saraswati? And this didn't refer to some distant future, but the present, based upon the past—who would she be had there never been a Saraswati in her life?

BEFORE NIVEDITA HAD come to Düsseldorf, she and Lilli had gone to Ruhr University in Bochum and majored in gender studies. Even back then, Lilli would've preferred to attend a school with more historic buildings, time-honored traditions, and the mustiness of millennia below its fancy caps and gowns. Nivedita, however, loved the place and its sleepy-suburb, commuter-campus feel. And then something happened that Nivedita had always secretly wanted without even knowing it, and it perfectly fit in with the functional practicality of this absurdly university-esque university: Lilli informed Nivedita that she was writing a short story, and Nivedita was a character in it! She was electrified by the idea that she was both capital-R Real and capital-R Romantic enough that someone had chosen to capture her existence with words on paper.

It was the same feeling she got from seeing the sheer heft of Saraswati's hair four semesters later. Just two weeks after Lilli delivered the apparently good news, the feeling rolled over Nivedita's body as she held the short story in her hand—actually in her hand, because it was printed out, not just emailed—with a handwritten dedication from Lilli, who instead of dotting her *i*s gave them puffy little hearts.

At first Nivedita figured Lilli had inadvertently grabbed the wrong document or printed the wrong file. Then it dawned on her that she was supposed to be the "Indian girl" who "just loved burning incense and cooking with yellow curry." Lilli had known her since their very first year and had never once seen her light any incense or use any curry powder, no matter what color, because actually Nivedita had a feeling she might be allergic to cardamom. How could all those real-life experiences count for less than such stereotypes?

Emotion oozed through and then trickled out of her body without leaving behind the anger or amusement it would in later years. Instead, it left her with a vague sadness, a twisted disappointment that she wasn't "the Indian girl" who "just loved burning incense."

Sometimes Nivedita wished she were Muslim because Muslim women, despite all the hostility they endure, at least exist in the collective consciousness. Muslim women were dangerous, veiled terrorists, a deathmatch between *One Thousand and One Nights* and the recent elegiac lament of Germany's end by Thilo Sarrazin titled *Deutschland schafft sich ab* (*Germany Does Away with Itself*). Indian women, on the other hand, belonged to a religion that ranked just a notch above Pastafarianism on the charts of German public awareness. And no wonder—after all, Hindus worshipped such implausible entities as flying monkey gods, women with a thousand arms, and roly-poly men with elephant heads. Who could take anything like that seriously? And then Nivedita realized she had fallen into the same logical trap as all the Hindu nationalists, because of course not all Indians were Hindus; they could just as easily be Muslims or Christians or Jains or Buddhists adherents of any other world religion or no religion at all.

"IN HINDUISM, EVERY soul is a circle with an endless circumference, and its center is the individual person's body," Saraswati explained, pointing through the terrace door and out over the roofs of Oberbilk. Nivedita, who up until then had always thought that a soul was located in a body the same way a heart was, began to feel dizzy sitting on Saraswati's yellow sofa.

"Dying only means that this soul has moved from this body to another."

"Why are we talking about Hinduism all of a sudden?" asked Priti.

"Because you're always the same soul, no matter what body you're living in," Saraswati clarified.

"Are you trying to say you're a soul of color, Saraswati?" Nivedita retorted, hoping to sound cynical but instead sounding panicked. "Do we have to call you an SOC now?"

"In Islam, there's a marketplace in paradise," Saraswati continued, lost in thought.

"How did we get to Islam now?" asked Priti.

"A marketplace, in paradise," Saraswati repeated, "where you can pick and choose the form you want to take that day. And, well, for now, I chose this one."

"Uh, sure—*in paradise*," Priti scoffed in protest.

Saraswati smiled at her magnanimously, and then her smile enveloped them all. "And, with my work, I aim to build a paradise on earth."

"Do we have to call you Jesus now?" Nivedita asked without making even the slightest effort to mask the panic in her voice.

"Jesus here wants to nod," Raji piped up. "See, Nivedita? Her entire body wants to give one big nod, and she has to expend all her effort to refrain from doing so." Nivedita had never met a man filled with so much resentment.

Saraswati stared at him with the kind of cold hard loathing only a little sister could feel toward a big brother—a brother capable of making her livid whenever he wanted, at a moment's notice. And then she collected herself again.

"The world needs me," she said, having regained her stately tone.

"The world doesn't need either of us, Saraswati," Nivedita said, on the brink of hyperventilating.

"Are you trying to say I *haven't* changed your life?"

"Oh, you certainly have!" cried Nivedita. "And now you've blown it. You've ruined my life!" Deep in her pocket, her phone started vibrating. Simon! Why did he always only call at the worst possible moment?

"Your entire life, or just a part of it, huh?" Saraswati asked before walking out onto the terrace. "Grow up!"

Nivedita had risen to her feet before Saraswati hurled that last insult. "Right! You're twice my age, and have probably read ten times more books . . ."

"A hundred times more," Saraswati corrected her.

"A thousand times more, I don't care! That doesn't undo the fact that you hurt me . . . that you did something to me . . . that you . . . took something from me." And then—since it was the sole thing she could do better than Priti, and was far better at than even Saraswati—Nivedita burst into tears.

Back when she was in seventh grade, a new teacher had humiliated her in front of the whole class. She could no longer remember why, or what had started it. She only remembered how, during the break, he'd come to apologize to her. But what he ended up saying instead was, "You need to see that you made a mistake, Nivedita. Why don't you even look at me when I'm speaking to you?"

She then turned her tear-streaked face to him and said, "Because I'm crying and I don't want you to see. That's why."

The shock on his face back then made as deep an impression on her as Saraswati's cayenne-red mouth did now, as all irony slipped away and her lips formed words that took longer to reach Nivedita than Saraswati herself did.

"Forget what I just said to you. Raji knows he brings out the worst in me."

"Oh, so now it's my fault you deceived Nivedita?" Raji said.

But Nivedita didn't even hear him, because now Saraswati held her in her arms and whispered into the locks of hair covering her ear, "I'm sorry, Nivedita, I'm so very sorry."

Who'd have thought just a few tears could so swiftly turn the power dynamics upside down?

That's only because Saraswati's a nice person, Kali's pedantic voice said inside Nivedita's head.

Shut it, Nivedita said back.

She breathed in the salty smell of Saraswati's skin and the sandalwood scent of her hair. In no other confrontation had she ever been so acutely aware of her own power. And then she noticed her phone had stopped vibrating.

4

Early on in their relationship, Nivedita had been fascinated whenever she and Simon had issues, if *fascination* was really the word she meant. She knew it started with F, at least—oh, right: no, she meant *frustration*!

Simon said "I'm in therapy" the way other people said things like "I'm learning a foreign language." His exact formulation was actually, "I'm talking to someone," and he'd say it softly, his hands at his chin with fingers meshed together, lips positioned just above, like Benedict Cumberbatch in *Sherlock*. In fact, Simon had actually played Sherlock in a campus theatrical production, but that had been before Nivedita's time, so she could only fig-ure he had acquired the gesture there.

After the debacle on the way back from the airport, they had agreed to meet up again soon, in the park, to have a proper relationship crisis–type talk. The day they met in the Volksgarten was cold enough that each of them was wearing too many layers to really be able to get close to the other. They sat on a bench surrounded by little kids feeding a bunch of ravenous ducks. Nivedita felt an urge to run over, rip the paper bags from their hands, and explain how bad it was to feed ducks bread, especially in the wintertime. But then the gesture of feeding ducks filled her with such a satisfying sense of species-transcending friendliness that to give in to that impulse would have broken her heart.

Simon was wearing fingerless lambskin gloves, and when he withdrew his fingers from his lips and folded them behind his head, Nivedita read it as a sign of disagreement. "We did some trance work. I'm really good at it. Have you ever been in a trance?"

"I thought we were going to talk about Marija," Nivedita counteroffered, uncertain whether her decades-long, constant conversation with Kali counted as being in a trance.

"Why are you so fixated on Marija?" Simon asked, his irritation audible. "I haven't seen her in months."

"I'm not fixated on Marija—I thought you were."

"We separated, okay? Isn't that enough?"

"Well then why did you say you're not done with her yet?"

Simon thought about it as the now-sated ducks waddled back to the pond and plopped into the ice-cold water. When Nivedita was the age of those kids now shaking the last few crumbs out of their bags, she'd always daydreamed about being one of those fountain figures—a bronze, naked little nymphette frolicking in a shower of sprinkling water, hands held high, eyes ecstatically beaming. In her fantasy world, these statues weren't rigid or immobile in the least. Instead, they were lively, real people who had just been frozen here in the human realm by a torrent of time standing still that had been spewed at them by a dolphin. Back in their own realm, they were still performing the dance of eternal youth and all its wondrously seductive moves. Nivedita had been particularly rapt by their bud-like breasts, greened by oxidation, lactating droplets of water. And of course the bird's nest between their wet thighs also caught her eye. Every time she looked back up, she could've sworn the water nymph's upper body had moved slightly forward, looking narcissistic and autoerotic the way only nymphs from the Art Nouveau period could, formed as they were by artists who systematically chose to ignore the pain of the world all around them.

Simon was a little bit like these sculptures, too: striking and electrifying and at the same time totally out of reach. Shifting a bit on the bench after what felt like an interminable five minutes, he finally came to a decision. "Well, if you really want to know . . ."

"I do," said Nivedita, steeling herself for whatever would come next.

"I heard a voice."

"What?"

"In my last trance session. I heard a voice."

It was worse than Nivedita had thought, but at least she was getting some clarity on the situation. "Marija spoke to you in your last therapy session?"

"No, it was a male voice, coming from up above. At first I really didn't want to listen, because I didn't want God to give me any good advice. But he kept on talking, and at some point I realized it was a little weird. Of all people, why had he chosen to talk to me? But then when I finally decided to listen to him, he stopped talking. And I have no idea what he actually said."

The pond smelled like animals, or musk, or homeopathically diluted essence of dog. It had a fountain, but even that was more like just an aerator—it wasn't adorned by a bunch of mythological statues gyrating around any-and-everything phallic, like in some naughty-aughties rap video—and even that was shut off, given the wintry temperatures. So, in lieu of any such lasciviously writhing figures, it now seemed Simon was the only guy here wrestling with angels and demons. Kali yawned, bored.

"And that's the moment I realized my yearning for Marija originated in an anger I still felt from a very early, primal experience of abandonment."

It dawned on Nivedita that Simon had just regurgitated his therapist's assessment, although he presented it as his own self-diagnosis. And since Saraswati had given her pretty much the same interpretation shortly before, on the wooden steps outside the economics department back on campus, she gave him an encouraging nod. "And?"

"And, whenever anyone gets close to me, one of my deep-seated fears pops back up, and I'm afraid of being abandoned. I then desperately look for reasons for why I don't actually love that person. That's what God was trying to tell me: since nothing else could help me, my ability to cut myself off emotionally saved my life. And all of a sudden I was immensely grateful for that."

Nivedita thought: *This isn't about Marija, it's about me. He's talking about me. I'm really important to him, but this is the only way he can express it.* She reached for his hand. He held on to her like a lost little boy.

"And what are you going to do now, with this newfound knowledge?" she asked with real warmth and openness.

"Then the hour was up, and we decided I should start by just taking that feeling with me."

BUT THEN THE next therapy session was also all about Simon's past, not his present—ditto for the one after, and the one after that, and the one after that. Meanwhile, of course, the present just kept going. And since Simon had shared his fear of commitment with Nivedita as if it were some precious treasure, she felt 50 percent responsible for it, and 0 percent competent regarding what changes Simon might make, and how fast, if any were called for at all.

The only one who had anything like an understanding of her situation was, surprisingly, God—the God who had specifically advised Simon, during one of his weekly trance/therapy sessions, to hang in just a little bit longer amid his issues with Nivedita. Mind you, he said *hang in*, not *solve* or anything like that. But by that point their relationship status was shaky, which made Nivedita feel so worn out and weary that she was grateful for the friendly word, even if it came from a God who wasn't her God.

(DRAFT) This whole Simon-and-God thing is really a thing. He talks to him. Not like other people talk to God (aka praying), but the way God speaks to a chosen prophet. And no, this isn't a breach of trust, because Simon talks to basically everybody about it. Women, above all. His signature greeting is: Has God ever spoken to you? It works every time. Maybe Simon does it because he isn't the nerdy, asexual, God-helps-us-all kind of prophet—no, he's more like the Patagonia-clad-outdoorsy variation on that theme: survival and visions. No Hallelujah, yes Campact NGO. The Lawyer, Mother Nature, and the Supernatural! He actually doesn't even want to talk about it—that's why he ALWAYS does, nonstop—because it's so intimate, so incredibly personal, y'know, and by then all the ladies are already spilling their much-more-intimate guts out to him.

And, well, hands up! I, too, am also constantly talking to my goddess.

"I should hope so!"

"Yeah, but I don't use you to make myself seem sexier, Kali. My motto isn't: hey, peeps, I'm in convo with Kali, so all y'all can just call me Kamasutra!

"But of course the fact that you talk to me does make you sexier!"

Nivedita had never posted this draft, because of course that would've been a breach of trust. But apparently even just using Simon's hand as the Hand of God in her cute-kitty-pic post now qualified as a mortal sin.

"So *that's* the kind of person you are," Simon had exploded at her over the phone as she headed home from the radio on that fateful day when everything had changed, when she and Simon officially became exes, when Saraswati became Ex-Saraswati.

Back then, Nivedita had thought the worst part of that day had been Simon totally forgetting/ignoring her radio interview. Upon hearing his indignation, she responded in kind. "Since when has it ever annoyed you if people find out about your one-on-one chats with God? You're the one who waves them in the face of every single complete stranger you meet, after all, as long as they're female."

The bike lock she had shoved onto the rear rack slithered between the metal bars like a snake, landing in a coil right next to a pile of pigeon shit on the asphalt. Nivedita held the phone in one hand, the handlebars in the other, and gazed jealously at a woman who'd wedged her phone under her headscarf and now sauntered into the main train station, both hands free.

To Nivedita's surprise, Simon's temper quickly calmed as he explained, almost reverentially, "That triggered a traumatic memory from Vanessa's childhood." Vanessa was the not-exactly-complete-stranger who'd hosted the party Simon had taken Nivedita to the week before. The traumatic memory was a vision of the Virgin Mary that Vanessa had experienced as an eight-year-old girl, after she and a friend had chugged her grandma's Advocaat, an egg-and-brandy liqueur. (Vanessa pronounced *grandma* "gramma" and *mother* "mmuther," which is why during the party—despite the fancy-pants, historic-enough-to-be-landmarked building Vanessa lived in, not to mention her apartment's grand-ballroom-scale dimensions and a sideboard arrayed with more types of cheese than Nivedita could even name—Nivedita had felt a kind of kinship with Vanessa. She thought of it as a We-Daughters-of-Essen-Against-the-Rest-of-the-World-type bond, until Vanessa turned her full attention to Simon and his experiences with the Trinity.) At least Simon hadn't called her Nessa or, worse yet, Nessie. Whereupon Nivedita realized maybe she should start calling her Nessie, aka the Monster of Loch Advocaat.

"Well why'd she tell you, then?" Nivedita huffed, just as her bike finally decided to join its lock, although not without ramming its pedals into her shin on the way. Simon managed to avoid his classic, endless pauses—they were bad enough when you were sitting next to him in the car, but downright deadly over the phone—and coolly replied, "Clearly you know nothing about trauma."

"Oh, spare me!" Nivedita shot back, rubbing her shin. "This Vanessa can trust you about as far as she can throw you, and I saw her skinny arms. She's just like all the other girls who're constantly coming up to you and are just *so* understanding and *so* important to you—just another pretext for you not bothering to treat me like your partner when we went to parties together. Marija is yet another. And, if you're honest with yourself, even your very own God knows that."

"I shared something very personal with you. And I'd just like for you to be a little more respectful with it," Simon said, his voice weighty.

"No, you never shared a thing with me—because if you actually had, then you'd have been interested in what I thought about it," she said, her voice just as weighty, or at least she hoped.

"I see," he said, and hung up.

Whereupon Kali launched into song:

Fell in love with a narcissist
lost 10 pounds
still I couldn't resist
lost my mind
didn't give a shit
lost my pride
digging in this hole
I'll go on 'til I lose my soul.

"That's not super helpful," Nivedita opined.

Nor was it meant to be, said Kali, still bored. *Why do you keep replaying the same scene, kiddo? Fight, fight, nah-no-worries-everything's-fine, then he plays the I'm-leaving-you card, and—poof!—he's the Big Bad Wolf and you're naïve Little Red Riding Hood. But once you're on the sixth, or . . . tenth go-around, you can't really be so naïve anymore, by then you're just reckless and maybe also a little soft in the head.*

"Isn't that ableist?" Nivedita asked.

So sue me, said Kali.

Nivedita had a recurring dream that she'd wake up and Saraswati's deceit would hurt her more than Simon's had, but that never happened. Saraswati was there, irritating yet reachable, whereas Simon had disappeared into a vacuum that was suckier, more gaping, and more painful than any of their fights had ever foreshadowed.

"D'you think it's painful for him, too?" she asked Saraswati as they enjoyed a glass of wine out on the terrace, since nothing more to say about Saraswati's delusions of grandeur came to mind.

Saraswati took a cautious sip from her glass, and then another, before replying, "Pain is a continuum. It's impossible for you to be hurt without him having been hurt, too—not on your watch, mind you, but by *something*, at some point in the past—and then he's passing that pain on to you, quite effectively."

"Or he just has some hidden agenda," Priti chimed in.

"Simon, you mean—or Raji?" Saraswati pointedly asked.

"*You* tell *me*."

"There's also a political reason you're feeling the way you do, Nivedita," Saraswati continued. "Although that doesn't mean that all your feelings are automatically political."

Nivedita automatically nodded.

"It just means that your feelings sometimes are based on political parameters."

"Saraswati, Nivedita has a broken heart. How about we try a little less hermeneutics and a little more actual advice?" Priti suggested, swinging herself up out of the hammock to go to the kitchen for some cookies.

Saraswati watched her go. "Okay, Nivedita, look. Your problem isn't that any given relationship might end—which in this particular case, entre nous, would be a goddamn blessing—but rather that that would constitute an emotional catastrophe, because you lack a fundamental sense of security. And why do you? Because you've never really felt you belonged anywhere, with anyone—except for maybe with your cousin, who in turn shamelessly takes advantage of that. How's *that* for actual advice—am I being real enough for you?"

"I once had a professor who taught me that people who start sentences with the words 'Your problem . . .' are privileged pricks," Nivedita remarked, to balance out her automatic Tourettic nodding.

"Sure, but only when those people aren't me," Saraswati smiled. "Generalizations are only accurate ninety-nine percent of the time."

"Are you one hundred percent certain about that?" Nivedita quipped.

Saraswati blew her a kiss. "Feeling like you don't belong, by the way, has a lot to do with racism, but usually it isn't primarily the racism you see out on the streets every day. You and Priti and Oluchi and her crew are trying to change the streets, but what we really need to change is the system."

"Does what you say ever actually have meaning, or are you just saying it because it sounds good?" Raji drily asked, ensconcing himself in the hammock Priti had just gotten out of.

"Oh come on, it's not like it's that hard to understand," Saraswati said in the voice she reserved solely for Raji, a mixture of lures and barbs. But it had been a long day, and Raji's self-control was showing signs of wear and tear, just like the thin veil separating them all—if not from truth itself, from truthfulness, at least.

"You are obscene!" Raji replied.

"You know that what our parents did isn't my fault."

"*Your* parents," Raji's voice turned cold.

"If it were really so easy, then everything would've been just fine," Saraswati explained, and Nivedita wished she could just pause her breathing so it wouldn't constantly remind them of her presence. "But your problem is that Konstantin and Josefa arranged things so that they were your parents, too."

"Stealing—kidnapping!—is not the same as adopting!"

"And wishing something were true doesn't necessarily make it so!"

Now Nivedita was gasping for breath. She felt found out, because for years she had identified with the First-Nations children in the USA and Canada who'd been taken from their parents under what was essentially a "Kill-the-Indian-to-save-the-Man" policy pursued right up through the nineteen-seventies. They'd been snatched and put in *white* orphanages or placed with *white* families to be "cleansed" of their culture. They weren't allowed to learn their own languages and weren't told their own histories. And then—if they managed to survive all that, which many didn't—they often spent the rest of their lives feeling guilt and shame for not being "real Indians."

Raji looked at Saraswati in disgust. "Says YOU?!"

Saraswati tried not to look at him with too much sympathy, because she knew nothing would infuriate him more than that. Whereupon Raji, perhaps because he'd spent so many years decoding her glances, grew even more infuriated. "Of course what our parents did was despicable, Raji, but they did it with the very best intentions. They did it for you!"

"Stop lying to yourself—they did it for themselves! They did it just because they wanted a kid! And then right after, when they realized Josefa was pregnant, well, they couldn't just give back the baby nobody wanted."

"It's not true that nobody wanted you!"

"Well then why did I have to leave when you came along?"

"You got sick. Tuberculosis. And you had to quarantine for a few days."

"*Days?!*"

"Weeks?"

"A half year. I obtained written confirmation from the pulmonary clinic. It was a half year."

"You were sick!"

"And what if it had been *you* who was sick, huh? Would they have shipped you off for six months?"

For once, Saraswati was speechless.

"Do you have any idea how hospitals in the late sixties treated babies?" Raji murmured, his voice sounding disembodied as a hologram.

Yet again, Saraswati was speechless.

"Don't kid yourself. You three were the perfect family, and I disturbed that balance."

Silence spread over them, swallowing all the space between them, creating as much of an internal bond as words would have.

Than Saraswati began to laugh. "You're such a liar!"

"It must run in the family," Raji said, his voice not exactly warm, but with the potential for warmth at some point in the future—the very distant future.

"Sure, but I only lie about me."

"Yeah, so? I only lie about you, too."

"Are you also getting the impression we aren't hearing the whole story, Niv?" asked Priti, who for quite some time now had been standing behind Nivedita, holding a plate full of Cookie Monster cookies.

"Have you ever felt you've heard the whole story with Saraswati?" Nivedita asked back.

BUT YES, LITTLE Konstantin had disturbed the balance. When he came back from the clinic, he wouldn't speak. ("Nonsense, of course it wasn't half a year, who on earth would ship a baby off to quarantine for six months?"—"Well how long was it, then?"—"It was . . . too long.") He broke everything he touched and was always having accidents. ("Sure, there *are* a ton of scandals with international adoptions, the baby trade *is* a lucrative business, but that doesn't automatically mean that Raji is one of those stolen babies.") And he took all his annoyance and aggravation to school with him—Saraswati had confided that to Nivedita at some point. And not only did his perfect little sister do everything better than him, she also wanted to do everything together *with* him. So that he could witness her flawlessness, her perfection, her future-yet-already-essentially-guaranteed stardom. She was as spectacular as the story of her conception, when heavyhearted Josefa and Konstantin Sr. had given up on having a child of their own and, after years of effort, adopted a child radically different from themselves, a little foreign boy, who was then enthusiastically trailed by the little baby girl they finally were able to have. She was a miracle, and from the very start she was sweet as honey to her difficult, adoptive big brother. How Raji must've hated Saraswati's loving adoration. Except it wasn't Raji who'd hated Saraswati, it was Konstantin Jr., and it wasn't Saraswati he'd hated, it was Sarah. Sarah, who called little Stan "Satan" when she wanted to make him cry. And Satan had been ahead of him from birth on, even when it came to the one thing his little sister could never take from him. Or so he'd long thought. But then Sarah/Saraswati not only became a POC like him, she became nothing less than a Professional POC.

6

The infamous Hay Festival debate had ended with Jordan Peterson asking the following penetrating question: "To what extent are my accomplishments the result of my White Privilege? What would you say—five percent? Fifteen percent? Twenty-five percent? Seventy-five percent? And how should I make up for that? Should there be a tax levied against it, so I can just pay up and stop having to hear about it?"

That had been just over a year ago, but now it felt like another lifetime, and Nivedita had taken that to mean Peterson thought of it as ransom—he wanted to buy himself a clear conscience. But here was Saraswati, seated next to her out on the terrace, on yet another balmy night, explaining, "It's not my fault I was born *white*. It's not like I'm *white* because of some character flaw."

Nivedita had drunk so much wine already—maybe it was the same night Priti had brought that plate of cookies, just much later—that she retorted, "Nah, but you're definitely brown because of some character flaw."

Saraswati gave her a stern look. "The *post* in *postcolonialism* refers to the consequences of colonialism, not the end of colonialism. And a guilty conscience will do nothing to alter those consequences. We don't need revenge, we need recovery. We need to heal."

"Yeah, but you want the healing to come before we've even had a chance to process our anger. And Raji's really damn angry at you," Nivedita countered, reprimanding Saraswati with her eyes.

But all Saraswati did was pick up the leather pouch of tobacco Raji had left on the warm cement floor of the terrace after he'd gone back inside, palpating its contents with such yearning in her fingers it was as if she'd forgotten she'd quit smoking years ago. "I don't want to be German."

"There's nothing more German than that," Priti proffered from the hammock.

Instead of answering, Saraswati extracted her phone from her pocket. "Have you two seen this?"

» Contra @CountercultureBlues *#Saraswati dances on the souls of Black folks @SoulEater*

"I thought we'd all agreed to steer clear of Shitter and In-Your-Facebook and Instagrief for the sake of our mental health," Priti observed.

"Those—but not only those." Nivedita thought back to the flurry of hate-filled articles, all of which she'd of course read on her phone, plus the endless rabbit hole of radio and video clips she and Priti dove into for an entire night. From the start, news of the Saraswati scandal had boiled up and spread the world over, and if you chose to believe the media—old media, new media, social media, asocial media—the entire world now regarded her as a racist. And the entire world included US populist Donald Trump. (*Unattractive both inside and out. There has never been so many lies, so much deception. There has never been anything like that.* And then a mere two minutes later: *While @Saraswati is an extremely unattractive woman, I refuse to say that because I always insist on being politically correct.*) It also included Indian populist Narendra Modi, who couldn't decide whether to condemn Saraswati (*Saraswati's mind is not the problem, her mindset is.*) or feel flattered by her (*The infamous German scholar pretending to be Indian has shown that India does not need to become anything else. India must only become India. This is a country that, once upon a time, was called the Golden Bird.*). That's why it was so surprising to find Saraswati scrolling through this very thread, as if it were more devastating than any other.

"*Being white* means killing people of other skin colors. But their souls come back in your children. Their trauma is reincarnated in your wombs."

Nivedita wondered whether she was reading to them from something, or just verbalizing her masochistic interior monolog.

"That's why I chose to take a karmic shortcut: no kids for me, and I didn't wait to be reincarnated. Instead, I opted to pay the price for my sins in this same lifetime." *Nope, that definitely wasn't a reading from anyone else.*

"What do you mean by 'my sins'?" Priti asked, incredulous.

"I thought you'd never ask. We did do something to Raji—Josefa and Konstantin and me—we forced our charity upon him. And I can't think of anything more violent than people who want to save someone who does not wish to be saved." Saraswati gazed up into the night sky, which was already incubating the heat of the following morning, and changed the topic. "The indigenous peoples of Australia believe that if you kill a person, that person has a right to your soul—they can ride your soul, so to speak."

"What are you getting at?" asked Nivedita.

"That Raji is riding on my soul."

Nivedita thought back to what Saraswati had told her about the Hindu concept of the soul, and pictured Raji on the circumference of an endless circle, the edge of perception. But at the same time, in this vision, Raji was very here, very present. Even now—while he was in Saraswati's home office, a mere two terrace-doors away, either sleeping or preparing to take vengeance, or whatever it was he was up to off in the darkness—he was here.

A flame flickered, tongue like, right next to her. Saraswati was holding Raji's lighter, meditatively staring at its flame. "I'd say it's time for an exorcism."

DECOLONIZING THE MIND

NIVEDITA'S CLASS NOTES:

"When we speak, we are afraid our words will not be heard or welcomed. But when we are silent, we are still afraid. So it is better to speak."—AUDRE LORDE

"By making whiteness the colour of oppression, the colour that defined a person's right to own other human beings, to rape and kill and steal with impunity, white supremacists had paradoxically opened up the way for blackness to become the colour of freedom, of revolution and of humanity."—AKALA

"So decolonization in my view is about having access to information and narratives which re-frame our understanding of how to relate to other peoples, other countries and other cultures."—PRIYAMVADA GOPAL

1

20 DAYS POST-SARASWATI

The arrival of the university's second letter brought measurable time back to the bird's nest high above the vendors lining Kölner Straße. This time, the legalistically ultra-proper signatories were the administration's legal department *and* the dean. This time, Saraswati's friend Simone wasn't on the phone; she beamed in from her law office via Skype. This time, there were two additional pairs of eyes watching as Nivedita opened the envelope, since

Saraswati refused to touch it, as if the paper had been infused with some evil magic that would begin taking effect on contact.

"Well?" Saraswati asked, her voice flat.

Nivedita nodded.

"Take a picture and send it to me on WhatsApp," Simone instructed.

Nivedita's hands were shaking so badly that Priti had to take over, using Saraswati's phone, while Raji stared at the two über-official-looking sheets of letterhead as if hypnotized.

Simone didn't look like Nivedita had imagined a lawyer would—meaning like Linda Fairstein and Elizabeth Lederer, the prosecutors who did everything in their power to convict five Black boys of a crime they didn't commit, in Ava DuVernay's Netflix series *When They See Us*. She felt a vague distrust toward lawyers, but the only Lederer-like thing about Simone was her tight perm. She ran her fingers through her curly locks so frequently while reading that her hair poufed out, its outline framing her head with question marks when she finally looked up. "Okay, there are a few ways we could frame our appeal. There are precedent-setting cases like the professor in Leipzig who they tried to fire because of racist tweets."

"Yeah, I remember him—that AfD-prof. guy," Nivedita said.

"No, you're thinking of the AfD-prof. *gal* who taught at a university in the Lower Rhine region, who took her school to court. I'm talking about the law professor who openly fantasized about a '*white* Europe' in his tweets. Neither school managed to get rid of either of them, because both firings basically violated the law protecting freedom of opinion and expression."

"What about the professor who tried to force a Muslim student to take off her headscarf?" Priti asked.

"All he had to do was apologize."

Saraswati, whose mouth had hung open this entire time, finally found her voice again: "How did it come to this? Are you really comparing me to racist . . . *racist!* . . . demagogues? I'm the polar opposite of . . . them."

"Not according to this document here," Simone held her phone up to her webcam, resulting in little more than a bright rectangle of light on the screen of Saraswati's laptop.

"They're accusing you of mocking minorities," Nivedita explained. "And saying you fraudulently obtained your endowed professorship, under false pretenses."

"How could I have fraudulently obtained my endowed professorship, under false pretenses, when said facts demonstrably made it harder for me to get this or any other job? And when did I ever stipulate my race? I never once said or wrote 'Name: Saraswati; Race: Indian.'"

"That will be our first grounds for appeal," Simone decided.

Saraswati shook her head, blinking eyes now so bright they looked suspiciously teary. "I am *not* going to file a countersuit over my dismissal!"

"Oh yes you are," Simone said. "You don't have to win, but you absolutely must appeal."

"WHY DON'T YOU just apologize and close this whole case?" Nivedita asked as soon as Simone left the Skype call to draft a strongly worded response letter.

Saraswati tightly wrapped herself in her dupatta, as if trying to secure her unstable place in the universe. "They don't want an apology, they want blood," she said, her voice so tight it came out as sharp and glittering as a diamond. "Or, to put it a little less dramatically, they want me to leave, to resign my professorship. If I apologize now, they'll just take it as a sign that I've done something that justifies the action they've taken against me."

Priti cast an urgent glance at Raji, but he was still staring at the now-black rectangle of Saraswati's laptop screen, as if spellbound.

"I'm better than them, and one day you all will understand," Saraswati declared.

"Come again?" said Nivedita, tired of her own indignation.

"That's the best way to respond to a shitstorm—just stand tall and say, 'I've made a decision and I'm standing by it.' Once you start apologizing, you can never do anything but keep apologizing."

"That's not true," Nivedita countered, unsure of whether it wasn't, in fact, true. "I wanted . . . I still want an apology from you."

"See? Once you start, it never ends." Saraswati tossed her dupatta over her head as if that could cancel out all further argument—but halfway through, her gesture lost its oomph. Her arms sank, and instead she gave Nivedita her sweetest smile, a smile you'd have seen on the face of a Virgin Mary crying tears of blood.

Or on the face of Sita, before she forgave that damn fool Rama yet again! Kali suggested.

Or Sita, Nivedita concurred.

"But I don't mean you, of course," the now weepy Saraswati/Sita/Virgin Mary benevolently added. "I'll apologize to you in a heartbeat, whenever you want, for as long as you want."

"Really?" Nivedita asked, bewildered—and then, a second later, "Are you apologizing to me because I'm the one you hurt the most?"

Raji gave a scornful huff without taking his eyes off the laptop's black screen.

"No, I'm apologizing to you because in your case you *really do* deserve an apology. Whereas with everyone else, I could apologize until I'm blue in the face, but . . ." Saraswati turned to her brother. "But you don't want an apology—you just want me to suffer."

Raji finally looked up, directly into her eyes. "Need," he corrected her. "I *need* you to suffer so that I can survive."

"And *that's* our cue to leave," Priti said, extracting Nivedita from the living room.

"DON'T TELL ME you want to eavesdrop through the door . . ." Nivedita said, surprised.

"But *of course* I do," Priti replied.

"*I'm* the Indian here," Raji said on the other side of the door, sounding more emotional than enraged. "Your goddamned best seller should've been dedicated to me—*Decolonize your Soul* my ass!"

"Are you sure you don't mean that *you* should've written it?" Saraswati shot back, with a hint of her old trademark irony. And then nothing—that was it. Nivedita imagined the two siblings seated, facing one another, like perfect mirror images, neither of them able to take a breath or make a move without the other doing exactly the same, neither able to say a word without the other repeating it right back at them, until both vanished into the eternity of their endless echo chamber.

And the Saraswati said, without the slightest hint of irony, "Then why *didn't* you write it?"

"Okay, let's make a deal," Priti whispered. "You clear up whatever it is you need to clear up with Saraswati. I'll talk to Raji, find out why he dragged all of us into this, and what he wanted those fucking photos for in the first place."

Nivedita was so impressed, she was at a loss for words.

"I'm so glad you're my cousin," she said, finally.

"For real? I thought I was just your certificate of authenticity."

Nivedita was again at a loss for words, but this time it was because she was taken aback. All these years, Nivedita had thought Priti was using her, and now it turned out that Priti thought Nivedita was using her, too—but just to feel browner?

"Don't give me that sad puppy look," Priti said, looking unperturbed, although she didn't quite sound entirely unperturbed. "It's so funny to watch how you constantly accuse Saraswati of not being authentic enough—you, of all people! You, who fear nothing more than hearing the phrase, 'Nivedita isn't an *authentic* Indian.' *That's* your Voldemort. That's why it was always so tantalizing to say something like that to your face, just to see you *cringe*. Haven't you ever noticed that people presumptuous enough to judge your authenticity are total fucking idiots?"

Nivedita tried to process what Priti had just said, and felt a grinding deep within, as if her perspective on her own life was radically shifting yet again. "Great, so you're saying I'm an idiot-magnet?"

"That doesn't mean you necessarily become one yourself," Priti said with her trademark 'I'm-better-than-you-because-I'm-more-Indian-than-you' grin—yet another thing Nivedita would now need to reinterpret.

"One *what*?"

"An idiot!" Priti whispered, albeit rather loudly, and suddenly turning quite serious. "Why should we care what skin color Saraswati's parents were? Her brother is brown enough."

But that was a bit too charitable and altruistic for Nivedita's taste. "Why are you turning the other cheek all of a sudden? By which, of course, I mean: Why are *you* turning *my* other cheek *to Saraswati* all of a sudden?"

They were still standing just outside the door to the living room—and maybe Saraswati and Raji suspected as much, since they were both standing silent as well as super emotional just inside the living room.

"Because there's no need for Raji to hurt Saraswati any more than he already has," Priti said.

"Come again?"

"That's what always drove me so nuts about Saraswati—that she always acted so superior to everyone else, I mean, so superior to us. Which is why I wanted to push her off her pedestal! Just to see if I could. But now, here, all this . . . *alles ist eine Zelebra . . . ein Zebra . . . eine . . .* it's a celebration of trauma." Priti gestured like a magician toward all the furniture in the light-filled hallway. It had all been designed back in the day when Saraswati was still *white*. And now the works of art, so full of dots and lines, looked like maps of a bygone world. Nivedita couldn't help but think of all the enamel pots and pans that couldn't help Saraswati's mother die, and her heart melted. Or maybe that wasn't exactly it, but something in her heart softened where before there had been nothing but cold, hard, implacability. Even Priti had shed her protective coat of untouchability, which now dangled, temptingly within reach, from the oh-so-retro, oh-so-yellow Schönbuch Quadro coatrack. All Nivedita would've had to do was stretch her arm out, grab it, and put it on.

She stretched her arm out—but held her phone screen in Priti's face instead.

IDENTITTI

(DRAFT) I'm a total Hannah Arendt fangirl. I mean, how cool is she? So cool that it doesn't even faze me that she's *white*. I'll write another post soon about her being Jewish, but for now let's stick to . . .

"Racism. How do you come to terms with the fact that your beloved, oh-so-cool Hannah is such a racist?" Yeah, that was Kali—who else could it be?

"No she's not. Hannah isn't racist," I counter, even though I know better.

"Yeah she is," Kali insists. "How else are you supposed to understand sentences that claim the people of Africa are the only peoples with no history, no consciousness of their own past, who sit idly by, or whatever it was she deigned to actually write?"

What do I say to that? "That's not Hannah, that's Hegel or one of those guys!"

"But that is Hannah—that's from *The Origins of Totalitarianism*." Kali tosses her necklace of men's severed heads over her shoulder and, just for a moment, looks like the embodiment of how Arendt described Black people in her book: like a primitive, an animal, racially degenerate.

And of course Kali is right. But I'm right, too, because Arendt was just unquestioningly passing along what she'd learned from the so-called Enlightenment.

"Does that make it any better?" Kali asks.

And I know the answer to that is: yes, because she, personally, didn't lay the philosophical groundwork that paved the way for the European colonial "project"—that was her forebears, Kant and Hegel—oh, and Hume, and so many other big thinkers of the aforementioned so-called Enlightenment.

And so I say: "No, a thousand times, no! That doesn't make it any better—but it also doesn't erase all the other amazing things she wrote. Hannah Arendt spread a ton of horrifying, racist bullshit though her work—but she also made a lot of important, life-affirming observations about power and the abuse of power and the leeway we all have. The former doesn't invalidate the latter."

"You only forgive Hannah because she's dead," Kali says dryly. But that isn't really what Kali is getting at. What really counts for her is what she says next: "Does Saraswati have to die before you'll forgive her?"

"Why didn't you post this?" Priti asked. "*Ich meine*, it's a bit highbrow, but whatevs, right?"

"I don't dare," Nivedita said, now that they were getting down to core truths. And since others had already expressed it so much better, she let the Internet speak for her:

> » **Kübra Gümüşay @kuebra** *We condemn people so quickly, absolutely, and definitively here in the digital realm. Of course we can and should debate and even criticize Saraswati's behavior. But our culture isn't one in which she could ever learn from her mistakes. 1/2*
>> » **@kuebra** *Nor one in which we can say what she did was wrong without reducing her to her mistake, negating her personhood— maybe for the rest of her life. 2/2*
> » **Magda Albrecht @magda_albrecht** *In political debates, people often argue with their own history as if their interlocutors had no history of their own or only one that's perforce 'privileged.' We'd all do well to grant folks a little more room for disagreement. #Saraswati*

Priti nodded. "That's exactly why I'm here. I'm not really interested in turning the other cheek. At all. But I'd like to make things right. Geez, I just wanted to find out whether Saraswati would bleed if I stabbed her. I mean, I never wanted a pound of her flesh."

Nivedita felt the urge to hug Priti and never let her go, but she still had to clear something up. "Well then, will you promise me something, Shylock?"

"Promise what?"

"That the next time you want to just disappear without saying a thing, which has been your MO with me for, like, forever . . ."

"Yeah?"

"Well, just don't," said Nivedita. She'd long since quit whispering. After all, Saraswati and Raji might as well hear it all since it was about them anyway.

"But I always come back," Priti replied, surprised, which in turn surprised Nivedita, since it sure as hell seemed like Priti could see right through their conversation.

"I know, but I don't want to be the kind of Nivedita people always just come back to whenever they feel like it. I want to be the kind of Nivedita people can confront without having to run away! How did it make you feel when I was totally unreachable for the first few days after I came to stay at Saraswati's?"

"I just figured you were sulking."

That was an entirely new perspective for Nivedita. The idea that someone would fall silent not out of a sense of superiority, or to overpower others, but rather out of a sense of helplessness or powerlessness was news to her. Another ray of sunlight fell through the kitchen door's frosted panes of glass, casting even brighter reflections onto the square yellow components of Saraswati's high-design coat rack. "Just stick around, okay? Stand by me."

"I'll try my best," Priti smiled, shyly.

"Don't try—just do it," Nivedita smiled back.

2

"The university wanted to get rid of me so the AfD would leave them alone," Saraswati stood in the kitchen, pitting cherries with a furious degree of precision. Simone had sent the cherries over via bike messenger: part expression of sympathy, part bribe, just to get Saraswati to sign the enclosed letter addressed to the university administration. "But they're forgetting that concessions won't shut the AfD up—to the contrary, any concession would just send a signal that they got their foot in the door, and next time they'll demand even more firings."

As for what Priti had said—well, talk is cheap. No matter how much Saraswati bled, she still controlled every situation and dominated every conversation. But at least Nivedita could take some consolation in the idea that Priti was now discovering the same about Raji. Nivedita had seen them leave the building together. Priti's exemplary mask of disinterest was swiftly replaced by a solemn friendliness, as if she were Mahatma Gandhi, as Raji became the perfect British gentleman, holding the door open for her with ironic, flamboyant courtesy.

"Could we just forget the AfD for a sec?" Nivedita pled.

"Wouldn't *that* be nice."

"Saraswati, I know I've been asking you this for almost three weeks now, but could you just give me an answer now, for a change? Why did you . . ."— and here Nivedita raised an arm to gesture at Saraswati's mascara, Saraswati's dupatta, and Saraswati's whole persona—"do all *this*?"

Saraswati shrugged with a nonchalance that, for a full six semesters, Nivedita had considered the epitome of Indianness. "*White* guilt?"

"Are you fucking kidding me?"

Saraswati was dead serious—but she didn't exactly mean what other people meant when she used the word *guilt*. "*Being white* is a flaw, a defect. *Being white* is an absence of identity. How can that be, you ask? *Being white* includes so many different histories, so many stories that have never been told." She took an avid step forward and slammed the colander filled with Simone's cherries onto the countertop next to the sink. "After all, we were the first people to be colonized, and then we were forced to become inhuman, and to colonialize others."

Nivedita began to get that frenzied feeling that conversations with Saraswati so often sparked—the dizziness that was a sign of all certitudes falling away, as every single thought sprouted eyes, and all those eyes stared right back at her. The only difference was that usually these conversations were about being *non-white*, not *being white*. She instinctively reached for the windowsill, and inhaled a deep breath of basil and cilantro. The dill had disappeared.

THE AMAZING THING about Saraswati's seminars had been that they not only made Nivedita more real, they also made her more Indian, because her professor simply knew so damn much about India.

"We need real, deep cultural knowledge in order to recognize one another." That had been the motto with which Saraswati assigned more readings, films, and songs as homework than all Nivedita's other professors combined. And even when Nivedita grumbled to Oluchi and Iqbal about the workload, she still absolutely, albeit secretly, agreed with Saraswati's approach. In order to be able to become Indian, she needed someone who at least had an inkling of what *being Indian* might mean. In Germany, people with such knowledge were so few and far between that she sometimes caught herself wishing that India had been a German colony instead of a British one, because then at least Germans would have a clue. And if they knew a tad more, they'd know not to say "Indians are such wise people," or "Indians are so very numerous," or "Indians are such poor people." But, nothing doing. Germans couldn't even properly pronounce the names of the yoga positions they practiced.

One time, walking down the street with Lilli, Nivedita had run into Lilli's therapist, who had enthused about how Indians breathe so naturally. Nivedita took a polite breath as the therapist stared at her, awestruck.

Why are you talking to me, anyway? Kali interrupted her train of thought, plucking one choice cherry from Saraswati's cherry-filled colander.

"Why am I? Talking? What?" Nivedita stuttered, unconscious of the fact that she'd just spoken to Kali.

Why me, exactly? Why don't you talk to someone else, like, say, a Polish goddess, for instance? Kali said, sucking the pit from the cherry.

Whereupon Nivedita began to grasp that this really was about fundamentals. But she was still offtrack because she had to ask, "You mean, like, the Virgin Mary?"

I've got nothing against the Virgin Mary, but what about all the pre-Christian Polish gods and goddesses? Ever heard of the Slavic deities?

Whereupon Nivedita had to admit she hadn't a clue. "Who?"

Ex-act-ly! See what I mean? You don't talk to them because you don't know them, because you've never heard of them, because not a single trace of them remains—not even their names.

"Names?" Nivedita repeated, her eyes vacant.

So much for cultural knowledge! Kali widened her stance into a super-stable straddle right in front of Nivedita, as if she'd just come from a Wen-Do self-defense class. *966!*

"Nine sixty-six?" Nivedita repeated.

966, Kali nodded, *that's the fateful year Poland was converted. The Poles were forced to watch as missionaries laid waste to their holy sites and tied ropes around the necks of their deities' statues.*

"Ropes? What for?"

To kill them! Kali replied impatiently. *There are historical accounts of the "heathens" weeping as they watched their gods being toppled and dragged off by horses. The death of their gods was the death of their whole world. That's what Saraswati meant when she said* whites *were the first people to have been colonized.*

Nivedita looked at Saraswati, frozen, midgesture, much like the water nymph in the park. In the split second just before Kali had begun to speak, a cherry had slipped from her fingers and now hovered, in free fall but also frozen, as Saraswati winked at Nivedita.

But people only truly, fully become subjects of other people when they begin to see themselves as inferior. Write that down, too, Kali continued. *Which explains why, after initially destroying the* bodies *of the Poles' deities, their conquerors went on to dismantle their* significance. *You know Greek, Roman, and at least a little about Celtic mythology. But what about Slavic mythology— what's survived? Nothing. It's been completely wiped out. Haven't you ever wondered why the word* slave *comes from the word* Slav?

"For real?" Nivedita asked.

Yup!

For the first time in her entire life, Nivedita thought about why she was so fixated on India but, until just now, had never really given any thought to Poland. When Birgit fried up pierogi or sang the gospel duet "Joshua Fit the Battle of Jericho" along with Magda Piskorczyk—"and the walls came tumbling down!"—Nivedita had dismissed it, suspecting it might be merely yet another instance of *whites* culturally appropriating the Black songbook. Just like she'd never really thought much about Essen, a town she was always itching to get away from, only to be overcome by sappy nostalgia, missing it badly—as long as she wasn't actually there. The only time she'd even mentioned the Ruhr region, as far as she could remember, was back when her blog was finally getting some attention, and a little kerfuffle had erupted on Twitter:

» @highonheels *Can we clear up this NRW hype once and for all? What's so great about North Rhine-Westphalia? It doesn't have a single interesting city, its natural areas aren't even pretty, and the whole place is one big construction site.*

THE RUHR REGION might not be Poland, but it was one of the few topics she and Birgit could talk about for more than five minutes without making Nivedita want to go all Texas-Chainsaw-Massacre on her mother.

"If I were capable of making anyone fall in love with Essen, I'd do it in a heartbeat," Birgit had said to Nivedita during her last visit, as they took one last loop around the block, the way they did every night. "One last loop around the block," that was their phrase, and it meant exactly that: it was the shortest distance for a stroll, and while they were out Nivedita's father would finish washing the dishes, drying them, and meticulously putting them back in the kitchen cabinet, each plate in its place. Birgit kept everyone sated, and Jagdish kept everything organized.

Walking arm-in-arm with her mother, Nivedita pictured describing Essen-Frillendorf the way she'd describe London or Berlin or all the other places where she had wandered through so much history. Everything in those places was steeped in history, and all that history was still so very present that even Nivedita grew pale trying to take it all in. But the place she had grown up in, where she'd imagined all the bedtime stories she'd heard throughout her childhood taking place—well, it had no history. In her mind, it was as if nobody had lived, loved, and labored in this area for centuries already, with an emphasis on *labored*.

"The Zeche Zollverein is still there, but most of the mines and factories of the massive industrial complex were decommissioned and dismantled in the eighties," Birgit continued. To its right loomed a massive dark brick building, the Schutzengelkirche—despite being named for a guardian angel, it had taken a historical preservation designation to safeguard it from being razed. As a child, Nivedita had always thought the church was a renovated industrial building. Her mother nodded at it like an old friend, and Nivedita was amazed to notice that Birgit's knack for filling her environment with life—regardless of what that environment looked like—reminded her of Barbara. When she was in their shared apartment with Lotte, Nivedita usually felt like she was there alone, but with Barbara that was impossible—she filled the space with life. There was a similar dynamic between Birgit and Frillendorf. Whenever Nivedita visited her parents, Jagdish usually wanted to talk about her studies, although his interest focused mostly on Saraswati's success, since the only other Indian he could think of who was famous in Germany was scientist Ranga Yogeshwar—and even though spoke German, he actually lived in Luxembourg—the list was shorter than short. But it was Birgit who really made her feel like she was *home*.

And then, in a very un-Birgit way, Birgit looked at the Schutzengelkirche and suddenly said, "I always struggled with this total absence of history. With every brick, every factory gate that got carted away, it was like a piece of my childhood was disappearing. As if nothing in my life were worth remembering, just a bunch of vacant lots."

My mother's memory is made up of fallow land and smoke-blackened skies, dark plumes of smog spewed from smokestacks that have long since been razed, Nivedita thought—at least, that's how she later phrased it on her blog. Back then, standing in the shadow of the Schutzengelkirche, all she thought was: *so that's why Birgit is such a master of forgetting, of suppressing memories*. And then she noticed something exceptionally odd: her anger toward her mother was morphing into melancholy, into a desire to write a dirge for Frillendorf, a teary lament.

EVERY LIFE IS a song. Nivedita had read that somewhere, at some point (maybe in some Nick Hornby paperback?), and it immediately resonated. Not even the fact that she had no song nor soundtrack whatsoever for her own life cast any doubt on the idea. She just read it as a sign that she wasn't really living, or that her life didn't count as much as everyone else's—meaning everyone who was constantly sending her their Spotify playlists, writing rousing posts about the importance of arrests within immigrant communities despite said posts' sexism, and communicating solely by quoting song lyrics, like speaking some secret code, as if feelings were only really feelings when they came with a beat. Of course Nivedita *listened* to music. After all, music was everywhere—the communal kitchen of her student apartment, the Gauguin, the everyman-and-everywoman-and-everyperson's phone, Saraswati's CD player, Kali's lips—but she'd never sought out that one song she'd heard during her first semester at Heinrich Heine University, or the one that was playing when she and Anish had permanently life-altering sex ("Indian both outside *and* inside, even *in my vag*: who's the coconut now?"), or the one playing when she and Simon had their first fateful yet triumphant make-up sex ("Every breakup brings a new beginning—everything is predestined"). She'd never sought out the song that lasted just a few earthly minutes—no, what she was after was THE SONG, something akin to the music of the celestial spheres. And if she were ever to actually find THE ONE BIG SONG, she was certain its timbre would perfectly encapsulate the entirety of her behaviors and relationships and thoughts and feelings. A song like that could only exist in your dreams, in the kind of twilight state as you drifted off to sleep, as the world slipped away and your entire being somehow cranked up its huge internal dial.

So it came as quite a shock one night, as Nivedita was wide awake and scrolling through YouTube, when she finally heard *her* exact song:

> *I am as brown as can be*
> *my eyes are as black as sloe*

A woman Nivedita's age sang onstage. Her utter uncoolness, plus the average attendee's median age range, led Nivedita to correctly surmise it had been recorded at a folk festival. Nivedita wasn't really into folk, but she didn't really have anything against it, either. But what she did have a thing against was lying, and the chick singing this was white as white can be, with eyes of blue or green, you couldn't quite tell from the lo-res video, but they sure as hell weren't black as sloe. Nevertheless, Nivedita couldn't help but keep listening:

> *I am brisk, I am brisk, I am brisk as can be*

She'd had to look up the word *brisk* on linguee.com, and then she'd had to look up *doe*:

    I'm wild as any doe

Up above the unusually appreciative string of comments she read "Georgia Lewis *The Brown Girl* (Child Ballad 295)"—apparently people actually were capable of being polite on the internet, as long as race, sex, and homeopathy weren't involved. That header led her to deduce that Georgia Lewis was the singer (correct), "The Brown Girl" was the song (correct), and that it was a ballad for children (incorrect). A frenzied bit of googling resulted in the discovery that Francis James Child had been a kind of One-Man-Brothers-Grimm who, back in the nineteenth century, had gone around England and Scotland and collected 305 traditional ballads. "The Brown Girl" was apparently added toward the end of his life, like an afterthought: oh, yeah, there's this one, too, if you really must. And supposedly *brown* referred to the fact that this girl didn't have the lily-white skin of a lady, but rather the sunburnt skin of a fieldhand—or so said the website mainlynorfolk.info.

    Nivedita was appalled. Surprise, surprise: even the folk-music community claimed to be colorblind, and preferred not to acknowledge racism unless a song was not explicitly titled "Racist McRaceface." Child had added the song to his collection at the height of the British Empire, and of course the girl came from the colonies, where else?! Weeks later, Nivedita even discovered she'd had a name—drumroll, please—Priti! Her name was Priti, although back in her day it had been spelled *Prithee*, and that's why her *white* lover didn't want to marry her—the racist, classist, lazy, navel-gazing coward! So far, so Simony. But in the song this "lover once so bold" ultimately succumbed to a broken heart and became so love-sick that he couldn't live (not just figuratively, but literally) without his "brown girl." So then he summoned her to his deathbed to beg her forgiveness. And, as if all that weren't implausible enough, she just laughed at him. The song ends with her dancing on his green, green grave.

• • •

RIGHT AT THAT moment Nivedita's phone rang, and the cherry that had slipped from Saraswati's fingers plummeted to the floor with a *plop* and rolled underneath the buffet table.

"I'm coming to get you," said Simon, his voice warm and authoritarian.

"Sure," said Nivedita, "just not quite yet."

"A-*ha*," said Saraswati.

"What?" asked Nivedita.

"Nothing, just: a-*ha*."

In order to evade Saraswati's gaze, Nivedita kneeled down onto the cream-white floorboards and groped under the cabinet, to fish out the cherry.

"To you, *being white* means being racist," Saraswati continued right where she left off, as if she'd never been interrupted, because in reality she hadn't.

"Being entitled," Nivedita, still down on all fours, corrected her. "To me, *being white* means being entitled, being able to feel like the world revolves around you."

"Whatever you want to call it, your take basically means that if I don't want to be racist, I have to give up *being white*."

Nivedita held the captured cherry under the flowing tap, washed off all the schmutz, and wished she could do the same with her head.

"So it's no wonder *whites* don't want you to call them that," Saraswati went on, coming so close Nivedita could feel her breath on her skin.

"Them?" Nivedita cynically raised an eyebrow.

Saraswati simply nodded, which could mean just about anything, and maybe did mean just that. "*White*, as an identity label—as you so superbly illustrated in one of your papers, for which you received an A+, if memory serves—was only created for the purpose of justifying white supremacy. That's why *white* isn't really a descriptor for people with pale-colored skin, it's more like the n-word in this discourse."

"*What?!*" Nivedita felt like she was back in class, where Saraswati was never satisfied until she'd driven every last student to totally lose it.

"Let's call it the w-word," Saraswati said, so self-assured you'd have thought she had no clue a formal letter of dismissal lay right there on the smaller of the two tulip tables in her living room. "Just like the n-word excluded Black people from the group of humans granted basic human rights, the w-word justified that dehumanization. *Whites* who don't back the concept of *white* supremacy—indeed, those who are disgusted by it, and revolt against it!—can only turn away, alienated, and full of self-hatred. In this view, being *white* means always and forever having to be a perpetrator."

"Why do you always have to know everything?" Nivedita shrieked, tossing the cherry into the sink. It swiftly disappeared into the pile of dirty dishes, whereupon Nivedita—who'd been raised to never ever waste even the tiniest scrap of food, because kids were starving in India, you know—guiltily began fishing around for it.

"It's my job," Saraswati said sweetly. "I am your professor, you know."

"Not for much longer," Nivedita shot back, taking a deep breath and then holding it one second. And then two. And then three. And then four. And then five. And then six. And then seven. And then eight. And then nine. And then ten. And then eleven. And then twelve.

And then she was relieved when Saraswati finally said, "So, why are you here then, Nivedita?"

She was relieved she could exhale, and carry on, but she was rather less relieved upon hearing Saraswati's pointed question. Why *was* she here?

Yeah, really: why? Had she thought she'd get any answers from Saraswati, or had she only come in order to delay the consequences of those answers? Kind of like people who break off a relationship and then can't stop constantly talking about why they broke up, solely so they don't really have to think about what they're going to do with the rest of their lives. Similarly, Nivedita was still incessantly swirling around Saraswati's deception, Saraswati's betrayal, Saraswati's lie, Saraswati's motivations, Saraswati's apology. Secretly, she hoped to find a fulcrum that would enable her to undo it all and just revert to the almost Edenic state that had preceded Saraswati's fall.

And then she felt a sharp pain, and saw she'd torn a thumbnail. The tear was deep.

"Hold on!" Saraswati carefully trimmed the nail, ran out, dug around in her medicine cabinet, ran back in, and then sealed Nivedita's nail bed with a droplet of something that, in the sunlight, looked like pure blood. Her thumb looked a whole lot worse after that, but it felt a whole lot better.

"What's that?" she asked a bit stunned.

"Sangre de Drago," said Saraswati.

"Maybe I wasn't clear enough: what *is* that?"

"Dragon's blood—resin from the Dracaena draco tree. It's anti-inflammatory."

A vision struck Nivedita: with each wound she'd learn more about Saraswati's secrets, until one day, finally, she would completely understand Saraswati because she'd be shorn of every last protective layer. But by then she'd have no skin left.

"So, what am I supposed to do now?" she asked, doubtful.

"Nothing," Saraswati said. "All you have to do is wait."

AND WHILE NIVEDITA was waiting for her thumb to heal, Saraswati prepared tea. And as they were both just waiting and sipping, Nivedita's phone rang.

"Umm, sooo, your mom called. She was worried because she couldn't reach you." It was Lotte, breathless as ever. Nivedita groaned. In the almost three weeks she'd been at Saraswati's, she'd only sent her mother WhatsApp texts, because she didn't feel grown-up enough to face the challenge of explaining to Birgit what she'd gotten mixed up in.

"What did you tell her?"

"That you were with your professor."

Nivedita groaned again. Zero chance of evading Birgit's interrogation now.

"Because you're all on a field trip, that's all I said. Does your mother think you're studying art history, for some reason?"

"Why do you ask?"

"Because after I said that, she said, 'Ah, then they must be out studying Mughal-era miniatures.'"

Suddenly Nivedita was overcome with profound gratitude for Lotte's unflappable friendliness, whereupon she stumbled into an equally profound void where she expected to find the words to express this new gratitude. Had she ever said a kind word to Lotte? Had she ever even tried to acknowledge Lotte's perpetual desire to be a good person?

"So, uhh, how's your . . . mom doing?" she finally managed to say.

A long pause followed, in which you could hear that question rattling around Lotte's brain.

"She's okay," she said, surprised. "Next week we're going to South Tyrol together, to a spa resort."

3

The evening progressed and the sun sank below the horizon before a brightly colored backdrop, setting the stage as a new night came on. Priti and Raji still weren't back from their showdown, so Nivedita and Saraswati were the only two out on the terrace, drinking wine. The sky stretched broad in all directions as the sounds of a strumming guitar and a man's voice drifted up live—albeit a live recording, so not *live* live—from an open window one floor below:

> *We weren't lactose intolerant* (laughter)
> *we weren't gluten-free* (louder laughter)

"Yeah, yeah—go ahead and get all flustered about Generation Snowflake . . . Kids these days, how dare they? They're allergic to all these foods, all this racism . . ." Nivedita quipped.

But Saraswati wasn't laughing with Nivedita nor with the faraway audience of the recording. "As a ten-year-old girl, I had always imagined I'd grow up to be an adult in precisely that time and place, that bygone world where of course nobody had ever heard of lactose intolerance, and all the furniture was orange and brown. And now I'm . . . an adult, but the seventies of my youth are as long gone as the GDR and the Raj."

Upon hearing the word *raj,* Nivedita gave a Pavlovian wince. That had been the period in which India was the crown jewel of the British Empire, but Indians themselves had been little more than dirt stuck to the soles of the British rulers' boots.

"Even if I were to give up virtually every part of my body, I could never go back to live in that past," Saraswati said. "In the seventies, I can only ever be a kid."

"Would you really want to go back there?" Nivedita asked, surprised. Nothing she'd heard up until now about Saraswati's parents and their pent-up, Protestant household somewhere in the vicinity of Karlsruhe seemed to warrant the longing audible in Saraswati's voice. As far as Nivedita could tell, Josefa was always laughing without actually being happy, and Konstantin Sr. was just a blank spot, never really even mentioned, which was totally cliché—middle-class families always seemed to center on the same dominant-albeit-absentee father figures.

"Back?" Saraswati said, with such a snap that it scared Nivedita. "I can't go *back* there because, back then, *I* didn't even exist yet!"

"You didn't?" Nivedita asked, until suddenly it clicked, *"Ohhh."*

"I *am not* Sarah Vera! But that's what you've wanted this whole time, isn't it? You want me to tell you about Sarah Vera," Saraswati complained.

And because that was precisely what Nivedita had wanted from Saraswati this whole time, she found no suitable words with which to reply.

"The problem, of course, is that back then so many books hadn't yet been written, so many notions hadn't yet been thought," Saraswati sniffed. Whereupon Nivedita thought, *Oh yeah? That's what you're going with?*

"Back when I was a kid, the chain you know as Netto Marken-Discount was called Plus, Kaiser's was called Kaiser's Kaffee-Geschäft, and Edeka was . . . Edeka, a name based on the initials EDK, which stood for *Einkaufsgenossenschaft der Kolonialwarenhändler*—meaning "Purchasing Cooperative of Colonial Goods Retailers"—although of course we weren't really conscious of what that meant. And had we been aware of it, it wouldn't have troubled us in the least. That's just how the West Germany of my childhood was. Despite the peace movement, and the women's lib movement, and the anti-nuclear movement, and the Red Army Faction. Dealing with racism didn't interest us in the least."

"And what about Raji?" Nivedita asked.

"Raji was as nonexistent back then as I was," Saraswati said, her saffron-yellow silk blouse blazing in the last burst of evening sun. "There was only Stan. And the problems Stan had were all his own damn fault. He did poorly in school because he hated studying, not because our teachers were racist. He had run-ins with the police because he was a pot dealer, not because he was watched more closely than any of his friends. He was aggressive and suspicious because he was aggressive and suspicious, not because other people were aggressive and suspicious toward him. That's how everyone saw it—including Sarah Vera. Yeah, you know, if *I* had been there back then . . ."

The air was sharp with the scent of mint and yearning. And suddenly Nivedita couldn't help but think of her father, who, during her last visit to Frillendorf, had said, "Nivedita, this is the great question of the diaspora," only to enigmatically fall silent, as if he'd forgotten what the question was.

"Yeah?" she'd said, steeling herself for some totally banal answer like *Where can I get basmati rice here in Germany?* Her father could drone on for hours about his attempts to find even barely edible rice back in 1980s Germany. The story always ended the same way: *In the end, I settled for Uncle Ben's parboiled rice—why not? If Native Americans can be Red Indians, then why can't Uncle Ben be a Black Indian?*

"What's the great question of the diaspora?" Nivedita followed up, prepared to risk having to laugh at that same joke again.

"If my children grow up in this country, who will they be?" her father said. "I was always a bit sad, knowing you wouldn't grow up in the same world I had, Nivedita. But that's impossible, anyway. Even if we lived in Kolkata today, it wouldn't be the same Kolkata I grew up in."

"Then why don't you ever talk about it?" Nivedita asked, getting emotional.

But then the little window of communication that had unexpectedly opened up was shut tight again. Jagdish didn't know what to say about the world of his early childhood and youth, or any world, for that matter. He just carried them all around, deep within.

Saraswati rinsed the aftertaste of what-if from her mouth with a nice gulp of wine and looked at Nivedita. "Okay, what do you want to know about me?"

This was Nivedita's chance—she'd finally get answers to her countless *why*s. But, instead, out came, "What was it like, the first time you went to India?"

Basically, in Nivedita's mind, the equation went more or less like this:

- Women are the subjects of repression
- Postcolonial countries are the subjects of repression
- Ergo, postcolonial countries are feminine

The first time she traveled to India, when she was nineteen—not counting the time when she was a baby, which she decided definitely didn't count—she had expected to discover some secret, mythical, amazing, ultrafeminine world. Basically the equivalent of the noble savage, just in feminine form: the heroic savage woman. Instead, she spent three exceedingly uneventful weeks with Jagdish's older sister, Priti's grandma, who took great páins to make sure the only part of Kolkata she saw were inside the walls of her *pisi*'s abode.

But instead of stoking Nivedita's envy with exciting insider tales of India, Saraswati said not a word.

"Saraswati?" Nivedita asked, as the air between them grew more viscous.

"The food was . . . amazing," she hesitantly said after a long pause.

Nivedita couldn't believe her ears. "What? India was nothing more than a lifestyle choice to you? You sound like some German tourist, enthusing about how amazing Indian cooking is."

"Well, you know, it really is amazing when suddenly pretty much everyone around you is vegetarian," Saraswati added dryly. "You probably can't even imagine. But the first time I went to India, Germans were still regularly cracking jokes like 'How many vegetarians does it take to change a light bulb? None, 'cause they're all too weak to even lift a finger . . . hahahaha!'"

"I know—and I can't even remember a time when Michael Jackson was Black!" Nivedita yelled, suddenly hating Saraswati as absolutely as Oluchi did, and both their absolute stances were rooted in the same pain. How could it be that Saraswati felt at home *both* in Germany *and* in India, but Nivedita herself didn't feel at home anywhere? And then, much to her own horror, she heard herself say, "How can it be that you feel at home *both* in Germany *and* in India, but I don't feel at home anywhere?"

"At home?" Saraswati shouted, just as incensed. "You want to know how *at home* I felt in India? What it felt like when I first landed at Calcutta's Dum Dum Airport?"

"You mean Kolkata's Netaji Subhas Chandra Bose International Airport," Nivedita automatically corrected her.

"Not in my day! Back then, I stumbled out of the airplane, strode out into the heat, and crossed the runway, and on that momentous, life-changing occasion I thought I'd gone nuts, because all I could think about was how the sparkling, speckled tar looked exactly like the decorative-arts glass pieces that Charles Rennie Mackintosh and Margaret Macdonald designed around nineteen hundred. And why was I thinking that? Because my mother Josefa collected art nouveau—that was all that was left of all her goddamn art history studies after she married Konstantin Sr. We take our Josefas with us, no matter where we go."

The wave of hatred drained from Nivedita as quickly as it had swept in. "Birgit loves art nouveau, too," she said softly. It wasn't true—the only time Birgit was interested in "art" was when she could make it herself, so she only loved the kind of stuff she could transform by painting or felting or, most recently, turning into DIY oilcloth. Nivedita still had an entire drawer full of silk paintings Birgit had done on handkerchiefs. But, right now, being truthful was less important than being kind, and being understood was less important than being understanding.

And Saraswati got it. "The problem with memory is that it doesn't really work the way we're taught that it does. It's not a bunch of select episodes or islands floating upon a vast sea of forgetting. Instead, we have far too many memories, and there's always more than one version of the same story. When I think back on my life, I recall moments when I open up the storage boxes of my memory, and the cat inside them is simultaneously both alive and dead."

"What cat?"

"Schrödinger's cat, of course!"

"What . . . are you trying to tell me?"

"That I simultaneously lied to you and didn't lie to you. Being a trans Indian woman gave me a chance to be me—a me that I, as a Germ . . . as a *white* woman, could never have been. Not only that, but I could even be more than just me, myself, and I."

Nivedita was simultaneously furious and not furious at Saraswati. She felt around for Saraswati's hand, and would've liked to yank it to her bosom, but the mere thought made her picture Raji's hand on her heart, and Nivedita turned her flushed face toward the setting sun.

Even in terms of body language, Saraswati automatically took control, petting Nivedita's fingers with long, slow strokes. "You have something I don't."

"What?" *My total inability to size up the world and then tell people what's good for me and what isn't?*

Meanwhile, Matti Rouse's velvety voice sang another folk song:

Oh, I do forgive you but it
won't forget the pain,
And every time the pain returns
I will forgive again.

"Let me put it this way: we all have a deep-seated need to experience what being discriminated against feels like, because we know that *being white* isn't good for us."

"And just who's this *we* supposed to be?" Nivedita needled her. The sun, now a heavy orange ball, shone directly into her eyes. Instead of looking away, she tried to remember Saraswati's sungazing exercises—something about how the UV rays were so weak by the time the very last hour of daylight came around that they wouldn't hurt your retina, or something like that, and so your body could . . . what? Absorb a bunch of luminous flux? Whatever it was, as usual, she felt like she was hooked up to one humongous battery.

"Well, y'know, us . . . *whites*."

Nivedita blinked, hard. "Wow!"

"Don't ever make me say that again."

"No worries, you'll never have to say it again . . . Or, hang on a sec, did you seriously just say that *being white* isn't good for *you all*?"

"Elementary, my dear Watson."

"For *you all*?"

Saraswati nodded emphatically from over in the corner of Nivedita's field of vision. The scent of sweetgrass intensified in the late evening sun. Nivedita remembered that Saraswati's syllabus for the next semester included an entire unit on postcolonial ecology, and in the first class they were supposed to braid sweetgrass and read Robin Wall Kimmerer's *Braiding Sweetgrass*. Whereupon she desperately wanted the class to take place despite everything.

Saraswati extended her arm and laid her hand on Nivedita's heart. "Of course Raji focused his ultra-concentrated, vast charm on you, Nivedita. That's how he works. He's always been a hanger-on with the people I'm closest to, in order to destroy our relationships. It doesn't hurt that you're outrageously hot, either."

Nivedita wondered how Saraswati knew . . . but the question that really interested her was quite another: "So . . . I'm one of the people you're closest to?"

"What do you think?"

And the terrace fanned out, offering up a kaleidoscope of possible new spaces and futures she might inhabit.

"Why me? I mean, why did you choose me?" Nivedita asked, and heard her voice echo, booming through all the endless parallel universes within this terrace of possibilities. *Say you recognized my unrealized potential!*

Saraswati laid her other hand on Nivedita's heart—becoming the sole anchor in this world of wavering realities—only to cast her out into the disorienting sea with this answer: "Because you're the one who needs me most."

Nivedita felt like she was falling backward, even though the back of the chair was right there, steadying her. "So then you think I'd also be the one who worships you most?" *The way I worship Kali? THE WAY I WORSHIP KALI! DOES EVERYBODY WANT ME TO FUCKING WORSHIP THEM NOW?*

Once again, as if she'd read Nivedita's thoughts, Saraswati said, "I am your Kali."

Nivedita looked at Kali, terrified: *What do you say to that?*

Does that make me your Saraswati? Kali giggled, just off to Nivedita's left.

And then that would make me your Durga, or is there some other goddess you prefer? laughed the Kali just off to Saraswati's left, as she raised the arm holding a man's severed head, whereupon all the Kalis behind her also raised their arms, just with an infinitesimal delay, creating an endless wave of arms, a Mandelbrot macarena of sorts.

Nivedita thought: *So that's why Indian goddesses have so many arms.*

"Never underestimate your power," Saraswati said, and all the Kalis collapsed into one Kali again.

"My *what*?" asked Nivedita, impressed at how Saraswati's every sentence seemed to catch her off guard.

"Your power. Your pain can move mountains. My pain will never be anything more than the whining of a privileged *white* woman, a target of everyone's scorn, just barely trumped by the whining of privileged *white* men, but at least they have other privileged *white* men whining along with them in the chorus. It's true: I was a privileged *white* woman, and I became a privileged brown woman, and now . . ." Saraswati's voice broke off.

"What am I now?"

4

ze.tt—the online magazine for anti-racism, queer life, feminism, and inclusion

What do academics think of the Saraswati Affair?

The controversy surrounding the professor from Düsseldorf who lied about her ethnicity shows no signs of stopping. Here, we try to sort things out.

By Şeyda Kurt

What does it mean to be Black in a world dominated by *whites*? Structural racism, police violence, and the battle against *white* privilege—the transnational Black Lives Matter movement and debates about the removal of monuments and how to deal with historic statues and memorials have brought the experiences of Black people and other racialized peoples back into the mass-media limelight.

So the notion that now, of all times, a scandal from provincial Germany has set international headlines ablaze sounds rather absurd: a professor who teaches intercultural studies and postcolonial theory—a little-known field outside of niche circles—had long been known as Saraswati. And as a POC. But now it's come to light that Saraswati's official name is Sarah Vera Thielmann. From Karlsruhe.

This case perfectly exemplifies the conflicts that inevitably arise when it comes to questions of identity and identity politics. Is Saraswati no longer Saraswati? Can people choose to be *white*, of color, or Black? Can an individual's answer to questions regarding their own identity be deemed true or false by anyone but that individual? And, above all, who gets to decide?

We've invited colleagues of Saraswati/Sarah Vera Thielmann from the fields of postcolonial theory and postcolonial sociology to give us their take on this.

PROF. NIKITA DHAWAN, PhD, AND PROF. MARÍA DO MAR CASTRO VARELA, PhD

"This is not about passing moral judgment on Sarah Vera Thielmann. This is about asking what benefits she gains from her chosen identity while others with that same identity must fight to survive precisely because of it. This is about the unequal distribution of power and disempowerment in our society."

Nikita Dhawan is professor of political science and gender studies at the Justus Liebig University Giessen; María do Mar Castro Varela is a professor of general education and social work at the Alice Salomon University of Applied Sciences Berlin. The revised and expanded edition of their widely adopted textbook Postkoloniale Theorie: Eine kritische Einführung *was published by UTB's Transcript Verlag in 2020.*

PROF. PAULA-IRENE VILLA BRASLAVSKY, PhD

"The reason Saraswati's deception strikes our very core is because social inequities are often expressed in aesthetically subjective ways. In a nutshell, people see and hear one another on the basis of many signifiers rooted in our corporeality, which often determine our social role, our place in the world. But when a person so radically switches places, when they play with the keys that determine these signifiers, and do so with such virtuosic skill, then it becomes clear that these signifiers and their meanings are highly conventionalized and tied to the time in which that person is living. Bodies like Saraswati's are unthinkable today, but maybe they'll become a more accepted possibility tomorrow or the day after."

Paula-Irene Villa Braslavsky is chair of the Sociology and Gender Studies Department at Ludwig Maximillian's University Munich. Read more on this topic in her book The Future of Difference: Beyond the Toxic Entanglement of Racism, Sexism and Feminism, *co-authored with Sabine Hark, translated by Sophie Anne Lewis, and published by Verso in 2020.*

PROF. RONNIE GLADDEN

"In spite of presenting as outwardly black and male—by in *[sic]* large I view myself as white and female. Of course I am aware, however, that many critics may view my identifications as nonsensical at best— misguided—and at worst, depraved. And many others are likely to be apathetic or overwhelmed with what might be viewed as an assault from the 'identity politics campaign.' In the face of these realities, I still fully acknowledge that my identifications are deep-seated—and I believe that Saraswati, too, is living as her true self. But before we can concede that that is true, our whole society must work through its many injuries and its immense pain surrounding the issue of race."

Ronnie Gladden is a professor in the English Department of Cincinnati State College. Read more in "TRANSgressive Talk: An Introduction to the Meaning of Transgracial Identity," published in Queer Cats Journal of LGBTQ Studies *in 2015.*

5

21 DAYS POST-SARASWATI

The next morning, the previously uninterrupted streak of sunny days came to an end. Nivedita felt like she hadn't slept a wink, because she'd spent the whole night feeling around the bed next to her to see whether Priti had come back. By morning, the wrinkles on her side of the bed indicated some-one had lain there, but Priti herself was gone. Nivedita got up and walked barefoot across the wood floor, which had stored up and was still transmitting the heat of the past week. The feeling catapulted her back to the summer she was eight, and had gone everywhere barefoot, be it advisable or inadvisable, because she wanted to be an Indian girl. That was also the same summer they'd gone to Birmingham for the first time, and she had been convinced her bare feet were the magic good-luck charms that had brought that trip about.

The kitchen was empty, the mixer was empty, it hadn't blended any coffee and butter to concoct Raji's bulletproof breakfast, no squeezed-out tea bags lay on the saucers by the sink as signs of morning life. But the terrace door was open. The air already smelled of rain, but the long-awaited storm still kept everyone in suspense. After three intense weeks together, Nivedita got the feeling a sudden emptiness was reaching out to get her with its wet and lonely fingers, so she ran back into the living room.

Inside, the light was hazier—if that were even possible. Shadows appeared here and there, like ghostly frames for half-remembered sunny surfaces on the walls, only to vanish again before she could really notice them. Saraswati lay on the sofa, curled up into a question mark. She was still wearing the saffron-yellow blouse from the night before, and a tweed jacket served as her blanket—the same jacket that had been sitting on the living room table all week, next to a bag of new buttons, waiting to be taken to the tailor. Nivedita sat down next to Saraswati's dreaming body, almost as if to keep watch and make sure nothing happened as that body's inhabitant wandered distant realms. So she nearly jumped out of her own skin when she suddenly felt a hand on her shoulder.

"Niv," Priti said, and Nivedita could immediately tell something wasn't right.

"What?" Saraswati croaked, her voice still sleepy as she swung her feet down to the floor. Her long, flowing hair fell in her face, making her look like a mermaid—a mermaid whose eyeliner was a mess after a late night at the pub along the docks.

"You're no longer breaking news, Saraswati," Raji said. His voice had an odd undertone—half scornful, half pained—as it left the depth of the ball chair. Apparently, that was his favorite chair since it made him almost invisible. He swiveled all the way around, and held his laptop out toward them. Nivedita bowed toward it as if spellbound.

And time stood still.

Not the way it had when she'd visited Anish's parents. Not the way it had when Simon said the words *I'm leaving you*. Not the way it had when Kali waltzed into her head, interrupted a conversation, and froze everyone around her like a game of red-light, green-light, only able to move a foot or an arm a little every now and then. Instead, time stood still in the sense that Nivedita was frantically trying to delay her next heartbeat, because it was going to be too painful. She read:

Terrorist Attack in Hanau

Months later, she would still remember the first thoughts that ran through her mind. They were seared into her memory like a time capsule she could open at any point, only to find the contents unchanged:

Hopefully the perpetrator isn't an immigrant, or come from a family of immigrants, or else we're in for another endless round of talk shows where people will debate whether immigration is the mother of all society's problems.

Murder in the Hessian city of Hanau: the suspect is a German . . .

Thank Kali!

Who around 10:00 p.m. went to a kiosk and two shisha-bars and opened fire on the crowd of . . .

People like us!

Immigrants and presumed immigrants. A xenophobic hate crime has not been ruled out . . .

That's not xenophobic, it's racist, dumbass! I'm not a foreigner but he'd definitely have shot at me if I'd been in Hanau.

At this time, we have confirmation that nine are dead, and six are wounded, one critically.

How could she be relived about that?

That was the end of her self-imposed, albeit already super-spotty, attempt at abstaining from the Internet. Over and over, Nivedita read the same reports, with only tiny variations in wording, all of them with the same video in the background. It was a YouTube clip that, once she'd seen it, became an endless loop underlying all her thoughts.

Last night in the Kesselstadt neighborhood, at the Arena Bar, we heard five or six shots ring out. And then I saw the guy run in. I had been eating. We were all eating, said a young man from a hospital bed with tubes hooked up to his shoulders and hands. *The first ones he saw, he shot in the head. He dropped to the floor, and then he came toward us, shooting. I tried to hide. That's when my shoulder got hit. Then I lay on the floor and somebody else lay on top of me, and so on. We were all piled on top on one another, like a little mound.*

Nivedita could not get that little mound of bodies out of her head, nor the pale-faced young man, as he kept going, talking right through his tears: *The guy underneath me had been shot in the throat, there was a hole in it. He'd reached up for a sweater or something, and said to me, "Brother, please hold my wound, keep it shut, please, please," he said. My arm hurt so bad, but I held it shut, and then he said, "Brother, I can't feel my tongue anymore. I can't breathe."*

NIVEDITA SPENT THE entire next day searching the newspapers and Twitter to find out whether the guy with the hole in his throat had survived. Even though that wouldn't have changed a thing, even though that wouldn't have reduced the number of confirmed dead, even if it only would have meant that some other guy had died instead. But this young man, who'd lain there in a mound of dead and wounded, and couldn't feel his tongue anymore, had somehow worked his way into her heart, so when she learned that just a few minutes after saying those words, he'd died, her heart broke, shattered into a million pieces. Only months later did she ultimately discover that the report of him dying had been false. Miraculously, Said Etris Hashemi had survived.

But on that morning after the attack, when she saw the video for the first time, the only thing she could do was turn to the omniscient Internet to sift through more and more information, even though it was only trickling in. Who had died? Who was alive? The digital realm was full of names—some true, some false—and she was filled with horror and pain and grief but also the daily routines and usual abuses and dreadful normality. Nivedita lay on the high-pile carpet holding her phone, scrolling and scrolling, with Priti by her side. Nivedita wanted nothing more than to be with Priti at Oluchi's, or with Priti and Oluchi in their campus students-of-color group, anywhere with her fellows. Instead, there was Saraswati, seated on the sofa, still as a statue. Raji had been cradling his face in his hands for a good long while already, as if trying to shut out the world. And Saraswati's books sat on their shelves, utterly useless. Nivedita typed a message into WhatsApp: *How you doing, Oluchi? With the news? N.*

But before she could even decide whether to send it or not, Iqbal shared an Instagram post. White lettering on a black background:

From *thefirenexttime*

Let's never talk about Saraswati again.

Never, ever, ever again.

This sad month, which started out with us fighting

over her absurd disguises—

it's now ended

with a racist in Hanau indiscriminately

shooting nine people dead.

But no.

It wasn't indiscriminate.

He shot nine people who bore racialized features.

The existential question of who is POC,

who belongs and who doesn't,

who's oppressed and who isn't

in this society—

now that question has been answered.

WE are the ones who get thrown to the wolves,

used for target practice.

Let us always bear that in mind.

We must resist.

Yes, thought Nivedita, *yes, yes, yes.* But also, *No, no, no!*

She watched as the likes on his post rocketed all the way past 17K. Translations into English, Spanish, French, and Bengali spread across Twitter and Facebook faster than Saraswati could say, "So now you have to be dead to be a POC."

Nivedita hurled her phone to the floor (but onto the carpet, not the wood) and screamed at the top of her lungs, "Shut your trap, Saraswati!" It felt good to have a clear and present nemesis, a focal point for all her anger and fear and, sure, for the guilt she felt knowing that she felt personally attacked even though she was way up here in Saraswati's luxury penthouse. "Please just shut up, for once, and give us a little time to grieve."

"And what about my grief?" Saraswati asked. Her voice sounded strange and hollow, as if she were far away. Nivedita looked at her, utterly uncomprehending. What did Saraswati's grieving have to do with her?

But Saraswati wasn't expecting an answer, at least not from Nivedita. "Are you thefirenexttime?" she asked Raji.

Raji let his hands fall from his face, as if the oh-so-familiar rancor he felt for his sister was like some kind of injection capable of saving him from his apathy.

"Regrettably, no," he said, his voice full of spite.

"You liar," Saraswati said.

"He just can't handle not being the biggest victim anymore," Priti whispered to Nivedita. But something had happened to Raji, and to all of them. As thefirenexttime so aptly wrote: *News of the shooting in Hanau changed everything.*

"Will you ever finally see that I don't even have to do you any harm?" he answered, as if on the lookout for familiar terrain—strike and counterstrike. "You're already doing sufficient harm to yourself, all by yourself." So then Saraswati's answer caught him off guard.

"Surely I'll understand one of these days, as soon as you stop harming yourself," Saraswati said with so much honest sympathy in her voice that Raji automatically spit on the floor.

Nivedita looked at the little white puddle of saliva, growing darker and more reflective as the invisible sun finally sank behind a thick wall of clouds. For one agonizing, terrifying moment, she was certain that, amid all the fighting and aggression and talking that had taken place here in the living room, she actually saw the shooter in that little white drop of liquid: a reflection of the man who, blinded by hatred, had shot at people who were eating and smoking shisha and just chatting—

—and then a teensy little bubble of spittle burst, and she saw herself and Priti and Oluchi and Iqbal and Saraswati pacing back and forth before them in her lecture hall, giving a fiery talk about the importance of love in political battle jargon. Because all these heady, exciting conversations had to mean something. Because the sheer beauty of all the disagreements among her classmates—a bunch of students who of course closely resembled the group in Hanau, where there had to be at least as many anti-racist groups as there were anti-fascist groups, and where shisha bars, OTBs, and teahouses were a way of life—outshined the perpetrator in that little bubble of spittle. Even though now he was entirely in Nivedita's head, projecting onto the wad of spittle on the floor, he was still aiming his weapon at innocent people just out for a meal, bursting, getting back up again, fading again, only to cast his shadow over everything, or maybe not exactly everything . . . This feeling of being bound to Priti and Oluchi and Iqbal was probably the only logical answer to the question of why she was lying here on the carpet in Saraswati's living room: because Saraswati, too, was a part of that WE—a WE that bore all the controversies of the outside world in its heart, but still had room for both Oluchi's off-putting anger and Saraswati's all-commandeering love.

And maybe it was also the only logical answer to the question of why Saraswati still let Raji stay here: because she loved him. But she loved him the way Saraswati always loved, unpredictably and arrogantly. And Raji, for his part, felt like he was Saraswati's savior sibling, conceived, born, and brought up solely in order to provide essential organs or stem cells to his ailing sibling—only in Saraswati's case of course the organ was the skin, needed for its color, and in Raji's case he didn't even have to be conceived and born, they'd just had to adopt him, or whatever it was they'd done.

Saraswati kneeled back and wiped Raji's spit up off the wood floor with the saffron-yellow cuff of her blouse. Her face was expressionless, as if the news had hit some reset button and her system hadn't fully rebooted yet.

"Don't play the martyr," Raji said, aware he'd done wrong.

"I have to wash it anyway," Saraswati explained.

"And don't play the simple, native girl next door, either."

"Can't I ever do anything right?" Saraswati asked, and then added, as her old talent for mimicry slowly returned, "Why do you hate me so much?"

"Why . . . ? In Hanau—multicultural Hanau!—a bunch of POCs were murdered, in public, right there in the shisha bar. And the only thing you're interested in asking is *why-don't-you-love-me*? That's so . . . so . . . *white*!" Raji snarled.

Saraswati turned her next words into a crude joke: "But you're *white*, too."

He stared at her, failing to understand.

"White. *Blanco. Comprende*?"

"No, I don't understand."

"You might be brown when you're looking for an apartment . . ."

"Or applying for a job," Raji added dryly.

"Or applying for a job. Have you ever even applied for a job in your entire life? Or did you get your gig as the savior of all London's brown youths the usual way, through a friend of a friend?"

"That doesn't change a thing."

"Maybe so. But when you're all alone at home, you're not the son of some Brahmin Indian—once again, goddammit, you're just the son of a *white* German dentist." Like a protective layer she no longer needed, Saraswati shed her spit-stained blouse.

Nivedita held her phone tight as it comfortingly vibrated each time new messages came through on WhatsApp or Signal:

Nivedita, have you heard what happened? (Lotte)

Nivedita, will you sign this petition? Right-wing terror in #Hanau: Appoint a federal official to fight antimuslim racists, now! (Iqbal)

Nivedita, are you okay? You're from Hanau, aren't you? (Richard)

Nivedita, please call me, it's been sooo long since we last spoke. (Birgit)

"That's really what you refuse to excuse our parents for, Raji, isn't it? You can't forgive them for turning you into something you hate," Saraswati said, now in the yellow top that was underneath her yellow blouse. Each layer revealed another, of an identical color.

"No, that's not it. I take offense at the fact that they *took what I am from me*, and gave it to you, with your insatiable greed!"

"Now there's something you really can't accuse Josefa and Konstantin of."

"You're right—I can accuse you of that, and you alone." Raji tried to give Saraswati a hostile look, but there wasn't really enough energy behind his eyes. Ever since he'd heard the news, he'd seemed weak and shaky, like the before pictures you see on those self-help, life-hack websites full of before and after pics that he was always looking at when he wasn't busy reading online articles about racial disparities in youth justice.

Priti poked Nivedita's ribs with her phone, "Mum has just asked me if we're safe." That was the old-school SMS text message that made this surreal situation realer than real: If even Leela back in Birmingham was worried, there was no chance that it had all just been a bad dream. No, flip that around—it wasn't a bad dream—the nightmare that behind every door lurked some pervasive, omnipresent danger had now sunk its claws into their real, everyday lives.

And then the living room door opened, but it was just Kali sashaying in, nonchalantly swinging one of the severed arms back and forth between her swaying hips.

"What's *she* doing here?" Saraswati asked, and any sense of reality flew right back out the terrace door.

"You . . . you can see her?" Nivedita stammered, even though she'd honestly thought nothing else could ever faze her. But obviously Saraswati's greatest talent was shaking Nivedita up.

"Seeing, hearing, feeling—what's the difference?" Saraswati enigmatically asked. "Of course I can see her. Sorry, Kali—of course I notice you. After all, you're the goddess upon whom all my research is based."

Kali nodded, clearly pleased, and caressed her own blue shoulders with a lick of her tongue. When it came to expectations of obeisance, both Saraswati and Kali were second to none.

Nivedita felt Priti's phone poke her ribs yet again, only this time Priti was sliding the screen over so Nivedita could read the limerick it looked like she had written right then and there:

> There was a goddess from Calcutta
> Whose tongue was so long she could suck her
> own beautiful cunt
> And she said with a grunt
> If I'm in the mood then I'll fuck her.

"So you can see her, too," Nivedita flatly said.

"*Beautiful* cunt," Priti nodded, nearly swooning.

"And since we're on the subject," Saraswati continued, "Kali, can you perform an exorcism?"

Of course, Kali replied. When it came to self-confidence, yet again, they were two peas in a pod.

6

The procession was led by a blue-skinned, blood-smeared, laughing, naked woman with long, flowing black hair, and had there been anyone else in the park on this stormy Tuesday around noon as they went from the Volksgarten to the Stoffeler Cemetery, they'd have caused a commotion. Saraswati brought up the rear so she could keep an eye on Raji, who had cocooned himself in skepticism, and make sure he didn't take off. Then came Nivedita, still not fully capable of processing the fact that, after all these years, she wasn't the only one who spoke to Kali all the time—not counting, of course, the entire population of Bengal and the millions of other believers spread around the globe. Then came Priti, almost dancing as she walked, rapt in a state of ecstasy brought on by . . . religious enthusiasm? "You really didn't make up all those blog, entries, Niv! Everything in *Identitti* is true! Wow, Kali! If my mum knew! But for real, are you the actual Kali?"

Sure am, Kali confirmed.

"May I touch you?"

Of course, I love being touched, Kali purred, beyond pleased—whereupon Nivedita wondered why *she*'d never had that same idea.

"*Ist das . . .* beneficent?" Priti reverentially asked.

Yes, although of course not quite as much as when I touch someone.

"Of course," Priti hastened to agree, only to then cautiously loop back: "Might you . . . deign to . . . touch me?"

Oh, but I usually touch people not with my hands, but with my eyes.

Counting on Kali, Priti stood before her and closed her eyes. "Go ahead!"

Kali cast a furtive glance at Saraswati and Raji—who, despite the racially motivated terrorist attack, despite her supernatural presence, and despite her divine intervention, were still totally absorbed in each another's issues. She then winked at Nivedita, and then moved her palms over Priti's head in tender, rapid strokes, as if wiping water, or maybe a very tasty alcohol, from her face and hair.

Priti vibrated with excitement. "Wow!"

Let's get a move on—this exorcism won't take care of itself, Kali said, stepping forward and leading the group out onto the large lawn from which air balloons used to launch, still barefooted but not bothering to avoid the bright green, little curlicued Canada goose droppings that dotted the grass.

While Priti was still savoring the aftereffects of her benediction, Nivedita ran after Kali. "Why did you lay your hands on her—I mean, can't you, y'know, touch her with your eyes?"

Of course I can, Kali gave a dismissive laugh, *but I need to focus my energy on what now lies before us. And we don't have much time left.*

A gust of wind struck Nivedita and she noticed that the clouds were no longer gray, they were now a sulphury green, and starting to roil in a rather sinister way.

"Don't we need some kind of expedient for this exorcism, something to help banish the evil spirits? Maybe a drop of two of holy water?" she anxiously asked.

Oh, I almost forgot, said Kali, leaning over to pick up an empty bottle of everyone's favorite local swill that—Nivedita could have sworn—hadn't been lying on the lawn a second before. Kali shook out the last few drops and then dipped it into the pond, which had now taken on the same sulphureous color as the sky.

"Holy water?" Nivedita asked, incredulous.

Weiherwasser, Weihwasser—*pond water, holy water—you say potäto, I say potato.*

"So did you, like, choose Nivedita, so to speak, as your interlocutor?" Priti asked, sounding only slightly envious as she ran to catch up with them.

Well, to be honest, Priti . . .

"Wow, she called me 'Priti.' Kali called me 'Priti.' You called me 'Priti,' Kali!"

"Uhh, I always do, too, y'know," Nivedita mumbled.

"Yeah, but you aren't . . . *anyway!* Kali called me 'Priti.' Sorry, did I interrupt you, Kali? Could you please say my name just one more time?"

Priti. So, in all honesty, I can speak to countless believers—and nonbelievers—at the same time.

"But Nivedita's a little bit like a chosen one, right?"

Of course, Kali nodded, *just like you are, too.*

Priti beamed.

And Saraswati. And Raji. And all living beings on this planet.

"Yeah," said Priti, "but it's not like I asked you about all of them."

"Here lie Josefa and Konstantin," Saraswati said, following them onto a chestnut-lined lane into the heart of the cemetery. "Don't you think it's time we truly laid her to rest, Stan . . . I mean, Raji?"

Raji looked off in the direction his sister was pointing, then he looked at Kali, who was cheerfully shrugging.

It's up to you. I'm not getting involved. But if you'd like, I can give a lamentation, she offered.

Meanwhile, the shroud of clouds had taken on all the colors of a nasty bruise. A wind rose with such force it seemed eager to sweep away any doubt that the storm might break at any moment, it was here already, but still not a single drop of rain. Raji stared at the grouping of grave stones—two massive crosses, a black granite slab with a white inscription, three light gray headstones, a boulder—and couldn't bring himself to get any closer.

Nivedita followed his gaze and asked Priti, "Before I forget, amid all this big news: how was last night?"

"Who knows? As long as you're talking to Raji, everything sounds totally logical, but as soon as you're no longer sitting right next to him . . ." Priti skillfully sidestepped her cousin's question.

She slept with him, Nivedita thought, and couldn't help but wonder whether she was jealous, but then couldn't really say. *She slept with him after all—after all that.*

Or, if you'd prefer, I can just have sex with them, Kali generously said to Raji, twirling one of the severed heads on her necklace so that its lips latched onto the dark-blue nipple of her right breast.

Raji shuddered. Saraswati gently laid a hand on his shoulder and he didn't shake it off, even if it required such restraint that he looked like he was about to get a serious toothache.

"I know that Josefa and Konstantin did something unbelievable to you. But you're here, and they're . . ." Saraswati's other hand made a vague, broad arc in the air. "Who knows where?" Where had her *In Hinduism nothing is permanent, not even death* gone all of a sudden?

"That's precisely the problem: They can no longer be held to account," Raji said through clenched teeth.

I could bring them back to life, if you'd like, Kali suggested, pressing her thumbs to the Uerige Alt bottle top as it flickered a warm brown in the first flashes of still faraway lightening. Then she began sprinkling the pond water in a circle around herself and the grouping of gravestones. Her hair looked as if it were as electrically charged as the air, and it made a crackling sound. Priti slinked over and pressed a bright little bag of turmeric she'd swiped from Saraswati's kitchen into Kali's hand. Priti was thrilled the awe-inspiring goddess generously accepted this token, and used it to double the circle, sealing the ring with both water *and* turmeric.

"Is she crazy, or am I?" Raji asked. "Or are you the only one who's crazy, Satan?"

Saraswati flinched when she heard his old nickname for her. Raji turned to Kali, his shoulders trembling. "Once you've freed me from Josefa and Konstantin, can we perform another exorcism, to free Saraswati from . . . Saraswati?"

What do you think I'm doing here? Kali asked, busy doing her thing.

And as they all just stared at her, entirely uncomprehending, she continued, *Exorcism means casting out all devils and unclean spirits! And who's the devil? Satan!*

Priti was the first to catch on, and gasped for air. The exorcism wasn't for Raji, it was for Saraswati. Nivedita opened her mouth to intervene, but Kali had already begun singing:

And death shall have no dominion.
Dead men naked they shall be one

"In this case the word *men* means all human beings, of course," she whispered to Priti and Nivedita, and then licked her lips, and then licked her own nipples, since—why not?

With the man in the wind and the west moon;
When their bones are picked clean and the clean bones gone,
They shall have stars at elbow and foot;
Though they go mad they shall be sane,
Though they sink through the sea they shall rise again;
Though lovers be lost love shall not;
And death shall have no dominion.

And suddenly the thunderstorm had arrived. The first bolt of thunder exploded, and the storm started howling all around, hunting down the ring of brackish Düsseldorf pond water and turmeric, lashing the chestnut trees, making everything heave and sway—but Kali's singing kept it all in check. Saraswati arched her back like a cat about to cough up a hairball. "Don't you get it?" she griped, stretching her hands out to complain at Nivedita or Raji or Priti or Kali or the elements. "I hated being me so deeply that I had only one option left—to not be me! I had to flay my living body, shed that skin, and leave it behind!"

So, less Michael Jackson and more The Silence of the Lambs?

"And what skin did you then peel off of whom, in order to then take it as your own?" Raji articulated Nivedita's thoughts for her.

Saraswati straightened up, again assuming her trademark ballerina pose. "I changed the world!"

"Yes, but at what cost?" Nivedita called out.

"Whatever the cost, it's a price I'm prepared to pay!" Saraswati yelled back, and the truth of that pronouncement struck Nivedita to the core. Saraswati wasn't just ready to pay the price in terms of lost social respect and all the other entirely superficial privileges and forms of cultural capital—she *would* pay the price, over and over again, with interest, and even compound interest. *It's not about being in the right. It's about rights—it's about justice. There's a difference. Justice means everyone is seen, and everything needed to make amends and maybe even lead to forgiveness—Truth and Reconciliation . . .* Nivedita feverishly thought. And then she noticed she was the only one standing right in front of Saraswati. Priti and Raji were two steps behind them, backing them up, and Kali was wildly writhing all around them, stomping her feet, rattling the skulls on her necklace, enveloping them in her sweet, low voice. And Saraswati was crying. She was wailing without making a sound, as if for the first time in her entire life. Maybe they were tears of anger, but they were tears nevertheless, and there were a lot of them—countless, endless, salty tears. "Can't you understand? I just couldn't bear being Sarah Vera!" she cried.

"Sure, but then why did you have to be Saraswati? It's not like all *white* women are Sarah Vera. Life handed you so very many opportunities, you had endless possibilities," Nivedita whispered.

"No, I didn't!"

"Oh, Saraswati." Nivedita spread her arms to offer up one last long, all-encompassing hug, and Saraswati staggered over to her.

Her face buried in Nivedita's shoulder, she sighed, "And, no . . . not all . . . other . . . *white* women . . . are Sarah Vera . . . but she was the only *white* woman *I* could be!"

Why had Saraswati wanted to be a POC? *Because she wanted the pain*, Nivedita thought with a shrug. Because she had no other words with which to express the serious suffering that had taken over her life—except for the vocabulary of racism.

Kali sang:

And death shall have no dominion.
Under the windings of the sea
They lying long shall not die windily;
Twisting on racks when sinews give way,
Strapped to a wheel, yet they shall not break;
Faith in their hands shall snap in two,
And the unicorn evils run them through;
Split all ends up they shan't crack;
And death shall have no dominion.

"I am you," Saraswati said, turning from Nivedita to Raji. "Everything our parents did to you, they did to me."

"No, they did not," he shot back. "And don't you *dare* forgive them on my behalf." But as he said this, he nevertheless stepped toward her, and Nivedita took his place next to Priti. They felt the wind at their backs, but it was as if there were a pane of glass between them and the rain, which remained mere background noise. Nivedita reached for Priti's hand, and held on as tight as she could.

"It doesn't matter to me whether you forgive *them*, or *they* forgive me," Saraswati said in her best-trained voice, which rang out like a bell even though there was no echo in the cemetery. "But what does matter to me is whether you forgive *me*. That's why I did what I did."

"Oh, please. Don't exploit me and my life any more than you already have, to excuse all the messes you've made."

"Raji," Saraswati implored as best she could, which didn't sound particularly imploring. He gazed right past her, staring at the only headstone that lay inside the ring formed by Kali's dance and Priti's turmeric, a simply hewn black granite slab, perfectly fitting for Josefa and Konstantin. But the tension visible in his shoulders made it clear that he was listening to Saraswati with undivided attention.

"I couldn't change our parents, but I could change me. I went to India in order to change the past. I went there so that you wouldn't have to be the only brown kid who'd grown up in a *white* family. So that you wouldn't have to be all alone in a *white* family that hadn't the slightest clue about racism. That always thought you had done something wrong when people treated you differently than they treated me." Saraswati's voice got higher with every sentence, so she was now speaking in a crystal-clear soprano. "So that you wouldn't always and forever be treated differently than me!"

Now he looked right at her, but with disgust.

"And I teach what I teach so that people like you are no longer cut off from this knowledge," she persisted.

"Knowledge?" Raji yelled. "Knowledge? You're all knowledge, and no feeling!"

"That's not true," Saraswati countered, genuinely surprised.

"See, even that doesn't hurt you—you can't even feel enough to know what you're not feeling!"

"But I took your pain—onto myself!"

Raji gave a scornful huff. "No, you *stole* my pain, reclaimed it, and then exploited it for your career."

"How are we any different from one another? You used your pain for your career, too—after all, no one can understand juvenile offenders better than someone who was himself a juvenile offender once upon a time. Or at least would have been, back then, if Daddy Konstantin's lawyer hadn't always taken care of everything."

"But it was MY pain!"

"Stan . . . Raji, pain never belongs solely to one individual. As a child, I could never have grown up with you, lived under the same roof as you for so long, without your pain necessarily becoming an integral part of me. The same would hold true for anyone."

Kali gently nudged the two of them closer, so that they stood face to face, skin to skin.

"You've already taken so much from me—you cannot take my pain, too," Raji's voice went from a roar to a gasp.

Saraswati was out of breath, too. "Why not? What's so great about it, that you insist on holding onto it?"

"You're just playing with words. You don't even know what *pain* means."

"I don't? How do you think *I feel*?"

"Right—you mean how you feel *now*! Welcome to the world of the disempowered!"

Kali clapped her hands and sang on:

And death shall have no dominion.
No more may gulls cry at their ears
Or waves break loud on the seashores;
Where blew a flower may a flower no more
Lift its head to the blows of the rain;
Though they be mad and dead as nails,
Heads of the characters hammer through daisies;
Break in the sun till the sun breaks down,
And death shall have no dominion.

"Why do you think I had Priti steal all that vulgar photographic documentation, which was ridiculously easy, too? Why do you think I went public with all this?" Raji let loose, asking the million-dollar question. Kali gave him an approving nod, and then a lecherous smack to his behind, and he carried on with renewed courage: "I only did all that to give you a tiny taste of the immense pain you hungered after for so long. And I wanted to make sure it was your pain you felt, not anyone else's. And? Well? Aren't you grateful? Don't you want to thank me?"

Saraswati swallowed, swallowed again, and then haltingly, cautiously nodded. "And why do you think I didn't defend myself in public?" she finally asked. "Every day, I get umpteen interview requests. I could've gone on any of Jan Böhmermann's many shows, or Markus Lanz, or gone on the Feuer & Brot podcast and readily convinced the world to see it all my way."

Raji raised his head with a jerk, as if he wanted to disagree, or maybe bite her in the face, but then he just let it sink again. Just beyond the border of their dried-out turmeric circle, a bunch of shadows scurried down the lane, relatives fleeing the now driving rain outside, or maybe ghosts trying to ride the storm. The only place everything was utterly still was here in this little group. Josefa's and Konstantin's grave smelled of grass and oblivion. For just a second Nivedita got the feeling that Saraswati's, Raji's, and even Priti's skin was dissolving, and she could almost make out their peripheral nerves, raw and red, and all she'd have to do is reach her hand out and heal those centuries-old wounds. She really wished she could take away the rawness and redness with her mere mortal hands, thereby healing these siblings who were both equal and unequal, all at the same time. And she'd have healed Priti and herself, too, plus Oluchi and Barbara and Lotte and Lotte's mother, and everyone in Düsseldorf and out in the big wide world. She wished she could transform the world's trauma, bestowing everyone with the sense of humble appreciation they had long since lost, helping them remember the empathy they'd forgotten they had. She wished she could take all the people apathetically lying about and help them get up, stand up. She wished she could make the broken whole, bring the dead come back to life, and give all of them—every single one—just one more hug.

"Don't you see any good in me?" Saraswati's voice wavered, and even Raji couldn't fail to see that she was offering up her vulnerability to him like a gift.

"I don't know," he replied with complete candor. "What do the rest of you think? Should the four of us take a vote? Nivedita?"

Nivedita wondered whether maybe Saraswati loved her so much only because she wanted to rectify what she'd done to her brother, but . . . whatever! When all was said and done, Saraswati was still the mother she'd always wanted, and now it was only a matter of being sincere, so she simply said, "Saraswati is the best professor I ever had."

Raji nodded, not too surprised, and turned to Priti.

"Sure," Priti concurred, "but, you have to admit, most professors were total *Scheiße*." Then she added, "Saraswati is the best opponent I've ever had."

"Kali?"

Kali twirled her long tresses like a lasso high overhead, like a snake she was wrangling, like a river run wild. *Saraswati is Saraswati.*

"Three to zero—you win," Raji said with an inscrutable expression, extending his hand out to her.

"And you?" Saraswati insisted. "Do you see any good in me?"

Raji wavered. He wasn't ready for that, not quite yet. But he also couldn't just keep waiting for the right moment to arrive. He shuddered a second and looked down at himself, as if inspecting his own skin. Kali let out a bleating laugh, as if trying to buck him up. "It . . . it actually mattered to you . . . how I was doing . . . who I was. That's what I appreciate about you. That you saw— you knew things were wrong. That I had an eyewitness."

Kali whooped with enthusiasm, laid an arm over Raji's shoulders, and pulled him slightly aside. *Y'know, I could change your life, too—shift the timeline, or even make you* white, *if you'd like!*

"Under no circumstances!" yelled Raji, appalled.

As the rain suddenly penetrated the circle Kali had so enterprisingly established, it was like a curtain falling over a stage. From one moment to the next, the rain's countless wet kisses pressed into their skin, and the wind tried to tear the clothes from their bodies with a thousand groping fingers. Priti took a step toward Saraswati in order to repeat once again the apology she'd offered three weeks before, and Saraswati, speechless, took her into her arms. Nivedita walked over to the graves. The inscription on the black granite slab read *Josef*, not *Josefa*, and the last name wasn't *Thielmann*, it was *Hammer*. Konstantin wasn't mentioned at all.

7

Kali had actually announced that, on the way back, she'd take her four protégés by the *Tor zur Hölle*, as the denizens of nineteenth-century Düsseldorf had nicknamed the underpass leading from Worringer Platz to Oberbilk. It must've really seemed like a gateway to hell back then, since the passageway led under the railroad tracks to the wrong side of town, where the lewd, hard-laboring classes crouched in their hovels, let their countless little urchins play unsupervised in the streets, and typhus and cholera regularly made the rounds through the dirt streets that doubled as sewers. Kali wanted to gaze through the gate from Oberbilk, the hellish side, thereby flipping the script, reversing the presumed perspective. But by then everybody was too tired and drenched to the bone—even Saraswati looked exhausted of being Saraswati.

As she opened the door of her apartment, she turned to Raji. "Just because your childhood was so much worse than mine, it doesn't mean my childhood was so much better. I had to live with Josefa and Konstantin as my parents, just like you."

"And that's the real reason no one should ever envy anyone else," he said with a grin.

"So, you want to finally look through the things from their house this time? Maybe there's something you'd like to take with you."

Nivedita followed Priti and Kali into the kitchen, giving the equal and unequal siblings a little privacy.

"That was all . . . very impressive," Priti said to Kali.

Of course it was, Kali nodded, raising her foot to scratch her kneecap with one of her toes.

Nivedita turned her phone back on. The world rushed back in, bringing a tidal wave of pain and violence that had yet to be healed. Meanwhile, the names of the victims in Hanau had come out and were shared all over social media. *Right*, thought Nivedita. They were people with their own pasts, their own histories, and that horrible crime had robbed them of their futures. They were so much more than a bunch of nameless, storyless, lifeless dead.

Say their names:
Ferhat Unvar
Mercedes Kierpacz
Sedat Gürbüz

Gökhan Gültekin

Hamza Kurtović

Kaloyan Velkov

Vili Viorel Păun

Said Nesar Hashemi

Fatih Saraçoğlu

And there were photos—lots of selfies, pictures of people who not only looked like Priti and Nivedita, but were their same age, too. These images made the horror of it all seem so everyday, so palpable, so *close*, that it nearly tore Nivedita in two. She felt personally hit, deeply threatened, but at the same time found the pain and grief of all the relatives and friends impossible to gauge, let alone to take in as if it were her own.

Kind of like Saraswati? Kali asked, as if she'd read Nivedita's mind—which she probably had.

"Angela Merkel has expressed her condolences to the victims' friends and families," Priti announced, reading from her phone. "And she said it was a racist attack." Priti hadn't wasted her two semesters in Saraswati's class, so she knew full well that—here in the country she'd lived in for a year now, and in its entire history—that acknowledgment was something new. Helmut Kohl was still (in)famous for having skipped the funeral service for the victims of the 1993 arson attack in Solingen because he had an "important meeting" and didn't think much of "condolence tourism."

Nivedita lost the thread of all the other conversations as she clicked around, trying to find out whether a vigil was being organized in Düsseldorf. When she finally looked up from her phone, she heard Priti say, "And that song you sang, Kali . . . was that some ritualistic Bengali dirge?"

Kali handed Priti a tea bag and pointed to the kettle. *Nope, that was a poem by Dylan Thomas.*

"By who?" Nivedita asked, curious—but at the same time finding her curiosity rather frivolous in light of the catastrophe committed in Hanau.

Everyone has their own way of grieving, Kali said, as if she'd read Nivedita's mind—which of course she definitely had, yet again. *And why isn't the mother of the shooter on the list of victims? After all, he murdered her, too, before he shot himself dead.*

"Dylan Thomas—Welsh national poet," Priti said. "The one who wrote *fishing boat bobbing sea*."

"Who? What?"

"Super sexy." Priti did a Google image search. "No . . . huh, umm, here he actually looks kinda like your uncle Hans . . . nope, let's not go there. I can't find the pic. But Dylan Thomas was def. super sexy."

And now the sky looked like a sheet of wrinkly grease-proof paper someone had stabbed over and over with a pencil, as the last drops of rain now fell through all the little holes.

"A Welsh poet? *Wales*?" Nivedita repeated.

Welsh, Bengali—they're like six of one, half dozen of the other, Kali said with a dismissive wave of her hand. *The English always confuse Welsh accents and Indian accents anyway, and we needed a song. The last time I sang a dirge . . .*

And as Kali said the words *the last time*, something in Nivedita's brain clicked. She ran back to the hallway, and of course no one was there anymore. She ran into the living room, where Saraswati and Raji both looked at her with the same, identical, magnetic smile. It seemed like they had both spent an entire life, maybe two lifetimes, just waiting for her. There they stood, with their two different and yet not at all different ways of conquering the world with their charm—but did she mean *conquering* in the sense of *seducing* or *colonizing*? She had to think about it for a second. Gazing out through the terrace door, she couldn't see a single drop falling, but the rain was still streaking down the kitchen window behind her, each drop leaving a track as thin as a spiderweb in its wake.

"You said you hadn't seen Raji in thirty years?" she confronted Saraswati.

"No, he said that," Saraswati smiled. "To which I replied that he's a liar."

"So you two have been in touch . . . every now and again?"

"Of course."

Raji looked at Saraswati, embarrassed. "Are you mad at me?"

Saraswati hesitated, and then said, "It depends."

"On what?"

But before she could answer, Nivedita's phone pulsed, making a sound that seemed a lot like a pounding heartbeat. It was a WhatsApp from Barbara: "Did you see this?"

> » **Adrienne M Brown @adriennembrown** *any good sci-fi explanations or transformative justice responses for #Saraswati?*

Nivedita tweeted right back:

> » **Nivedita Anand @identitti** *Identity is a spectrum. Identity politics is a spectrum. Cultural appropriation is a spectrum.*

And somewhere on that spectrum lay the point at which approximation turned into appropriation, help into manipulation, solidarity into self-centeredness. That was the point where Saraswati stood in perfect equilibrium. One foot on the constructive side, one on the destructive side.

PART III: CODA

THE ACADEMIC FORMERLY KNOWN AS SARASWATI

"Is this a fake meme I see before me?"—William Shakespeare

The next morning, Raji was gone.

"He'll be back," said Priti, who was the first to notice that the door to Saraswati's home office was ajar and who had dared to open it all the way.

"Yeah, but not for another couple of years," Saraswati scoffed, not bothering to join Nivedita and Priti in their search for a note, a scrap of paper, anything that might explain his sudden absence.

"For another couple . . . *years*?" Nivedita asked, incredulous.

"Yeah, one-and-a-half to three years or so—that's his usual timing."

Nivedita and Priti also began packing up their things, which had been strewn all over the apartment. Simon rang at 11:00 a.m. and waited out front, standing next to his blue Clio with the characteristically paradoxical #Fri-daysForFuture decals on the back, as Nivedita and Priti showered Saraswati in so many hugs and kisses that you'd have thought they were never going to see each other again. Unwilling to be ignored by anyone, Saraswati then slid over to Simon and admonished him, in a voice that made her sound like an entire cadre of older brothers: "Watch how your treat Nivedita, understand?" Simon wrinkled his forehead, looking dour or maybe just insecure. Saraswati swung her dupatta over her shoulder as she turned and headed for the train station, off to Berlin to see Toni one last time before she headed to Nicaragua.

And to appear on an episode of Maybrit Illner's talk show—about Hanau.

INSTEAD OF DRIVING to the seaside with Simon as they had originally planned, Nivedita headed back to her apartment and watched the show along with Priti and Barbara. Priti was staying in Lotte's room while she was in South Tyrol, trying out the resort's various wellness treatments as her mother did a round of ozone oxygen therapy. Onscreen, Saraswati seemed more compassionate and affable than usual. Draped in her deep red wedding dupatta, it felt like she was trying to send an affirmation to the entire audience, one big YES, as if to say, "I'll answer all your questions about me and my identity—just not here and now. Today is all about the victims. Today is all about why, here in Germany, people with *presumably* visible immigrant roots are interpreted as a threat even though they're actually the ones *living* under a daily threat. Today is also all about why such people so rarely obtain professorships in German universities, and why so few of my colleagues reflect the actual demographics of the country we live in. Today is all about racism's omnipresence and the very concrete steps we need to take to change that on both the individual level but also, above all, structurally."

Saraswati kept her promise. Over the following weeks, she spoke with all the media outlets that, up until then, had competed in vain for her time and attention. Nivedita read the interview on the website of the *Guardian*:

"*I, as a privileged white person, have offered up my privilege in service of the oppressed.*"

Nivedita listened to the interview on WDR public broadcasting:

"Before, there were only three channels on TV. Now we can choose from among countless channels, and not just on TV. It's the same with identity."

Nivedita watched the interview on *Tagesthemen*, one of Germany's main daily news broadcasts:

"Imitation is the sincerest form of flattery."

"What exactly *does that mean?"* Caren Migosa prodded with her trademark directness.

"That imitation is the highest form of respect."

"Okay, but you still said 'flattery' just a second ago."

"So? Situations and—above all—we ourselves can be one thing, without necessarily losing the ability to be something else entirely."

After that, the mass-media carousel spun ever faster. Nivedita heard a production company was planning a documentary film about the whole thing—and Saraswati catapulted out of Nivedita's orbit.

9 MONTHS POST-SARASWATI

Nivedita rode her bike through the Indian spring night. Everyone's windows were open to let the city in, and a charged air hung over Düsseldorf, as if someone were throwing a party somewhere and Nivedita was the guest of honor. The feeling was so intoxicating that even Oluchi smiled at her as she walked over from the other side of Sonnen Park—Saraswati's side. But it had been a long time since Nivedita had seen lights on up in Saraswati's penthouse during her little detours biking down Kölner Straße. Nearby was a playground where families sat all day, cracking open sunflower seeds as kids played. The wall around that playground now had some new graffiti: *It's not the meek who shall inherit the earth—it's the mixed who shall inherit the earth.*

Nivedita had only seen Oluchi once since that afternoon back at Saraswati's, when Priti moved back into her old room, and Oluchi moved to Giessen to start her studies with Nikita Dhawan at Justus Liebig University. It had been such a chaotic afternoon that Nivedita and Oluchi hadn't even had a chance to chat. Nivedita, too, had briefly toyed with the idea of going to study with Nikita Dhawan, but ultimately decided against it, because it would've felt like some kind of betrayal. So she stayed in Düsseldorf and, after a thousand-odd long walks, decided to title her draft thesis "Sex & Love in the Ruins of Empire: The Effects of 'Race' on Intimate Relationships." She also wrote a few articles for the media outlets who had reached out to her during the Saraswati Affair.

"Hey, Nivedita," Oluchi said. Her tone made it sound like they were on the same level, but then—as if that weren't enough of a surprise—Oluchi stayed on her feet, opting not to sit down next to her in the grass.

"Hi," Nivedita said, utterly unprepared. Thinking her own chilly tone a little too unfriendly, she added, "What're you doing here?" Then, since that was *definitely* too unfriendly sounding, she added, "I mean . . . *here* . . . back in little old Düsseldorf?"

A cloud of parrots shot by like a bolt of bright-green lightning and landed with the usual frenzied fluttering of wings on the young cherry trees in bloom, showering the ground with white petals.

Oluchi plucked a few petals from her hair and said, "I'm thinking about coming back."

"To Düsseldorf?"

"Maybe."

"To campus?"

"I dunno. I'm thinking about it. For now, I'm back on Höhen Straße. Since classes are all online this semester, it doesn't really matter where I live."

"You're back on Höhen Straße?" *With Priti?*

A gust of wind rattled the white sunflower seed shells scattered on the ground by the wall and rustled the flower petals.

"Anna-Lena's room is free. And we still want to do the film."

Over the last several months, Priti had talked nonstop about all her "mind-blowing experiences" in the world of Tantra—"everything's super-safe, ultra-hot, and extra-hygienic!"—so Nivedita had to wonder why Priti hadn't even mentioned that they were going to go ahead with *Kinky Tantra* after all. Nor had she mentioned Oluchi's return. It was especially odd because Nivedita's relationship to Priti had grown a lot more symmetrical after the time they spent together at Saraswati's. Nivedita felt the old pangs of entanglement and slightly envious longing, a knot rose in her throat, and she looked away—ostensibly to pick out a twig that had gotten stuck in her spokes. Dust had covered her front wheel, making it not gray, but a wan white, like chalk letting through bits of the slate blackboard underneath, and before she could stop herself, she said, "Just because I wrote an awful poem once, it doesn't mean I'm some imperialist state authority."

Oluchi moved one foot, using the tip of her shoe to draw a figure eight in the scant layer of sand that kids had tracked over from the playground. "My critique isn't about you," she said with a hint of regret.

Nivedita sat up straight and gazed directly into Oluchi's brown eyes. "Uh, yeah it is," she said, knowing full well that both of them were right. She wished there were a way to negotiate these things without paying such a hefty price— without so much pain, hurt, and suffering.

The parrots prattled loudly as they flew from tree to tree. Nivedita and Oluchi fell silent. They were so close to one another that Nivedita could smell the Moringa oil she had given her as a present, back before . . . everything. Apparently, Oluchi was still using it instead of her old facial cream.

"Would you maybe want to be part of our porn flick?" Oluchi finally asked.

"I'll think about it," Nivedita said, mounting her bicycle. Ten paces later, she turned around. "Hey, Oluchi?"

Oluchi was still standing next to *the mixed shall inherit the earth.* "Yeah?"

"I never got a chance to say thanks."

"Thanks? For . . . ?"

"For that time you tried to warn me about Simon."

"It didn't exactly help."

"Oh, it totally did—just not immediately."

"It never does, right?"

Things hadn't worked out with Simon. Of course things hadn't worked out with Simon. The only difference between this last time and all the other times was that Nivedita now saw it that way, too. It didn't make their breakup any less painful, but it did make it a lot less meaningless.

"What's he up to now, anyway?" Oluchi asked, less because she actually cared, more because she just wanted to prolong the conversation.

"Who knows?" Simon and Nivedita had shared so much of their lives with one another—although in his case it was less like he'd shared, and more like he'd just temporarily lent a bit of it to Nivedita—that it was surprising how little their paths crossed now.

In the meantime, other pressing issues arose. New catastrophes had cropped up and proceeded to run through town like mad cows. The TV experts on racism had been replaced by experts on virology. Then, after yet another video of yet another non-*white* man saying "I can't breathe" went viral—this time, unlike Said Etris Hashemi, George Floyd did not survive—the experts on racism temporarily reappeared, only to be replaced by a whole new slew of furious debates.

Meanwhile, other pains and other ecstasies quickened Nivedita's heartbeat. Saraswati still hadn't been fired and was now on temporary leave, but the search for her successor wasn't moving forward much since several international intellectuals had closed ranks and expressed solidarity with Saraswati in an open letter to Heinrich Heine University. So, officially speaking, she was still Nivedita's doctoral advisor. Even the emails Raji sent from the London Southall flat he was squatting in became fewer and farther between. He wrote that he'd "seen her soul," and although Nivedita never replied, she did read them, rapt. Moreover, Priti had a Kali tattoo now, and Nivedita had a column in *der taz*.

Oluchi hopped up, taking a seat atop the low playground wall. "I read your article in *Die ZEIT online*—the one about . . . well, you know which one."

"Well, what did you think?" Nivedita asked, walking back, pushing her bike by her side.

"It was very . . . you."

10 nach 8: Die ZEIT online's magazine for politics, poetics, polemics
Racism
How can we disagree and still love each another?
Saraswati's life as a POC hurt many of us, deeply. But hurting her back can't be the answer. What might healing look like?
BY *Nivedita Anand*

What I am about to tell you is true. I can tell you how it went down *because I was there, and saw it with my own eyes.*

That sounds great, doesn't it? But I didn't write it. I cribbed it from the *Ramayana*. And the *Ramayana* is an Indian epic that originated sometime between 500 BCE and 100 CE on the Western calendar. Nobody knows the exact date. What we do know, or at least believe we know, is who wrote it—one Valmiki (no last name, just Valmiki, much like Saraswati is just Saraswati). And the sage and poet known as Valmiki didn't just write the *Ramayana*, he wrote himself into it. He even wrote scenes in which *he* recounts the *Ramayana* to the son of the hero of the *Ramayana*. Bona fide postmodern lit way back in ancient India—look it up.

And, just like Valmiki, I saw with my own eyes what I'm about to tell you. Really! Really truly! But . . . what is it we see when we see? And how do we understand it? Anyway . . . here goes:

As the news of Saraswati's passing—let's stick to this rather more neutral term, since "deceit" and "deception" imply specific intent, and no matter what I might think about Saraswati, I don't think her intent was to deceive anyone, at least not the way we picture deception—exploded across the mediasphere, I went to her. I didn't go to her place as a pushy fangirl planning to hold her little hand, as some have accused. I went to get answers—answers from Saraswati herself, not from articles or threads or anything else that came out in the outburst of online rage. Or so I thought at the time. In the meantime, I realized that, above all else, I wanted answers to the question of why *I myself* felt so horrifically betrayed by Saraswati. Because of course I felt betrayed. I still do. But, as time has gone by, that has begun to subside. Betrayal is no longer my main feeling about the whole thing.

The hardest thing for me over these past few months has been waiting until I developed a discernible stance on Saraswati's whole carefully constructed illusion, and only then writing about it. There are reasons that—amid all the other challenges of the present day—this whole thing has struck me particularly hard, struck many of you hard, struck *us* so hard. I found a very moving statement about it by *empathy_galore* on Instagram. I believe it's a poem. In any case, I think it's a really, really great poem:

The opinions
of so many
BIPOC re.
#Saraswatigate
express a degree
of sorrow
that shows
how desperately
we seek out
role models in
German
universities.

I found it so on point that I printed it out and hung it over my desk. (It doesn't hurt that the background is Baker-Miller pink with white text, super sweet.) And then I took it down—and re-hung it over my bed. It describes what I always felt was missing, and what Saraswati signified to me, what she was for me: a role model, an example—at the university but also in magazines and on TV—a voice that spoke *for us*, but above all a voice *from among us*. If we had more role models of color, no single one of them would be in the unfortunate position of needing or trying to meet all of our expectations. If we had more role models, they wouldn't have to be infallible. They'd have room to be . . . human.

Seriously, I still find what Saraswati did to be totally wrong. I still wish she'd chosen a different approach. But passing was the path she chose. And the knowledge that she's *white* (or *was*? You decide) changes a whole lot about the things she taught, and how she taught them—but it doesn't make them all worthless.

I still love Saraswati, even though I disagree with her.

That very sentence, and the subtitle of this article, expresses yet another notion I can't take full credit for—I cribbed it from James Baldwin. He starts with "We can disagree and still love each other," but then he goes on to say, "unless your disagreement is rooted in my oppression and denial of my humanity and right to exist."

That second part is something Saraswati never did, and we should acknowledge that. Even though the things she did may well make it easier for others to take our humanity less seriously. After all, in the wake of Saraswati's scandalous crash landing, some people seem to be claiming that anybody can be BIPOC for a day and come out knowing more about our complicated, contradictory life experiences than we ourselves do. And hey, sure, if I add up all the articles about Saraswati and then compare that number to the total number of articles written about BIPOC researchers and academics in Germany over the last nine months, then Saraswati wins—not only in terms of sheer number, but also in terms of article length and the prominence of the bylines, mastheads, and publications. After all, the media just love letting *white* people explain racism and who we are.

Is that Saraswati's fault? No.

Should she have taken that into consideration? Yes.

Had I already known three years ago what I know about Saraswati today, would I still have studied with her? Oof, well, probably not.

But that would've been the biggest mistake of my life—a real loss, an enormous, gaping hole. And that's the best lesson I can take from this whole debacle: that your politics *don't* actually have to be perfect in order to make a real difference. And, well, Saraswati has made an enormous difference in my life, and in the lives of many,

many others who've grappled with her and her ideas. Even if that difference is based on a fake of sorts, it is nevertheless very real.

If Saraswati has shown us anything, it's this: being non-*white* has become cool, and that's a sign of our success.

Just like the title and subtitle of this article, that notion isn't mine. Since this is all about her, it's only fitting that she have the last word. Saraswati says: *being non-*white *has become cool*. Indeed—on that, at least, she's absolutely right.

Nivedita had written that article a month or two before, but *Die ZEIT online* had held on to it, and chose to publish it to coincide with the launch of a new book: *Post-Identity: Why I No Longer Want to be White*. It was the book whose first few pages Nivedita had spotted back when Saraswati had rashly shoved the manuscript from one of her tables, scattering the pages on the floor. *Post-Identity* was now about to have an international launch, appearing almost simultaneously in English, French, Spanish, Hindi, and German. Saraswati had, rather poignantly, dedicated the book to Nivedita, giving her a superb reason to obsess over whether the dedication had been written before or after those three weeks they'd spent together at the eye of the shitstorm:

FOR NIVEDITA ANAND, MY STUDENT AND TEACHER.
I KISS YOUR EYES, NIVEDITA!

The book's pièce de résistance was the suite of photographs—*the* photographs Priti had stolen—showing a whole lot of exposed skin ranging from alabaster to brown. Saraswati had been really gorgeous as a twentysomething. The dust jacket was printed on both sides, so that the reader could decide whether they wanted the cover of their copy emblazoned with the ash-blond, pre-Indian Saraswati curled up in the sheets at her parents' house, or the post-op incarnation draped in a blood-red sari.

Nivedita would've loved to talk to Oluchi about it, but instead they were busy talking about Nitty Scott and "For Sarah Baartman," Cardi B and "WAP," and May Ayim and *Blues in Black and White*, which the Düsseldorfer

Schauspielhaus had invited Oluchi to stage as part of their Schwarzes Haus—Black Culture initiative.

And then they kept the conversation going, heading to Oluchi's place to watch the "Be(com)ing the Other" panel at the Hay Festival, which was being livestreamed for the first time this year.

"Have you heard? The protest-vigil for Hanau has been banned," Oluchi said as she opened the door upon their arrival.

"Yeah, it's scandalous," Nivedita nodded, steeling herself for a confrontation with Priti. But Priti wasn't there, and then she remembered Priti had gone to Berlin for a Tantra meetup, something about yoni and lingam mindfulness. The event had been postponed so many times that Nivedita had totally lost track. The relief she felt—upon realizing not only that Priti hadn't been keeping things from her, but also how glad she was to have Oluchi back in her life again—was so clearly written all over her face that Oluchi couldn't help but ask, "Is everything okay?"

"You know what? I think I'd like to participate in your film," said Nivedita.

"What would you say is the most colonial cocktail we could serve at tonight's party?" Oluchi grinned. "Planter's punch?"

"Gin and tonic?" Nivedita grinned back.

Three red heart emojis popped up on Oluchi's phone screen and she smiled as she replied.

"Is that . . ." and then Nivedita remembered his name, "Bijan?"

"Mm-hmm."

"Are you two still together?"

Oluchi smiled again. "I actually do find Black men . . . better. You should meet him, he'd definitely like you."

Then, as Nivedita gave her a skeptical look, she specified, "I mean meet him *under different circumstances.* Hey, have you heard that Rachel Dolezal is back? Now she's selling skin-color face masks, in all skin tones," Oluchi said it in a completely neutral tone, as if it were just a matter of time before somebody expanded the definition of the term *skin color.* Or she ditched all irritation as a peace offering of sorts. Nivedita couldn't be sure.

"Is she also hawking Black Lives Matter masks?"

"Of course, duh! Hey, how about we invite Barbara and Lotte tonight, for a real reunion?"

"Why not?" Nivedita replied, realizing that this would be a real party, with her as guest of honor.

"MANY PEOPLE THINK racism is a thing of the past, and there's a good test for convincing them to reconsider: just ask who among them would switch places with a Black man," Saraswati's voice streamed from Oluchi's laptop, free of all the shakiness and insecurity it had had over the past few months. Nivedita and Oluchi sat side by side on Oluchi's bed watching Saraswati onstage at the Hay Festival, exactly as both of them and so many others interested in justice on this unjust planet had watched the famous bullfight between Saraswati and Jordan Peterson on the same stage a mere year ago. This time Saraswati wore a white dupatta, but this time the theme was also *whiteness*. "Who here would be prepared to give up *being white*?" she asked, looking into the camera—directly at Oluchi and Nivedita, who didn't exactly feel like she was talking to them. "Well, that's what I did. I mustered up my courage, and said: I'm Spartacus!"

Nivedita felt someone gasp, but couldn't tell whether it was she herself or Oluchi.

The camera zoomed out, only to immediately zoom back in, this time centering the author seated next to Saraswati.

"What do you say to that, Kwame? Is it possible to choose one's own *race*?" the moderator asked. Kwame Anthony Appiah leaned in and held out his hands as if gently holding some invisible object in front of the audience. "As a philosopher, the question I always have to ask is: what are we really talking about when we talk about *race*? Our conception of *race* is relatively new, since we use it to refer not only to different people, but also to people who are supposedly *biologically* different. But that means we need a concrete understanding of biology, but the field of biology was only established in the early nineteenth century. To be exact, the word *biology*, in the strictest sense of the term, was coined in eighteen hundred."

The dark shadows dancing around Appiah's eyes made him look more Indian than Nivedita, even though he wasn't the slightest bit Indian or German—he was actually Ghanaian and English and also a tenured professor at New York University—but, just like Oluchi and Nivedita, he first and foremost belonged to the same great big family clan of people with unclear, complex identities. "Of course people had studied flora and fauna before then, but the idea that people could be studied in the same way, and divvied up into different types and races, was a real shift in thinking—a fork in the philosophical road. The latest step down that same path came in the twentieth century, with the rise of genetics and the idea that any- and everything biological was determined by genetic heritability. With that, genes purportedly proved the supposed differences between people."

"Does that mean *race* is nothing but a social construct?" the moderator read from her next cue card.

Of course—what do you think, pea-brain?

"Yes," Appiah softly said, "but the fact that it is inherited socially instead of genetically doesn't mean it is arbitrary."

The camera zoomed back out, and then zoomed back in again to the next guest. Clearly every guest was expected to come with a brief introductory statement. "Hi, I'm Shappi, and I'm an Iranian comedian. Backstage, my fellow comedians call me the Quota Queen."

"Who's that?" Oluchi whispered, as if she and Nivedita were among the hundreds of audience members under the big top in Hay-on-Wye rather than in Oberbilk, nestled on her assemble-at-home bed.

"Shappi Khorsandi," whispered Nivedita, who was well versed in BAME comedians thanks to Priti. "She's . . ." Nivedita racked her brain for the right adjective but felt a bit guilty when the only one that came to mind was "sweet." Whenever she saw Khorsandi on the BBC, she was riveted: her languorous brown eyes were reminiscent of Oluchi's, her irony-tinged overbite was reminiscent of Priti's, and her subtly turned-up nose made it look like she was always pooh-poohing something or other, which was oh so reminiscent of Saraswati. "She makes it seem easy to laugh about racism—and *of course* everyone laughs along, since racism is *beyond absurd*."

Whereupon Shappi set out to prove it: "When our little son was born, we were in the hospital, and the midwife came along with a little clipboard and she goes, 'What is the ethnicity of your child?' And I looked at my baby boy and I said, 'Well, if I had to guess, I'd say he's half otter, half squirrel monkey.' And she goes, 'Look, we really need to know for our records. . . . Look, where are his parents from?' And I said, 'We're both Middle Eastern—I'm from Iran and my husband is from Nottingham.' And she goes, 'Right, so he's mixed race.'" She flared her nostrils as if she could stealthily smell a stench no one else had noticed. "Mixed race? What does that mean? I don't know what that means. It means nothing . . .'cause we're a mixture of all sorts of things." It must be her nose, Nivedita decided—if that nose smelled racism, then everyone else followed suit, crying, *Eew, ugh, disgusting!* "I don't think you should call someone mixed race unless that person is really, truly, undeniably mixed—like a mermaid."

> » Nivedita Anand @identitti *Moinjour fine folk, @OutsideSisters and I were just chillin', drinking down some guys' brains on the rocks, livestreaming #BecomingTheOther at the Hay Festival—tune in.*
> » Nivedita Anand @identitti *OMG #ShappiKhorsandi is THE queen: Mermaids of the world, unite!*

"I know I'm a little too PC, but I think mermaids are an underrepresented minority in Great Britain. We only ever see the beautiful, *sweet* mermaids!" And with that, Khorsandi's set was a wrap.

Nivedita's simple little tweet immediately garnered twenty likes. Meanwhile, the Hay Festival moderator wasn't sure whether nodding was an appropriate reaction so, somewhat helplessly, she turned back to Appiah. "Do you think we'll ever really get away from relying on labels and attributions of this sort?"

"We likely won't. Identities appear to be important to people, but they aren't the only thing that's important to us. We're constantly coming up with new solidarities that cross all group boundaries."

"Which is what you write about in your book, right?" the moderator said, turning to pass the mic to Saraswati.

"Precisely. It's about the concept of radical empathy," Saraswati said. But before she could elaborate any further, the buzzer rang. Nivedita left Oluchi staring rapt at the screen, and got up to open the door. She had heard the term *radical empathy* before—she was certain she'd already heard it somewhere else. *Of course!* It was in one of Saraswati's classes on the historian Quinn Slobodian. She had intended to google that name and that term immediately, but then immediately forgot again. Nevertheless, the name had rattled around at the back of her mind: Slobodian, like Slobodan, but with an *i* stuck in it.

She heard Lotte's long legs bounding up the stairwell. The familiar sound was enough to make Nivedita start feeling nostalgic since Lotte was about to head to Dublin for a fully funded postdoc at Trinity College—just like the privileged characters in *Normal People*. Looking back, Nivedita realized she was really going to miss her.

"Sooo, Barbara says she's coming later," Lotte said, out of breath from the climb.

Nivedita briefly wondered whether she had treated Lotte as a scapegoat for *all white* women all semester, and whether Saraswati had now stepped in to occupy this same position in her mind. Then she decided her character was simply so refined by now that she loved all people, even if they were *white*. And then she realized this love still included Barbara, who was hardly ever at home anymore because she'd fallen in love with a media artist in Wuppertal who had a house with a yard, and then when she did make the rare reappearance at their shared apartment, she spent all her time on the phone talking to Paul, who was in a bit of a crisis and had taken the semester off in order to save his foundering relationship, a move Barbara found a bit abusive, although none of that really had anything to do with this—it was just that Nivedita felt a bit abandoned by Barbara, so didn't really love her at all at this particular moment.

Nivedita handed Lotte a glass of Grasovka—*Did you know the blade of grass in the bottle is sweetgrass?* Kali asked—and led her into Oluchi's room just as Appiah said "Everyone will do certain things based upon their identity, but not everyone will do the *same* thing. However, it remains true that we treat people differently based upon their identity. In short: identity does not determine the things we *do*, but it does determine the things other people *do to* us."

The moderator's next question was drowned out by the noise in Oluchi's room—greetings, glasses clinking—but clearly it was a rather more academic formulation of *oh really?* because Khorsandi answered, "People always ask me if I'm really from Iran. Nah, pal, I only say that so you'll like me more. . . . But when you have a really foreign name you have to shorten it so people pronounce it better. So I shortened Shaparak to 'Shappi.' I went to school with a guy named Mir Abdul Bari and he shortened his name to 'Jim.' I have a cousin called Mohammed and he's had to change his name to 'Wasn't Me!'"

This time even the moderator couldn't help but laugh.

"Like I said, she makes it easy to laugh at racism," Nivedita whispered as she sat back down next to Oluchi. Lotte smiled as if she got it—or, if she didn't get it, as if it didn't bother her—and played along like she was in on it. Then it was Saraswati's turn again to speak. "You can't talk about *race* without talking about *whiteness*. But we constantly talk about the former without talking about the latter, just like we talk about sex and gender as if they only applied to women. So it's incumbent upon me to talk about *whiteness*, and to do so from a central perspective, since I've only ever known *being white and being nonwhite*. I believe quite deeply . . ." Nivedita took a gulp of vodka from her teacup and thought: *Yeah, everything you think and say is deeply believed, Saraswati. You aren't even capable of feeling feelings that aren't deep and profound and larger than life. Don't go galloping off too fast now on your new hobbyhorse.* Despite Nivedita's own racing mind, she still caught almost all of what Saraswati had to say about her latest deep belief: "*Being white* isn't a character flaw, it's just another designation within the social hierarchy, and it's assigned—like POC, or gender. Just as other social designations are now changing, our conception of what *being white* means must also change and expand. What it means to *be white* must be *allowed* to change and expand, otherwise none of this means anything."

Oluchi held her phone out to Nivedita and sent a tweet. "What do you think?"

> » **Call me Zadie @OutsideSisters** *Being white isn't what it used to be, either.* #Saraswati #BecomingTheOther

A FEW DRINKS later, after the panel had ended, Nivedita's phone rang: *Arise, ye wretched of the Earth.*

"Nivedita?" It was Saraswati, sounding almost hesitant.

"Yeah?" Nivedita replied, trying to infuse this single syllable with as much warmth and acceptance as possible.

"Did you just see the 'Becoming the Other' panel?"

"Yeah," Nivedita replied, whereupon she realized she was having trouble formulating full sentences. She had never gotten really drunk, not even after her last and final breakup with Simon. How did Saraswati manage to affect her in a way no one else could? "You were very . . ."

"Very . . . ?" Saraswati asked in her trademark old tone, half flirt, half enigma, plus a bonus third half interrogation.

Nivedita wanted to say "impressive," but her tongue had other plans, and ended up saying "intimidating."

"I hope not so intimidating that you won't come visit me again soon. I'd like to invite you to my going-away party."

"Going away . . . ?" Nivedita slid down the wall until she was sitting on the scratchy blue carpet that covered every last square inch of Oluchi's apartment, including, most regrettably, the entire bathroom. "But you can't go," she whispered, retrospectively realizing that she had finally forgiven Saraswati. Nivedita had spent months wishing she would somehow be able to forgive her, and then it had actually happened, in the blink of an eye, when she wasn't even thinking about it.

And then she experienced one of those breathtaking moments when you can see into the future—more specifically, she saw *herself* in *her own* future. She saw the woman she would become: softer, more compassionate, a bit more round and rounded out, but still unmistakably *her*, with the same part separating her long hair right down the middle of her head, the same A-line skirts echoing the signage on women's bathroom doors, only they'd sit a bit tighter on her hips—a detail that, amazingly, didn't bother her—and, even more amazingly, she looked *more Indian*. Future Nivedita didn't wear a bindi, but something about her was nevertheless, fantastically, unmistakably Indian. And then it hit her: the Nivedita of the coming decades had . . . an aura of belonging. The vision vanished as quickly as it had appeared but, like all precious moments, a flicker of this flash-forward remained in her mind forever.

"You don't have to go," Nivedita repeated, louder this time. "I . . . I could start a petition. Are you . . . really leaving?"

"Not the way you're imagining," Saraswati replied, touched. "I accepted an offer from Jesus College in Oxford."

Nivedita was so drunk she just had to snicker. "Jesus?" *Has god already forgiven you, too?*

"In Oxford," Saraswati explained, audibly elated. "They've made me the inaugural Identity and Solidarity chair. I'll build their new program."

"You'll do WHAT?"

"And it'll offer a concentration in *whiteness studies*."

The pungent taste of sweetgrass suddenly flooded Nivedita's mouth, but she managed to suppress her gag reflex.

"You could consider doing your doctorate here with me in Oxford," Saraswati's voice enticed her, promising gorgeous medieval college quads and leatherbound books chained to library shelves. "After all, the City of Dreaming Spires is the very heart of the Empire."

"*Whiteness* studies," Nivedita repeated softly.

"That's only one concentration. Identity and solidarity are *the* conflicts of our time. If the hullaballoo surrounding my debunking proved anything, it's that."

All of a sudden, Nivedita was certain Saraswati had planned the whole thing: all the disclosures about her, all her humiliations, all the poking and prodding into her past, all the hate and drama, all the debates and non-debates, all the free promo and advertising for an academic who—without all that—would've had a predictable future leading right up to retirement. Becoming professor emerita after such a career would just be a wonderful, interesting, luxurious . . . dead end. Saraswati was always on the lookout for new challenges.

In the *Mahabharata*, there's a battle between . . . somebody and somebody else. Nivedita had heard the story as a child, and even then, she had found the warring parties rather less exciting than the people who experienced the effects of such battles. And in this case that was EVERYBODY, because the battle was so violent that it sparked the Doomsday Fire, Vadavagni. Nobody could put it out. Even the gods and goddesses couldn't keep it from burning the entire earth, reducing all life to ash. In desperation, they turned to Saraswati and begged her to turn herself into a river, extinguish Vadavagni with a flood, and carry its remains out to sea.

Nivedita ran her hands over the scratchy blue carpet so hard and fast it raised a bunch of dust and crumbs, and then she imagined Saraswati turning into a river, swiftly sweeping away the opposition. And then she thought about Miss Jean Brodie from *The Prime of Miss Jean Brodie*—that redheaded, charismatic, universally convincing, awesome teacher who just happened to be more than a little sympathetic to fascism. And then she remembered how, after the Marcia Blaine School for Girls in Edinburgh had kicked her out, Jean Brodie just changed her name, got a gig as Professor Minerva McGonagall, and ended up as director of Hogwarts. So it was totally fitting that Saraswati was now headed to Oxford. And maybe, just maybe, so was Nivedita.

IDENTITTI

I don't long to be Indian because it's somehow an integral part of me, or because my soul is somehow POC or Indian. What I long for is the ability to picture someone like me in my family's history, among my parents and grandparents. But that doesn't work if I'm only allowed to imagine myself as almost German, as a German without any history of her own, as if I were some kind of new species that, through some evolutionary accident, suddenly sprung up from a void. I'd like to know about and share in what made my ancestors who they were. If I were in a Doctor Who movie, I'd love to be able to just hop into the TARDIS and plop down in their past, without being an intrusion, a what-doesn't-belong-in-this-picture element, wherever I go.

I'd like to lay claim to the history of the people who came before me without having to make any excuses, without any limitations, exactly the way other people here freely lay claim to entire parts of Germany and its history and culture—coining evocative comments on belonging in so many colorful dialects, no less—as if it were part of their emotional estate, so to speak, even when such people often possess neither land nor property of their own . . .

"What's the difference?"

"Stop constantly interrupting me, Kali!"

"Since when do you minded me interrupting you?"

"You're right, I'm sorry . . ."

"I bet you don't even know the difference between land and property, do you?"

Ah, right, that's where we left off! Even if the vast majority of them own neither land nor property, and consequently had and have little chance of influencing the politics and history of this country, they can at least imagine they might.

They can imagine being one of the men or the very few women whose dreams and fears shape this country—the people in whose image this country is made, and whose soul it reflects. Different leaders would mean a different land, a different society, over and over. There may not be continuity, but there are stories and histories drawing connections between all the discontinuities. Stories about *who* people are and *why* they are who they think they are.

The eternal *Where-are-you-from?* Mantra (pardon the loanword!) reveals nothing about who you are—but if you don't know the answer, that lack of knowledge will inhibit your exploration of who you are and all that you can be.

Judith Butler says . . .

"Phew! It sure took you a while to finally get to Judith Butler!"

I always save the best for last, Kali.

"But I thought I was the best . . ."

I always save the very best for the very last—be patient!

So, as I was saying, Judith Butler says what really binds us all together is our vulnerability. Being human means being vulnerable. But we're united not only in and by pain—we're also united in and by love—our interest in one another, empathy, and sympathy. Which makes all of us everything. We're all sexes, genders, races, classes, castes. We all are—and I say this in an utterly unreligious way—the miracle of creation, and as such, every now and then, we should pause for a moment to really experience the awe, the shiver of reverence, that our complex existence inspires.

All the really important Hindu gods and goddesses—and no, not just the Hindu ones, you wiseasses, these are all just examples here—have always crossed all the thresholds: they've blurred the boundaries of sex, gender, species, even physical states like liquid, solid, gas. We are creation and we are life itself, hence all our goddamned guilt and the responsibility we all have to love one another. It's like you always say, Kali:

Let love flow like a river.

AFTERWORD:
REAL AND IMAGINED VOICES

This is a novel. All characters are fictional, and some are meant to appear *almost* real.

The issues tackled in this novel are also the subject of ongoing, heated debate in (for lack of a better term) the real world. The concept of *race*—which the German language rather misleadingly adopted as *Rasse*—is a fiction that continues to have a huge, concrete influence on our everyday lives: how we perceive others; how we are perceived; and, last but not least, how we perceive ourselves.

The process Saraswati would call *decolonizing* is so urgently needed precisely because the phantom of *race* exists not only "out there," but "in here." It is in our heads and bodies and souls, it is an unavoidable part of our shared social self-image, and it significantly affects the roles of state and government.

This novel grapples with all that and more.

In recent years, the struggle for self-determination and visibility has often been called *identity politics*, and this term has been applied to a vast variety of opinions—some more vehemently expressed than others. I wanted *Identitti* to reflect the extreme polyphony of this phenomenon, which is why the novel owes its existence first and foremost to generous contributors who wrote some of the social media posts included here—tweets, as well as

Instagram and Facebook posts. Their brief was to imagine they had read about the "Saraswati Affair" on the Internet, and then to donate their commentary, exactly as they might have spontaneously responded to a real scandal of this sort. Therefore, I owe one thousand and one thanks to: René Aguigah, Magda Albrecht, Carolin Amlinger, Fatma Aydemir, Simone Dede Ayivi, Patrick Bahners, Christian Baron, Felix Dachsel, Felicia Ewert, Berit Glanz, Kübra Gümüşay, Meredith Haaf, Sarah Fartuun Heinze, Arne Hoffmann, Fatima Khan, Ijoma Mangold, Jacinta Nandi, Madita Oeming, Ruprecht Polenz, Aidan Riebensahm, Jörg Scheller, Sibel Schick, Antje Schrupp, Hilal Sezgin, Nadia Shehadeh, Ralf Sotscheck, Regula Stämpfli, Ralph Tharayil, Minh Thu Tran, Lars Weisbrod, and Hengameh Yaghoobifarah. Their real names and the social-media posts they donated to this book appear in the entirely fictional scenario of this novel.

Equally heartfelt thanks to Steffi Lohaus, Enrico Ippolito, and Peter Weissenburger, who make cameo appearances as themselves and ask Nivedita for articles on #Saraswatigate for *Die ZEIT online*, *Der Spiegel* online, and *taz*. Special thanks to Verena von Keitz for agreeing to make a cameo appearance interviewing Nivedita on national radio—Verena has also interviewed me many times, and her dog Mona was always at our side in the studio, observing us with her melancholic eyes. Şeyda Kurt wrote the *ze.tt* article about Saraswati specifically for this novel, just as Nikita Dhawan, María do Mar Castro Varela, and Paula-Irene Villa Braslavsky specially formulated their reactions to the Saraswati Affair for *Identitti*.

I cannot overstate how valuable all these collaborations have been and continue to be for me. What's even more valuable is that so many of my fine colleagues have been engaged—both online and offline—with the topics broached in this novel for so long now, enriching and advancing the public discourse. Additional thanks to Andrea Auner, Leila Essa, and Nina Anuschewski, whose thoughts on life in Germany for people with immigrant backgrounds—either visible or invisible—have been directly and indirectly incorporated into this book.

Barbara is based on my former roommate and current fabulous neighbor Sandra Röseler, aka Randy Texas. "The Brown Girl" is an actual folk song that, despite its seemingly obvious title, is almost never read as a song about a girl from a British colony. British singer Georgia Lewis not only recorded a great version of it, but also enlightened me about the song's history. Matti Rouse remains invisible, but is nevertheless audible: his song "The Stories of All and Every" plays while Nivedita and Saraswati lounge on the terrace high above the rooftops of Oberbilk; I myself make a cameo appearance as a backing vocalist in that same scene.

OF COURSE SARASWATI herself didn't come into existence out of nowhere, either. While she is entirely fictitious, in crafting her ideology my numerous inspirations include: Gayatri Chakravorty Spivak, the godmother of postcolonial theory, whose call to "unlearn one's privileges as one's loss" is Saraswati's lifelong motto; Audre Lorde, who as a guest professor at Freie Universität Berlin in the 1980s kicked all *white* students out of her seminar; bell hooks, who is as impossible to capture in words as Saraswati, so I'll just name *all about love* and *Belonging: A Culture of Place* as two of her works that influenced this one; and Priyamvada Gopal, whom I really wish I had studied with in Cambridge.

And then, when it comes to Saraswati's deceit, there have been real people who have been in the news in similar ways: Rachel Dolezal, president of a local branch of the USA's National Association for the Advancement of Colored People (NAACP), who in 2015 was outed by the press as *white*. She herself, the public outcry in response, and the heated discussions surrounding her identity left me with countless questions, all of which provided some of the impetus for writing a book about so-called reverse passing. This story is set in Germany, and the entirely fictional character Saraswati has opted to live not as a Black person like Dolezal, but as a Person of Color.

Many of the reactions to Saraswati are based on actual quotes about Rachel Dolezal that I applied to the events in this novel in a fictitious manner as tweets—including comments by political analyst Melissa Harris-Perry, gender and sexuality scholar Kai M. Green, *New York Times* critic Wesley Morris, Black feminist (and author of books like *Pleasure Activism: The Politics of Feeling Good*) adrienne maree brown, scholar and talk show host

Ronnie Gladden, philosopher Justin E. H. Smith, and sociologist Rogers Brubaker, whose book *Trans: Gender and Race in an Age of Unsettled Identities* I'd have loved to have quoted in its entirety. All credits and sources appear in the bibliography.

All the places in the novel are real, as are all the books mentioned—except, needless to say, the ones written by Saraswati. Where real public figures appear, they are applied to the novel in an entirely fictitious manner. The tweet by J. K. Rowling is inspired by a real tweet by Rowling that sparked a scandal. The tweets and quotes from Donald Trump and Narendra Modi, who were president and prime minister of the United States and India, respectively, as I wrote this novel, are based on famous statements by both of them. Jordan Peterson, who debates the fictitious Saraswati at the Hay Festival, is an actual and highly polarizing public intellectual. Equally real are Saraswati's debate partners at her second Hay Festival appearance: Kwame Anthony Appiah, whose great book *The Lies That Bind: Rethinking Identity* should be required reading in schools and universities; and Shappi Khorsandi, who, by the way, has also written a wonderful novel titled *Nina Is Not OK*. All statements by Peterson, Appiah, and Khorsandi are comments they actually made in other contexts—including interviews, books, and comedy club stages—just transplanted into this made-up world, as part of the fun of this novel. I translated and paraphrased their comments for the original German edition, and did my best to dig up the English sources for this translation. I did not fabricate their sentiments—this novel reflects *what* and *how* they *think* or *thought* about these issues—for real—just in an imaginary context!

THE STRUGGLE OVER identity is the struggle over fiction in reality—and sometimes these struggles have very real victims. Hence the right-wing terrorist attack in Hanau is based on the unfortunately all-too-real right-wing terrorist attack in Hanau on February 19, 2020, in which a *white* perpetrator with racist motives shot nine people who were visibly non-white immigrants, before murdering his mother and killing himself.

The Hanau murders occurred while I was working on this novel. The horror, fear, anger, and grief I immediately felt helped me realize that my fiction had to end with just such an attack. I made this decision because attacks like the one in Hanau have occurred, and continue to occur, all over the world. Most BIPOCs are all too aware of this fact because it's like the soundtrack of our lives—not always audible, but always there. I'm not afraid to go outside or walk down the street here in Germany, of course, but when I walk past a man alone at night, my first thought is: *Is he a Nazi?* It's not: *Is he a rapist?* It's not even: *That's just some guy, we live in a safe society where people express social solidarity with one another.* But that's exactly what we should all think or at least be able to think.

Everyday life in Germany doesn't consist solely of horrific violent crimes, but such crimes are indeed a reality here, and therefore I consider German literature's overwhelming silence on this topic an unacceptable omission. After long deliberation with many colleagues regarding issues of reverence and appropriation, I decided to include the real attack of Hanau in this book—although in my fictional reality, I moved it to the height of summer, simply because the debates between Nivedita, Saraswati, Raji, and Priti occur under the pressure of summertime heat, and their brains and souls inevitably had to boil over at some point.

But, of course, the attack isn't the end of the novel. The show goes on—it's unbelievable but true—much as life always goes on. Because *Identitti* also grapples with what we commemorate, what we choose to remember, and who we want to be as a result, it was important for me to create a memorial to the victims—albeit only in the very small, modest way most readily available to me. Germany does not exist without us, so our dead must also be mourned in German literature. At this point, my German editor Florian Kessler—to whom I owe the greatest thanks for his diligent and sensitive work on this book—pointed out to me that it might sound as if I'm resorting to an essentialist *we* in these last sentences by referring to "we POCs"—a term I was careful to deconstruct in so many other places in the novel. So allow me to unpack this once again: the point isn't that we should mourn the dead of

Hanau and all other victims of racism and other forms of discrimination because they're somehow extraordinary, but rather because they are so very ordinary. The only extraordinary aspect is the nature of their deaths. They were and are ordinary residents and citizens of this country—my country, Germany—just like Lotte and Nivedita and Barbara and Priti and Oluchi, my fictional characters. We, as in *all of us*, are this society. There is no living together and getting along without *all of us*, so we all have to keep empathetically speaking up, arguing with, making up with, and celebrating one another—in all our many different voices.

Similarly, in the English-speaking world, white supremacists continue to terrorize with their violent, racist attacks. And each attack is added to our painful soundtrack even as it is unpacked and explained endlessly in the media. At the same time, more and more cases of BIPOC-passing women, especially in academia, continue to surface in the United States. In addition to Dolezal, Jessica A. Krug—an associate professor of history at George Washington University—allegedly claimed to be part Algerian, part German, part Afro-Boricua, but was actually white all along. BethAnn McLaughlin purportedly pretended to be a Native American anthropology professor at Arizona State University. Andrea Lee Smith—formerly an assistant professor of American culture and women's studies at the University of Michigan at Ann Arbor, and currently a professor in the Department of Ethnic Studies at University of California, Riverside—has been accused of falsely claiming to be Cherokee since at least 1991.

I don't know their personal stories, and I don't want to fuel any additional scandal around them. For me they are part of a bigger picture. Being white is no longer the end all be all. Something is moving and I want to acknowledge that, while at the same time not losing sight of the vastly different opportunities and the lasting legacy of racism. I have been told that some English-language readers might want me to weigh in on who is right and who is wrong at the end of my novel. Or at least to say whether Saraswati was right or wrong in doing what she did. But I won't. It's the system that's wrong.

THANK YOU FOR reading. I love you all so much.

TRANSLATOR'S POSTSCRIPT: MITHU AND MYTHS AND YOU AND ME

Mithu Sanyal wrote every word of the novel you just read, occasionally adapting quotes, tweets, speeches, and other statements originally made by various people in German and English, and applying them to her fictional account. The only catch is that she wrote the book in German, and then I did my damnedest to bring all her German into English, which is obviously an impossibility. But it wasn't even that simple, because her text was remarkably polyphonic, featuring German, English (i.e., British and Indian and North American Englishes), French-via-English-translation, and sprinklings of other languages, not to mention a whole lot of slang and other super-loaded language. Readers of the German edition could witness Priti's evolving elocution as her English was supplanted by German—an amusing mix that couldn't be translated "exactly," as that would've had the *exact opposite* effect of the original. So, I struck as careful a balance as I could—lest the character who spoke the least German now appear to speak the most—and if the balance wasn't successful, that's on me. The evocative pun on *Priti* and *Prithee*, on the other hand—like so much of the humor in this book—is entirely the author's brilliance.

I opted to restore French West Indian philosopher Frantz Fanon's book title to its original language as a way of maintaining the "foreign" flavor of the German edition, which featured that and other titles in English. I made dozens of other decisions following that same logic: where colonization has occurred and capitalism has had its way, one should respect the highly human mess that results (e.g., notions like "French West Indian"). You'll see names like Birmingham and Bombay alongside both Calcutta and Kolkata— Mithu and I went with Bombay not only because the name Mumbai has been so heavily politicized by Hindu nationalists, but also to preserve the alliteration.

My main way of channeling the text involved going overboard and being reined back in, so I'm indebted to the author and editors for the open dialog and their careful attention to detail and register, especially with the intriguingly inventive social media handles. Made-up social media handles that appear to refer to real people, inserting their statements into this fictional account, are marked by asterisks.

À propos of appropriation and adaptation, both the author and I took great liberties. Allow me to expand on just one such instance: in the German edition of this book, Jordan Peterson's persona is inserted into an entirely made-up setting. The author watched videos of various public appearances he made over the years, extracted phrases here and there, and then combined them to compose fictionalized responses to the invented scenario of this novel—all in German, of course. Her German translation of these phrases had a certain flow that would have been lost had I transcribed, verbatim, the passages from his public lectures given in English. Therefore, I chose instead to be faithful to the way the author wove his actual spoken words into her fictional story. Similarly, the passage featuring Trump and Modi are based on (in)famous statements made by both of them. But if you still want to track down what everyone said, the sources are all laid out in the bibliography.

Now, let's talk about sex: specifically, *The Joy of Sex*, a book by British physician Alex Comfort first published in English in 1972. The scene where Priti reads from it was based on the German text, but English has an entire spectrum of terms beginning with *n*, from *negro* to the *n-word*, whereas German does not distinguish between them. This is important because writers like James Baldwin, also quoted herein, used both terms with extreme precision in English. I found it plausible that the 1972 edition used the former, but I had to eliminate all doubt as to whether it had used the latter. The argument could be made that it didn't matter, since the characters were focused on the incendiary language in German, but I still needed to know. The matter was complicated by the fact that no fewer than five revised editions have since been published. The latest is "revised and updated for the 21st century," which means (you guessed it) *Oriental* has become *Eastern* and all the tidbits Priti and Nivedita marvel at have been excised—well, not *all* of them. The 1986 edition, heavily revised during the AIDS epidemic, still had what would've been the n-word in German, but the English edition had used a French term (I'll let you do your own digging there, if you so desire). So, was it deemed not incendiary solely because it was in French? And would that have been because the editors didn't know what it meant, or *did* know, but thought it was neutral? We're left with a conundrum, but editorializing or speculating about things I cannot know is not my job; I partially unpack these quandaries here so you can appreciate the complexity of this novel, in whatever language you might read it.

I'VE OBSERVED A TENDENCY—IN the Anglophone world, at least—to lament what is purportedly lost in translation without acknowledging what is undeniably gained. There are many new voices in German that have yet to be heard, and my sense of urgency grew each time I saw people's reactions when I told them I was translating a German satire about identity politics— the words *German* and *identity* produce so many presumptions, everywhere. And then I recalled how, two decades ago, many North Americans reacted to my study of German by asking why I wanted to learn the "ugly language of the Nazis," instead of a "beautiful language, like French"—as if French speakers had never committed any atrocities, or as if English speakers are somehow exempt from humankind's unkind, highly fraught history . . . to not even touch upon what it means to read this book from within a culture where, *every week,* thousands of people experience some form of gun-related violence, and invariably underreported hate crimes are hard to quantify. So here we are. A little like the Wizard of Oz now peeking out—*pay no attention to that person behind the curtain!*—I remain fallible even as I strive to do this rich novel justice. It's a story about so many forms of misunderstanding and injustice, but also love—so I tried to make it understandable, and maybe also misunderstandable, and hopefully also lovable. As Saraswati might say to Nivedita and her other seminar students, *class*: *discuss.* I can't wait to hear what you think.

SARASWATI'S LIT LIST

QUOTATIONS AND INSPIRATIONS

P. 57 "Not in the least. I merely . . ." This and all subsequent statements by Jordan Peterson regarding order and chaos were adapted by the author from statements made by Jordan Peterson in the BBC radio cultural discussion program "Jordan Peterson: Rules for Life," May 14, 2018, www.bbc.co.uk/programmes/b0b2gsct. They are being applied to the made-up events in this book in a fictitious manner.

P. 58 "What is happening right now at universities . . ." This statement by Jordan Peterson was made in the "Munk Debate on Political Correctness," May 18, 2018, www .youtube.com/watch?v=ST6kj9OEYf0. The author has woven it into a fictitious scene for this novel.

P. 58 "The main point of this ideology . . ." ibid.

P. 72 "Practically the only star I had to steer by . . ." Zadie Smith, *Feel Free: Essays*. New York: Penguin, 2018, 31.

P. 106 "There was England, a gigantic mirror . . ." Zadie Smith, *White Teeth*. London: Penguin, 2017 (originally published 2000), 266.

P. 106 "The people who think of themselves as White . . ." James Baldwin, in his preface to the 1984 edition of *Notes of a Native Son*. London: Penguin, 2017, xxii.

P. 119 "Once you go Asian . . ." Tez Ilyaz, TEZ Talks Podcast series 2, episode 7, Feb. 7, 2018, www.bbc.co.uk/programmes/b09qfwt3.

P. 119 "The personal is not . . ." Michele M. Moody-Adams in the panel discussion "Who are we? Identity politics dissected," Nov. 8, 2016, www.youtube.com/watch?v =sSkItnTni5I.

P. 119 "I'm honored . . ." Homi Bhabha, "On Global Memory: Thoughts on the Barbaric Transmission of Culture," a lecture given Apr. 14, 2008, www.youtube.com/watch?v =5Fp6j9Ozpn4.

P. 123 "Don't expect to see any explosions today . . ." Frantz Fanon, *Peau noire, masques blancs*. Paris: Éditions du Seuil, 1952. English translation by Richard Philcox as *Black Skin, White Masks*. New York: Grove Atlantic, 2008, xi.

P. 134 "When someone shows you who they are . . ." Maya Angelou in conversation with Oprah Winfrey in Pajamas, *The Oprah Winfrey Show*, Jun. 18, 1997, www.youtube.com/watch?v=Pa-QE_bIvNk.

P. 146 Quotations from *The Joy of Sex* by Alex Comfort were drawn from Wilhelm Thaler's German translation, *Freude am Sex*. Frankfurt am Main, West Berlin, and Vienna: Ullstein, 1981 (based on the 1972 English-language original).

P. 150 "@ShappiKhorsandi *If you find me* . . ." The fictional tweet was inspired by a tweet from Shappi Khorsandi on Jul. 17, 2020, twitter.com/ShappiKhorsandi/status/1284134444266389505.

P. 156 "Trouble with the Engenglish . . ." Salman Rushdie, *The Satanic Verses*. New York: Viking, 1988, 343.

P. 156 "Europe is literally . . ." Frantz Fanon, *Les damnés de la terre*. Paris: François Maspero, éditeur, 1961. English translation by Richard Philcox as *The Wretched of the Earth*. New York: Grove Press, 2004, 58.

P. 156 "The mythologies of empire . . ." C. L. R. James as quoted by Priyamvada Gopal in "Changing the stories we have inherited from colonialism," a talk given Jun. 24, 2019, www.youtube.com/watch?v=wOnBiHHPLm4.

P. 164–165 Quotations from Cynthia Heimel's *Sex Tips for Girls*, originally published in English in 1983, were taken from the German edition, translated by Gabriele Becke as *Sex Tips für Girls*. Munich: Goldmann, 1994 (reissue of the 1985 ed.).

P. 172 "The individual may be . . ." The fictional tweet quotes Roger Brubaker's *Trans: Gender and Race in an Age of Unsettled Identities*. Princeton, NJ: Princeton University Press, 2017, 140.

P. 177 "Our world is suffering . . ." The fictional tweet quotes Ibram X. Kendi, *How to Be an Antiracist*. New York: Random House, 2019, 234.

P. 182 "The parallel with Michel Foucault's discourse analysis . . ." cf. Michel Foucault, *Histoire de la sexualité 1. La volonté de savoir*. Paris: Gallimard, 1976. English translation by Robert Hurley as *The History of Sexuality, Vol. I: The Will to Knowledge*. New York: Pantheon, 1978.

P. 187 "In so far as I reacted at all . . ." James Baldwin, "Stranger in the Village," *Harper's Magazine*, Oct. 1953, 43.

P. 188 "Knowledge never was . . ." Aziz Al-Azmeh, *Islams and Modernities*. London: Verso, 1996, 182.

P. 188 "Where there is power . . ." Foucault, *History*, 96.

P. 188 "Where there is resistance . . ." Nikita Dhawan, "Heimatphantasien. Die Beheimateten befreien," lecture given Aug. 19, 2018, www.youtube.com/watch?v=DZdruYFpuqE.

P. 204 "boundary work," cf. Brubaker, *Trans*.

P. 205 Noel Ignatiev quotes are from "Treason to Whiteness Is Loyalty to Humanity," in John Garvey and Noel Ignatiev (eds.), *Race Traitor*. London: Routledge, 1999 (first ed. 1996), 10.

P. 211 "You can help . . ." Amiri Baraka, *The Autobiography of LeRoi Jones*. Chicago: Lawrence Hill Books, 1997 (first ed. 1984), 285.

P. 211 "those *white* kids . . ." ibid.

P. 211 "that seeing whites as the enemy . . ." Joseph F. Sullivan, "Baraka Drops 'Racism' for Socialism of Marx," *New York Times*, Dec. 27, 1974, 1 and 67.

P. 228 "Caring for myself . . ." Audre Lorde, "A Burst of Light: Living with Cancer," in *A Burst of Light*. New York: Dover, 2017 (first ed. 1988), 131.

P. 228 "We are porous beings . . ." Ann J. Cahill, "Disclosing an Experience of Sexual Assault: Ethics and the Role of the Confidant," unpublished lecture, 2019.

P. 228 "You can remove all the threat . . ." Stephen Porges in conversation with Dave Asprey, "The Nervous System Circuitry of Safety, Sound and Gratitude," Bulletproof Radio episode 573, Mar. 7, 2019, www.youtube.com/watch?v=k4NnJ6eJPjg.

P. 240 "Rachel Dolezal, Caitlyn Jenner . . ." The fictional tweet quotes a phrase in Wesley Morris's essay "The Year We Obsessed over Identity," *The New York Times*, Oct. 6, 2015.

P. 240 "If sex isn't real . . ." The fictional tweet quotes a tweet by J. K. Rowling, Jun. 7, 2020, twitter.com/jk_rowling/status/1269389298664701952.

P. 240 "We are all responding . . ." The fictional tweet quotes a phrase in Kai M. Green's article "'Race and gender are not the same!' is not a Good Response to the 'Transracial'/Transgender Question OR We Can and Must Do Better," *The Feminist Wire*, Jun. 14, 2015.

P. 256 "The idea that passing . . ." The fictional tweet quotes a phrase said by Melissa Harris-Perry in an interview with Rachel Dolezal, "Rachel Dolezal Exclusive Extended Interview," MSNBC, Jun. 17, 2015, www.youtube.com/watch?v=USr_bm39hrU.

P. 272 "To what extent are my accomplishments . . ." These statements by Jordan Peterson were made in: Stephen Fry, Jordan Peterson, Michael Eric Dyson, and Michelle Goldberg, *Political Correctness Gone Mad?* London: Oneworld Publications, 2018.

P. 273 "Unattractive both inside . . ." The fictional tweet by quotes a tweet by Donald Trump, Dec. 28, 2012, twitter.com/realddonaldtrump/status/240462265680289792, as well as one of Trump's statements in the presidential debate held Oct. 9, 2016.

P. 273 "While @Saraswati is . . ." The fictional tweet quotes a tweet by Donald Trump, Oct. 28, 2012, twitter.com/realdonaldtrump/status/262584296081068033.

P. 273 "Saraswati's mind is not the problem . . ." The fictional comment references an oft-quoted statement by Narendra Modi, "Mind is never a problem, mindset is."

P. 273 "The infamous German scholar pretending . . ." The fictional comment by quotes a statement from Narendra Modi's interview with CNN's Fareed Zakaria, Sep. 21, 2014, www.narendramodi.in/pms-interview-to-cnns-farid-zakaria-2865.

P. 275 "When we speak . . ." Audre Lorde, "A Litany for Survival," in *The Collected Poems of Audre Lorde*. New York: W. W. Norton, 1997 (first ed. 1978).

P. 275 "By making whiteness . . ." Akala, *Natives. Race & Class in the Ruins of Empire*, London: Two Roads, 2018, 104.

P. 275 "So decolonisation in my view . . ." Gopal, "Changing."

P. 281 "The people of Africa . . ." paraphrased from the German edition of Hannah Arendt's *The Origins of Totalitarianism*, which originally appeared in English in 1951. Cf. *Elemente und Ursprünge totaler Herrschaft. Antisemitismus, Imperialismus, totale Herrschaft*, Munich: Piper, 1991 (first German ed. 1986), 323.

P. 281 "animal . . ." ibid., 322.

P. 304 "In spite of presenting . . ." Ronnie Gladden, "TRANSgressive talk: An Introduction to the Meaning of Transgracial Identity," in *Queer Cats Journal of LGBTQ Studies*, 2015, 75.

P. 306 "Last night in the Kesselstadt neighborhood . . ." from an interview with Muhammed B. on TRT Deutsch, "Überlebender des Blutbads in Hanau," Feb. 20, 2020, www.youtube.com/watch?v=GY08s12pD4c.

P. 317 "And death shall . . ." Dylan Thomas, "And Death Shall Have No Dominion," in *The Poems of Dylan Thomas*. New York: New Directions, 1943 (first published in 1933).

P. 327 "Any good sci-fi explanations . . ." The fictional tweet quotes a statement by adrienne maree brown excerpted in Green, "Race and Gender."

P. 342 "As a philosopher, the question I always have to ask . . ." The comments by Kwame Anthony Appiah are from on a conversation with Gideon Rose for *Foreign Affairs*, Apr. 7, 2015, "Kwame Anthony Appiah on Race," www.youtube.com/watch?v=EEOQcVLvnKo, and are applied to the events in this novel in a fictitious manner.

P. 343 "Of course people had studied . . ." This and all subsequent statements by Kwame Anthony Appiah were published in the German edition of Kwame Anthony Appiah's *The Lies That Bind: Rethinking Identity—Creed, Country, Color, Class, Culture*. New York: Liveright, 2018. Cf. *Identitäten. Die Fiktionen der Zugehörigkeit*, translated by Michael Bischoff. Berlin: Hanser, 2019. They are applied to the events in this novel in a fictitious manner.

P. 343 "Hi, I'm Shappi . . ." Statements by Shappi Khorsandi are from "Shappi the Box Ticker," www.bitoffun.com/video_vault/shappi-khorsandi-standup.htm, and are applied to the events in this novel in a fictitious manner.

P. 344 "When our little son was born . . ." Statements by Shappi Khorsandi are from "Shappi Khorsandi: Stand Up Against Racism," Apr. 23, 2010, www.youtube.com/watch?v=M7c9CxwSWlY&t=6s, and are applied to the events in this novel in a fictitious manner.

P. 346 "People always ask me . . ." Statements by Shappi Khorsandi are from "Shappi Khorsandi Live At The Apollo," Jul. 13, 2018, www.youtube.com/watch?v=hgTZ0VY0dYk&t=150s, and are applied to the events in this novel in a fictitious manner.

ADDITIONAL SOURCES AND RECOMMENDED FURTHER READING

—Soul food and comfort food: see LeRoi Jones (Amiri Baraka), "Soul Food," in *Home: Social Essays*. New York: Akashic 2009, 121ff.

—Kali's theories about vibrations: see Thaddeus Golas, *The Lazy Man's Guide to Enlightenment*. Encino, CA: Seed Center, 1971.

—Nivedita's knowledge about mixed-race, first-person narrators in novels: see Zadie Smith, *White Teeth*.

—Saraswati's explanations of Blackness/Whiteness and Australian Aboriginal people: see Patrick Wolfe, *Traces of History: Elementary Structures of Race*. London: Verso, 2016.

—Resistance against empire and its affects on the notion of freedom: see Priyamvada Gopal, *Insurgent Empire: Anticolonial Resistance and British Dissent*. London: Verso, 2019.

—Fundamental reflections on passing and the position of Amiri Baraka: see Asad Haider, *Mistaken Identity: Race and Class in the Age of Trump*. London: Verso, 2018.

—The idea that in India nothing is final or eternal—not even death—and what that means for notions of sex and gender: see Devdutt Pattanaik's essay "Introduction to the Karmic Faiths" in Jerry Johnson (ed.), *I Am Divine. So Are You: How Buddhism, Jainism, Sikhism and Hinduism Affirm the Dignity of Queer Identities and Sexualities*. London: Harper Collins, 2017, 1–38.

—More about the goddess Saraswati: see Devdutt Pattanaik: *7 Secrets of the Goddess*. Mumbai: Westland, 2014.

—A classic on decolonization: see Ngūgī wa Thiong'o, *Decolonising the Mind*. London: James Currey, 1981.

—The reasoning behind Oluchi's Twitter handle: see Audre Lorde, *Sister Outsider*. Berkeley: Crossing Press, 1984.

—More about German colonialism and the so-called Salt-Water Thesis: see Mark Terkessidis, *Wessen Erinnerung zählt? Koloniale Vergangenheit und Rassismus heute*. Hamburg: Hoffman und Campe, 2019.

—Additional references to identity discourse other than the aforementioned treatise by Kwame Anthony Appiah: see Florian Coulmas, *Identity. A Very Short Introduction*. Oxford: Oxford University Press, 2019.

—Reflections on *POCness*: see Jaswinder Bolina, *Of Colour*. San Francisco, CA: McSweeney's, 2020.

—Racism and its history: see George M. Fredrickson: *Racism: A Short History*. Princeton, NJ: Princeton University Press, 2015.

—Gaytri Chakravorty Spivak's famous essay on the subaltern: see Rosalind C. Morris (ed.), *Can The Subaltern Speak?: Reflections on the History of an Idea*. New York: Columbia University Press, 2010.

—The debate on connections between culture and identity: see Stuart Hall and Paul du Gay (eds.), *Questions of Cultural Identity*. London and New Delhi: Sage Publications, 1996.

—Another foundational text: see Stuart Hall, *The Fateful Triangle: Race, Ethnicity, Nation*. Cambridge, MA: Harvard University Press, 2017.

—Sexual identity/identities, the lack of any such notion, and homoerotic experiences in India: see Madhavi Menon, *Infinite Variety: A History of Desire in India*. New Delhi: Speaking Tiger Books, 2018.

—White Privilege: see Kalwant Bhopal: *White Privilege: The Myth of a Post Racial Society*. Bristol: Policy Press, 2018.

—The "Third World Diva Girls": see bell hooks, *Yearning: Race, Gender, and Cultural politics*. Boston: South End Press, 1990.

—Other significant works by bell hooks that influenced this book: see *Belonging: A Culture of Place*. London: Routledge, 2009; and *all about love*, New York: William Morrow, 2000.

—Reflections on being mixed race: see Will Harris, *Mixed-Race Superman*. London: Peninsula Press, 2018.

—Additional thoughts on mixed-race identities: see Afua Hirsch, *Brit(ish): On Race, Identity, and Belonging*. London: Jonathan Cape, 2018.

—Reflections on being Indian: see Amartya Sen, *The Argumentative Indian: Writings on Indian Culture, History and Identity*. New York: Farrar, Straus and Giroux, 2005.

—What sweetgrass has to do with colonialism: see Robin Wall Kimmerer, *Braiding Sweetgrass: Indigenous Wisdom, Scientific Knowledge, and the Teachings of Plants*. Minneapolis: Milkweed, 2013.

—All you need to know about breathing, oxygen, and carbon dioxide: see Michael Eze, "The Oxygen Paradox and the Place of Oxygen in our Understanding of Life, Aging, and Death," in *Ultimate Reality and Meaning* vol. 29, no. 1–2. Toronto: University of Toronto Press, 2016.

—The course Saraswati is developing for Oxford was inspired by Linda Martín Alcoff, *The Future of Whiteness*. Cambridge: Polity Press, 2015.
—The book I currently consider most up to date in the question of how we can *unlearn* colonialism is: Ariella Aïsha Azoulay, *Potential Histories: Unlearning Imperialism*. London: Verso, 2019.
—Reflections on healing and decolonization: see Resmaa Menakem, *My Grandmother's Hands: Racialized Trauma and the Pathways to Mending our Hearts and Bodies*. Las Vegas: Central Recovery Press, 2017.

AND SO MANY more . . .

ABOUT THE AUTHOR

Mithu Sanyal is a cultural scientist, journalist, critic, and author of two academic books: *Vulva*, which was translated into five languages, and *Rape*, which was translated into three languages. This is her first novel.

ABOUT THE TRANSLATOR

Alta L. Price runs a publishing consultancy specializing in literature and nonfiction texts on art, architecture, design, and culture. A recipient of the Gutekunst Prize, she translates from Italian and German into English.